The Chair

By

GB Williams

Black Bee Books Ltd.

First Published in Great Britain in 2020 by
Black Bee Books Ltd
Bryn Heulog
Talley
Llandeilo
Wales SA19 7YH
Copyright © GB Williams 2020

Cover Image © Mumemories / Shutterstock.com
Cover Design © Huw Francis

ISBN: 978-1-913853-02-0 (Paperback)
ISBN: 978-1-913853-03-7 (eBook)
Printed and bound in Great Britain by Clays Ltd, Elcograf S.p.A

www.blackbeebooks.wales

Acknowledgements

Writing is generally a lonely experience, but writers don't do it all alone. So here are just some of the people who have supported and encouraged me to get this novel out into the wild. To my family and friends who pushed me on, put up with me grumbling when things don't go well, and celebrate with me when they do. To structural editor Tony Fyler - a man who will not let me get away with anything.

Mostly I have to say thank you to Black Bee Books, for liking my book and publishing it. Let's hope it's the first of many.

Dedication

This one is for Jonathan. The man who made me stay in Wales, introduced me to the wider country, and supported me through everything. Thank you for believing.

JANUARY
Chapter 1
Alex – Belsize Park

"Why on earth would I agree to that?"

"I made you!" Mark was adamant, indignant even.

Alex disagreed. Mark Levinson wasn't the major music journo he liked to believe. And he dressed like a teenager from the eighties, Alex thought. Faded blue jeans, white t-shirt, leather blouson, and a thinning mop of curly hair, treacherously showing the dye marks. But Mark knew too much. At the time, Alex had considered it a worthwhile risk. Now he wasn't sure. Mark could prove dangerous if not kept on side.

The journalist sat forward, snarling. "I could unmake you."

Unlikely. The truth would unmake Greebo K, but there was a very good chance Alex Berenger's reputation would be enhanced. It was a different truth that could drag them both into the mire. Thankfully, Mark didn't know that one. At least Alex hoped not.

"Look," said Mark, trying a placating tone. "Think of it this way: after the theft of Greebo K's single, this can be his right to reply. He's known for not giving interviews, so releasing one now could get public sympathy on his side."

Alex considered. Mark was good at looking after Mark. If Mark got an exclusive interview, it would put his editor on side, and if that meant looking after Alex et al, then so much the better. "I can't guarantee anything."

"You're his golden boy." Mark smiled, apparently thinking he'd won. "He won't say no."

There was no guarantee of that either, and disagreement could be fatal. If he was lucky.

***

The silence made Alex uncomfortable. He liked sound, had always been enchanted by music. It wasn't just something he made, sound was his life, his everything. Still, sitting in Granger's office was better than being taken to the other room. Alex didn't even let his eyes wander to that door. All he knew was that behind that door was a chair. That was the only common reference. The Chair. He didn't ask and the information wasn't volunteered. He'd never been in there, but he'd seen the difference in the people who had. They weren't the same after.

Granger sat before him, behind the impressive glass desk, in a massive leather desk chair. The chair had been specifically constructed for the big man. Two podgy hands ran up and down the length of the padded arms. The record label boss sat with feet flat and knees apart. The protruding belly didn't yet fill his lap, but one day it might. He sat there as king of all he surveyed.

Granger held more than a record deal over Alex. Alex knew more about Granger than Granger wanted him to. That mutual understanding explained why Alex had never had to visit the other room.

"Do you know who that is?"

Alex glanced to the newspaper the older man had indicated with the slightest flick of a finger.

Alex looked. When he wanted to make his way into the music world, he had made it his business to find out everything he could about the big hitters, and most of them stood quietly away from the microphone and the press.

"Bradley Pill."

"Bradley Pill," Granger said with a sneer. "That little scab used to be my assistant. He told lies and they were believed. Sony Music cut me because of that runt. Me! All because he wanted my job."

From what Alex had been able to find, Pill hadn't lied. Granger had been guilty of all the accusations. That was one of the reasons Alex had approached the newly formed Nemesis Records. Granger's corruptibility gave Alex the opportunity of increasing his own coverage and income, and his scheme needed the greed and drive that Granger had in abundance.

The real money, Alex knew, came from elsewhere. Granger had a backer. Who the money-man was, Alex couldn't uncover. It was self-evident that Granger would never have re-established himself without signing Alex Berenger and Greebo K. Mutual need assured mutual protection.

"Yes, sir. What's your point?"

"The point is, I won't be crossed again."

Alex suspected Granger would be, but kept his mouth shut. This time Granger picked up a thin manilla file.

"Do you know what this is?"

Alex felt blood drain from his face. "No, sir, I don't."

"This is the police report into our little incursion last month."

That incursion had been a hacker who had stolen the next Greebo K single file. That bastard hacker was now selling the recording at half the price they could. The hacker had sold enough copies in one week to make a fortune and ensure that when the official release happened, sales didn't. No longer viable, they'd pulled the release, but still people were lapping it up. They didn't care about the music, or integrity, or that creatives needed to make a living. They only wanted to dance.

"Tells me fuck all." The file slammed into the bin.

Alex suspected the file didn't contain any actual report, possibly not even a single piece of paper, but was just a display for dramatic effect.

"That's why this interview has such potential. We use it to tell Greebo K's fans how much damage that pirate has caused, say it means delaying the album because we need a new song, that increases cost, which of course we won't be passing on to the fans, and thus we get the audience back on our side."

Granger considered the point. "But you want to record that interview on the same server that got hacked last time."

"The server is less important than the firewall, and we've increased security on that and file retrieval. We're tighter than the Pentagon."

Granger didn't look entirely convinced.

"Think of the exposure the first ever Greebo K interview will bring. The public have been asking for one since we started, and there's only so long the reclusive act can work. If we finally give them what they want, then even Bradley Pill will have to sit up and take notice."

Granger's eyes slid to the newspaper. His lips twitched up.

Gotcha.

Chapter 2
Simons – Home Counties

From the quiet office, Simons looked out over the immaculate garden. Immaculate thanks to no work of his own. All he'd done was pay the gardener. He might potter out there, deadhead a few things when necessary, but that was as green-fingered as he got. He did appreciate the result, however. The restful view provided a point of calm when his thoughts failed to find any. Now the garden wore the colours of winter, it matched his mood to perfection.

The business was successful, his clients were happy. But one failure bothered him. Letting a friend down was never good enough.

Letting one die was worse.

Now another case bothered him. Though it wasn't strictly speaking a case, no one was paying him to investigate, but far too many times there was a name muttered around the edges of his other investigations. The name stuck, echoed, nagged. Simons recognised that accusations could be unfounded, but not this many. Not this…consistently. And not with so much fear from the accusers that they barely dared speak the name, as though a single utterance might conjure the devil.

So Simons crept carefully around the perimeter of the other man's life. He kept his eyes and his ears open. If anything happened, he wanted to know, wanted to be ready.

He also wanted to be sure he wasn't enacting some vindictive persecution. A chance existed, slim though it might be, that the man was not the villain he'd been painted. Simons didn't want to drive an innocent man into the ground, but if the accusations, and the fear, and the whispers were true, he'd find a villain hiding beneath the veneer of money and power.

Chapter 3
Branwen and Cobb – Cader Idris

Steep and rugged, the rough ground was treacherous under foot. The spiky grasses stood angled and hard, ready to strike. The mountain skeleton lay exposed as rock, dictating shape, demonstrating obstinance. Frozen winds howled, buffeted, bit extremities, searched for routes through layers of clothing, sought to drag intruders to the edge and beyond. Icy poniards rained into eyes. Then, quick as a finger-snap, the mountain might turn, as the Welsh would say, proper nasty.

Slogging up the track, the volunteers of the Mountain Rescue reached the coordinates they had been given. Looking over the ledge, no lost walker came into view. As suddenly as it started, the rain stopped, the mountain offering them a break. The big grey dog who had obediently stayed by the tallest man's side padded two more metres along the ledge. Its sensitive nose tested the air till it looked down. Irish Wolfhounds weren't bloodhounds, but they still detected scent better than any human. The group looked down the steep edge of the mountain. The low hanging cloud around Llyn Cau parted like curtains, and the bright yellow of the man's jacket marked him where he'd slipped down to the scree. Even from where they stood, the unnatural bend in the man's leg was obvious.

"Woolverton, you and two there." Cobb pointed to a flat stable area two metres to his left. Finn, the dog, whined in response of the call to heel to get him out of the way. "The other two here with me. Jones, you'll go down with the stretcher and get him on it."

Cobb stood at the ledge, the toes of his walking boots peeking over. While not his place to order this crew, he'd done it automatically. He was the most familiar with these situations, he knew how to get men back. The dry heat of Kamdesh was the opposite of the cold wet of Snowdonia. Here on Cader Idris, the elements froze his bones, but retrieval was retrieval.

Stepping back, he turned to see Branwen Jones preparing her harness. The only woman in the group and the local vet, in the absence of the doctor on this call out, she was the best first aider they had. Even as Michael Woolverton, group lead, called down reassurances to the walker, Cobb moved to face Branwen. Her nose glowed red, her cheeks white, and that was pretty much all of her that was visible under the thick four-season clothing and the hat tied over her ears and under her chin. Some would say it looked ridiculous; he thought it looked warm, sensible.

"You okay with this?" he asked as she buckled the climbing belt.

"Of course!" she shouted over the wind and didn't look at him as she checked the buckles of the belt. "You belaying for me?"

Naturally. Any of the team could do it, but he felt more confident with her life in his hands. "I will." Easing his pack to the ground, he got into his own belt. Once the rope was sorted, they checked each other's harnesses for security and hold. Branwen took his waist buckle and pulled it tighter for a firmer fit.

"You never do that tight enough."

He did, he just liked when she tightened it. She checked again and looked up at him.

"Ready?"

She nodded. "But do me a favour, don't stand so close to the edge as you were before. That's scary to see when you're on your own, I don't want to see it when my life is in your hands."

He nodded as she stepped back. The lifting cage would be lowered down to her, but the med kit she'd need was strapped to her back. Ropes were thrown down towards the mark and when she was ready, she looked to Cobb. He braced, took up the last of the slack then she started to lean back, to abseil down to the fallen walker.

***

Branwen pushed down the inevitable bile as she crested the edge. She trusted her abilities; she could do this. She'd learned to climb for two reasons: firstly, this was her mountain, and secondly, the fear of heights must not be allowed to control her. Another step, then another, she'd take each one and finally she'd do what had to be done. The fear, however, never went away, she just had to control it. So she placed her feet carefully and looked up at the edge of the rock.

She couldn't see much of Cobb; thankfully he was standing further back than he had before, just as she'd asked. But she saw Finn. The big wolfhound lay on the edge, one front paw and that big stupid head looking over the ledge, watching her. The dog's mouth hung open, and she suspected he might be overheating with the exertions of getting up here, even in this cold weather. She just hoped that didn't mean she'd get a faceful of drool next time she looked up.

Instead, she looked down. Looked towards her feet, made sure they wouldn't slip on the scree, then she checked she was headed in the right direction for the fallen man. She was, and as she continued, her fear of heights diminished beneath her concerns for the man's life. Little blood showed on the rocks – most likely it had soaked into the man's salopettes, but his face stood out as very pale, and his lips seemed to be turning blue. His wide eyes watched her as he clung on for dear life and imminent rescue.

That was good. In a situation like this, tenacity often pulled people through, more than physical strength. With a bit of luck, it would get him through the fact that she was going to have to straighten that leg without anaesthetic.

***

Unable to get the helicopter anywhere near the fall site, the Mountain Rescue had to get the fallen man back to Pen-Y-Cwm Farm – the nearest place with an area that the chopper could safely land. That the farm also happened to be Branwen's home made little difference.

Cobb carried his share of the rescued burden and while the walker talked with Woolverton – whose conversation was really about making sure the man remained conscious and lucid – Cobb watched Branwen. She walked ahead, Finn at her side. The dog stood tall by any standard and against a short woman, it was particularly striking.

The sight of the house as they carried the now heavy stretcher was a welcome one. Golden light spilled from various windows. As they rounded a twist in the path, the blade and nose of the flying machine in the farmyard came into view.

Less ferocious though it was, the wind still muted other sound, but Cobb doubted there'd be much since the rotors weren't rotating. Darkness crept slowly over the land, though four o'clock had yet to arrive this afternoon. A figure appeared at the edge of the building, paused – Cobb suspected the flight-suited individual had stopped to call back an update – then rushed forward. The memory of another time, another helicopter, men in fatigues, the soul-freezing – *No!*

He pushed the memory aside. *Not now.*

The man reached them and Branwen started reeling off facts and figures. For a heartbeat the memory of the same in the Highlands threw him. There the shock of seeing a loved one murdered had blunted his facilities, here it was just a minimal understanding of the medical. He took a deep draw of the present cold air into his lungs. He must not live in the past.

The exchange made, the fallen walker became the responsibility of the Air Ambulance crew. The man was safe. Cobb mechanically followed Woolverton's orders for returning the equipment to the storage container they held here at the farm, the highest residence on Cader Idris. When all was safely packed away, the shout was over, all bar the paperwork.

"You'd best come in."

Cobb and the crew turned to the deep-voiced man. At five-nine, he stood thickset and solid as a rock. He was as hard and unyielding

as the mountain on which he lived. Iolyn Jones, Branwen's father.
***

"Oh no, you don't get to slink away now," Branwen told Cobb as he started towards his car. The rest of the Rescue had already gone into the farmhouse – her father always had hot soup and a warm kettle to greet them with. Iolyn always grumbled about it, but he'd never been asked to do it and he always did it and they were always very grateful that he did. While getting Cobb to join them never proved the easiest task in the world – she'd only managed it a handful of times in the last two years – today she was determined he'd join them again.

Cobb stopped and turned back to her. Alone in the shelter of the quadrant formed by the farm buildings, the wind sounded around them, but for once it didn't pound them. She moved up close.

"It's not far home," he said.

"It's not far home for any of us." She reached out and took his hand. Like her, he had removed his gloves and while the two sets of fingers were exposed, recent activity kept them from being cold. "Please, this isn't about how close home is."

Cobb sighed.

She saw him searching for a way out. "Don't you dare try the whole Marlene Dietrich 'I vant to be alone' act again."

"Greta Garbo said that," he corrected with a small smile. "Doesn't it ever occur to you that I actually *do* want to be alone?"

It more than occurred to her. She knew he wanted to be alone, she just got the sense that that wasn't necessarily the best thing for him. It certainly wasn't for her.

"We all need some alone time, but we also all need some time with others. Don't forget it was being on his own that got that walker into trouble. If he hadn't lucked out by not breaking his phone and somehow getting a signal up there, he would have died on this mountain. But he got lucky, and we got him back. As a team. It's time for you to be part of that team." She stepped even closer. "*I* want you to come in."

His expression as he looked down at her didn't change, but she felt the increased pressure on her fingers and took that as a good sign. Taking the chance, she turned and headed towards the house. Cobb followed, and at a single whistle, Finn trotted by their side. Then, realising their goal, the dog ran towards the open door.

"Dumb dog."

"He's showing more sense than you are." She turned and grinned at him. He said nothing.

Inside, Branwen let go of Cobb's hand to take her coat off while he closed the door. When he turned back she looked at him, and his eyes went to the full rack of coat hooks on the wall. All the other team members had hung their coats up. The reluctance Cobb showed was a reflection of the man himself, but he unzipped the coat and she realised that that was a recognition of the importance of being a member of the team rather than just a part of it. She suspected he knew more about such things than she ever would. The kind of command he occasionally demonstrated could only be learned one way.

He hung the coat up, paused. Again, she reached for his hand, felt the gentle return hold and drew him down the hallway, straight into the kitchen. The big oak table filled one end of the kitchen, flanked by benches on both long sides and carver chairs on the end. The five other rescue members had arranged themselves along the benches and even now chatted as they sipped the hot soup and tore into the fresh made bread. It was one of the things she liked most about farm living – proper food. And her father was a fabulous bread maker. Branwen led Cobb straight to the nearest bench, and Woolverton budged up to give them room as they joined. Iolyn placed full bowls of thick soup before the two of them.

No one said anything about the unusual appearance of Cobb, they continued to talk and eat and the whole thing seemed as natural and normal as could be. For Branwen it wasn't normal, because Cobb was here and that made it very different.

An unexpected knock on the front door quickly turned into the sound of it being opened. It wasn't unusual for a lot of people just to wander into other people's homes in the village, though only one person did it up here – Doctor Peter Pearson.

"Hi all!" he called through, then he appeared from the hall. "Everyone okay? I saw the Air Ambulance go. Hi Branny."

Pete bent over Branwen and dropped a kiss on her head. Branwen noticed the way that Cobb stilled at the act, but he didn't know the past, he'd never asked, so she'd never told.

"Sorry I missed all the action," Pete said as he sat on the opposite bench. "I was on a house call. But you all alright?"

The conversation resumed. Cobb returned to his soup, but already Branwen sensed the increased distance between them.

Chapter 4
Baron – Fulham

There was something very satisfying about watching a good fight. Not that this was a good fight, more a public beating. David versus Goliath. The only sling David was going to have use for would be the one that supported what looked like a fractured wrist – the smaller man had stopped jabbing with it a minute ago. Goliath on the other hand had hardly broken a sweat. Being an illegal bare-knuckle fight didn't lessen the excitement of the event, instead it added to the piquancy. The potential for a raid was part of the draw.

The warehouse had been boarded up years ago; condemned, but yet to be demolished. The owners were a development company, builders who had sold a good story and a beautiful development plan, selling shoebox homes for hundreds of thousands of willing investors who thought they were getting the new best thing in modern living in the heart of London. What the developers got was easy money. What the investors got was shafted. The directors of the building company hadn't been seen in years. The only way one would ever be seen again was if the Council decided to dig up the footings for a certain bridge, and even if they did, the skull had been so thoroughly fragmented it would be an anthropologist's life's work to rebuild it.

A mobile generator buzzed at the far end of the big empty space, its rumble nothing to that of the crowd around the makeshift ring.

Standing at the back of the roaring crowd, in his chinos and shirt, Baron should have looked more out of place. Half this clamouring audience consisted of booted and suited types, ready to play in the dirt a moment, desperate for the thrill of blood to compensate for their own damn impotence.

David hit the canvas with a thump so hard it shook the building. The crowd reached a crescendo and money, real money, paper money, untraceable money, changed hands.

Baron looked at Goliath.

Real name, Gary Shoreham. A big Scot with more sense than people gave him credit for. Shoreham got paid by the fight, any fight, so if some little wimp wanted to try his luck, as far as Shoreham was concerned, that was okay by him. Money for an easy fight was still money.

Baron knew the fighting Shoreham liked best didn't take place in the ring, and that usually paid even better.

***

Pressing an on-screen button ended the call. Baron put the phone in his jogging bottoms and walked back into the gym. There were

10

lots of meatheads without anywhere better to go. The place stank of sweat and testosterone. He knew steroids were pushed in the changing rooms here. It was one of his more lucrative income streams, given the lack of effort it took. He walked back over to the lockers, not that there were any lockers. Bare knuckle fights were illegal, so these were hardly great facilities. Still, they padded the pocket.

"You get the cash?" Baron asked as Shoreham rubbed salve into his red and swollen knuckles.

"'Course I did." The taller man turned to Baron. "Who called?"

"Granger." The music boss paid them a retainer to do his dirty work. Sometimes to show people the chair in Granger's anteroom. Shoreham particularly enjoyed that, he wanted to use the chair the same way Granger did. Thankfully, so far, Granger had had the sense to refuse the muscleman, and Shoreham was smart enough not to push it. "He's got a job for us. Let's get cleaned up." Baron didn't tell Shoreham about the call he'd made after Granger signed off; Shoreham didn't need to know Baron answered to Granger only because he answered to someone higher up first.

Chapter 5
Simons – City of London

The alley was cold, but Simons couldn't get the view he wanted from the car. The stinking thousand-litre bins wafted their stench as Simons made his way up the fire escape. The smell released its stranglehold on his nostrils only as he reached the first floor. The cold gave him one thing to be thankful for – in hot weather that stench would have a much higher reach.

He stopped at the third floor. Then, with the wind whipping around him, he brought out the camera and hooded the telescopic lens which he trained on the window of interest.

Yes, the mark was in. It was a moment's work to set up the gorilla pod to hold even this weighty lens. Next out came the handheld parabolic microphone. Simons doubted he'd hear much with the windows closed and the winter wind rushing down the street, but he had to try. At least it wasn't raining.

The man he watched was in his late fifties, but he looked younger because he kept himself fit and active. Enough grey stood out in his hair to suggest that he didn't dye the rest, but it was a close-run thing. Always immaculately dressed, he rarely appeared out of a suit and tie. At the moment, he was alone in his office, looking through various ledgers. That was interesting. A computer sat on his desk, but it was off and the man, O'Rourke, focused on the bound ledgers with handwritten figures. Simons knew of only two reasons to do that in this electronic age; having either a small, easily managed business, or a large illegal one. O'Rourke's empire was neither small nor easily managed.

Simons pulled on the headphones – if nothing else they were protection from the cold. He watched through the camera and listened, but all he heard was static generated by the passing winds. Then the door to the office opened and a woman walked in. Her subdued navy dress didn't hide the fact that like O'Rourke, she was into her fifties, but didn't look it. Her hourglass figure was enviable, even on a younger woman.

Rebecca Keel, O'Rourke's long-time personal assistant. She seemed to be one of the very few people that O'Rourke kept close. It might even be possible O'Rourke actually trusted her.

Simons saw Keel's pink coloured lips move, and O'Rourke responded. Even this state-of-the-art microphone picked up too little to be sure what was said. He should have brought the laser microphone. It felt like watching a movie in an open car with the speakers on a dodgy connection. Like a bad imitation of Norman Collier's faulty microphone act. Simons wondered if anyone else even remembered the comedian now, a thought that made him feel very old, despite being younger than O'Rourke.

For two hours he stayed and waited, watched, hoped for something. Got nothing. O'Rourke and Keel worked, talked sometimes, but he heard nothing, and no one else came near. This was getting him nowhere, so when O'Rourke packed up for the day, so did Simons.

Chapter 6
Jay – Paris

Ah, Paris in the Springtime! Nothing like it.

Unfortunately, it was January and a bloody freezing winter. Still the frosted air made the lights of the Eiffel Tower sparkle just that little bit more romantically.

Romance was far from Jay's mind though. He'd used the first free Wi-Fi connection he could log into, redirected the IP addresses and then delivered five thousand pounds worth of pirated music. Two weeks ahead of the official release date, but he didn't care. Five big ones for one night's work was a sweet little pay-out and nothing was getting between him and that.

Time to relax.

He returned the smile to the girl on his right. Though not the best of places, it wasn't the worse. She moved over. As chat up lines go, her opener lacked a certain *je ne se quoi*, but luckily his fluent French allowed him to take advantage. In every way possible.

***

Even free sex had a shelf life and the girl was getting clingy, so a week later, Jay left Paris and headed home. Now he stood in the foyer of the flats and looked at his mailbox, willing it to provide the answer. He'd posted the application online weeks ago. There had been an acknowledgement email, but no follow-up. Would they do things by physical mail? It was possible, though likely only for rejection. He didn't want a rejection. Now the lack of response was holding his life in limbo. In university, no one had ever doubted the class of degree James Whitney would get. He had always been a first-class student. Only one term into his Masters, he'd already had four job offers from top software houses. His future seemed secure, except –

Except he was still waiting for what he wanted. He wanted NASA. Space exploration by remote computer-driven robots. Automatons to do man's dirty work. Robots with brains designed by J Whitney. That was Jay's dream and he wasn't ready to give up on it, not now, maybe never.

He stood alone, with people passing on the street outside. Another resident appeared and left the building. There was no exchange of pleasantries. Few people ever noticed him. He had always been a loner. Too smart behind those thick-framed glasses. Too wimpy in the jeans and oversized T-shirts, sweatshirts that never hung to a fashionable length on his over-tall, over-thin frame. Girls had never found his sort of looks particularly appealing, which was irritatingly inconsistent when in the next breath they would say he looked a lot like Alex Berenger, then go on to coo over the pianist. Jay didn't let it get to him.

Even hacking wasn't that important to him. It paid, so he did it; student debt was difficult even with the Bank of Mum and Dad for support. He had his dreams. He wanted to build artificial intelligences. To do that, he had to be the best. If that meant building diving bots to mine other people's data, for the time being, that would do.

Chapter 7
Alex – St John's Wood

They met at the Nemesis Records recording studio. It seemed appropriate. For the backup plan, if nothing else.

Mark Levinson arrived like a strutting peacock. He'd supplied his questions and Alex had tutored Greebo on what to say in response, also giving strict instructions for the journalist not to deviate from the script. Being on the spectrum, Greebo didn't work well with surprises.

Alex looked on as the two sat together and Mark went into his usual spiel to greet and relax the subject; it had the opposite effect. Greebo shifted uncomfortably in his chair. Alex pressed one of the many buttons on the console in front of him.

"Greebo, you're in a recording studio, I can hear pretty much every move you make, please sit still."

Through the glass, Greebo flipped him the finger.

"Thanks. Mark, shall we make a start?"

Half an hour later, Mark looked up at Alex. This wasn't working and they both knew it. Alex watched as Mark smiled at Greebo and excused himself. He left the studio and appeared at the desk a moment later.

"I can't use this, he sounds retarded."

"I believe we're supposed to say mentally challenged." Alex glared at the older man, knowing Mark was right. While Greebo wasn't dumb, he was no genius. Greebo sounded like what he was. The bastard son of a dole-sponging lout. Alex understood the bit-of-rough philosophy, and even the idea of a rebound revenge fuck, but he'd never understand why his mother had kept the baby. Greebo K, real name Graham Kasaval (after his father) Berenger. Greebo had been a school nickname that stuck. Still, Alex sighed, Mother had kept the child, and like it or not, Alex was stuck with a half-brother that looked and was nothing like him. Yet they remained brothers, even if the best they could do for one another was publicly hide that fact.

"Fine," Alex agreed. "You'll interview me and I'll synth my voice to sound like him." He sat forward and pressed the intercom button. "We're done, Greebo, you can go home if you like."

Greebo K did, in fact, have two talents for which Alex was very thankful. He could dance better than Michael Jackson – a claim the press had made several times – which explained why his performances were always so well received. Then there was the second talent – he could lip sync better than any other artist Alex had ever seen.

***

16

Granger called shortly after Mark had left.

"It's all in hand," Alex assured him. "The interview's complete, all sorted."

"Mark Levinson interviewing Greebo K is complete, is it?"

The tone spoke volumes on Granger's unhappiness. Alex had to be careful. "It is."

"How's that then, when I've been sitting in the same room with Greebo K for the last half hour?"

Ah. On the positive side, half an hour was an improvement, usually ten minutes was about all Granger could stand. "You know what he's like, even coached he can come across like an untrained monkey." Mother had done her best, but the influence of his father had been stronger, and the various beatings about the head for being a half-breed couldn't have helped. Greebo wasn't stupid, he just didn't articulate well. "So, I did the interview, I'm just remodulating the voice now to sound like Greebo K. It's not going to take long, it's the same program I use for the singing."

Granger's angry breathing throbbed threateningly down the line. "So now Levinson knows."

Alex sighed. "Levinson always knew. That's why we paid him for the first stories, remember?"

"How much more would he get now to sell this story?"

"Not enough to make it worth his while," Alex said with certainty. "Because part of the recording included the preamble he didn't know I was recording and that proves he was aware of what was going on from the start. And he openly admitted that he only did it for the money and to screw over that, and I quote, 'bitch-faced editor Severine Du Lac.' I played it to him once we finished and told him if he said anything about us, I'd send that to every entertainment editor in the country and he'd never work again. Don't worry boss, we're safe."

Again, the slow response. He heard the start of the boss's smooth riding Merc. "Okay, well make sure you delete the original files. I don't want some smart-arsed shite hacking in again and finding that or any of my other files."

"Don't worry, Mr Granger. I'll remodulate and delete the original. It'll all be fine. Besides, we rebuilt the firewall, upped the safeties and encoded those… other files. We're wrapped up tighter than Fort Knox. No one's getting in."

Alex put the phone down with a sigh after Granger rang off without a word of farewell. So much for "manners maketh man."

The remodulation program was 90% complete when the phone rang again. Alex frowned to hear Greebo's call tone. He took it up.

"You gotta get 'ere, man." Tears and sniffs filled Greebo's voice.

"It's Ma."

Alex's throat ran dry even as the file finished, and he automatically hit save. He didn't have to ask where or why. "I'll be there in fifteen." Hopefully, that would be quick enough.

FEBRUARY
Chapter 8
Branwen and Cobb – Pen-Y-Cwm Village

The Mountain Rescue Annual Fundraiser Ball was early this year. As ever, it was a Valentine's Ball, but this year they were celebrating a week in advance since Michael Woolverton, the organiser and chief officer of the Rescue, had had a ball with his Valentine nine months earlier and the resultant due date was Valentine's Day itself.

The Woolvertons were leaving the next day to stay with family in Bangor, to be near a hospital rather than risk getting stuck in the village. Most mothers expecting at this time of year stayed. Doc Pearson had delivered two winter babies and Branwen had once been called in when the Doc was unavailable. For the Woolvertons, the situation was different: much as they trusted both Doc and Branwen, they weren't taking any chances. They had already lost one baby for lack of immediate incubation facilities. It was something the whole village knew and they totally supported the couple's choice, though no one ever mentioned it.

Cobb arrived late, and when they saw him, he saw money change hands, though he had no idea why. He hadn't planned on coming at all, but he had received a text from Branwen that said if he wasn't there by eight, she'd drive up to his place and drag him down herself. He believed her. She would do just that if he gave her cause. So, he turned up, at seven fifty-five because he didn't want her thinking she was getting everything her own way. After greeting the Woolvertons and wishing the couple good luck, he turned to look at the array of drinks on offer.

"That one isn't spiked."

He looked down at the blonde, Emma, as she smiled up at him. Ivan Evans lurked close by, scowling at Cobb. The man need not worry; Cobb liked Emma, but not that way.

"Thanks." He leaned forward and poured a cup of fruit punch – it was suspiciously bright orange and somewhat cloudy. "Branwen not joining us tonight?" She'd better be, or he'd go and drag her in.

Emma's broad grin suggested he had failed to achieve the attempted nonchalance. "She called to say she'd been held up by an early lambing, she'll be here as soon as she can. I told her I'd be sure and tell you."

That made him frown. "She wanted me to know she'd be late?"

The smile dimmed a little. "Not specifically, but I knew you'd want to know. Now I've told you." Her eyes moved beyond him. That grin grew. "And now you get the full impact."

He turned to where Emma was looking. Branwen had stepped in and was already chatting, smiling with the Woolvertons. She wore a fitted gown of midnight blue velvet. It displayed a curvy full-bodied figure that usually hid under loose trousers and baggy tops. Long black hair that shone with midnight highlights curled softly around her shoulders. Freed from its usual tight braid it looked soft and seductive, and new. Little wonder then that every man in the room began to salivate, and that there were a few women distinctly unimpressed with their partners. Yet no man rushed to her side. Did that mean she had always intended to come alone? He'd not heard of her having a date as such, but then he didn't tend to indulge in village gossip. And the Doc always looked at her like he'd eat her for breakfast.

Mind, last year she had arrived and left alone. Cobb didn't dwell on why that pleased him. In the two years he had been here, he had never seen her look so good. He could go over.

No, you can't. Don't risk it.

The discomfort started when Fred Ogden stepped up to her. The knot in Cobb's gut was in no way an acknowledgement of a wasted opportunity. He turned away as Ogden took Branwen's hand and led her to the dance floor. The vet and the hill farmer. It was a good match. Sod the punch, it was too damned cheerful; he needed a beer. Unfortunately, the beer tasted ever more bitter as he turned from the crowd and pulled heavily on it.

Five minutes later, Cobb stood outside the back of the hall, listening to the music from inside, watching the stars in the surprisingly clear sky and trying not to think about why he had come here tonight, searching for a better reason to leave. He heard the rapid open and close of the door from the hall.

"God save me from hill farmers."

Cobb smiled at the heartfelt sigh. "Come on, Branwen," he told her softly, enjoying her start. "Fred's not that bad."

She smiled, coming to stand beside him. "He'd be better if he didn't have such a huge crush on Em."

Cobb raised an eyebrow, looking at the dark crown of curls. "Looked like he was more interested in a brunette tonight."

"Shows how little you see." She turned her eyes heavenward, gazing up at Orion, and Cobb watched a deep frown carve itself into her forehead.

"What's wrong?"

"Nothing. In fact, there's a lot right." She gazed at the stars, her expression distant and wistful, her sigh sad.

He studied her for a moment. This wasn't like her. Usually she at least had a smile on her lips. "What's wrong, Branwen?"

Her lips turned down more and she turned away, hiding her face.

"Branny?" he asked. "Come on, you can trust me. I'm hardly the village gossip."

"True," she admitted, but took a moment before she lifted her head up and looked at him. "I'm selling the business, the vet's. I'm leaving the area."

The calm announcement hit Cobb like a punch in the gut, leaving him shocked and winded. A million questions shouted for answers in his head, but only one question formed. "Why?"

"There's nothing here for me."

The certainty in her voice, the absolute conviction, surprised him. "What about your work? The practice you've built up?"

She shrugged shoulders turned to alabaster by moonlight. "Any vet could do that. It doesn't need *me*."

She had a point, but it didn't help him. It wasn't the heart of the problem as she studied the stars again.

"What are you looking for, Branwen?"

The frown grew deeper. "I don't know. The practice used to be enough, it's just... not anymore. I'm twenty-nine years old and except for a few years in university studying, I've spent my whole life here. I've never been anywhere or done anything."

Cobb considered all the places he had been, the things he had done. It didn't make him any happier than Branwen. He was still lonely. There was a time when –

No, going there won't help. Don't let those memories intrude. You know where they always lead.

"Doesn't even make sense. Pen-Y-Cwm. One of the few places in Wales that really doesn't match its name. Means top of the valley, possibly end of the valley, depending on your translation. Either way it doesn't work. We're just *in* the valley. We're just... Cwm. The road out is the road in, most people don't even realise they've driven through."

"A one man and his dog kind of town," Cobb tried to joke.

Branwen's small huff of a laugh rang with bitterness. "Little wonder you like it then."

That cut. It shouldn't, but it did. Like he'd told her before, he'd come here to be alone. Just him and his dog. That was what he wanted. Solitude. She was the one who kept dragging him back into the world. Maybe, when she left, he'd find that place, that isolation. But now the word conjured images of cells and lock-ups.

"Emma," Branwen announced suddenly, "thinks my problem is that I don't have a man."

The left fielder hit it out of the park. He swallowed. "What do you think?"

She considered for a moment. "I think there are six bachelors in this village and that's not enough."

"Why not? You and Emma are the only two eligible spinsters-"

"Spinsters! We're not maiden aunts."

"Okay, bachelorettes. It's still an average of three each."

"Well, yes, but take a look at the six," she told him. "There's Dai Jones, fifty if a day and hardly ever sober. Besides, he's some kind of relation of mine, though it's difficult to tell when most of the family stopped speaking to my family generations ago. Paul Davies is only interested in engines, and besides, we ran out our romantic possibilities in our teenage years. Fred Ogden is only interested in Emma, who's only interested in Ivan Evans. Then there's Doc and he's – well, he's Doc."

Cobb understood what she meant, though he was pretty sure he didn't know all there was to know about Doc and Branwen. Doc Pearson always struck him as a nice enough guy, but something odd lurked about the man. It probably had to do with the spiky-leafed plants he grew in his conservatory and the occasionally odd-smelling tobacco he rolled in his cigarettes. For now, Cobb concentrated on Branwen. "That's only five bachelors."

Branwen looked at him. "Well, you're number six. I didn't think I needed to point that out."

Even after giving that idea a moment of digestion, it didn't acquire any flattering perspective. He needed to ask. "What disqualifies me?"

Looking up at Orion again, Branwen didn't even pause to answer that. "You do."

Cobb considered – it still didn't make sense. "Would you care to elaborate?"

Branwen's smile twisted. Did she realise she'd hurt him? He wasn't ready to examine that himself.

"You only come into town once every other week for grocery shopping, usually when we have a Rescue team meeting. You barely even speak to anyone. You made it clear from day one you're not interested in human contact. You even reminded me on Wednesday that you want to be alone. Finn's the only one you care about and he's a dog." She shivered in an icy blast of wind from the frozen mountaintop. Her words were having a similar effect on him. "Em's pointed out that I'm about the only human you ever talk to and that's either about the Rescue or Finn." She shivered again. "It's cold out here."

And getting colder with every damning word, Cobb thought, hating the fact that every damning word was also true. When she looked up at him, she offered her usual forthright friendship. "You coming in?" she asked. Then, when he said nothing, she grabbed his hands in hers. "Please? Save me from the other bachelors I don't think so eligible."

***

Only one dance had been worthwhile all evening, and her feet were killing her. Branwen thought Cobb had been all too eager to let her go and pass her on to the next man. Since then, she had been squeezed and trodden on by too many men who seemed to have forgotten they had other women to consider. Finally, Doc Pearson had decided to cut in and she relaxed again. They'd known one another most of their lives and been friends for the majority of that time, a weird and varied friendship that had survived many a trauma. Which probably explained why having a joint surgery built to their mutual specification had worked so well for them.

With one hand on his shoulder and the other in the warmth of his hand, they stood close, dancing to some waltz she didn't recognise. They had been laughing together for a while and his arm at her waist brought comfort. She wasn't worried about any trouble from him. He always behaved in public.

"So, what do you say? Dinner, Thursday?"

She frowned for a second. "That's Valentine's Day."

The way he smiled warmed her, the slight lopsided nature of the expression was a favourite quirk of hers. "Exactly. What better day to start."

"Start?"

"Yeah. You and me…"

Was he actually asking her out? "Oh." She turned her head away for a second before looking at him again. He hadn't done that, asked her out, for a few years now. Quite a lot of years, actually. "You don't think that it could ruin a perfect friendship?"

"Nope."

She had to smile at his confidence.

"Well it hasn't up to now, has it?" he asked. "And think of all the free breast exams." Her brows shot up, her jaw slackened, even as Pete's face screwed up in self-disgust. "Yeah, okay. Even I heard how creepy that sounded."

"Good." She laughed and rested her forehead on his shoulder by her hand.

"So, Thursday?"

With a sigh, she picked up her head and looked at him. So far Cobb was the only one who knew she planned to sell the business and leave the area. It seemed unfair to string Pete along, but she didn't want to hurt him either. "Not Thursday," she said. "There are too many expectations on Thursday. Another day?"

He smiled. "We'll work something out."

***

Watching the easy hold and obvious connection between Branwen and the Doc tied Cobb's stomach in knots. Just because he didn't want another woman in his life, didn't mean that he wanted her going off with some other man.

Hypocrite.

He ignored the internal voice.

Dog in a manger.

Gritting his teeth was starting to hurt as Branwen looked up at Doc and laughed.

They were too close. He wanted that closeness for himself. He missed being that close to another human being, to a woman. How could he risk it? How *dare* he? Being close to him is what got –

No, don't think of it.

He had to. He had to remember why he'd come here, buried himself in the back of beyond, to be alone. He couldn't face another loss like that one. He couldn't watch another someone he cared about be torn away because an idiot decided to use a gun. Her face smiling across the road at him one second, the splash and smear of red on bricks –

No, don't dwell on it.

The cold expressionless face of the man who'd shot her.

No!

That was then, this was now. Around here the only guns were the twelve bores the farmers had licences to keep. And he'd seen several of them in action. Snipers, these people weren't.

He concentrated on Branwen instead. With no reason to lie to him, Cobb didn't doubt that she would sell up and leave, in which case, better she led Doc on than him. Not that he could be sure what Branwen told Doc. As a doctor, the man knew how to keep secrets, perhaps he already knew. Besides, Branwen had said they'd been friends since childhood, perhaps their closeness was innocent.

The way Cobb wanted Branwen wasn't innocent, just too dangerous in every respect. Especially with her leaving. He could barely deal with the world in Pen-Y-Cwm, facing the reality of the wider world was beyond him.

The music stopped, the dancers parted company. Doc brought Branwen back against his side with an arm around her waist. Cobb watched her shake her head, words were smiled up at the man. The Doc's arm didn't move. Cobb braced. Then Branwen moved the arm, moved away from the Doc. Only when he realised Branwen was moving towards him did Cobb relax.

***

24

Leaving Pete shouldn't have been such a relief. Branwen didn't want to date him again, but a night out with an old friend wouldn't be so bad. It would give her a chance to tell him her plans.

She turned away. She needed a drink and a sit down. Cobb standing alone at the side of the room glowering caught her attention. Nothing new there. But he was the one focused on her, so what if she decided to use that?

"I need a drink and you're nearly empty."

She pointed to the tulip glass in his hand, and trusted that he'd follow her over to the bar. He did. She ordered, they took their drinks and sat at one of the few unoccupied tables at the side of the hall.

"Should you be drinking?" he asked as she took a long first drink from the cold wine.

"Why not?"

He frowned. "What about driving home?"

"I've made up the bed in the surgery that I use when I have to monitor animals overnight. No driving for me. What about you?"

"Booked into the Pig and Whistle."

If he had a double room, maybe – *Stop it!*

"I meant to tell you." Yes, good, be business-like, great seduction technique. "That group that booked for the Winter Survival Course week after next, they called to cancel."

"Did they give a reason?"

"Not really, though frankly I was up to my elbow in sheep uterus at the time, so I was concentrating on other things."

"Probably too cold for them."

She smiled. It never ceased to amaze her how often she had last minute cancellations on winter survival courses when people realised that they would be going out into the wild, on a mountain, in the snow. What they thought winter survival was actually about she wasn't sure. *Indoor* winter survival? With coffee and biscuits, perhaps?

"I did remember to point out that at such short notice they wouldn't get their money back."

"So, I'm out a week's wages."

"You'll get paid. That's why they don't get their money back. If you feel guilty about earning without working, I'm sure Dad can find you something to do up at the farm. It is the start of lambing season."

He curled his lip. "Unlike you, I don't want to be elbow deep in sheep uterus."

"How deep would you like to be in my ut–" His shocked look and her realisation cut her off. "I think I've had too much to drink." She rushed from the table, from Cobb, and her surprisingly empty glass.

Chapter 9
Jay – Lambeth

Jay was bored, he had to do something. No current pet project. He started the MacBook and remotely accessed a laptop in Wisconsin that was always turned on even when the owner left the house. He didn't know the owner, and frankly didn't care, but he knew enough. Mr Wisconsin had insufficient sense to be a hacker, he used too many porn sites, and clearly didn't have the slightest idea that a hacker could use his PC as a cover.

A certain gentleman in Wisconsin appeared to start looking at the systems of Nemesis Records.

Jay stared at the layers, the firewalls and passwords. All new since his last incursion. The smile spread across his face. There might not be much of value on the other side of those walls, but he was going to have fun challenging his opponent.

It turned out that the company had invested in a state-of-the-art fish tank for the office, meaning that a mobile phone app controlled things like temperature and pump settings. Jay smiled. Some people didn't have the vaguest idea.

Using the app as a backdoor, he hunted for ways to bypass the firewalls and new security access. Tricky, but he'd get through, however grainy his eyes. He reached for and chugged the canned energy drink, these hours made the others worthwhile.

***

He had it.

Okay, he didn't technically have the files yet, but Jay had passed every level of security and he could see everything that could be had. The encrypted ones stood out. That was important. An unencrypted file wasn't worth stealing.

He popped the lid of another Relentless energy drink. He hadn't stopped in twenty hours now and he needed the boost, but he wasn't about to quit at this point. He was in and he had to download these files. All of them. He sipped and enjoyed the surge of energy through his thin body.

He'd break into each file at his leisure. Right now he just needed to grab them.

***

Warning lights and alarms sounded as the completed bar hit 95% through the download. Jay's slouch straightened up, his eyes wide and desperate. He watched the progress bar and the journey of the trace. He'd routed it through enough hubs to keep it busy for a while. Hopefully long enough to finish this download.

Heart racing like a sprinter, Jay sat on the edge of his seat. The

26

guard dogs had got halfway through his diversions. They were unnervingly fast. Jay bit his lip, considering coming out of the download. If he did that, he'd lose the files and whatever had this much security around it had to be worth having.

Finally, the download completed. But Jay knew he had been traced. He knew too that any time now the police could be at his door. He knew from the press that the record label was already baying for his blood. Bye bye, NASA…

Jay pulled the plug on his connection to the world and tore modem leads from the phone line. Knowing that the box in his hands contained what fortune was his to be had, Jay scrambled, slamming the lid and finding the neoprene case. Then he scrambled again, this time for clothes. Stuffing what he grabbed in his bag, he tried frantically to figure out what to do, where to go.

He had to get out of here, but if the bastards traced him and his address, finding his dilapidated car wouldn't be a bother.

Frankie. Frankie had a car.

The now full knapsack went over his shoulder, Jay left his home and headed down the stairs. Jay was concerned about waking Frankie at this hour by pounding on his door. Frankie worked as a nightclub barman, he would only have got home in the early hours, so he might still be in bed. An angry, groggy Frankie was not a thing he contemplated with much optimism, but on the other hand, he might be about to give Frankie the heads up on the possibility of the police turning up, which, since Frankie used and occasionally dealt substances that the police would not view kindly, might work in his favour.

A few moments later, Jay suddenly found that the target of his hand fell away from him.

"This'd better be good, man," Frankie growled, leaning on his door, glowering at his neighbour.

Jay shifted, glancing every few seconds at the front door, desperate to see the arrival of authorities in time to make his exit though the back. "I've got trouble," Jay succinctly pointed out. "I need to get out of here fast." Jay looked back at Frankie. "I need your car, man, mine's in the shop. I'll send the keys back with details where it is, Frankie, I promise. But I gotta get out of here, like now." He checked the front again. "It's the police! Frankie, please!"

Frankie frowned at his neighbour. They had lived in the same building for three years, so they had a fairly clear idea each of each other. The lack of answer wasn't a no, it was a need to compute. "'Old on."

Jay shifted, uncomfortable in the hall, panicking each time a car

27

passed.

Suddenly Frankie reappeared, holding out his spare set of keys. "It's out the back."

"Cheers, Frankie." Jay grabbed the keys and ran.

Chapter 10
Branwen and Cobb – Pen-Y-Cwm Village

"So – what happened?"

Branwen looked up from her paperwork to see Emma had stepped into her office. "Knocking too much effort for you? Sorry." She hung her head and put her face in her hands. "It's been a bad day." For the umpteenth time that day, she wondered why she had ever come back to this Godforsaken Welsh valley. Why was she traipsing around, working her socks off only to constantly run into male chauvinist attitudes like the one she had just turned out of her consulting room?

The fact that the chauvinist in question happened to be her second cousin once removed didn't help matters either. Nor did the fact that he'd rather lop her completely off the family tree, but that was her experience of family, so nothing new.

She pushed away the annoyance and turned back to Emma, who closed the door and came to stand in front of her desk. "Don't avoid the question."

"I'm not," she lied, turning back to her notes. "I'm working. See? Look – working." She finished the entry, sighed and looked up. "What do you want, Emma?"

"I want to know what happened last night."

"I went to the dance alone. Came back here alone. Slept here alone. Got up this morning alone, now I'm working, unfortunately not alone. Shouldn't you be in your shop?"

Emma shrugged. "At this time of year, selling houses is a less than thriving industry."

"What about all the local crafts you sell to counter for that?"

Emma looked at her askew. "Crafts? You mean the homemade tat?"

Branwen smiled. "Now is that the way to pull in customers?"

Emma shrugged. "To them it's 'lovingly made traditional craftwork' or 'locally inspired artwork of the highest calibre.' Whatever I feel will best sell anything. But I didn't mean generally, I meant what happened with Cobb?"

The smile became fixed. "Nothing."

"Oh, come on."

Branwen looked away, the shame burning her insides.

"We danced once. Spoke twice." She shrugged, though less casually than she would have liked. "Nothing you'd be interested in happened."

"Maybe you should give him more of a green light."

Her eyes widened, and her cheeks burned at the memory of the green light she'd given. Emma's eyes brightened.

"Oh, something did happen! Come on. Tell your Aunty Em all about it."

Branwen hung her head, covered her face in her hands, unable to look at Emma as she told her best friend what she'd said.

"Wow."

Even the solitary word trembled with the laughter Emma was struggling to contain. Branwen looked up.

"Wow." Emma's face split in a wide grin. "That is one hell of a green light."

"Green light?" Now Branwen laughed too. "You should have seen the horror on his face! It wasn't so much a green light as a total stop sign. I tell you Em, if I ever had a hope, I don't now."

"After a line like that, probably not," Emma laughed. "On the other hand, you did basically announce you want sex with him."

"Yeah, great. A man whose first name I don't even know."

"That never stopped a woman jumping a man's bones before."

"Em!"

"Well it didn't." She seemed then to drift off. "I wonder what it is."

"What what is?"

"Cobb's first name."

Branwen frowned at her friend and this pointless diversion. "I haven't the foggiest. But how do you not know his name? Surely you had to have it for the house sale?"

Emma shook her head. "My records are complete with Mr E Cobb, and he paid with cash, so no mortgage paperwork to give the game away either. Even his bank card only says 'E Cobb'."

"I know, he's paid here with card a few times. What do you think it stands for?"

"Eric," Emma mused. "Or maybe Elvis." She laughed. "Thankyouver'much."

Despite her tension, Branwen found herself laughing too. "Enoch!"

"Edgar," Emma returned.

"Not stuffed shirt enough," Branwen declared, adding an imitation upper-crust accent. "Edward."

"Oh no," Emma frowned. "He doesn't look much like a Teddy to me."

"I wouldn't mind cuddling up to him."

As they both realised what Branwen had let slip, they fell into peals of laughter.

"How about Emlyn?"

"Nah, he's more Ernest." Branwen posed like a scowling statue.

"Oh, this is silly," Emma said. "Come on, let's go to the pub, commiserate and work out how we're going to hook you up with the unnamed hunk with the inviting elbows."

Thankfully it was half twelve and afternoon surgery didn't start until two.

***

Cobb's Jeep skidded to a halt in front of the Surgeries as Branwen turned to lock the door. She and Emma looked at each other as Cobb jumped from the driver's seat. Even in that small move, Branwen saw blood on his green coat.

"Hold the door open," Branwen told Emma as she rushed to the back of the car, meeting Cobb as he pulled Finn from the open boot area. The big dog was awake and snarling, blood covering his front paws. "Good God! What happened?"

"We went walking," Cobb grunted under the weight of the large animal as they headed towards the door Emma had open. "A sodding mantrap."

Pushing aside worries about the illegalities of those, Branwen started thinking about treatments as she rushed ahead to open other internal doors, taking Cobb and Finn straight through to her surgical room. As soon as Cobb was through, she covered the table in a disposable cloth and told him to put Finn on top. Then she started scrubbing up. "Emma, go see if Pete's upstairs, ask him if he'll help."

Finn kept trying to sit up, Cobb had to hold him down, and the big dog was showing the worst of his temperament, even snapping at Cobb. That worried Branwen; Finn was usually of the soppiest temperament of pretty much any animal she'd ever known. He still acted like a puppy. She suspected Cobb overindulged him like one too.

"It's okay boy," Branwen soothed as she dried her hands and threw the paper towel away. "We'll get you sorted soon as." First thing she had to do was get the animal sedated. Though not strictly necessary for a plastering, with Finn in obvious distress, she didn't want to have to deal with wolfhound bites as well. She opened the cupboard and selected the appropriate sedative, then as Cobb tried to calm the big animal, she grabbed the scruff of Finn's neck and administered the small dose quickly. It took a few heartbeats, then the dog started to feel the effects. Carefully, Branwen eased the grey head to the table, making sure nothing got bumped on the way.

Doc appeared at the door, immediately scrubbed up and pulled a green plastic apron over his head.

"Cobb," Branwen said. "Cobb!" Shouting the second time got the big man's attention. "Why don't you go sit in the waiting area?

There's cleaners on the counter you can wipe yourself down with while Pete and I take care of Finn."

Cobb stared at her, and she could see the effort he had to use to focus, to understand. That was fear, heart-stopping fear. Finn was the thing he cared most about in the world and he was now faced with the prospect of losing him. Finally, Cobb nodded once and turned away. His long stride was measured, nothing rushed or uncontrolled. That one moment of skidding into the carpark was the closest Branwen had ever seen Cobb come to losing control.

"What do you need me to do?" Pete asked.

***

Cobb felt sick. Finn was hurt and he could do nothing to help him. He moved to the waiting room and waited as he'd been told. Orders, obey orders. You didn't question it, you just did it.

There's cleaners on the counter you can wipe yourself down with.

He stood up and moved across to the counter, found the spray bottle and the hung roll of blue paper towel. For a moment he just stood there with the two in his hands, uncertain what to do. Two slim hands with bright red nails came and took both from him.

Emma. Emma was here.

She squirted the cleaner on the cloth and then started to wipe the front of his jacket. He stepped back and she stopped. Confusion showed in her eyes as she looked up at him.

"Cobb?"

The voice seemed to come from far away. He lifted up his hands, saw the bloodstains. Just like before. Just like when he'd run to her, held her, cradled her. They'd made him give her up, but he'd not wanted to wash her blood away. He'd sat for so long they'd called her stated next of kin. Unfortunately, that was him, Cobb, so they'd called her emergency contact. Their business partner had come to the hospital, yelled orders at him until he'd stood to attention and done what he'd been told.

"Cobb?" Emma's voice intruded. "What's wrong?"

No explanation came to him. No explanation could. He could no more wash Finn's blood off his jacket than he could ever have washed her blood from his hands. He'd seen the face of the man, the murderer. He'd sworn to kill the bastard, but never identified him, never had the chance.

"Mantraps are illegal." The softly spoken words seemed to echo in the waiting room.

"Yes, they are."

"Call the police, I want to report one."

Emma put the cleaner and the towels on the counter. Moved

around him, her heels clicking on the linoleum flooring. She appeared again behind the counter, and from there she used the vet's landline to call the police.

It was unlikely that anyone other than PC Johnson would respond. And less likely that he'd do anything. But Cobb would obey the law and if nothing happened, he'd find the man who'd hurt his dog and make him pay.

Cobb reached over the counter and put his finger on the rest to cut the connection.

Emma looked confused. "Revenge isn't worth it."

"No."

She put the phone down properly as Cobb finally felt his brain kick into gear.

"However, mantraps are illegal, it needs to be reported."

Cobb nodded. "Once I know Finn's going to be okay."

"Fair enough." Emma looked pointedly at his hands. "You do need to get cleaned up. Why don't you use the bathroom?"

Cobb frowned. "Up in the doctor's surgery?"

"Well you could, but I was thinking of Branwen's private cloakroom. Come with me."

He followed her into Branwen's office and the door he had always assumed was just a cupboard, but was actually a compact toilet. Emma asked for his coat and he passed it over. Then he was on his own. This room might work for Branwen, but it made him claustrophobic. He reached back and reopened the door while the other hand turned on the taps at the basin. The water ran red as it washed blood off his hands. There wasn't much, not like before. Guilt filled him. How dare he let go of Finn so easily? He wasn't letting go, Finn wasn't going to die. He'd be a grumpy guts for weeks with an injury like that, but he wasn't going to die. Branwen would make sure of that.

Cobb looked in the small mirror. Strain marked every feature, his eyes looked every bit as haunted as they felt. Could Branwen be right? Did he need some time to be with others? Had separating himself from the world been a mistake? Branwen kept pulling him back to the world, back to her.

No.

He'd thought long and hard about his decision. It was the right one. This was just a moment of weakness. Besides, Branwen was leaving, there was no future in any idea of being with her.

He leaned down, cupped water in his hands and plunged his face in, scrubbing the sweat and dirt, the day's growth of beard he hadn't bothered to shave this morning. Be calm, be patient,

33

Branwen would bring his dog back to him.

Returning to the waiting room, Cobb was surprised to see Emma at the counter, rubbing the blue paper towels over the front of his jacket. She looked up.

"I've got the worst of it off." She picked the jacket up and showed him. "It'll still need washing, but..."

"Thanks." Cobb stepped over and took the coat from her. He sank onto the waiting benches and the coat went down beside him. Elbows on knees, he covered his face with his hands. He didn't see, but he sensed Emma coming to his other side, sitting beside him. "I can't lose her again."

"Him."

Cobb frowned and looked at Emma.

"Finn's a boy dog. That's him, you said her."

Had he? Yes. Returning to the world would be like losing her again, like trying to forget her. He couldn't do that. He forced a small smile. "You're right. That's what I meant... I can't lose him."

"Good thing you're not about to, then."

He looked up at Branwen's voice and saw her coming into the room. She shifted his coat to sit beside him. She looked concerned, but not like she was about to deliver bad news.

"Finn's going to be fine. In fact, he was really lucky. The skin and muscles were torn by that trap, but it didn't fracture the bone, so it's about as good as it could be. Did you take note of the condition of the trap itself?"

"It worked well enough."

"Unfortunately," Branwen agreed, "but what I need to know is what kind of condition the blade was in. Was it clean or rusted? What kind of ground was it on, what could have got into the wound?"

Cobb swallowed and considered it. "The mechanism was oiled, but the blade was rusty. We were up on common land, so..."

Branwen nodded. "He should be fine then, dogs are largely resistant to tetanus and I know his shots are up to date. I don't like forcing antibiotics on animals unnecessarily, and I know how strong Finn is, so I'll keep away from that for the time being. I am, however, going to keep him here for a few nights, I want to make sure that he's kept inside and that wound is kept clean."

"I can do that," Cobb insisted, not liking the idea of being without the animal for any length of time.

"No, you can't. Finn's a big and determined dog. If he wants to get out, he only needs one unguarded moment from you and he's through the single doorway between him and outside. Here, there are a minimum three doors he's got to pass to get out. It's better he stays here."

There was little he could argue with, so he nodded instead.

"Because of the nature of the injury, this has to be reported to the police. Have you called them yet?"

He shook his head.

"Given that the most likely responder is Constable Johnston, do you want me to deal with that?"

Cobb nodded.

"Okay." She looked to Emma. "Em, you were looking for a drink earlier and I think Cobb needs one, will you take him over to the pub and don't let him drive home until he can do so safely?"

Chapter 11
Alex – St John's Wood

Alex booted up the computer and ran his hands over his face. God, he was exhausted. Mother wasn't recovering. She wasn't *going* to recover. She was dying. Had been for a while now. Some days he wished she'd just get on and do it.

Unable to face another hour at that hospital bed, he'd come back to the recording studio and five minutes peace. The next booking started in two hours, he should have time to eat some lunch, do some remixing. He looked up to the screen, logged in and headed to delete that bloody file. Ridiculously, he'd forgotten about it till now, but he'd had a lot to deal with and now he had to deal with this. He clicked on the file and hit delete.

Nothing happened.

Perhaps too many programs were running concurrently and slowing the machine down. He shook his head at the stupidity of that. He'd only just logged in, hadn't started doing anything yet. The only program running was file explorer.

Movement caught the corner of his eyes. The red and green modem symbol flashed in the bottom right of the screen, giving the game away.

Somebody had linked his machine into the Net – and it wasn't him.

Alex explored the network. He checked the guardian program and let out an explosive expletive that would have shocked fans of classical pianist Alexander Berenger. Classical pianists didn't swear, according to their fans, apparently. According to Granger, it was the Clayderman Effect. Alex pushed the irrelevant concept aside, activated the tracer program and set the dogs on their intruder. He sat glued to the screen as the world map appeared and the program started drawing lines back to the intruder's base.

This guy is good, Alex thought, but he'd known that from the hacker's ability to bypass the guard dogs when he'd hacked the latest Greebo K single. They'd upped the ante on the firewall and the security, but the hacker had still got past it all. The new system had already picked up five would-be intruders, all of whom had been investigated by the police but found not to be connected to the original theft.

This time the tracer jumped all over the globe like an overexcited flea. Alex scraped his hair back. It felt like forever. There – Wisconsin. No, that was a hacked system too.

It took twenty minutes, but the tracker found the originator. The bastard was right here in London.

"Bingo," said Alex.

Granger took some time to answer the phone and while he waited, an odd track of the hard drive caught Alex's attention. He was just quick enough to tell that another file had been downloaded before the hacker jacked out.

"This'd better be good," Granger snapped.

"It is," Alex said, ignoring the grunting and clamping the phone against his shoulder, trying to identify which files had been copied. "The defence programs have been breached. I think this is the same hacker as before. I've traced the guy."

"Who? Where?"

"Calls himself CyberousRex. Records have him as a James Whitney." He reeled off the address.

"Right." Now Granger was already dialling on his second line.

"Want me to call the police?" Alex asked.

"No!" Granger snapped down the phone at him. "Leave this to me. I'll deal with it."

Chapter 12
Simons – City of London

This wasn't what Simons expected; after finishing another assignment, Simons headed straight to O'Rourke's office, unsure if he'd catch the man. He arrived just in time to see O'Rourke stepping into a large black limo. The dark-suited chauffeur who held the door looked vaguely Italian, but was probably English through and through, several generations UK born and bred.

The darkened windows of the limo blocked virtually every detail, but Simons saw O'Rourke wasn't alone. The tinted windows and the five to five evening lack of light conspired to quickly rob him even of that view. He held two cars back in the choked London traffic and kept an eye on where the limo went. The multi-storey carpark surprised him, not least of all because he would have hesitated to have driven that long wheel base vehicle into that space. The limo continued up the spiral towards the parking, and Simons pulled quickly into a space. The benefit of the Golf lay in its being nippy and easily parked, and after the work he'd done on it, it also drove faster than it was designed to. Grabbing the backpack, he rushed from the car, remotely locking it, pulling the bag onto one shoulder as he ran up the stairs. At each floor he checked to see if the limo had stopped. By the sixth level his thighs burned. More importantly, there was the limo, at the far end of the level, exactly where no overhead lights shone, a convenience Simons assumed O'Rourke had a hand in.

The only other vehicle on the level was a small Belingo van stuck up on bricks – that the carpark attendants hadn't had that carted away was a minor miracle.

With no other vehicles in sight and no movement from the limo, Simons could just about make out the driver still at the wheel. Crouching in the small gap between the Belingo and the wall of the carpark, he readied his camera and the parabolic microphone. The earphones slipped easily over his ears.

"… n't a clue."

"And the other guy?" That voice he recognised as O'Rourke's.

"No, sir. He's good for muscle, and not as stupid as he sometimes pretends, but he believes we only work for Granger."

"Hmm, Baron?"

"Yes, sir?"

"Keep it that way."

"Of course, sir."

Simons noted the names, Baron, Granger. The distinct sound of another car coming up the ramp. Its speed varied with the need for caution on corners, but it slowed as it came to level six.

The second car stopped perpendicular to the Belingo. Simons was reasonably sure that the driver hadn't seen him. This driver flashed his lights three times. Then the limo did the same before it turned its lights off. The new arrival drove halfway down the car park, and parked in line with the road way, over three spaces. It was a personal bugbear of Simons when people pulled crap like that, but tonight he said nothing, just watched and listened.

From the second car stepped a man. A big man, protuberant belly, double breasted suit that didn't suit him. Simons saw the way he worked his hands; this guy was nervous. Meeting O'Rourke in a place like this, the man had good reason to be. He walked carefully toward the limo.

Headlights flicked on full beam, the fat man stopped, shielding his eyes, Simons squinted, the camera would be useless now.

A large figure stepped from the back of the limo, walked around the vehicle and opened the other rear door. The first figure remained by the door, insufficient ambient light making him only a silhouette. The second man to exit the vehicle moved forward, forward enough for the headlights to back light him.

"So, you messed up again, Fat Man."

Every word came through crystal clear into Simons earphones and thus the recording. The fat man's back straightened, his shoulders shifted, he must be rankling at the description.

"The situation is under control. We have the hacker."

"Explain," O'Rourke demanded.

"Alex Berenger traced him."

Simons wondered if the fat man realised how his voice shook.

"I've sent my men to get him. I'll have all those files back within the hour. It's under control."

"You're lying."

"No! I swear I –"

"You said it was under control last time. You also said that about the incident with your last employer."

"This is different!"

"Yes, it is," said O'Rourke calmly. "This is your last chance. Get those files back. Or it will be the last thing you don't do."

Despite protests from the fat man, O'Rourke returned to his car, the other man closed the door and went to his side. The limo was moving away. Simons noted the number plate as the fat man, dejection written in his every move, returned to his car and also left the car park. Only when both were gone did Simons pack up and leave.

Time to find out who the fat man was.

Chapter 13
Baron – Lambeth

At one time, Baron thought as he pulled up before the Victorian terrace, this would have been a lovely area. Substantial homes for large families. Now it was all dive-flat studentville with all the accompanying problems of mess and decay that came along with that.

The house they were heading for was mid-terrace, the tiny front garden covered in greening pavers and the only thing growing was a wheelie bin and an overflowing box of empty beer bottles. The front door was ajar, like someone had rushed out and forgotten to pull it closed. Baron didn't care who or why, only that it meant he could just walk in. They wanted flat 4, on the first floor. He paced up, with Shoreham at his heels. There was no answer to his knock. The Yale lock was solid, but it was only a Yale lock and he was through that in under a minute.

Flat 4 was empty.

Baron turned to leave. Shoreham stood sentinel in the doorway, filling it almost as completely as the door. In a discrete black suit, with a shirt and a tie, he looked like a million other East End bouncers who thought they'd look good in the West End.

Without a word, he tipped his chin, Shoreham stood back, and Baron led the way downstairs, the big man close behind. Flat 2 was the closest to hand, Baron knocked on the door.

"Oh, for fuck's sake!"

He didn't know who lived here, but they clearly weren't in a good mood. The door opened a crack, there was a chain from the door, but the man didn't use it. Without a shirt on, joggers just about clinging to his hips, it was clear the man was fit, but not bulky, there wasn't a spare ounce on him. He had a square face, wide nose typical of black men, and close-cropped hair. Judging from the pungent aroma and dilated pupils, he'd been smoking something relaxing.

"Yeah?"

Baron pushed down the tension. Why did the young adult age group refuse to use full words, 'yes' was hardly difficult. "We're looking for James Whitney."

The black man's lip curled, he frowned. "Who?"

"James Whitney."

The man blinked like thinking was just too difficult. "Oh! You mean Jay, man?"

Baron just looked at him. Saw the man's eyes flick to Shoreham. "Wrong flat. Jay lives upstairs. Number four."

40

The man tried to close the door. Baron's boot stopped him. "We went there first. He's not in."

"Maybe he's out, then."

Baron didn't have much time for wasters and this waster was wasting his time. He didn't like that. "Maybe you know where he's likely to have gone, Mr...?"

The frown suggested the man's uncertainty of his own name, then Baron spotted it. There was actual intelligence in there somewhere; this man might have had a drag or two of pot, but he wasn't potty, he was just playing it up. He was helping hide Whitney, Baron was sure of it.

"Where's Whitney?"

"Man, I'm the man's neighbour, not his keeper. How the bloody 'ell do you expect me to know where the guy is?" He tried closing the door again, but again Baron's foot stopped him.

This time Baron put his hands up and forced the door back, following the man as he was forced to stumble back into his flat. A torrent of abusive language was launched at them in the cannabis heat. Shoreham stepped inside, picked Frankie up by the throat as Baron carefully, quietly closed the flat door.

**

Baron looked at Granger. The guy paid, but not as well as O'Rourke. Granger didn't do lots of things as well as O'Rourke, hell there were lots of things Granger didn't do as well as Granger thought he did. The whole throne thing in this office, the chair in the other room. These weren't symbols of success, but symbols of Granger's need for success, of his own stupidity. However much the fat man sat there drumming his fingers and trying to appear stern, he just looked like an overstuffed baby in a suit, a petulant child who deserved a good slap. Baron figured O'Rourke wasn't a million miles away from ordering that smack down either.

The only thing Granger had right was what a mess this all had become. O'Rourke was not a happy man, he might not know exactly what had been stolen, but he understood it might seriously damage Nemesis Records and that might in turn affect O'Rourke's business. Money laundering needed viable businesses to cover it.

Baron glanced at Shoreham. The taller man stood straight and looked not at Granger, but directly ahead, over Granger's head. Baron wasn't sure what Shoreham took in at times like this. He didn't respond but he'd act in the field when it mattered.

"You will find him." Granger's voice rang with certainty. Opening the top drawer of his desk, the producer picked out an unmarked buff document wallet. With a small flick of his wrist, Granger threw the wallet to the other side of his desk. Shoreham stepped forward to take it. "You will find him, and you will get my files back."

"Whatever it takes," Baron nodded.

"Exactly."

A perfect match to O'Rourke's order. He flicked open the file and saw more details on James Whitney's life. He closed the file and looked at Granger.

"We're on it."

***

Wanting to read the file on Whitney, Baron gave Shoreham the address and let the big man drive. Thankfully that meant he didn't have to watch the road, as Shoreham drove like he did everything else – aggressively.

The aunt's address in West London was closer, so worth trying first, though Baron suspected that Whitney would scurry home to his parents' estate in Hampshire. They arrived at 22:45; catching people off guard and unsociable hours worked in their favour. Baron considered what the aunt might be like; the picture suggested straight laced, the job – librarian – suggested quiet and easily manipulated.

The house was an Edwardian three-storey in an area rapidly becoming fashionable with the trendy set. Number 23 had an air that suggested neither it nor its occupant would ever stoop to being fashionable or trendy.

As Shoreham parked in front of the house Baron thought this was just what a maiden aunt's home should look like. Moving from the car, Baron shrugged his shoulders, and the dark tailored jacket fell easily into a comfortable and smart hang from his well-developed breadth.

Shoreham came from his side of the car and in silence the two men measured the pace to the front door.

Chapter 14
Branwen – Pen-Y-Cwm Farm and Guesthouse

Tension made Branwen shake as she drove up to her own home. Generations of Joneses had been born, grown, worked, loved, played and died at Pen-Y-Cwm Farm. She was the last. Of the last four generations, only she had been born within wedlock, but the life here, the control her grandmother and great-grandmother had tried to wield had set an unpalatable air over the place for her Tuscan mother. Now all three women were gone. Two to their graves and one back to her homeland. Branwen had no memory of her mother, who had been forced out before Branwen's second birthday. Branwen's knowledge of her mother came from searches in university, from the letters they had exchanged, when she had a separate address so father wouldn't get to the post.

The past worrying her as she parked, was the one between Cobb and Pete. They were both standing by the container in which they stored the Mountain Rescue equipment. Michael Woolverton had asked that while he was away they do a stock take. Looked like they were doing it now and not happily.

She glanced to the cowshed, the animals were down from the fields now, the snow last night had been deeper than predicted and more was on the way. The lambing shed was full too, she'd had to bring the other ewes off the mountain for safety's sake.

The wind tried to force her door closed again when she opened it. Then it turned, let her out, allowed her to step from the vehicle. She raised a hand in acknowledgement to the two men, and for a moment she heard a word or two before the wind whipped them away again.

"… friends a lot longer…"

Well, yes, she had been friends with Pete a lot longer than she had been with Cobb, but she'd intended to greet them both with that wave. At the front door, she turned back to see her father stomping over from the cowshed towards to the house, so she waited.

"Neither of you is good enough for my daughter. Ever considered that?"

The annoyance on Iolyn Jones's face seemed permanently carved, but his being annoyed enough to speak out was rare. Especially on such a topic. For a moment she saw the surprise on the two younger men's faces, then her father filled her vision and shooed her inside.

Chapter 15
Jay – Chiswick

The nail gave way, Jay pulled the strip of keratin from his thumb, wincing as it tore into the cuticle. But that didn't stop him sitting in his aunt's back bedroom chewing on his thumbnail and wondering what the hell he was going to do next.

Aunt Sophie had always been a straight-laced old woman, which left Jay somewhat surprised to find her housing a Vaio complete with Wi-Fi connection. Last time he'd been here, she'd had a tower so old upgrades were impossible.

"Information Superhighway," she had trilled when he had expressed surprise. "Got to move with the times." And move she had, well regards the technology she had, shame about her attachment to the twin set and pearls.

But Sophie wasn't the problem. Taking a risk Jay called Frankie, to sort out returning the car. Frankie's girlfriend informed him that the barman was laid up in hospital after a vicious and unexplained attack at his home. She'd also explained in graphic detail the injuries Frankie'd incurred and what pieces of description he had been able to give through a broken jaw.

The police, Jay could deal with. Sort of. If the police caught up with him, yeah, he would be arrested and put in clink. Despite rumours to the contrary, he believed widespread police brutality to be a fallacy – please God let it be a fallacy! Yes, he would face charges – being his first offence, he would likely make police bail. Then in court he would be given a hefty fine. Mummy and Daddy might be of assistance again there. The only problem might be a ban from computer use or ownership or some other equally pointless punishment like community service, but probably he'd be relatively unscathed by the encounter.

Except that it wasn't his first offence, and if the police found him, they'd probably figure that out.

Steroid-pumped goons, however, were a completely different prospect.

He could obliterate his entire MacBook memory, but that would lose him the files he'd worked so hard to get, something he wasn't ready to do. Goons meant that the recording company had not only traced him and knew who he was, but that they (a) had not called the police and (b) wanted to play hardball, which led to the conclusion that (c) they probably weren't too bothered about rules. Jay considered pulped features, broken bones, mangled bodies, having his balls ripped off and being left to die, bleeding in some forgotten alleyway.

Jay swallowed bile, hugged his drawn-up knees, frowned and bit his nail. The only respite the persecuted extremity had was when he ran that hand through his hair. If he kept the data, he might be able to use it as a bargaining chip.

Jay worried about (c). No rules.

No rules – no police. No police – no rules.

$$X + Y = Z$$

In this case, Z equalled they had something to hide.

***

They had something to hide.

The thought resounded in Jay's head. They had something to hide and he had the key to it. That had to be why they were after him. Okay, there was the pirate Greebo K single he had grabbed, selling thousands, but the police knew all about that and if they were after him for piracy then it would have been uniforms who turned up on his doorstep, not slap-happy goons.

So it must be something in the files he had down loaded from Nemesis Music's recording system. The largest was GKINT1220.

Jay figured since he had cracked the rest of the codes, he would easily crack the encoding on these files. Whatever he had must be worth a fortune and he couldn't start bargaining for it or his safety until he knew what he had.

With Aunt Sophie out at bingo, Jay used the study at the back of the house. The overly cute chintz suite and large rose-bloom wallpaper battled with the over-patterned carpet to give him a headache. Volumes of Windows for Dummies and Jane Eyre seemed uneasy neighbours behind the bevelled glass of the antique bookcase.

He had never seen a laptop so out of place as on that mahogany writing desk. Still, the choice was Sophie's as was the laptop, so he moved it out of the way and put his own MacBook down instead. Code was all that stood between him and the file so he had to break it. Hard as getting the file had been, this might only be a case of finding one more password. Jay hoped for such ease.

Running the password finder on the encryption took only seconds; after quarter of an hour he had grown stiff sitting still and his eyes ached from watching little screen movements, but the flashing asterisks indicated progress through potential passwords.

Eventually, he had to bow to Mother Nature, and wandered off to the bathroom. Releasing the contents of his bladder, Jay scraped long blond hair out of his eyes. He really should get it cut. The thick foliage of fir trees in the backyard helped make the small window before him a poor mirror. Jay studied himself with a critical gaze. Okay, so he was no Mister Universe, but he had a distinctive look.

With the pressure on his bladder relieved, Jay completed his ablutions before turning to the proper bathroom mirror. Thick glasses didn't help. He pulled them off and leaned closer. The effect was quite surprising. Jay rarely looked at his face without glasses. Being short-sighted meant he needed them even when he shaved to avoid cutting his own throat.

Contact lenses.

He had never seriously considered them before, but they would help change his appearance. Maybe a beard too, which for no explicable reason always grew ginger. Maybe change the hair, dye it to match the beard. No more shaving.

Whoever the goons were, they had to have his description, so changing his look had to be a good idea. He should at least try some disposable lenses. How hard could finding a hairdresser to change his hair be? Or even a box dye.

Yes.

He would do it first thing in the morning.

That decision made, Jay slouched back to the study. Stopping in the doorway, he saw the file open. Back at the keyboard, Jay first checked the finder program. The password surprised him. BERENGER.

Jay frowned. That made no sense – usually passwords displayed some logic, otherwise the users forgot them. Okay, Greebo K and Alexander Berenger were both signed with Nemesis Music, but why use the name Berenger on a file that had more to do with Greebo K. It didn't make sense.

An hour later, it made all too much sense. It also explained why goons were coming after him, rather than the police. Nemesis Records really did have something to hide. A big something.

But was it really that big? Fakes filled the entertainment industry and the world knew that. It could cost an artist a career, but would a record company care that much? Jay wasn't even sure how to classify the crime.

He Googled "musicians that fake their music". The returned list wasn't inspiring, but he clicked the first link: "15 Most Outrageous Faked Musical Performances" from Rolling Stone. Turned out to be a list of people who had basically lip-synced on stage. The worst thing he found was a band called Milli Vanilli being dropped by their label. He didn't see anything that bad. He looked the group up again. Ah. Bad. Lead singer might have killed himself. Yeah okay, bad, but still only bad on an individual basis, not a record label basis.

Closing everything down, Jay pondered his next move. Would

the individuals send thugs? They were successful enough to have the cash, but would they have the contacts? He didn't know. He did know Richard Granger had a shady past, rumours abounded of dark clouds and shadowy figures when he set up Nemesis. Of course, the interview wasn't the only file he had. What if something dangerous lurked in the other files? He'd have to find out at some point. Or was it better to leave them?

Jay considered taking the whole thing to the police. Only then he would have to explain how he had the recording and that would lead to even more trouble for him. He had to stop second guessing himself. His already tortured thumb nail took another beating.

Perhaps the music press – but then the interview proved they were as involved as any of the others. Where could trust be safely placed?

He had to move on. That at least was clear. He considered where to go as he hurriedly packed. One night sleeping rough would be manageable, then what? Hating himself for it, he raided Aunt Sophie's moneybox, taking two hundred pounds. He'd need the cash to change his appearance.

***

Coming down the stairs with his bag, Jay froze hearing the knock at the front door. Sophie was due back any minute, but she wouldn't knock. She, of course, had her own key. No visitor would call at this hour. Or at least, no welcome visitor. Stuck on the bottom step, Jay's heart started to race. Instinctively he knew who it was. Large shadows moving into the opaque window only confirmed his worse fears.

Thanking God and Aunt Sophie that she lived in a terrace, Jay crept carefully, picking his way to the back of the house. At the end of the surprisingly long garden, Jay opened the gate in the high wall and entered the narrow alley between the backs. The shortest length of alley lay to his right, but that was also likely to be the way the thugs would come if they decided to try the back of the house.

Jay set off to the left at a brisk pace.

Chapter 16
Baron – Chiswick

The door remained obstinately shut; a large panel of opaque glass filled the top half. Baron thought he saw movement beyond, but with no accompanying sound or answering of the door, he couldn't be sure.

"Can I help you two gentlemen?"

Baron turned at the voice. The woman stood tall and erect, steel hair short and curled. Genteel suit, low heeled, sensible shoes. All she needed were glasses on a chain around her neck and she'd be the cliché of her job type.

"Are you Sophie Whitney?"

Sophie's eyebrow arched like the question surprised her. She looked him up and down. If not a librarian, Baron figured she'd make a great teacher. Or copper. "Who's asking?"

Shoreham shifted, like he might try some intimidation. Baron stopped him by getting there first, taking one step closer to Sophie for all she didn't give an inch.

"We're looking for James Whitney."

She sized him up, classifying him and deciding how to catalogue him under the Dewey Decimal system. Would she put him under physical health or true-life crime?

"I haven't seen Jay in months. He doesn't like being called James. He called a few weeks ago, when term started up, but I've heard nothing since. He has his own flat in the centre of town. Try there."

Baron smiled in the face of her cool response. "Why don't we discuss this inside?"

"Because there's nothing to discuss," Sophie told him evenly. "Jay is not here and I have no idea where he is."

Shoreham stepped up to the woman's side. "It's not an option." The big man grabbed her arm and pushed her to the door, moving to stand far too close behind her. "If you don't unlock the door and let us in, I'll break it down. That will make me angry, and you won't like me angry."

The urge to roll his eyes only just remained controlled, Baron doubted Shoreham even knew he'd just quoted Bruce Banner before he turned into the Hulk. Clearly Sophie did however, and she gave Shoreham a look that would have turned a more sensitive soul to a pillar of salt. Shoreham's lack of sensitivities only heightened the threat in the moment.

"Prove Jay isn't inside, and we'll go away."

Shoreham didn't usually say such things, because usually they didn't go away, they stayed, did what had to be done, but the old lady seemed to believe him and opened the door with a trembling hand. Inside, Shoreham pushed Sophie to the front room and sat her down. Moving away, he drew the curtains. Silently, Baron followed them in, propped the door open to ensure he got a good view of the hallway, just in case. Then he sat, watching Sophie and the opened door. Baron glanced at Shoreham; the nod of his head sent the blond man searching the house.

"So where is Jay?" Baron asked.

"In his flat, I should think."

"We already tried there. He's packed and gone."

"Then I don't know." Her back ramrod straight, she looked at Baron as though he was nothing more than dirt beneath her feet. His lips pursed, his eyes narrowed. Even beneath that imperial sneer, he could see her fear.

"Guess."

"Well he won't have gone to his parents' house," she stated. "They're out of the country again."

"I want to know where he is, not where he isn't."

"Try his friends."

"Which friends?"

"I don't know," Sophie informed him as if speaking to a backward five-year-old. "I don't know his friends. We don't exactly move in the same circles."

For a moment Baron wondered which of them the uneven glare favoured. Shoreham reappeared, walked straight over to Sophie and whacked the back of his hand across her face. She fell to the side, crying out and holding her throbbing face.

"Where is he?" the tall blond growled. "He's obviously been here. So where is he?"

"I don't know!" Shifting away from Shoreham, Sophie sat up again.

Two large hands easily encircled her throat. "When did he leave?"

The grip was tight. Baron watched the wide-eyed Sophie struggle for breath.

"She can't tell you if she can't breathe."

Shoreham pushed her towards the back of the sofa. She looked back up in fear, finally understanding the precariousness of her situation.

"I'm not sure." Her voice shook, fear filling her eyes. "Please. I swear. I don't know where he is."

"Was he here?"

Weakly she nodded. "Was when I left this evening. He said nothing about leaving or where he might go. You have to believe me."

"Oh, I do."

49

Shoreham reached down, grabbed her again by the throat despite her ineffectual protest.

The neck snapped loud and quick.

Chapter 17
Branwen and Cobb – Pen-Y-Cwm Village

No one enjoyed admin, but it had to be done, and Branwen had a plan for the rest of the day. Get it and a few other necessities sorted. She sat at her desk and tried to carry on.

In the other room, only two cages had occupants: a castrated cat slept in one large cell and a few feet away in the big floor pen, Finn lay on a blanket, whining occasionally and generally feeling sorry for himself. Once she'd finished the drugs stock take, she'd let him out to pad around the office.

Branwen smiled at the big dog from behind her desk. She had left the door open to the adjoining room. The back door of the surgeries opened, but that didn't surprise her. Doc Pearson shared the building with her. Humans went upstairs for their health check, the animals stayed downstairs. The only point of connection was the back door she and the Doc used – otherwise known as the emergency exit. At 11:46, she assumed it was Pete's receptionist leaving after the last patient, it was Saturday after all, half day for the pair of them. A second set of footfalls didn't surprise her either. They would probably belong to the sometimes-scary male district nurse.

Branwen turned back to her papers, not looking up as Finn shifted noisily in his cage and whined in false patheticness.

"Cry baby," Branwen called through to the mutt. Then with more sympathy, she went on. "I know you miss your daddy, but you can go back to him just as soon as you're better. Maybe, if you're a good boy and get better, I'll call him Monday and your daddy can come pick you up."

"You know-"

Branwen jumped at the voice. Startled, she looked up to see Cobb standing in her doorway.

"–I've always hoped my offspring would come out better-looking than that mutt."

Branwen had no doubt that they would, should Cobb ever get close enough to a woman to have kids. "Bloody hell, Cobb. How'd you get in?"

"Came in with Stan."

Stan Fairbrass, the district nurse. "Fair enough, but this is the second day in a row you've visited the village, are you unwell?"

He rolled his eyes at her.

"Just so you know, I reported the mantrap, and gave the position you gave me. Johnston said he'd look into it."

"Do you think he will?"

"It is his job."

"Yeah, but do you think he will?"

She wished she had a better answer to give than a pathetic shrug. Johnson wasn't that interested in doing his job. Except when it meant booking her for speeding on her way to emergency call outs.

Cobb half-smiled at her as he sauntered through to hunker down and fuss the large animal, who pushed his head into his master's hand, loving the attention and playing for sympathy.

"Looks like your daddy's been missing you, Finn."

After less than a day. Coming to the doorway, Branwen leaned on the jamb and watched the unusual display of affection. If only she could show him a fraction of that affection. Still some things just didn't work out that way. She sighed.

"You know, boy, I think Mummy's jealous of all this attention you're getting."

Branwen frowned, focusing properly on Cobb, then she gave a half-hearted smile. "Nah, it's just any excuse to avoid the paperwork."

Cobb petted Finn one last time and rose to stand before her.

"Would an offer of a drink in the 'Pig' be similarly distracting."

Oh, tempting idea. She really should be getting the paperwork done though. She looked at the crowded desk, then back to the man. Cobb didn't voluntarily spend time with anyone. "I'll get my coat."

***

Predictably quiet in the middle of the afternoon, The Pig and Whistle had a roaring fire keeping the place wonderfully warm, and the alcohol-free larger Cobb bought them proved deliciously cold. Sitting together in the snug, their knees brushing under the table, neither felt any urgency to talk.

After the first quarter-pint, Branwen sighed and thanked Cobb again.

"My pleasure."

"Really?" she asked.

"Why not?" he countered.

She shrugged, looking into her beer. "Normally you shun most human contact, and here you are inviting it."

"You're not most humans."

"What am I then, an alien?" She didn't seem to be enjoying the joke. "No, don't answer that," she quickly added. "I probably am alien to this lot." She glanced at the village beyond the glass.

"That makes two of us, then." Cobb understood completely. "Are you still planning to leave?" he asked after a few moments silence.

She nodded. "I've made a few calls, there's a couple of interested parties who are considering the business. Selling a practice like this is never going to be a quick shift, I guess. And once it's gone, so will I be. For good."

Seeing how she gazed out of the window, a look of longing in her eyes, Cobb seriously doubted that. "You'll be missed."

She turned to look at him.

"The village knows you, your clients will miss you."

"They'll have another vet and will soon forget me."

"Your friends won't."

She snorted at that. "You miscounted." Bitterness tinged her small laugh. "That should be my 'friend' will miss me. Besides, Em'll be too busy. She came running round to tell me how wonderfully she and Ivan are getting along. She even said she thought he might propose, and if he did that she'd like to start a family straight off. Em may miss me, but she'll cope."

"What about your father?"

"He'll survive. He managed while I went to Uni."

"He knew you would come back then."

She seemed about to say something, but the phone in her pocket started ringing. As she apologised and pulled it out, Cobb noted it wasn't her usual ring tone, but something new. Her greeting explained the disparity.

"Pen-Y-Cwm Farm and Guesthouse, can I help?"

Apparently, she'd redirected the business phone to hers, must mean her father was doing something that precluded him answering a phone. Cobb sat in silence, listening to her take a booking for the guesthouse.

There was no question, he and Finn would miss her if she left. She would almost certainly miss Pen-Y-Cwm and village life too. Having spent enough time in towns and cities, he knew what survival there required. He didn't doubt Branwen would make it, but she would be a fool to think simply moving away would make her happy. For once, Cobb agreed with Emma – Branwen wasn't suffering from the location, but the absence of affection. He'd seen the need in his own reflection too often not to recognise it in her. After what had happened to Mary -

He pushed down the rising bile and tamped on the accelerating heart rate. Over two years and he still couldn't think back on what had happened without being overwhelmed by this sense of grief.

Suddenly a warm hand covered his. He looked up to see Branwen looking at him a little too closely, her phone call obviously over.

"You can talk to me."

He wanted to do a damn sight more than just talk to her. *She's*

53

leaving. Maybe that was a good thing, he could tell her now and not have to face her once she knew the truth.

"Cobb, we all have things in our past we'd rather not think about, sometimes I see you drift away and I get scared you won't come back."

He understood, sometimes he got scared he'd not make it back. He'd come to Pen-Y-Cwm in part to ensure that he never had to. His method of control. Don't feel, don't risk. And right now, the woman who challenged him to do both held on to his hand like she needed him too. She's leaving. He pulled his hand away. She looked away and sat back, withdrawing from him. It's for the best.

"So, when can Finn come home?"

Branwen sighed. "Monday probably. The stitches are holding, he's started walking well, well, as well as can be expected at this point. His temperature is still a little high, so I'm watching for infection, but as yet I'm not seeing any, which is good. If I have to send him home now, I'd have to give you a course of tablets for him, and we both know how likely Finn is to actually take them."

"Yeah," Cobb agreed, thinking about the number of times the wolfhound had preferred to starve than eat food with crushed tablets in. If he tried to force the damn things down the dog's throat all that usually achieved was a lasting irritation for Cobb complete with claw and/or tooth marks and a palm full of soggy tablet remains, glaring at a couple of hundred pounds of sniggering dog.

"So, Finn stays with me at the Surgeries for the weekend and if all's still okay, home Monday evening."

"Fine," said Cobb. "I'll pick him up after four, then."

"No need." Branwen smiled. "I can drop Finn off on my way home. It's hardly out of my way and won't be a bother."

"The car's MOT is booked for Monday, I'll be down anyway."

"Oh, okay."

For far too long they sat and sipped in silence. There had been a time when Cobb had been confident enough to actually talk to intelligent, attractive women. Now he felt like a heel for thinking her attractive, like he was betraying Mary.

"You know, I really rather admire your control."

Cobb swallowed and turned to look at Branwen. *Control? What control?* He couldn't control the way he reacted to anything these days. Not even a woman who had shown no romantic interest in him. Yes, she was a concerned friend, and one who thought he eliminated himself from her lists of possible men. The control he'd tried to take by burying himself here was the control she took every time she dragged him into something new. Or put her hand on his.

"Control?"

"Yes. You're always in control. Of yourself, and those around you. Even when you should be letting Michael be in control. You always know exactly what to do when we're called out. You regiment your life, I've seen your shopping lists, your weekly menu plan. I see how much control you have over your life and I envy it. That control is part of what I lost, part of why I can't stay. I'm not in control of my life here, I'm just trapped by it. I'm trying to take back control, figure out who I am. I need that."

Suddenly she made more sense to him. Everyone needed some control. Without it, no one could live the dream of a fulfilled life, a meaningful existence. He'd never really considered she might be unhappy, but if she believed being here had somehow been forced on her, then her recent demonstration of disaffection was a natural build up.

This time he covered her hand with his. "You're a good woman, Branwen Jones. You need to know that."

***

The sermon hadn't been the best she'd ever heard, and it hadn't inspired her either. Branwen had a lot of things to do, not least of all checking on Finn. It was lunchtime, he needed feeding. The last thing Branwen expected was Cobb leaning against the door of the surgeries.

"Three days in a row?"

He shrugged. "Can I see Finn?"

Of course, the man loved his dog. She smiled and unlocked the door, letting him in and leading him through to the recovery room. Finn, being a big dog, was in the largest cage. The keening whine because a thumping wag and a bark as Cobb knelt down and opened the cage, nearly crawling inside to greet his dog.

I should lock him in. Keep him here.

She turned away and went to her desk.

"Still okay for him to come home tomorrow?"

Branwen kept her eyes on the paperwork. "Hopefully. His temperature's still a bit high, but no other sign of infection. I want to be sure it stabilises lower."

"I can take care of him at home."

She smiled and looked up. "Would you like me to lend you a thermometer, so you can keep a check on his temperature?"

Cobb stood and moved over to her. "Don't see him letting me put that under his tongue."

Her eyebrows rose and for a moment she held her lips between her teeth. "Wrong end."

It took a moment for confusion to turn to realisation, to turn to mirth. "Okay I'll leave him here another day."

"Don't worry, I'll charge you as little as possible."

"I can afford to take care of my own dog."

Apparently, she'd offended him. "That wasn't an insult. But I have to ask. Do you let Finn sleep on your bed?"

"Not as a rule, but sometimes he doesn't give me a choice."

She nodded. "I stayed here Friday night. But Finn kept whining and whining, so I went to check on him, opened the cage and he was out like a shot. Jumped straight on the bed." Her grin widened. "Quite funny actually, it's a zed bed and it collapsed in. Scared the living daylights out of him. I had to make it up again. With all the doors closed, I let him roam, figured he'd sleep on the floor, but as soon as I was settled on the bed, he jumped up and lay down. He took over the foot of the bed and I had to curl up at the top end."

Cobb nodded and grinned. "Sounds like Finn. The real fun habit he has is getting on the bed while I'm asleep and laying on my feet. I wake up in the morning and my feet are so numb I can't stand."

"Sounds joyous." Branwen tipped to one side looking past Cobb to the big dog. "Remind me never to sleep with your master!"

The dog whined, and the door banged shut behind Cobb's exit.

Chapter 18
Simons – Home Counties

Simons looked at the screen. Richard Granger; Nemesis Records. Not an obvious arena for O'Rourke to connect to. There again, profit ruled, it had to be made and live events meant lots of cash. It was possible that the business was perfectly legitimate. Simons had to keep an open mind.

Scrolling through the list of artists, he didn't recognise a single name; Banshee, Alex Berenger, Dotty Whirl, Greebo K, Madeline Turner, Shan Sh'Kara, Zeedamn. He sneered at the list and the photos of the all too eager. These weren't real names, half of them didn't even sound like real musicians. Perhaps he was just getting old.

Music was a background to him, but the state of the company might be of more interest. It took time, but he managed to find the published accounts of Nemesis Records.

He looked through them, looking for inconsistencies. He didn't find any. Then he looked at turn over. He looked at turn over and looked at the artists list again. Then back and forth between the two. Things didn't add up right. These figures suggested platinum records, but he saw no sign of those being awarded. He wasn't a forensic accountant, but he knew one, so made the call.

Chapter 19
Alex – Belsize Park

The dream enveloped Alex in warmth and joy. The sound of someone entering the house didn't bother him; Greebo often stumbled about at odd hours.

A big hand smothered his mouth, startling Alex from his comfortable dream to a stark and frightening black reality. As he tried to struggle, the strength of the intruder blocked every twist and turn. A punch in the gut blew the air from his lungs, insulation tape shut his mouth denying him easy oxygen. His hands were grabbed, twisted behind his back and zip tied together. The covers thrown back, he was pushed to his back as his feet were grabbed and bound together with zip ties. Unable to resist, Alex found himself rolled into his duvet; bucking and struggling in the suffocating darkness of the roll was useless. Alex felt himself carried from his bedroom, down the stairs, out of the house the back way and bundled into the boot of a car.

The drive could have been ten minutes, ten miles or ten hours; time meant nothing to Alex stuffed into the suffocating darkness. He was only thankful that he could still breathe, though barely. His heart thumped, desperate to struggle, to fight free and flee. Of course, that was not an option now.

He wondered who his unseen captors were. What did they want? Fear tasted foul in his mouth as he lay in the soft surrounding darkness and his overly vivid imagination wrought scenes of horror. Were they going to dump him somewhere, so he died helpless in his pyjamas? Was this a ransoming? If so, who would pay his price? What if they simply planned to torment, torture and kill him? Why?

It slowly reached Alex's conscious mind that the damp on his face was his own tears, the warmth about his hips, fear-soaked urine.

If they didn't kill him, in that moment he wanted to die of shame.

Eventually, the vehicle stopped. It seemed like forever before the boot opened. The duvet muted all sounds for Alex. The first tug was on the fabric above his head, then a pull by his knees. He was manhandled out of the car, but when first lifted, he heard an indistinct curse and found himself dropped back into the boot. They had discovered his embarrassment. Then came a deep frightening laugh.

Lifted again, this time he was quickly dumped in a chair. There was movement, and he realised he was sitting in a wheelchair. They moved perhaps fifty metres. The duvet covered his head, muffling everything. He could get no feel for where he was. Then they stopped abruptly. Finally, his captors pulled the duvet from over his head. Before his eyes adjusted to his surroundings, a switch clicked, and a bank of lights blazed on right in front of him.

The halogen screen was obviously meant to hide the man sitting before them in a chair with a wide triangular back. Images of old Bond movies jumped irreverently to mind. Since the man was only about two or three feet away, Alex could have told them not to waste electricity. Being so long-sighted, without his glasses or contacts, anything this close was a total blur.

"Good evening, Mr Berenger." The man before the lights spoke with a well-cultivated accent that nonetheless betrayed traces of a less privileged upbringing.

Alex tried to answer coolly, but his fear seemed to have frozen his vocal chords.

"Well, Mr Berenger, I hope you soon recover your voice. I have some questions I'd like you to answer."

Alex tried to swallow his fear as the man loomed over him. A big man, the outline suggested muscle not fat. He didn't want to get hurt, there was little in life worth that. "Okay." Less squeak would have been preferable, but the silhouette nodded. He took that to mean he had answered correctly.

"I understand you traced a hacker for Mr Granger, is that correct?" At last, Alex found his brain. "Who are you?"

"Your worst nightmare. Answer the question, Mr Berenger."

"Y-yes," he stuttered.

"Well?" The man demanded after a few seconds silence.

Alexander realised what the man wanted and gave all the details he had on James Whitney.

"Good boy," the menace praised. "I'm glad you understand. You're an intelligent man. Now you'll also understand why you're going to tell me everything you find out about this man Whitney. Why you're going to tell me everything you tell Granger, and, of course, why you're not going to tell Granger of your contact with me."

Numbly, Alex nodded.

Chapter 20
Jay – City of London

Jay surveyed the difference. Yesterday he had gone to an optician for the contacts, they felt strange, but no more than expected. The copper hair took getting used to, but it matched well with two days' growth of beard.

Last night, a little before midnight, he'd used his credit and debit cards to gather as much money as possible, and repeated the process an hour later. He believed this to be the typical MO of a wallet thief, so he wouldn't be able to use the cards again as it would set off an alert with the card companies and banks. Now he had a full wallet and a load of survival gear he'd got from an outdoor shop as soon as they'd opened. He had no idea how long he would have to hide out, but however long it took he wasn't stupid enough to risk being tracked by using his credit card. Not one of his own anyway.

He had had the idea during the night as he had wandered on the cold streets. The cold had reminded him of the school field trip he had once been forced to attend in Wales. In turn, that reminded him of the working farm his parents had visited last summer. His father had mentioned that the place was so remote it would be cut off during the winter. Remote and stranded sounded good to Jay at that moment. More importantly, the chances of the goons guessing he would go there were between slim and non-existent.

Jay knew his mother's car would have been left at her office car park, and his father's would be at Gatwick while the couple holidayed in Malta. Getting a car from Gatwick posed a couple of issues – the greater distance, his lack of keys and Gatwick was riddled with CCTV. Not that central London wasn't, but for once it represented the lesser risk.

As he neared the security lodge of the underground car park, Jay spotted that the attendant today was Rory. Rory was as opposite to Frankie as two men could get, despite being roughly the same age. Almost as wide as he was tall, exercise was a complete mystery to Rory, and from the smell in high summer, so was deodorant.

"Good morning, can I help yo- Mr Whitney?" The other difference was Rory's propensity for jolly, chatty politeness. "Wow, do you ever look different. I nearly didn't recognise you."

"Yeah," Jay grinned, glad it worked. "It's me, I just fancied a change, and I keep telling you not to call me Mr Whitney."

Rory looked around and leaned closer. "I'd 'appily call you Jay, Jay. Problem is that the big bosses don't like it and one of the other guys got a warning from HR for calling Mrs Chandler Margaret, even though that's her name, so it's really not worth the risk. I mean this isn't much of a job, but it's better than nuffin'.""

"Sounds naff. Sorry you have to put up with that."

Rory shrugged. "What are you doing here? Your mum's on holiday."

"Well I hope so, otherwise there was no point in her allowing me to borrow the car this weekend. So may I have Mummy's keys, please?"

Rory looked doubtful, looked at the log sheets on the wall. "Erm, there's nothing in the log book about it."

Jay shrugged. "Oh, perhaps she forgot, what with the excitement of the holiday. You realise, of course, how unusual taking time away is for Mummy." 'Mummy' rarely got excited about anything, she found displays of emotion distasteful and was way too organised to forget to mention any arrangement to someone on whom it might impact. But Rory wouldn't necessarily know that. "I'll have the car back long before she returns."

Rory's podgy face rolled layers of fat into a smile that nearly obliterated his little dark eyes. "I guess it would be okay, Mr Whitney." Impossibly fat fingers plucked the keys from the locker. "I'll get the car."

Jay relaxed at that. "I need to make a quick call, may I use the phone?" He pointed to the standard company issue phone on Rory's desk.

"Sure – just keep it short, they monitor phone usage."

Problematic, but a risk he'd have to take.

Chapter 21
Branwen and Cobb – Pen-Y-Cwm Village

"Have you seen this?"

I'm never getting through this paperwork. Branwen sighed and looked up at Emma, who again had strode into her office without knocking. "Why do I pay a receptionist?"

"To man reception and see to your clients coming and going. But it's Sunday, so you don't have any."

Branwen sat back in her chair and looked at the desk. "So much for a day of rest. Why aren't you having Sunday lunch with Ivan?"

Emma frowned. "I did. You realise it's gone four, right?"

Wrong, but okay.

"Have you eaten today?"

"Of course I have. I just hadn't realised the time is all. You still haven't told me what you're doing here."

"Thought I'd show you this." She thrust her phone in Branwen's face.

Branwen sat back and moved the phone a little further away to focus on it. A podcast, the exclusive first ever interview with Greebo K.

"Who's Greebo K?"

Emma tutted and rolled her eyes. "How can you not know who Greebo K is?"

"Apparently, very easily."

"Oh yeah, I forgot your idea of good music is harps and indecipherable gibberish in Celtic -"

"We prefer to call it Welsh."

"- or at best some grotty last century pop."

"Nothing wrong with 1980s pop."

"You weren't even born then."

And her dad hadn't brought a CD since either. *Nope, he brought one last year – though it was a 1980s compilation.*

"Okay, so what's so hot about Greebo K?"

Emma went into full gush-mode as she extolled the virtues of this ebony skinned beauty as a fabulous singer, and an incredible dancer with the associated pumped body and the face of an angel. And never giving an interview, of any sort. An unusual stance for a newbie on the scene, but it had added to the mystery of his persona, so giving a recorded interview now had created a real buzz.

"Great," Branwen said when Emma finally finished. "Can you buzz somewhere else?"

"Can you cheer up?" Emma demanded. "Why don't you go see Cobb? Maybe a good shag would improve your mood."

"Maybe, but I won't be getting it from Cobb. He walked out again."

"What? When?"

Branwen shrugged. "He came down to check on Finn. Then left without so much as a by your leave."

"What did you say this time?"

**

Snow had covered Pen-Y-Cwm overnight, making the drive into town difficult, but Cobb had to bring the Jeep in for its annual MOT before lunch that Monday. Normally he combined his visits with his fortnightly trek down for supplies. But he'd shopped last week, and been hardly able to eat since Branwen suggested he should get deep inside her, then declared she never wanted to sleep with him. Slamming cupboard doors in the cottage made him realise she had meant she wanted to avoid sleeping with Finn. He was an idiot.

He had returned to the village and the garage, only to discover that Paul Davies, the mechanic, had been called out in his other capacity as the local vehicle recovery man. Cobb's MOT would have to wait. Cobb wandered the village – it didn't take long. There was only one street. He looked at the estate agent's come local craft shop. If he went in, Emma would run to Branwen with the news. It was tempting, just to find out if Branwen would react. His doubts stopped him. He saw Davies's truck returning, a Volkswagen Beetle hooked behind the tow truck. As the truck passed, he saw a couple of kids squashed on the bench seat beside the mechanic.

Cobb wandered to the garage, arriving to find Davies lowering the car, revealing two young women on the other side. Women, Cobb thought, was an overstatement, children seemed more fitting. Was he getting old?

The blonder of the two glanced up from the forlorn automobile and saw Cobb. Seeing his shadow Cobb was uncomfortably reminded that the breadth of his shoulders, the tapering to his hips and the distance his legs travelled to reach the ground, and all of it topped off by a fiery halo was, he had been told a few years ago, something women considered sexy. Except that the woman he wanted to think that, didn't. Cobb ignored the one girl's preening and come-get-me eyes. Her friend at least was more subtle. Once he would have been flattered by this attention, but now he simply wasn't interested, wasting all the preening and smiling.

"Cobb," Davies greeted him, looking for the reason behind the girls' sudden change of focus. "I haven't had a chance to get to the Jeep yet."

"I saw the sign." Cobb's gravel-deep tone seemed to appeal to the girls even more. He tried to ignore it. "Any idea how long?"

"This," said Davies, indicating the Beetle, "is a five-minute job. I just didn't have the right parts with me on the road. The test should take no more than twenty – thirty minutes."

"Oh, you could do Mr Cobb's car first," piped up the blonde, with come-hither eyes.

"We don't mind waiting," added the other, leaning forward to emphasise her breasts.

Emotionless, Cobb regarded the pair. "Thanks girls, but it's no bother." Turning back to Davies, he told the mechanic he would come back later as he headed to the Pig and Whistle.

***

Branwen met Emma for lunch in the quiet pub, trying not to notice Cobb the second that they stepped inside.

"What can I get you?" Dewi asked.

"Diet cola and a bacon and Brie panini, please."

"Same for me," Emma added.

"Usual then." Dewi walked away and Branwen turned towards Emma, towards the door to keep her back to Cobb. He'd walked away and she couldn't face him, didn't want to have to deal with the rejection right now. She tipped her head and they headed to seats in the front window.

As Emma started the conversation, Branwen didn't want to be aware that Cobb was drinking lemonade or that two pretty young girl's had walked in and headed straight to him. Walked? Sashayed would be a better description. Of course, he attracted them. Why not? He was tall, good looking, the deep kind of ginger that wasn't orange enough to be taken the mick out of. And he had a good body. *Stop thinking of his body.*

"Hello again."

Branwen cringed at the husky tone from the blonde, and she tried unsuccessfully not to watch Cobb turn to the girls.

"Sounding a little hoarse there," Cobb returned. Branwen tamped down her smile and looked down.

A glance at Emma showed the other woman grinning, then she looked up to see Cobb approaching. She swallowed as he stopped by their table.

"Mind if I join you?" he kept his voice low, so not to carry.

"Why?"

Cobb smiled. "Tourist trouble."

Branwen and Emma glanced at the two girls at the bar.

"Of course not." Emma smiled up at the tall man. Innocently, she continued, "You go tuck in beside Branwen on the bench there.

64

The cosier you get the less likely they'll be to move in again."
Branwen's glare had no effect on Emma's smile, as Cobb followed
her direction.

Branwen sat quiet as he and Emma chatted.

On the bench, Cobb's spread-legged stance pressed his thigh
against hers. Heat and awareness sizzled through Branwen with
every move. Another man did that, she'd tell him to move away,
especially if she thought he was getting something out of it, but not
Cobb. He obviously felt nothing as he spoke with Emma, deftly
avoiding answering any of her questions. Cobb shifted; heat burned
through Branwen. She told herself to get over it, get herself under
control. This was only for appearance's sake. But no amount of
telling helped when his arm moved around her. She started,
looking at him, at clear green eyes like the deep evergreen forests.
Looking into those depths, she saw forever, saw a wonder she could
never define, a box of secrets that would remain forever hidden
from her.

"For the floor show," he told her softly with a smile she had never
seen from him before. A heart-stopping smile the power of which
robbed her of her senses. The hand that had been wrapped around
her glass slid from the table to his thigh. The warmth of solid
muscle through the denim sent heat rising in her belly, burning at
her core, firing needs she had tried to forget.

He was looking at her. Really looking at her. Moving towards
her. She was imagining – no she wasn't. His lips were getting closer
and blood thrummed in hers.

The sharp rap on the window behind them had them both
turning suddenly to the sound. Davies stood outside the pub.
Through the glass, he told Cobb that his car was ready.

Chapter 22
Alex – Belsize Park

Hacking didn't come naturally to Alex, but he'd learned enough to be able to do it.

Sort of.

He'd been shown what to do by some seriously scary people he never wanted to meet again. Getting into the credit card system had taken time and a visit to people in places he'd rather not think about, but he had got what he needed. Mostly because the bank's own anti-fraud software picked it up.

Who to call first?

***

That O'Rourke took his call personally, was a sign Alex wasn't sure how to read.

"I'm starting to like you, kid."

At twenty-seven Alex didn't like being called a kid, but challenging the man in control wasn't a great idea; he wasn't that comfortable with the situation yet. Instead, he reported what he'd found.

"Friday night and Saturday morning, James Whitney drew out his maximum daily allowance on various bank and credit cards. He would have had around three grand in cash at that point. More than enough to lay low for a while."

"Smart kid," O'Rourke grated.

"Not that smart. There's been some unexpected transactions on his father's credit card. He booked a room for tonight at four different places: Glenshields B&B, Pen-Y-Cwm Guesthouse, Dales View Hostel and the Queen Victoria."

"Where are these places?"

"Scottish Highlands, Welsh hinterlands, the Yorkshire Dales and Cowes on the Isle of White."

"He's covering all bases," O'Rourke mused. "Where do you think he'll go?"

"Don't know him well enough to guess," Alex said. "Were it me, I wouldn't go to any of them, but if I had to, it would be the Highlands or Wales."

"Why?"

"The guy's a computer nerd, going somewhere where he'd struggle for phone or internet signal would be the best place to hide. Also, minimises the chance for ANPR."

Alex decided O'Rourke's silence indicated the man was thinking about things. "Does the hacker have a car?"

"Yeah, but it's still outside his flat, hasn't moved in days."

Damn. "Does he have access to any others?"

"Not that I'm aware of."

"Hmm, I can probably find out." Alex heard what he thought might be O'Rourke snapping his fingers.

"What do I do now?" Alex asked. "Do I tell Granger?"

"Yes, but don't tell him I know. Do, however, find out what those files Granger is so worried about contain."

Chapter 23
Jay – On the Road

Wales was a hell of a place to drive.

Jay had hoped to make better time, but a crash on the M40 and road works on the M42 had held him up, by at least 100 minutes according to the inbuilt SatNav. At least the wait had allowed him to remove the contact and put his glasses back on. Contacts might seem like a good idea, but they didn't half irritate his eyes. As the early dusk gathered and Jay moved across the country on the A458, he wondered if he would ever reach his goal.

This course was not a fun drive. Mummy's car thankfully had all the traction control and anti-lock braking it could get, which was just as well. These wet roads, in places still icy, jerked back and forth like the civil engineer had planned the route during a spasm. The SatNav proclaimed this to be an A road. Jay doubted that.

The sky had darkened considerably, and a light snow picked at the windscreen. By the time Jay passed Welshpool, the shower had become a full-blown storm. An hour and a half later, when Jay finally found the turn off for Pen-Y-Cwm, he wondered if he would ever get there. The sign said he still had thirteen miles to go. Thirteen, just his luck; he hoped it wasn't an omen.

Jay sighed with relief when the snow eased off as he entered the village, although 'village' might be an overstatement for a single street with roughly twenty houses on each side and little else.

A garage stood near the start of the village; a little way on was a pub, slap-bang opposite the church. The clean outstanding front of an estate agent surprised Jay. How a place like that survived in a village like this was a mystery, but that was the agent's problem not his.

Slush covered the road edges and by sheer misfortune, Jay drove through what in clear weather would have been an obvious pothole, kicking up icy water and dirt all over some far less fortunate individual. Jay saw the tall redheaded man's fury, and no way would he enjoy any encounter with said man at that time, so he drove on.

The directions to Pen-Y-Cwm Farm Guesthouse were easy – follow the road into Pen-Y-Cwm, turn right after the Surgeries, keep going. That would be fine, Jay thought, if the damned road didn't keep twisting all over the damned mountainside. Jay slowed to a crawl. Now the snowstorm had passed visibility had improved, but night was settling in with a fog, and he could barely see three feet in front of him.

The sign a few metres after the village had said 'Road Narrows'

– they weren't kidding. It didn't narrow so much as cease to exist. The track could be distinguished from the surrounding area, but only just.

Shifting in his seat, Jay hunched forward, frowning in concentration, trying to distinguish and follow the road. Suddenly he understood why nearly every vehicle he had seen in the village was a four-wheel drive; they needed to be on these roads. His mother's Rover 800 was a big bitch in these conditions.

Without apparent warning, the road crossed over the icy flow of a stream running off the higher peaks. The stone construction, although two car-widths wide, required a sharp turn in, so Jay slowed slightly, thankful to take the left fork up the valley rather than the right, which would necessitate a second very sharp turn.

A precious second was wasted realising that the two black dots weren't a mirage of strained eyes, but the defiant glare of a tough sheep. In instant reaction Jay stamped on the brakes – and an instant later, he lost control. The ABS failed on the iced road and the vehicle fish-tailed. Jay thought hysterically as the car slid sideways that a Rover 800 made a luxurious sleigh. The ripping, crunching sound of metal seemed like a distant devil's song as forces of inertia, momentum and gravity played war games with his body. Consciousness suffered the first casualty.

Chapter 24
Branwen and Cobb – Pen-Y-Cwm Village

Cobb swore as he stamped into the vet's. Branwen had unlocked the front door for him and currently stood behind reception, sorting papers and tidying.

"You look a little damp there, Cobb."

The only answer he dare give was a cold hard look.

"What happened?"

"Some idiot in a Rover. Hit that old pothole as I walked past."

"Come through, I've a towel here you can use." As Cobb came into her office, her hand towel hit him full in the face. After glowering at her laughter, he wiped his own dripping visage. "People like that deserve to have accidents."

"Perhaps," Cobb agreed, "but let's hope he doesn't do so on our mountain."

Branwen nodded; she didn't really wish the anonymous driver ill. "Em's been on to the Council to get the road fixed but – as expected – we're last in the list. Rhodri said if they haven't done it by June, he'll take action." The last time Rhodri took action, he'd dumped a truckload of organic fertiliser over the councillors' front door, and ended up spending a week in jail for it. Both Cobb and Branwen hoped it didn't come to that.

"So," Cobb asked, wiping his hands, "is Finn ready to go?"

"Yeah." Branwen sounded strangely reluctant. "Sure. I'm sorry you got soaked by some idiot driver. I could have dropped him off on my way home tonight."

Cobb shrugged. "No problem."

Ten minutes later, Finn lay happily installed in the back of Cobb's Jeep parked on the hard standing at the front of the surgeries. Branwen fussed the top of his shaggy head one last time before Cobb closed the tailgate. Though just past five, night had already settled over the village, the warmest lights spilling from the pub. Branwen raised her hand to acknowledge Ivan Evans as he headed for the Pig and Whistle. A second later, Emma came out of her own shop. She did a double take to see Branwen and Cobb together, before heading towards them, literally sliding to stop at their side.

"So," she laughed, using Branwen, and Cobb's Jeep for balance, "the invalid goes home today, does he?"

"Yeah," Cobb muttered, checking the tailgate.

"I don't suppose I can tempt the pair of you into joining me in the Pig and Whistle for a drink or two."

Branwen looked at Cobb, but he simply pointed out that he

needed to get Finn home. The vet turned to her college pal.

"And I want to get back before the road home closes." She pulled her coat closer. "Besides," she laughed, "playing gooseberry all evening to you and Ivan isn't exactly my idea of fun. So I'm going home."

Emma smiled. "Shame. Drive carefully. Make sure you look out for each other." She slipped again, skating skills coming to her rescue at one point.

"Right," Branwen said with a sharp intake of breath. "Guess it's time I was off too then."

"Yeah." Cobb didn't move.

"Tidy… Well, I'll see you whenever then."

"Yeah." Still Cobb didn't move.

"Tidy." Since she felt like an idiot for saying the same thing, and there was nothing more to be said or done, Branwen marched back to the surgery, made sure everything was locked up, headed to her Land Rover parked next to the Jeep, and jumped in. Thankfully the cold engine started first time.

Glancing his way, Branwen saw Cobb hadn't left. He frowned, looking at her. She put the car in reverse and began to bring the clutch up to biting point. Suddenly he was standing by her passenger window and banging on the glass for attention. Frowning, Branwen took the car out of gear as the electric window rolled down.

"What's the matter?" she asked.

"I was just going to say…"

Such awkwardness was unlike him.

"…that the roads coming down were pretty bad. I suggest you follow me up." His voice dwindled to nothing.

"Just to be on the safe side, like?" she asked, her brows raised at the idea of such chivalry. Given that they both drove 4x4s and which would perform better in these conditions was debatable the offer could be no more than chivalry, She wasn't sure if as modern woman she should accept it.

"Yeah."

"Okay."

He stepped back to move to his car.

"Cobb?" she called after him. She didn't speak again until he turned back. "Thanks." She smiled.

He offered an equally quick smile and sped off, jumping into his own car. His lights came on and when he indicated, reversed out and pulled slowly away, he was relieved to see she followed him.

The careful drive up the valley proved thankfully uneventful, with Branwen maintaining a safe distance behind Cobb. Reaching

Satan's Turn, as the bridge had always been known, Cobb experienced an odd depression that their paths here diverged, her to the left, him to the right.

Cobb slowed, denying that this was reluctance. Of course, she would know the only way to take Satan's Turn and make the right hand turn safely was at a crawl.

Suddenly realising that what lay ahead wasn't a figment of his imagination, Cobb stamped on the brake. Thankfully Branwen did too, though she stopped closer to his car than he found reassuring.

A dark blue Rover lay twisted at the edge of the bridge. Half the far-side wall was missing and the car listed dangerously, the whole back end hanging above the road, cradled by the stream's border. The front passenger side was an inch from the edge, held only by the remnants of the wall. The driver was slumped over the steering wheel and the deflated airbag, not moving.

"Iesu Grist," Branwen breathed.

Guilt assailed Cobb, as if his earlier wish had been forced on this poor man. But when Branwen moved toward the car, Cobb grabbed her, holding her back.

"There's a rope in the back of the Jeep."

Nodding her understanding, Branwen fetched the rope. The Rover balanced precariously; any move to pull the driver out might tip it over, taking the would-be rescuer with it. Finn stood in the back of the Jeep; Branwen ordered him to sit and the big dog obeyed as she pulled out the length of rope.

With one end secured to Cobb's bumper, she threw the other to the man who carefully found a holding place on the stricken vehicle.

As Cobb secured the car, Branwen returned to her own vehicle, retrieving the Rescue's folding stretcher and first aid kit that she should have replaced in the storage cabin. By the time she returned to the car, Cobb had forced the door open and checked the guy for a pulse.

"Well?"

"Faint, but there."

The now forlorn airbag had saved the man's life, but the rapid deflation had left the steering wheel open for a head to fall forward upon and get knocked out on by the second bash.

Carefully, Cobb checked the thin man's neck and back. Nothing seemed to be broken.

Supporting the man's head, Cobb manoeuvred the body upright. Taking a folded towel Branwen held towards him, he placed it like a brace around the man's neck. The vet worked carefully in the limited space to secure it with a length of thick electrical tape.

Branwen took the victim's weight as Cobb released the seatbelt.

Carefully, they worked together to lift the man from the driver's seat and lower him to the waiting stretcher. As Cobb secured the restraining straps over the prone form, Branwen reached into the car again to grab the rucksack strewn on the passenger seat. Slinging it over her shoulder, she rejoined Cobb, taking the other end of the stretcher.

"We'll have to take him to your place," she said as they lifted him into her car.

"What?"

"Your place is closest."

He didn't like visitors, something Branwen knew, but it was the best option they had. Nodding, he returned to the car and unhooked the line. As he began to gather up the rope, the Rover groaned; with a screaming wail of metal grinding against stone it tipped backward, to stand on its boot in the stream. An accidental grave marker.

Climbing into the Jeep, Cobb judged that by morning the force of mountain run-off and wind would have it on its rooftop.

The rest of the journey to his cottage took less than two minutes; just enough to crest this rise in the uneven reach for the mountaintop.

Once there, they quickly transferred the body from the stretcher to Cobb's big bed. Cobb set the fire in the cold hearth to warm the room as Branwen administered first aid.

She shook her head and looked up at him. "Bruises and broken bones I can deal with, but this large lump on his forehead – " she shook her head – "That I'm less sure about."

It was an angry red; the boy's right temple was covered by a lump, but here the skin had broken and was bleeding. She tried to clean it up, all the time worried about brain damage and worse. She was doing the best she could for the man, but that head wound was scary. Her hands shook as she pulled her mobile from her pocket and dialled Doc Pearson.

"Pete!" The evident relief scared Cobb. He hated the closeness he detected between Branwen and Doc. "Thank God. Pete, I've got a problem." She paused. Was Doc answering? "Pete? Can you hear me? Pete?"

Apparently, Pete couldn't. Branwen pulled the phone from her ear, looked at it.

"What did Doc say?"

She shrugged. "Not even sure he heard me."

"So what do we do with a head wound like that?"

"Pack it in ice. Do you have one of those plastic holders used for headaches?"

"No, but I've got ice cubes, zip lock bags and a tea towel."

She smiled. "That'll do."

***

As Branwen tended the man in his bedroom, Cobb set the other fire in the main room of the cottage that formed his living room and kitchen. Finn crept over, favouring the bandaged front paw. Flopping down on the rag rug beside his kneeling master, the big dog lapped up the affection shown by the absent ruffling of ears. Cobb stood as Branwen left the bedroom, shutting the door carefully behind her.

"How is he?"

Branwen shrugged. "Not good. I don't like the look of the bump on his head, but I've done all I can. Maybe we should get the Mountain Rescue out."

"In this storm?" Cobb pointed to the window. The white flakes had grown in both size and intensity.

"Oh, Duw."

"Pardon?"

She looked at him, that 'how stupid are you?' look, then she smiled. "Sorry, that was Welsh for 'oh God'."

Coming over to the hearth, she held cold fingers out to its warmth. "I can't be sure what Pete heard or didn't. I don't know if he knows what we know. And I don't know what he'll do if he does know."

"Given that we've done nothing wrong, it doesn't really matter what he does with the information."

"What about failure to report an accident?"

She always asked the most awkward questions. He pulled his phone from his pocket. "I've no signal to call, no landline either. You?"

Branwen checked her mobile. "I've got one bar." That was all she needed so she started typing numbers. "Now I don't even have that."

"So much for a local mast ensuring connection," Cobb grumbled.

"Well, it gives the farm a much-needed extra income." Her voice was absent, and she looked worried at she glanced back at the door to his bedroom, and the boy beyond.

Cobb stood looking down at her, but he said nothing. When Branwen turned to face him, she seemed about to say something, but she looked away, pushed her hair back and looked again at the window.

"If I don't go soon, I'm going to be stuck here too. I'll report the accident when I get home, the landline should still work."

Cobb nodded. If the police knew about the accident, they'd soon come calling. They or someone would come and take charge of the young man now filling his bed.

"I'll drop in first thing in the morning to check on the two patients."

"Yes," he said, not moving from the hearth while she strode to the door.

"See you then, then."

"Yes," he said again, but she was gone before he spoke.

Alone again, he sighed. Only he wasn't alone. He liked his solitude. He liked not having anyone around, no one to depend on him. No one to let down. That had apparently gone out the door with Branwen.

Chapter 25
Simons – City of London

The laser mike worked much better. Simons sat on the third floor fire escape in the shadow of the tall buildings around him; O'Rourke finished the call and called Keel in.

"Get Baron up here."

Simons considered. The Glenshields B&B in the Highlands, Pen-Y-Cwm Guesthouse somewhere in Wales, Dales View Hostel in Yorkshire and the Queen Victoria on the Isle of White. Covered all the major compass points.

While listening to the silence in O'Rourke's office, he had to disagree with the voice on speaker phone. If Jay Whitney was a really smart kid, he'd be heading to St Pancras and the Eurostar out of the country. Use the four bookings as total misdirection. Still he didn't know Jay well enough to make that call, he'd have to do more research. For now he texted the details through to his assistant and asked for full addresses, trace the bookings to see if a commonality could be found.

"Ah, Baron."

Simons looked up at the voice in his ear and focused on O'Rourke's office. Another man had entered. Simons judged him to be about five eight or nine. A solid figure, not so muscular he couldn't hold his arms straight. Looked like he knew his way around a fight though. The telephoto lens gave him a good image, with that and a name, he might well find out who the man was.

O'Rourke gave the man an update, and told him to be ready. He didn't say what to be ready for, just to be ready. Baron bore a confidence which assured Simons the man was always ready. Whatever was going on, this could be the way in to find what O'Rourke was up to.

Unhappy with their progress, Baron faced the punchbag man and jabbed into the heavy-browed plastic face that somehow managed to look more attentive than Shoreham the last time Baron had seen him.

The intention had been to scare Sophie into helping them, but Baron, and apparently Shoreham, had quickly realised that the old bird was tougher than expected. She wouldn't have scared easily, which actually made disposal the only real option. He didn't like leaving a trail of dead bodies, but sometimes necessity dictated.

Granger was spitting feathers, and Baron had sent Shoreham off to Hampshire to what would doubtless turn out to be an empty house. Still, it got the muscleman out of the way.

He had spoken to O'Rourke earlier and knew that the man had others working on the problem, so Baron had time to figure out what he would do with James Whitney when he found him. It would be slow. And very, very painful. The smile spread as ideas formed; his eyes fell on the black notebook on his sideboard. Collection time.

***

Baron took the call at eight-fifty. He watched with disinterest the bobbing head of the crying girl as she sucked him off. He didn't need the sexual gratification: she needed to be taught a lesson.

The woman on the end of the line identified herself as Keel. Apparently James Whitney had managed to get hold of his mother's car, and that car had been picked up by another of O'Rourke's contacts on the M40 and M54 near Telford. Apparently, Whitney was heading to Pen-Y-Cwm after all.

Baron signed off and looked down. Big wet eyes looked up at him.

The phone rang again.

"Keep going," he told the girl as he answered again.

Granger this time. Same information. Yes, he and Shoreham would be there in the morning. This time when he signed off, he grabbed the girl's hair and pulled out of her mouth.

"Do better next time or I'll double your debt."

Pulling up his zip he walked away to the sounds of her sobs.

Chapter 27
Branwen – Pen-Y-Cwm Farm and Guesthouse

The morning was slow to start and so was Branwen. Mornings were not her favourite, she'd got used to the early hours on the farm, but this morning was a non-starter. It followed a late evening waiting up with her father for a guest who never showed. It did occur to her that the man they had waited for might be the stricken one in Cobb's cottage. She had called the police, given them the minimum details of the crash, then spent the night tossing and turning, worrying about the man at Cobb's.

She had slept through her alarm. A late start was all she needed. Cursing, she looked forward to the prospect of being a town vet working nine till six with nothing bigger than an Alsatian to worry about.

Only right now she had a huge wolfhound and an accident victim to check on.

As she approached Satan's Turn at half six she spotted the parked Discovery and two men. A tall blond was using a torch to highlight the car lying in the stream, the other sat in the driver's seat looking at a map spread out on the dashboard with the car's inside light offering ineffective assistance.

Branwen slowed down, parking herself on the road. She had seen this type before. The big muscled outdoors type, who actually spent most of their time indoors, working out in gyms. They came up regularly to play in the winter wonderland. More often than not they were sensible and had fun, going home safe and sound. Still, more often then she'd like, they turned out to be the ones she and the rest of the Mountain Rescue had to go fetch back.

Switching off the engine, Branwen stepped out and walked over to the car.

"Morning," she greeted them as the guy wound down his window. "You guys okay?"

"We're fine, thank you," the driver said. The other, who had been looking at the crashed car, turned his attention to her. He sauntered over to stand closer to Branwen than strictly necessary.

Looking up at the big man, she reckoned him in the mid-six-foot range, taller than Cobb, and broader too. But the look in his eye left her with a chill.

"Morning," she greeted again. He nodded. She got the distinct impression that these two were ex-military. Probably why they were here. A few times they had had ex-army personnel stay at the Farm, using it as a base for going out 'on manoeuvres'. Turning back to the man at the wheel, she asked if they needed directions.

"We're heading for Pen-Y-Cwm Farm Guesthouse."

She smiled, relieved that these must be the guests who hadn't turned up last night. Mind, she had expected only one, but the line hadn't been the clearest. "You're in the right place then. Straight on." She pointed to the road she had just come down. "Over the next crest and you'll see the house. It's only a few minutes from here."

"You're staying there?" the man asked.

"I live there." No point hiding it. "My Dad runs that business, he'll check you in."

"Thanks."

"No problem. Enjoy your stay."

"The crash." The taller man spoke finally, stepping in front of her as she moved to return to her own car. "When did it happen?"

"Yesterday sometime," she told him. "I'm not sure when. It was long done when I drove past."

"What about the driver?"

Internal shivers juddered through Branwen as she looked up at the man. "I'm not sure. There wasn't anyone in the car when I drove past. Guess the driver must have faired better than the car."

"Yeah," the tall man said.

"Well," she said, pushing a smile onto her face, "I have to get to work, good day gentlemen." As Branwen paced back to her Land Rover, she heard a car drawing nearer. Stopping, she saw Constable Johnston approaching in the police Land Rover. The sigh and shoulder slump happened automatically. She lifted a hand in greeting to the patrol vehicle, noticing how quickly the two men got into their car and left.

***

Branwen pulled her coat closer around her, stuffing her hands into the deep pockets for warmth. She kept meaning to get some driving gloves, but she found wearing gloves and driving didn't work for her.

Finally, the police car parked and out climbed the reluctant PC Johnston. In his late thirties, Johnston had a rapidly receding hairline, of hair greying just as fast; add the extra pounds of middle age spread and he looked a good decade older. He smiled, the image of a congenial village bobby.

Branwen didn't trust him. She tried telling herself to lighten up on the man, he couldn't be that bad. Only she had good reason to know he really was.

"Miss Jones," he said, in a stiff greeting.

"Constable." Standing on the bridge, they watched each other with polite indifference. "You're out early." A lax attitude to time

79

keeping was only one of the things she didn't like about Johnson.

"There might be a life at stake."

"I reported the crash," she checked her watch, "ten hours ago."

"No point in risking police officers' lives in the dark."

"It's still dark." And would be for at least another hour.

"Well I had orders." Johnston glared at her. "Why didn't you call straight away?"

"Couldn't get through on the mobile," she said. "Had to wait till I got home to call from a landline." She shrugged. "Besides, I looked over the wreck, there was no one here and no followable sign of anyone leaving or getting away. It didn't seem that urgent."

Johnston grunted. "So, you found the wreck?" he asked looking over the bridge.

"Yes."

He turned piercing eyes back on her. "On your own?"

The alarm on her phone started blaring. She looked at it, any excuse to look away from Johnston. "I have an early appointment. Can I go now?"

Something about Johnston's manner put her on edge. The two had never found much common ground, and doubtless never would. Branwen never worried about that, she lived in a village where at least half the population refused to talk to her on the grounds that her father was illegitimate, so one more made no difference either way to her. Yet in this conversation, in this place and time, there seemed an underlying accusation, a hostility she couldn't fathom.

"Was he drunk?" Johnston demanded.

"Who?"

"The driver."

"I wouldn't know." Branwen didn't think he had been, but the prickling at the back of her neck counselled her to be non-committal. There had been no smell of alcohol about either the young man or the car. "Besides, from the skid marks in the snow and the marks on the bridge, I'd guess the accident was caused by a sudden braking, probably to avoid a sheep."

"I see no livestock remains and there are none on the car," Johnston pointed out. "Nor are there any discernible tracks, animal or skid."

"Maybe the driver avoided the sheep better than the accident." She shrugged. "I don't know, I wasn't here when it happened. As for the tracks, they would have been lost, destroyed by weather and people driving over them. After all, between now and then I've driven over here, so has Cobb. And there's the guys who just drove past. And it snowed again last night. I'm only telling you what I'd guess from what I saw. Have you managed to identify the driver yet?"

Johnston didn't sound so happy as he glared at her. "It's hard to trace anything without so much as a license plate number," he pointed out.

"Ah," she said. "Yeah. I suppose it is." She moved over to the edge. She read the now upside-down registration that marked the car as last year's model. "London registered." She turned back to Johnston.

He muttered, looking daggers at her.

"Right. Well." Cold and uncomfortable, Branwen had had enough of the grouchy PC clearly unhappy to be awake so early. "I've got a house call to make, so—"

"On who?"

Branwen leaned away from the viciously snapped-out demand. "Finn. You remember the dog who got injured by a mantrap. You done anything about that?"

"Didn't you keep the dog at the vets?"

"For a while. He's back with Cobb now and I promised I'd call in this morning."

"Did he see the crash?" Johnston bit out the question.

Branwen frowned. "Finn?"

"Cobb."

"You'd have to ask Cobb."

"Well make sure you don't bully him to silence when you see him."

Unable to believe she'd heard that, realising that telling a police officer where to stick it wasn't a good move, Branwen stormed off to her own car and carefully, if somewhat angrily, took the tight turn up to Cobb's cottage.

Chapter 28
Branwen and Cobb – Pen-Y-Cwm, Cobb's Home

Sleeping on the floor was always an option, but rarely a good one.

Especially not with a big dog that wanted the prime location next to the fire. So, Cobb got up at four. He checked on the boy. Still alive and the swollen lumps on his head were subsiding, darker in colour, but subsiding. That had to be good news. He spotted the rucksack Branwen had left by the bed, the one she'd taken from the wreck.

He carried it to one of the chairs by the table. The cottage came furnished, so the choice of a table and four chairs wasn't his, and in a place that only had one double bedroom, it seemed rather pointless. He returned with his coffee and opened the bag. The feel of the material and the sharpness of the clasp told him the rucksack was new. The manufacturer's tag hanging inside was more proof. He started with the top pocket and worked his way down until the bag was empty and the contents neatly piled on the table.

All new clothes. Two to three thousand in cash. A very nice looking, clearly used MacBook. And no identification whatsoever.

The laptop would tell him the most, but what this collection told him most loudly, was that the boy was running from something. He looked away from the stacks on the table to the closed door to the bedroom.

What was he running from? Who? Why?

The boy knew the answers. Chances were, the laptop would too.

***

Branwen was stewing from the encounters when she reached Cobb's cottage. The strain pulled across her shoulders, even her teeth felt tense. This far out there was little need to lock doors, and though it had once been Cobb's habit, he hadn't locked his front door in over a year. She slapped her hand on the doorknob, twisted and stepped straight in, surprised to find Cobb turning from the hearth, his phone to his ear.

Cobb appeared more serious than usual, and he was never exactly the jolliest joker in the pack. Branwen detected a dangerous edge too. He glanced at her, instantly took the phone from his ear. She had to push away this sour mood, none of this was Cobb's fault.

"Who did you call?"

"It didn't connect."

In other words, none of her business. More evidence of his control in who he dealt with, more evidence he didn't want her in his world.

"Anyway," she smiled. The forced expression drew a look from

Cobb that told her he wasn't falling for it. "Morning. How's the patient?"

"Judge for yourself."

Adjusting the grip on her bag, Branwen stepped forward as Finn struggled up from his place in front of the heat source to limp towards her, whimpering for attention.

"Humph," Cobb grunted. "He's been walking fine 'til now."

"Fine?"

"Well, better than that."

Branwen smiled, kneeling down and fussing the big dog. "You just love the attention, don't you baby?"

"He's a dog Jones, not a child," Cobb said. "Tea?"

"No thanks." Then to the dog, she said "What's Daddy say about you? He didn't mean it, darling. He's apparently woke up grumpy this morning." She spotted the sleeping bag dumped in the corner. "Probably didn't sleep too well last night."

Cobb glanced round and glared at her. She smiled at him and stood, which was when she spotted the piles on the table.

"What's that?" She pointed.

"His belongings. No ID. No phone."

Branwen frown. "Unusual. I'd best go check on him."

Beneath the white sheets and the heavy bedspread, the young man looked pale and drawn. The lumps on his head had gone down, but painted his brow in livid colour. Sitting on the edge of the bed, Branwen looked down at the white pillowcase. Where the cotton indented around his head, it had stained slightly orange. Branwen frowned. The one time she had tried to change her own black mop with henna, the dye had taken better on the pillowcases than her hair. But surely the man had to be a natural redhead. His beard was ginger. She didn't think men dyed their beards. Though if she could get her eyebrows dyed, dying a beard probably wasn't that much more difficult, it was only hair after all.

His regular, even breathing reassured Branwen. Reaching out, she tested his temperature, placing the back of her fingers along his cheek. The cold contact roused him, slightly. His eyes fluttered open. They seemed a little haunted. Branwen smiled, speaking softly and thanking God that the young man had not fallen into a coma. "It's okay. You're safe. Rest."

His eyes closed and he drifted back to sleep. Retrieving a small vial and syringe from her bag, Branwen made quick work of giving him an antibiotic. She wondered how the human medical profession would react to a vet doing this, but she was more concerned for this man's health than BMA ethics. Satisfied she'd done all she could, she left the bedroom.

Cobb awaited her. "Well?"

"He's improving. I've given him a broad-spectrum antibiotic, just in case. And don't tell Pete, I don't want to get in that kind of argument if I don't have to. I do think the boy will be okay though. I'll talk to Pete about it, get some advice."

"I suppose I'll have to have him up here too," Cobb grumbled.

"Not likely. It's Tuesday, remember? Tuesday to Thursday, Pete works over in Llanindra. At this time of year, he usually stays there too." Llanindra was a village two valleys away, where Doc shared another office, this time with a dentist. There he offered GP service to Llanindra and the surrounding area. "Given the improvement in the last twelve hours, I suspect your unwelcome guest will be gone by the time he's back. By the way, I think I know who he might be. Remember when we were in the Pig I took a booking for a Howard Lions? Well he didn't turn up at the farm and I think that's because he's here."

"That gives us his name at least."

"Possibly," Branwen agreed, sticking her hands in her pockets as they stood before the open fire. "By the way, PC Johnston was at the crash site. Not a happy man," she observed.

"Probably too early in the morning for him."

Branwen smiled and nodded. "He asked about the driver, what I'd seen, had I been alone, that kind of thing. I said I hadn't seen the driver, and didn't mention you, but chances are someone in the village knows you and I left about the same time."

"Emma certainly does."

"Exactly, so it's not going to take even Johnston long to realise that you might have seen something and come calling."

"Great."

"Yeah, sorry about that." She pushed her hair back. "Look, I don't know why, but I get the feeling that we shouldn't be mentioning this to anyone."

Cobb narrowed his eyes at her. Did he think something was off too?

"Look, call me a fool, but if this guys' not carrying ID or even a burner phone-"

"Burner phone?"

She looked up at him. "Yeah, you know -"

"I know what a burner phone is." Cobb cut her off. "I'm wondering how you do."

"I watch a fair amount of crime and spy shows on TV." She shrugged. "Anyway, my point is he's hiding, and yes, he could be hiding from the police, or he could be hiding from something worse. Anyway, in the state he's in, and not knowing what's going on with him, not even knowing who he is, I just think keeping him hidden a while longer might be a good idea."

She watched Cobb, looking for any sigh of agreement. Or disagreement. Any reaction would be good. But his damnable control held sway again.

He took a breath. "Unless we find something more incriminating than a lack of ID, I'm inclined to agree."

That shouldn't have been such a relief. "Good. Can I suggest you start locking your doors again? Oh, and sorry for just barging in, shouldn't have done that."

***

The second time Branwen reached the bridge, PC Johnston had gone, but Paul had arrived with assistance, to pull the wrecked vehicle from it watery grave. The winch had the many dented machine on the flatbed, but it still needed securing. Paul left that to his mate and moved over to Branwen's car.

"Nasty business," he said after greeting her.

"Yeah." Her non-committal reply felt stale. She had stayed longer with Cobb than expected so was running late and she had several morning appointments.

"Johnston sent us up this morning, but said nowt about the driver. You hear anything?"

"No." She smiled. "Sorry, Paul. I don't mean to be rude, but I can't stop. I've Mrs Jessop in first thing."

Paul rolled his eyes. The strictest schoolteacher the village had ever known, although now retired, was a stickler for punctuality.

"You'd best get going unless you want a half-hour lecture on the importance of time keeping. I'll move the van to the passing point, you should be able to get past then."

"Thanks." She smiled as she bade him farewell and waited till he'd got his vehicle off the road. They'd secure the wreck properly before they moved again.

***

"It's the Doc for you," Hannah, the receptionist, told Branwen a few hours later when Branwen picked up the internal transfer. The call transferred with a click.

"Hey Pete, you okay?"

"I was about to ask you that," the voice said. The steady connection suggested he was on a landline his end too. "I was worried after that call you made last night. What was the problem?"

"That I'm an idiot?" She tried to force a laugh, but it didn't work well. "I thought I had a problem, instantly called for your opinion, which was a bit lame, honestly. When you couldn't hear me, I applied myself and sorted it within five minutes. I also felt a right plonker for turning to you far too quickly."

His laugh was gentle and genuine. "Branny you can turn to me any time. I really rather wish you'd do so more often."

Warmth spread through her. "Pete, you really are such a nice guy."

The groan was unexpected. "Oh no, not the nice-guy epitaph. That's the kiss of death, that is."

For the first time that day Branwen genuinely smiled. "Pete, we haven't kissed for years." Though he was pretty damn good at it. He'd been the standard she'd measured all other guys against. "And besides, you are a nice guy. A good guy. I trust you. I like you. I enjoy being around you. I even think of you first when I have a problem. Don't see that as being damning of you. Bit weak of me –"

"Branwen Jones–"

Sounded like someone had called his attention at the other end.

"I've got to go," he said, "but this conversation isn't over, and you call me anytime you want to, you hear? I'm here for you. No matter how trivial the problem might or might not be. Promise you'll call me."

She wouldn't, but he made her feel good, so she promised him anyway. "Speak soon."

Chapter 29
Baron – Pen-Y-Cwm Farm and Guesthouse

The farm was, well it was a typical farm. Stone built house that had been variously extended over a couple of hundred years. One wooden barn stood decaying next to another with corrugated steel cladding and a pre-formed dome roof. A mid-size storage container to one side, bore the crest of the local Mountain Rescue. The buildings formed a square around a large cobbled, stone and beaten dirt square. A quad-bike and an aged Subaru waited near the house.

"Grotty," Shoreham pronounced as they drew up beside the car.

"We've both stayed in worse." Hell, Baron had lived in worse, and given Shoreham's army background, it was a safe bet that he had too. The guest house had a four-star rating, so had to be pretty good – or lying. It was a toss up.

As they got out of the car, a man's voice greeted them.

"Hello," Baron stepped towards the man, noting the oil stained rag he wiped his hands with. "We were looking for a room for a few nights."

The man looked between the two. "Is one of you Mr Lions?"

That, Baron knew, was the false name Jay Whitney had used. "Neither, sorry."

"You don't have a booking then?"

"No, is that a problem?"

The man shook his head. "Not this time of year." The cragged face shifted in what might have been a friendly smile. "Come on through, I'll book you in. I'm Iolyn Jones by the way. You are?"

As he led the way to the front door, the man checked his hands and threw the rag over his shoulder. The door was unlocked and he led them through to a small room that looked like at one time it would have been a parlour, but now acted as the office/reception.

"I'm Baron, he's Shoreham."

They got an acknowledging nod as Iolyn moved to the desk and opened a laptop. This was more modern than he'd been expecting.

"Right, you said you wanted one room, twin or double?"

"Two rooms," Shoreham snapped.

Iolyn shrugged. "I'm not judging." He looked over the screen. "Right, you can have rooms four and five. They're on opposite sides of the corridor, but they're both doubles. That okay for ya?"

"That'll be fine," Baron agreed.

"How many nights you staying?"

"Till the weekend."

"Four nights then. It's full payment up front, okay?" He entered a load of data on the screen. The door behind them opened sharply, and Baron was caught off guard by the appearance of a uniformed constable.

Iolyn looked up and scowled.

Interesting. Baron noted this reaction matched the daughter's. Unpopular officers often became good sources of information. The man looked at Baron and Shoreham.

"You were the ones at the crash site a few minutes ago?"

"Yeah," Baron confirmed. "Looked nasty."

"What were you told about it?"

Baron could see why the locals didn't like this guy. Didn't mean he wouldn't be useful. "The woman only said that there wasn't anyone in the car when she drove past."

"Woman?" Iolyn asked.

"Branwen," Johnston confirmed. "She was there when I drove up."

"On her way to work." Iolyn said. "Did you want something, Johnston?"

"You reported that car crash," Johnston said striding up to Iolyn.

"No." Iolyn didn't move from his seat at the desk or from the data input. "Branwen reported the crash, I know nothing about it. Now if you don't mind, Constable Johnston, I have guests to see to."

"What happened to the driver?"

Now Iolyn looked at the officer. "I don't know."

"What about Branwen?"

"Ask her."

"Where did she take the driver she pulled out of the vehicle?"

Iolyn slowly and carefully stood. He had a decade or more on the officer, and a couple of inches in height, but the farmer was easily hardier than the police officer, and apparently they both knew it. "I don't know anything of use to you, Constable Johnston. Now get out of my house and off my land."

Johnston squared up to the man, pointlessly. "This isn't over." But he turned on his heel and stomped away, so clearly it was.

Iolyn apologised and returned to the desk, hit a couple more keys and named the price for the stay.

Baron figured he'd be lucky to get one night for one in some London hotels for that little. He pulled out his wallet and paid cash.

A few minutes later, they'd been given keys and shown to their rooms, left alone with the house rules and indication that the house didn't provide lunch or dinner unless pre-ordered. Baron pre-ordered for that night, paid cash. Apparently, the locals weren't as yokel as he might have liked.

The room was surprisingly nice. Big and comfortable, recently decorated in a country style, but not too much chintz. The ringing from his pocket surprised Baron, the satnav had been warning of intermittent signal and unavailability of traffic updates for the last two hours of driving, so when he clocked the full five bar signal strength here, Baron frowned, even as he answered the phone to Granger.

"Hello, sir." Soon enough he'd be able to tell the man where to stick his demanded respect.

"Well? Have you got it yet?"

"We've found the car, but not Whitney."

"That's not good enough. I gave you those details, how hard is it for you to get the man and his computer?"

"We only just got here sir, and it seems no one knows what happened to the driver. At this point no one seems to even know who was driving. Whitney is missing, but the car is here so he can't be far, we're not out of options. I believe the local constable might be useful too."

"Why?"

"I've seen the way the locals react to him. People don't dislike a good cop. I'll make enquiries, he might be useful."

"Well hurry up, all that bastard needs is a bloody internet connection and we're all screwed."

Left listening to the silence of an empty line, Baron didn't know what the stolen files were, but the way Granger was wigging out, it had to be something major. He wondered what O'Rourke knew. And a local telephone mast wasn't going to help anyone.

Chapter 30
Cobb – Pen-Y-Cwm, Cobb's Home

The door handle turned, a thud sounded, then someone hammered on the door. Cobb stood for a moment in the bedroom doorway and let the person knock. Thankfully he'd locked the door after Branwen left.

Taking a steadying breath, he moved over to the door and opened it a little, PC Johnston. Strong winds buffeted the officer and meant Cobb had to hold the door tight to stop it being blown in.

"Johnston," Cobb greeted.

"Can I come in?"

"You got a warrant?"

Johnston frowned. "No."

"Then no."

"What are you hiding?"

"Nothing."

"Why can't I come in then?"

"I don't like you." Honesty could be so refreshing.

Johnston glared. Cobb just looked back, whatever the man might think, there wasn't a law against dislike, if there were Johnston would have to arrest half the village – and caution the other half.

"You saw the crash on Satan's Turn last night."

"Did I?"

Johnston's jaw clenched. "So, you didn't see it?"

"Of course, I did, but the first time you were telling me not asking. Thought the police had training courses on things like that. I left the village about five, the roads were awful so I drove real slow, then I came up to Satan's Turn, and I saw the car in the stream, looked out, couldn't see a driver, came home. Didn't have a signal so I couldn't call the police."

"What about Branwen Jones?"

"She's a vet, I've been dealing with her because Finn's been unwell."

"That wasn't what I meant!"

Johnston's snap revealed his lack of patience.

"What did you mean?"

"Did she see the crash?"

Lying to the police wasn't a great idea, but it was really easy. "I can't tell you what someone else saw. That would be hearsay."

"She called from the Farm, but she didn't mention anything about the driver to her father."

Cobb shrugged. "Any conversation between Branwen and Iolyn

90

Jones is their business, not mine."

He guessed Johnston would have ground his teeth if they hadn't been chattering.

"So, you saw the crash, but you didn't even report it, you just did nothing?"

"What else was there to do?"

***

With nothing else to do, Johnston stomped away. Cobb closed the door and opened the MacBook. The password wouldn't make opening it any easier. He noticed the fingerprint reader. Could it be that easy?

He headed to the bedroom and checked on the boy. Still asleep, which was a bit of worry. *Let's see if this disturbs him.*

Nope, apparently even trying thumb and two fingers didn't disturb him. But it did get him into the laptop. Leaving sleeping beauty to his recovery, Cobb took the MacBook back to the main room and sat down at the table to start looking through. The .exe files that caught his attention first these weren't off the shelf programs. Opening them up caught his attention more. He knew what he was looking at, and it was a damn sight more impressive than expected.

He looked at the MacBook, turned his head and looked at the bedroom door, wondering about the man in there.

Very interesting. Very.

Chapter 31
Simons – Home Counties

Simons sat at his desk. The suit felt a little tight around the waist. He needed to get out running more, he might be well into middle age, but that didn't mean he could let his fitness levels slip or his middle spread.

Judy knocked and entered. The trouser suit suited her, as did the pixie cut hair. No one would look at her and believe that she'd celebrated her fiftieth two weeks ago, and she'd drunk most of the lads under the table, and still been fresh as a daisy for work the next day. Well, maybe not that fresh, she'd flagged earlier in the day than normal, but she'd definitely been fresher than he had.

She sat before him and they ran through what they had on. Everything was entirely in hand.

"Sometimes, Judy I think you could run this place without me."

She smiled. "Only sometimes? My, I must be slipping."

Luckily, she was joking. She could definitely run the place without him, which was just as well given the number of times he had to go away on business on short notice. "Did you have any luck with the four hotels?"

She pulled and A4 sheet from the file in her hand and passed it across. "These are the addresses. I couldn't get into the Galashields booking system, but I got into the others, there were no name correlations. However, the only booking for last night at the Pen-Y-Cwm Guesthouse, was for a Howard Lions. That was marked 'pay on arrival', but I checked again this morning and Mr Lions hasn't arrived. I checked the other two as well, and they both had no shows too."

"So, either the man's gone to Scotland or out of the country some other way. No way of knowing which without being able to get into their system."

"Sorry boss, I'm good enough most of the time, but I was never the gifted hacker a certain other man we both know was. Is there really no way you can get him back."

"I wish." Simons really did, but it was made clear that the man in question wanted to get away and stay away. Said he would get in touch when he was ready and able.

"It isn't beyond the realms that I could trace him, if you just gave me the green light."

Simons smiled over at Judy. "I know." In truth, because of an unexpected call, he already had a rough idea where Cobb might be, and he would leave him in peace. For now. "But I made a promise that I wouldn't, not for first five years anyway. We're still within that. If he calls, that's different, but…" Something clicked in his mind.

"If he calls I'll do backflips across the hall." Judy stood as she spoke. "Right now, you need to review the plans for the Curzon test."

Curzon Creative Media. Another set of whizz kids who had yet to realise there was nothing new under the sun and believed that they could build an impregnable system. They'd contacted him yesterday, given him a week to break into their system and tell them what their non-existent flaws were. He'd got in within thirty minutes of hanging up the phone. Their system had more flaw than function.

The phone started ringing.

He glanced at the flashing lights, line one was solid, that meant Judy was dealing with that call, he reached out and connected to line two.

"CSC Securities."

A deep voice answered. "It's Cobb."

Simons nearly dropped the phone. "You're still alive then."

"Some might debate that."

Typical, and understandable.

"Simons, I need a favour."

"Somehow I didn't think you'd start with a social call."

***

Simons walked out of his office and into Judy's.

"Come with me," he said when she looked up. It was really rather gratifying that she did so without question or hesitation. He led her out into the hall. "Well?"

She looked at him, frowned. "Well, what?"

"Back flips."

For a moment her jaw dropped, he couldn't hold the smile back any longer.

"He called?"

Simons nodded.

Judy jumped up and down like a delighted school girl, she threw her arms around Simons' neck and hugged him tighter than he'd been hugged in years. "Oh, that's wonderful. Wonderful!" She let go and looked at him closely, piercingly. "And he's okay? Not in trouble?"

"He's fine. Safe and healthy. He just wanted me to share some of his old files with him."

"Where is he?"

"He didn't say, I didn't ask."

Now she rolled her eyes. "You two are hopeless."

"Actually, right now I'm rather hopeful. Hopeful of seeing you do back flips down this hall like you promised."

Another eye roll and she turned as if to go back to her office before performing three perfectly executed back flips down the hall, and another three back. Standing straight she smoothed down her jacket, her hair and stepped elegantly towards the door, pausing only at the last second to stick her tongue out at him.

Chapter 32
Alex – Belsize Park

"Oh crap."

Alex stared at the screen, fighting the nausea. When he'd discovered the hacking, he'd found another folder, all encrypted files. It had taken him this long to crack the code and get in, and now he had he wished he hadn't. Now he understood what The Chair was, how Granger used it, he wished he didn't. It wasn't right or natural. Some twisted bastard had dreamt that up.

His hand shook as he reached out and dialled the only number he dared. The strong desire to scrub his brain warred with the knowledge that the acid in his mouth wasn't strong enough to etch out these disgusting images from his mind.

"Yes?"

Alex didn't know how to read O'Rourke's neutral tone. "I found something, sir. And you're not going to like it."

Chapter 33
Branwen – Pen-Y-Cwm Village

Branwen needed a drink. She doubtless needed her head read too. She'd been going over the books for the vet business, making sure everything was ready for the sale, when she found some calculations she'd been working on for the Guesthouse. Occupancy was down to forty-seven percent. With the other income streams it would keep the wolf from the door, but her father wouldn't be able to afford help around the house. At the moment, they managed between the two of them, but would he manage alone? Did she need to stay and take care of that business? Of him? Was leaving a mistake?

No. She couldn't let such thoughts intrude. They still nagged her though. In her grandmother's voice. *Stay here. The farm has to be tended. Be a vet only because it'll serve the family. Family first.*

Family first.

What a joke. Her father was born out of wedlock and the wider family had shunned them for it. Her own mother had been so oppressed by the narrowness of the valley and its people's world-view that she'd left her year old old baby behind and never set foot in the UK again. Branwen had stood by her father all these years because he was her father, the one who'd loved her, gran and great-gran had only scolded her, told her what to do, what to think, what to be. Only her father had loved her when she messed up, when she went against the matriarchy. But even he wanted to hold her here when she would flee. She was terrified she was already trapped, she had stayed for others, now she had to go for her.

With a hopeless grunt she let herself slump forward, her head hitting the desktop harder than she intended.

"Coming down the pub?"

She shot back upright to find Emma standing before her. "Has Hannah gone to lunch?"

"Nope, she'd out there doing whatever it is she does. She did however say that your next appointment isn't till two-twenty, so I could come in and drag you all the way to the pub for lunch."

All the way to the pub; right next door. Branwen looked at the paperwork on her desk, much diminished after the weekend. "Oh, I think I can manage that."

Five minutes later they sat in the pub, pints of cola before them, paninis ordered and on the way. Emma watched her, all bright eyed and shiny. That was a worry – the prying was coming.

"So, tell me about Cobb."

Branwen frowned. "What about Cobb?"

Emma leaned conspiratorially forward. "Well, have you made

him notice you're a woman yet?"

"He knows I'm a woman. He's not blind."

"No, but he's not seeing you, is he?"

Heaving a sigh, Branwen slouched back. "Stop trying to set me up with Cobb. It's not going to happen."

Emma looked questioningly at her friend. "Whatever you've said this time, we can recover. We can make it happen."

Branwen rolled her eyes. "Cobb and I have an understanding. We're friends. Our paths don't lie on the same road."

Emma blew a raspberry at that. "You and Cobb suit each other. It's a waste that the pair of you aren't together. The downtrodden local and the mysterious, rich stranger." She smiled. "It's a great idea."

"Have you been reading trashy romance novels again? Anyway, where did the 'rich' come from?"

Emma raised her brow and leaned forward. "Well, I wouldn't as a rule discuss a client's financial details, but this is an exception, since you and Cobb belong together. Besides, I already told you, he paid for the cottage outright, one single cash transaction. And what work has he ever done in the last two years to support himself?"

"Well, he does work for me."

"Occasionally," Emma pointed out. "It's not regular and it's not enough to live on, not even for a man as frugal as him. He has money, but he never seems to earn it."

"Ever considered that maybe he took a redundancy package? Early retirement? I don't know, but really! His finances, like his past, are no concern of ours." But she wanted to know all the same. She pushed Cobb from her mind, concentrating again on her friend. "Why do you stay here?"

Emma paled. "What do you mean?"

"Well, you came back here with me after uni, I stay because I'm a vet, I work as a vet, I have a home and a purpose here. You're a biochemist selling real estate and handicraft. I know why you came here, but why do you stay?"

For a moment Emma couldn't meet her eye. They both knew why they'd come here, but that didn't make thinking about it any easier. Finally Emma looked up. "I stay because I like it. But mostly I stay for Ivan."

"Love's enough?"

Emma smiled. "Of course. Love is what matters. You have to love what you do. Or at least the people you do it for. And one day, it'll be love, family and roots."

Family and roots.

She had both, yet she felt unrooted.

***

The black of night flashed with red and blue, and the occasional white as a torch beam looked momentarily at something other than the ground. Branwen slowed her car as she neared Satan's Turn. Police vehicles, including one minibus, littered the area. There was no getting through because of the uniformed officers in their thickly padded hi-vis vests standing in the road. Halting the vehicle, she wound down the window as an officer moved to the side of her car.

"Any reason I can't get past?" she asked.

"Any reason you should?"

She glared at the officer. "Because I live up the road, as you full well know. So stop being a dick, Johnston."

Johnston glowered back at her. "And that attitude's really going to help you." He leaned back and started looking over her car.

"It was MOTed three weeks ago, no advisories. So don't even think of trying to trump up some charge to pacify your bloody ego."

"Attacking a police officer is never a wise move." Johnston advised as he moved to lean on her window.

She considered pointing out that it wasn't a wise move to piss off a woman on the edge with enough pentobarbital to drop a man dead, but she figured that was probably pushing things too far. "What are you doing up here anyway?"

"Fingertip search," Johnston grouched. "Inspector Perkins' idea."

She nodded. "Makes sense. Something could have dropped from the car. You might even find tracks, or the driver. Smart man this Perkins. Or woman."

"Man." The tone suggested Johnston didn't hold with this nonsense of a woman having the capacity to be smart.

"Found anything?"

"Wouldn't tell you if we did. That's police business."

Offering a saccharine smile she agreed with him. The way he glowered suggested it had unnerved Johnston. "Then please, kind Constable Johnston, might a young lady alone at night, please drive past all your hardworking officers to get home and do the milking?"

"Don't milk it, Jones." He falsely smiled back. "Your car may be fine today, but I'll be around tomorrow and a lot of tomorrows after that."

Hopefully she wouldn't be, but he moved from the window and waved her forward. She hoped the search gave his fingers frostbite.

The night was pitch dark by the time Branwen reached the secluded farmhouse, so the light spilling from the badly closed curtains, was welcome and warm. Shame she couldn't head straight in. The curtains moved in the front room and Branwen raised her hand in acknowledgement of her father as she moved to the back of the Land Rover to retrieve and don her wellingtons.

The cows, all six of them, complained about the lateness of her attendance.

"All right you lot, I'm only half an hour late. The wait obviously didn't kill you." Quickly she fed and milked them. As a dairy herd, they were far from being viable, but the novelty of feeding and milking cows helped attract some town and city school groups and they did make reasonably nice cheese, another learning novelty, and income stream.

Bovine bodies and emissions had heated the cowshed and warmed Branwen, making crossing the yard a plunge pool experience. Walking into the house was like putting herself in an oven, not too hot, more a proving oven to give rise to that sensation of home, comfort and wellness.

"Hiya."

"Hi," she returned her father's greeting as she struggled out of the second Wellington. "How's things?"

"Two new arrivals. Messers Baron and Shoreham. They've been asking about you. At least Baron has."

"One tall and blond, the other shorter, dark haired? Gym muscle?"

Her father nodded, like many who lived and worked with people muscled by the activity of life he easily saw when someone was more pumped by static weightlifting than activity.

"Met them this morning. They were looking over the car wreck on Satan's Turn."

"So I heard." Her father moved closer. Taking her arm, he moved her to the corner of the hall, his voice low. "What's going on, Branwen? You never mentioned pulling the driver out last night." He seemed upset she was keeping secrets. If only he knew.

A lifetime of not talking about what she was doing had taught Branwen how to lie, but this question caught her off-guard. "What?"

"And Johnston's been bending my ear about it all day," her father said.

"Why? You weren't there."

"And you aren't talking to him," he returned. "The little git came up here throwing his weight around when I was trying to check our guests in. And he's phoned since."

That sounded like Johnston. Why ask an actual witness when he could piss off the witness's family? "The man's an arse, but that's not news."

"He said you pulled the driver from the car."

She shook her head. "I've no idea why Johnston's saying that. The driver was already gone when I arrived at the crash site."

"Gone where?"

She shrugged. "Oh Dad, please. I've no idea."

Chapter 34
Baron – Pen-Y-Cwm Farm and Guesthouse

Shoreham had the room at the front of the house, where Baron joined him to watch for the daughter's return. The father hadn't known anything. They'd gone down to the village, and then Dolgellau, and managed to find Johnston. It didn't take much to find out how easily he was brought. No self-respecting bent copper in London would be so cheap, but there again, they weren't in London any more. Felt like Kansas wasn't exactly local. Looking over the farm yard Baron wondered if Earth was. From where they stood, they watched Branwen Jones drive in, then surprisingly, turn away from the house.

"Porcelain doll."

Baron blinked. Turned to Shoreham. "Pardon?"

"Branwen Jones. She's like a porcelain doll. Small, dark hair, white skin."

He considered the man, unsure where this was going. "Go on."

"When I was a kid, my mum buggered off to Spain for a week. I had to watch my little sister. When Mum came back, she brought this doll back. Shaz loved it. First thing I did was poke an eye out. Mum blamed Shaz because she'd never seen me so much as pick the doll up. Then I poked the other eye out. Shaz cried for ages, that only made Mum more convinced she'd done it. I did something to that doll every week for two months. Breaking or loosening something. Mum started smacking Shaz then. I had my first wet dream about that doll."

There was so much wrong with Shoreham, Baron didn't know where to start, and didn't really want to. He looked back through the window. Branwen was coming back to the house. That seemed like a good place to start.

"Let's go find out what she has to say."

Shoreham walked out the room and Baron followed. The taller man stopped at the top of the stairs, looking down but not moving. Baron realised he was listening to the voices from downstairs.

"How about a hot mug of soup and a cold pork sandwich?"

"Oh, yes please!" Hunger filled her voice. "I'll be back down in five minutes, I need a shower."

Baron watched Shoreham go down the stairs. Something happened as the two crossed, Baron didn't catch what, and he didn't care, but he started to walk down too. Branwen jumped at seeing him. Her unintelligible grunt acknowledged him as they passed. He headed to the lounge, where Shoreham stood on the rug, staring at the fire and saying nothing as his shorter partner eased himself into the big chair at the fireside.

"Do you think she knows where Whitney is?"

"Yep." The blond studied the fire as it lapped around the edges of the logs.

His taciturn nature was an occasional irritant to Baron. "Why?"

"She lied this morning."

No fuller explanation was forthcoming, and Baron didn't care enough to ask for one. Less than ten minutes passed before Branwen reappeared. Scrubbed clean, her wet hair was piled on top of her head, held in place by a large jaw clip. Gone was the over-large, thick Arran sweater, hard worn jeans and walking boots, replaced by soft moccasins, moleskin pants and a thick fleece pullover with a neck zip. The open zip revealed that the pale length of neck gave way to a tantalising glimpse of ample breast. Baron watched Shoreham; the taller man tipped up his chin, doubtless getting the best view his height would afford him. From what Baron could see, Branwen Jones lived on a mountain and carried two with her.

"Hello again," she said. "You found us all right, then?"

"Fine," Baron smiled. "Thank you."

Even as he introduced himself and Shoreham, Baron wondered how best to use her to find Whitney.

Her father returned, bringing a big mug of steaming oxtail soup and a thick sandwich of doorstop bread and broad cut pork. The same dinner they had been provided with, and it tasted as good as it smelt.

"Ah wonderful, thanks." With heartfelt gratitude Branwen took the two offerings, sinking on to the overstuffed and mismatched sofa. Reaching down, she lay the plate on the floor, unthinkingly providing him with a great cleavage shot. She wrapped both her hands round the mug and sipped carefully on the hot soup. In the silence, Branwen looked between her two guests. "So," she asked at length, "what're you two planning on doing while you're up here?"

"Having fun," Shoreham replied in a deep tone.

Branwen looked up at Shoreham as she lounged back. "And what's your idea of fun, Mr Shoreham?"

She really didn't want to know.

"You'd be surprised, Miss Jones."

Yes, unpleasantly so, Baron thought.

She met his steady gaze, didn't flinch from it. Baron liked that.

"Probably not," she muttered, as she turned back to Baron. "Will you be venturing out on the chair?"

"The chair?"

She smiled. "The mountain. It's what it means. Cader Idris. The Chair of Idris."

"Possibly." Baron smiled. "We'll wait and see how things pan out."

She nodded. "Make sure that if you do go out, you leave a route plan and time guide – just in case. There's a map in the hallway with all the best routes marked."

"Thank you."

"Is there anywhere to go on the mountain?" Shoreham asked.

"Just the mountain," Branwen answered.

"So there's nowhere to shelter?"

"Not really. There's a couple of caves around, sort of, some half collapsed dry stone walls. There's a shelter on the very top, on the other side, it's not much, without care you can still die of hypothermia up there, but that's about it. That's why the Mountain Rescue gets so many calls, there is nowhere to go and if anything happens while you're out there, you need help asap. So, leave a route and ETA."

"You're a member?" Baron asked. "Of the Mountain Rescue?"

She nodded as she drank.

"Is that why there's a container with the logo on in your yard?"

"Actually, no. This farm is the highest up the mountain, we've been storing their equipment here for ease of collection for years. Long before I joined up."

"Do they have much use for a vet?"

"Sometimes. It's not only humans who get lost on these mountains. We had five calls for sheep last year alone." She laughed, remembering. "The year before we got called out for a cow. Besides, some walkers take their dogs with them and they can fall too. Sometimes it's not just a fall." The laughter disappeared, thinking of the last dog that hadn't had to fall to get carried off the mountain in need of a vet.

"Could the driver of that crashed car have made it to the shelter you mentioned?"

She paused to consider it. "Doubt it. If it were me and I was still walking, which I supposed he must have been, I would have followed the river or the road down and back to the village. But that's the opposite direction. There again, that's rational thought and we don't know the driver was in a clear enough state of mind to think rationally. Guess that would depend on what shape he was in after the crash."

"What shape was he in?" Baron pursued.

Calmly, she shrugged. "How would I know? I believe I said this morning that the driver was gone when I got there."

"But you knew the driver was a man."

"I hadn't heard the driver was a woman, so I assumed it was a man. Which is pretty bloody sexist when you think about it." She shrugged. "Was it a woman then? As crashed the car?"

Baron watched the woman intently; she interested him. Shoreham had a point, with her short stature and pale skin, she seemed delicate, add the black hair and large eyes and she did have a doll-like cast. Yet the more he observed her, the more he discovered. Brains and spirit. Strength of character. She wouldn't easily give up Whitney. Not unless she wanted to. All he had to do was figure out how to make her want to.

***

For now, all Baron had to do was wait. Not his favourite pastime, but necessary. He paced in his room. The conversation with Granger had not been enjoyable, the following one with O'Rourke worse. What Granger wanted was impossible. Inaction wasn't an option, but he didn't want to unleash Shoreham just yet, the body count was already too high. Though with what he'd discovered, Baron couldn't be sure that the body would be Branwen Jones'.

The Joneses had left the sitting room downstairs at half ten, both claiming exhaustion. He waited until quarter past eleven.

The Jones's office door was clearly marked 'Private', and easy to get into. Not even locked. Baron scoffed at the naïve trust. The daughter should have known better. She, at least, demonstrated a certain wit, displayed a level of distrust higher than any of the other locals they had encountered. Her distrust meant she foresaw problems, and had the imagination to fear. That might be fun.

At the computer Baron discovered that it, like the house, had absolutely no concept of security. No passwords, no lockouts. And no contact with the files they sought. Every stored document clearly related to the businesses, bed and breakfast, farm and veterinary practice. *Bugger!* He spotted a regular monthly income from renting land for a telephone mast. That explained the good reception up here. That had to go.

Switching the PC off, Baron sat back, looking around the shelf-lined rooms. Thousands of places to hide a hard drive here.

Thousands of places, and each had to be searched. Sighing, he sat forward and started going through the desk.

Chapter 35
Cobb – Pen-Y-Cwm, Cobb's Home

Cobb fought the sleeping bag and the sleeping dog to get the weight of the wolfhound off his already numb feet. He had a perfectly good, comfortable bed only a few meters away and yet he was sleeping on the bloody floor and for what? Someone else. A few years ago that would not have been a problem, that it was now bothered him. It told him he'd become selfish.

He had a reason for stepping away from humanity. A reason that tore the heart out of him. A loss so painful that he'd been unable to cope. Seeing the murder was one thing. Seeing the murderer was another.

The man appeared from the sunroof of a car, what car he didn't remember. But the car crossed his path, he saw the blond man appear, thought it odd, clearly saw the man's profile and suddenly –

Bile stung his throat. The image haunted his nightmares. He'd spent six painful months looking for that bastard, determined not to let him get away with it. Graham Denham. The police proved useless, the car had been caught on CCTV, but the stolen vehicle had led to nothing. That was why he didn't remember what the car was, it was unimportant. Simons helped, but he hadn't seen the man. He'd gone to the grave. Taking flowers. It had become a ritual, everyday…

Even the day when they finally traced the bastard, found his death certificate, his grave. Cobb had been robbed of revenge.

On that day when he reached the plot, his knees had given way beneath him. The tears wouldn't stop, sobs quaked through him. The loss was too great to live with. The day had gone dark, and he had run out of tears. Finally he had dragged his bones to his car and driven. Just driven. Until he basically ran out of petrol. In Pen-Y-Cwm.

Circling his ankles, he tried to ignore the unavoidable pins and needles as he looked at his phone. Should he call Simons? Yes, he'd got what he'd asked for, but did the help he'd asked for differ from the help he needed?

He hadn't asked for Branwen to come into his life, to drag him back to reality either. But had he needed her? She kept trying, and he kept denying. That would stop soon, when she left. Why did that sound so lonely? Why wasn't he looking forward to the solitude he'd craved?

Because she's become what you crave.

Perhaps he should go up to the farm, take a chance. She'd discounted him, could he make her count him again? Could he stop her leaving? Did he want to? It made no difference, the boy couldn't be left alone.

The injured driver lacked the skill to handle a snowy road but, judging by the program Cobb had found, had the ability to hack the Pentagon. It was a conundrum Cobb needed a solution for.

He stood and stretched his back, his neck. Bones up his spine popped. *The joys of getting older.*

Finn yawned and stretched, occupying ever more of the space in front of the fire. Movement and a groan from the room next door drew Cobb's attention. He went through, switched the light on and saw the boy feebly turn his head, raise his arm against the sudden brightness. Skin pale where it wasn't livid, the boy looked better simply for opening his eyes.

"Where am I?"

"Safe," Cobb moved to the bed and the boy shrank away. Given his size, that wasn't unexpected. "Don't worry kid, you really are safe here. You crashed your car, we got you out."

"My laptop!"

Cobb pointed to the rucksack he'd repacked and left by the bed. "Your stuff's there."

The boy looked at it and visibly relaxed. Which showed too much trust since the laptop was currently sitting on Cobb's table, one of his own decryption programs running. Still, Cobb didn't need to worry the kid with such facts now.

"There was a woman."

Isn't there always?

The boy frowned. "Black hair?"

Branwen. "She'll be back in the morning. Now lay back and rest. We'll talk tomorrow."

He turned around, clicking the light off as he left, and closed the door. The rest of the night all he heard were Finn's grumbles for being kicked off the sleeping bag and deposed of his first position in front of the fire.

Chapter 36
Branwen – Pen-Y-Cwm Farm and Guesthouse

The alarm was far to rude. The usual urge to chuck the thing across the room nearly overwhelmed her. People thought that the upside of owning your own business was setting your own hours; the downside of owning a business was knowing every hour needed some attention, and that there was no one to cover if you decided to throw a sicky. Groaning, Branwen threw off the bed clothes, the equivalent to an ice plunge. She dressed in the clothes she'd worn the previous evening. The brush struggled through her hair, so she pulled it into a scrappy ponytail.

A run down to the cow shed sorted the girls. A return run to her bedroom collected the coat she'd forgotten, and back down to the car. Branwen concentrated on the list of things she needed, checking her pockets as she moved. Credit cards, phone, money –

She slammed into a rock wall otherwise known as Shoreham's chest. Ricocheting off him, she landed against her car. He moved, and she found herself trapped by two immobile objects.

Surprise and shock rooted her to the spot as she stared up at the tall blond man. Recovering quickly, she noted Shoreham was snugly wrapped in a thick fleece-lined Gore-Tex. Judging by the look of his face, the man could stay out here forever warm while she was chilling, the second fleece and her coat still in her hand. The wind picked up, cutting through both the fleece and the t-shirt beneath. Due in the surgery all day, she wasn't dressed for outside work. Her extremities and heart began to freeze.

The obvious threat, the gleam in his otherwise flat eyes, rippled ice down her spine. Why threaten her?

"Something you wanted, Mr Shoreham?" She didn't like the quiver in her voice.

He ran dark eyes down her body with insulting slowness. Despite the covering clothes, Branwen's skin crawled, as if she stood naked beneath his gaze.

"You."

He practically drooled, shifting forward an inch. With nowhere else to go Branwen pressed herself against the Land Rover.

"I-I'm not available," she stuttered. No man had ever been so blatant. Although she didn't want him, despite the implied threat, his overwhelming masculinity sent heat soaring through her. Sex was a thing of her past, yet this animal was affecting the urges in her. She disgusted herself.

"Really?"

The wind whipped around them and Branwen's ponytail swung

with it. The movement, not unlike the lashing of a true pony's tail, caught Shoreham's eye. One large hand snapped up, snagging the thick bunch, pulling it back over the top of the Land Rover, holding her in place, imprisoning her between the cold steel of the car and the hot steel of his body.

"I've learnt," he said quietly, looking down at her now wide eyes, "that everything, and everyone, is available. All you have to do is find the right way in."

"Well, this isn't it." She pushed at his chest. A move as effective as a flea trying to push a dog over.

Shoreham looked down at her. He didn't laugh, he didn't smile. He didn't react. It was so degrading, for one of the few times in her life, Branwen felt totally belittled. She almost wished he had laughed, it would have been less shameful.

"Isn't it?" One large hand slipped up under her fleece. The extremity had been chilled, exposed to the cold air. It froze Branwen's blood as it clamped over her left breast. His thumb played over her erect nipple. "You're aroused."

"I'm cold," she told him, careful to keep her chin up and proud, searching for the calm to out-bluff him in this power game.

"I'll warm you." He pressed closer.

Glaring up at him, she felt the large hand knead her breast. It had been a long time since any man had shown any attraction to her, and her sexual frustration worked against her. So, despite knowing that this man was little more than an animal, the animal in her responded resoundingly.

"Uummmm." Half murmur, half growl, he ground himself against her. "Not many girls fill my hands."

Branwen swallowed, believing him, though she wasn't sure how she felt about being in that distinguished group. The way he played with the weight of her flesh, squeezing and pummelling, burned her sex and churned her stomach.

He leaned closer, his voice a whisper in her ear. "I could lay you down, rip off your top, and sink my teeth into your breast while silencing your scream with my hand over your mouth."

"I'd bite you."

His laugh was low and sensual. "Better and better."

The twisted idea made her wet where it shouldn't. She needed to get a grip, to get out of his grip. "I'm sure you find this amusing, Mr Shoreham, but I have to go to work." It was grated through teeth she clenched to avoid them chattering. Her inner thighs clenched, she shouldn't be turned on by this. How had she become so desperate?

"Time to play vet?" he said, looking down at her.

107

She'd never felt smaller, he was a giant of a man.

"You're like a little dolly."

The surge of his groin pressed against her. The disgust spread – this wasn't arousing any more, it was sick.

"I don't play, I am a vet."

His dark laugh dried her throat.

He ground against her, effectively turning her off, though the length was impressive. That wasn't going to be as much fun as he seemed to think. Size mattered, but bigger wasn't always better. "I could take you right here."

"I'd gouge your eyes out for trying." She moved her car keys between her fingers. If she had to punch him she'd make sure she had some weapon to do it with.

"I like a woman with spirit." He leaned close to whisper in her ear. "More fun to break." She felt the flat of his tongue on her neck and shivered in revulsion. "Where's James Whitney?"

She frowned. "Who?"

He stood up over her, he looked about to snarl, then his head tipped and he frowned. "James Whitney. The driver of that smashed car."

Branwen swallowed. So what had happened to Howard Lions? "I, I told you last night, I don't know."

"Where did you go when we left you yesterday morning? The tyre tracks said you didn't go straight to the village."

"It's none of your business."

"If you can't tell me about Whitney," Shoreham said. "Tell me about McManus."

What little heat she had left deserted her body. For a moment it was only Shoreham's press against her that kept her upright. "You know what?" Red mist warmed her now. She reached into her coat pocket and picked out the lapel pin she'd stowed there after losing the back a couple of days ago. "I deal with sick animals every day. The ones that are really sick, I put down. That's why I have to carry pentobarbital. And you are the sickest puppy I've ever had the misfortune to meet." She reached up and put the point of the pin against the back of his neck. He looked startled by the cold touch. "Now you back off or you're the next one I put down."

***

Branwen only started to calm down as she stepped into her half of the surgeries. Her hands shook as she opened the door. She flicked on the kettle and hugged her coat to her. She moved across to her desk and sat down.

They'd found a wounded man. That was all. She'd tried to do the right thing, tried to keep him alive. What was it going to cost them? Why wasn't her keyboard right in front of her?

It should be right in front of her. It always was. It was where she left it. She nudged it two inches to the left. The mouse wasn't where it should be either. She needed to stretch to reach it, but she stopped as she did so. The chair didn't feel right either. She looked around the room. Everything was where it should be. Sort of.

She swept the place with another glance.

It felt like someone had been in here.

Stop it. Stop being stupid. The chair feels off because you're sitting on the coat you'd usually have taken off by now. The keyboard and mouse aren't out of place by a couple of inches, you are.

The place isn't off. You are. You're having a bad day.

She checked her watch. Not even half eight.

***

Branwen saw her clients and treated her patients and did everything she could not to think. Apparently, she wasn't even thinking when Mr Tiddles lived up to his name and peed all over her, and she didn't notice until way too late.

What is wrong with me?

McManus.

The name came out of the past like a demon to torment her soul. An accident. A bloody accident! And it would haunt her for the rest of her life. McManus being a secret didn't help either. She'd have to tell her father. Didn't want to, but she had to. Problem was, it wasn't just her secret.

The knock on the office door told her Emma wasn't visiting, though as per standing instructions, her receptionist, Hannah, came straight in, closing the door behind her.

"You okay if I go now?"

"Of course. I hope you enjoy the delights of Tunisia, I hear it's spectacular." Though she doubted Hannah would enjoy it much given the girl's propensity to wear everything black and that she complained about the heat in summer here. Or she'd totally surprise them all and absolutely love it. Stranger things had happened. Branwen sighed. "What time's my next booking?"

"Two."

"Great. Have a lovely holiday." She smiled. "Though you might not want to go out dressed like that." She nodded at the girl's heavy boots, black jeans and thick jumper.

Hannah looked back and returned the smile. "You either. See ya."

Branwen looked down at herself. All she had left to wear were a set of blue scrubs. She didn't do surgery here often, but such things had to be bought in multipacks. She usually kept a spare set of

109

clothes here for incidents like Tiddles, but she'd not replaced the set she'd taken home after stitching Finn's leg back together.

Still, she needed to talk to Emma, and a drink to do it. She texted her friend.

Be there in 5

Unfortunately, when Branwen arrived she found Emma had brought Ivan along with her. While she liked Ivan, she didn't want to talk about McManus in front of him. It became the longest forty minutes of her life.

Chapter 37
Jay and Cobb – Pen-Y-Cwm, Cobb's Home

Jay opened his eyes. Where was he? Why? He moved, a steamroller squished him. He remembered being lucky. Although everything hurt, carefully shifting one extremity at a time indicated nothing broken. When he moved his head, a steel band started playing the 1812 Overture inside his skull. It wasn't a good combination.

Laying back, laying still, Jay reviewed his situation. Stuck on a mountain in North Wales. In a cabin, thankfully, he supposed. But he had no idea who his dark-haired angel was, nor the man Cobb. He vaguely remembered someone tending to him in the night, not the raven girl. So Cobb. At least he hoped there wasn't a third figure out there he need worry about.

Immediate situation, not so bad. What about the Nemesis Records situation? They had traced him to his aunts – he hoped she was okay – which meant they might well have traced him to his mother's office and car. If not connected, he might be home free but for the crash. Of course, now the police had the licence plate, so he could be located again.

Yet the raven said he was safe and he wanted so badly to believe her. She said only she and Cobb knew he was here, never once did she mention the police. Even Cobb said he was safe. So perhaps he was safe. Maybe he couldn't be found. The maybe worried him. He didn't know who the Raven or Cobb were, what if they worked for Nemesis?

He swallowed. Was it possible? Anything was possible. Was it likely? Not very. But it was possible.

Carefully, he pushed back the heavy blanket and quilt that lay over him. The air chilled his skin and looking down he saw with horror how extensive the bruising was. All he wore was his green boxer shorts.

He inched carefully into an upright position, having to hold his ribs as he swung his legs over the side of the bed. Once sitting on the edge of the big bed, Jay took a moment to look around. Thankfully his glasses, miraculously unbroken, lay on the bedside cabinet. Gratefully, he put them on and the world came into focus. The walls were bare stone and only four items of furniture stood in the room. The bed, a two-drawer cabinet by its side, a big double wardrobe and an ottoman. On top of the ottoman, sat Jay's clothes. Apparently his T-shirt had been cut off.

Standing slowly, Jay grabbed the foot post of the bed to steady himself. The long, padded over-shirt was still intact, so Jay pulled that on, gritting his teeth against the pain. With the shirt on, Jay was grateful for its warmth, for all that he was sweating from the exertion. He took a few moments to catch his breath.

When steady again, he moved, slowly turning the knob to ease the door towards him and inching it back to look through to what was on the other side. He saw a large space, with a blazing fire giving a golden glow to a room lit by candles and one large oil lamp. The lamp currently sat on a rough-hewn kitchen table. One large chair, by the side of the fire, faced the room, with a high-backed dining chair in the reflecting position. He saw parts of a big dog stretched out on the rug between.

On the far side of the room was a neat kitchen area and beside that, a big Welsh dresser. But no display of matching crockery here. Just books. Lots of books.

The table had three chairs left and in one sat a big man with a slightly overlong crop of thick red hair. Real red, not an orange dye like his. Jay saw this man's bigness was a function of height as well as breadth. Cobb. He sat, concentrated on the laptop in front of him.

"Well?" The deep voice spoke without the man turning. "If you're coming out, come out."

Jay stiffened. He hadn't realised that he'd been spotted. Not a good sign. Slowly he opened the door. In nothing more than a shirt and boxer shorts Jay felt vulnerable, but then in his condition, he would be vulnerable whatever he wore. Tentatively he closed the distance between himself and the table. Each step sent shock waves of pain through his body, although each wave became gradually less fierce.

***

The knock surprised Cobb. Jay looked up, terror washing the blood from his cheeks. Though the day had brightened, the curtains remained closed. Cobb passed Jay the MacBook and nodded him towards the bedroom. Waiting until Jay softly closed the door again, Cobb moved to the front of the cottage. Opening it a crack he looked at the man beyond.

Dark and slightly shabby, office trousers not jeans nor walking trousers, the thick padded jacket practical and looking like it had been in use for a while. The high neck stood up to the man's chin, brushed his ears. Cobb wasn't the least bit surprised when the man raised a warrant card.

"Mr Cobb? I'm Inspector Rhodri Perkins."

Cobb scrutinised the warrant card. Looked real to him. "Apparently."

"Can I come in, it's less than pleasant out here."

The wind had picked up, the air was damp, the fine grains of rain were starting to discolour the well-loved coat.

"Do you have a search warrant?"

"Do I need one?"

"Not sure, but your PC Johnston threatened to get one."

Perkins didn't even flinch. "Yeah, he demanded I got one, but I figured simply talking to you might be more productive. So, can I come in or do I have to stand here getting wet?"

The rain gleamed like sweat on the left side of his face. Cobb stepped back.

"Bit early for a visit, isn't it?"

Perkins stepped in, shrugged. "Johnston saw me late yesterday and I have meetings this morning. This was the only available time."

Cobb directed him to the table. "Take a seat. Want a cuppa?"

Perkins accepted as he sat, and Cobb closed the door. The tall man walked to the kitchen area, a corner of seven cupboards and a built-in oven. Wall units sat above. Room for a large dresser too. A substantial space in a one room cottage. As he turned from the kettle Cobb noticed Perkins looking around.

"Searching for something, Inspector?"

Perkins looked back at him as he unzipped the coat. "Just getting the lay of the land. You've more room here than I thought."

"Yeah, the doors go to my bedroom and the bathroom. And no, you can't look in either without a warrant. I still have a right to some privacy."

The way Perkins tipped his head seemed both acknowledgement and acquiescence. Cobb made the tea and moved back to the table with mugs, milk and sugar, to sat across from the inspector.

"So, what can I do for you?" Cobb asked as he stirred milk into the strengthening tea, then offered the jug to Perkins as the other man spooned two sugars into his own mug.

"I'm sure you can guess."

"I'm sure that this conversation will work much better if you don't try playing games. What do you want?"

"I want to talk to you about the crash at Satan's Turn."

Cobb nodded. "What about it?"

"You saw it?"

"No."

Perkins frowned at him. "You would have had to drive past it to get here."

"I know. I saw the aftermath, not the crash."

Perkins looked at him, sucking in his cheeks. "Now who's playing games?"

Cobb risked a smile. "I reached Satan's Turn about ten past five, I think. It's not like I checked my watch. The crash had happened

113

sometime after I'd left in the morning – around ten, I don't have to be certain of times these days. Though I'd say from the fact that there was only a dusting of snow on the vehicle that it hadn't been there more than thirty minutes."

"Was the engine still warm?"

"I didn't think to check."

"And what about the driver?"

Cobb swallowed a mouthful of tea. "What about the driver?"

"Did you see him?"

"I saw no sign of anyone leaving the vehicle, but again, with the wind and snow, nature may well have covered any tracks. I looked into the car. Then it tipped over the edge. Branwen told me that Paul Davies from the village recovered the vehicle."

"Yeah, our recovery unit was dealing with a multi-car pile up between the A470 and the A494. Thankfully no fatalities, but it blocked all directions."

And since those were the only decent roads in the area, they had to be kept open as much as possible.

"When did she tell you?"

Cobb frowned. "Sorry?"

"When did Miss Jones tell you the vehicle had been recovered?"

"Tuesday morning."

Perkins watched him. Cobb could see him trying to figure out how Cobb might be lying. The fact that the man was even looking for the lie assured Cobb that Perkins was a better officer than Johnston.

"Why didn't you call out the rescue to look for him?"

"The driver was definitely a man, then?"

Perkins nodded. "We believe so."

Cobb considered. "It was dark, I saw no indications of which way the driver might have gone, so calling out the Rescue would have meant doing a circular sweep, and ultimately putting lives in danger without good cause."

"But you didn't call them in the morning either."

"Branwen, Miss Jones, came here first thing, she told me Johnston was at the Turn, which meant the Police knew of the crash and the missing driver. I reckon if you lot wanted the rescue to search for the man, you would have called us."

Perkins assessed again, seemed to accept what he said. "Why did she come here?"

"Checking on Finn." Cobb indicated the dog; the inspector turned and looked.

"What happened?"

"Mantrap."

"Have you reported it?"

"Yeah, well, actually, Branwen did. I phoned a statement in after. No one seems much interested, and the thing was gone when I went back the next day." Which probably meant that someone had been told to shift it, but he wouldn't say that to an inspector.

"How long have you known Miss Jones?"

Cobb shrugged. "A couple of years."

"How did you meet?"

The memory was clear as a bell, though he stared into his mug as he answered. "A week or so after I moved in I was out, walking Finn, and I saw her. She was standing by a crag edge. For a moment I thought she was about to jump, but she wasn't, she was just fighting the wind, which pulled her hat off her head and her hair flew out like a raven's wing." He'd been surprised by its length and that was still the only time he'd seen her with unfettered hair. The usual minimum was a bunch. "Then she turned around and didn't give me any choice but to help her with a walker who had fallen over the edge. She can be quite forceful when she has to be."

"So I understand." Perkins said.

Cobb got the impression something lay behind that darkly muttered comment, but he didn't know what.

"When did you join the Mountain Rescue?"

The smile was unavoidable. "About twenty months ago. Couple of months after I moved in."

"What's the smile for?"

"You said 'join', that might be too weak a word for it. 'Press ganged' might be more appropriate."

"Press-ganged by who?"

"Branwen Jones."

Perkins frowned. "Her name keeps popping up."

Cobb shrugged. "She's a busy woman, has contact with most of the villagers, and the surrounding farming families. She is the vet after all, and this community needs its animals, working and familial."

Now Perkins smiled. "Familial? Yeah, the English always think we Welsh are a bunch of witches and wizards walking around with their familiars."

"I used it to indicate their being part of the family," Cobb pointed out. "But you lot do tend to play up the whole wizards, bards and Eisteddfod thing a bit."

Now Perkins shrugged. "Anything for the tourist buck."

***

"You won't be able to hack into it."

Cobb looked up at the pale young man in his bedroom doorway. Jay had been asleep by the time the Inspector left, and Cobb had judged it best to leave him that way. It looked like the right decision, he looked steadier now than he had earlier. "I didn't have to," he said. His peripheral vision assuring him the decoding program was continuing to work, he twisted the machine to show the active screen. "Biometric locks unlock even when the biological decoder is unconscious."

Some of the arrogance washed off the young man's face and Cobb turned the screen back to him.

"Well you won't be able to decode the files."

Cobb looked at the screen, saw the files were already starting to appear in English rather than the Cyrillic they had been in. The boy's jaw dropped as he moved over to stare at the screen, leaning a little too heavily on the chair and table for Cobb's liking.

"I don't believe it."

"Amazing. A genius level intelligence doesn't believe anyone can do what they can't. There's a new event." Even he heard the sarcasm; it wasn't a part of his personality that Cobb was proud of. Especially since he'd been guilty of the same arrogance in the past.

The boy looked closer at the screen. "That's not one of my programs."

"No, it's one of mine." Cobb stood up. "Sit down, I'll make you a hot drink."

The boy moved to sit but froze at the bang on the door.

"Back to the bedroom, keep quiet." Cobb spoke softly as he closed the MacBook and waited until the boy was out of sight. Then he moved over to the window – the day wasn't light enough yet to have opened the curtains. Carefully he twitched the curtain. He saw the familiar Land Rover and the short woman at his door.

He moved to the door, unlocked it, opened a fraction, and quickly scanned the area to ensure Branwen was alone before he opened up and let her in.

"You alright?" he asked as she rushed inside. She looked pale and as she greeted Finn, her hands shook.

"Fine."

It really didn't sound like it and the way she hugged the dog cemented the idea. He reached out and made her look at him. "Branwen?"

For a moment she looked away, swallowed. "I'm fine. Is the boy okay?"

"He's conscious. Up. Sort of."

She nodded, not looking at him. "That's good. It's good."

If it was so good, why was she back to fussing Finn? Why did she sound so distant?

"Branwen, he's right –"

"Right. Good. He's right."

Why wouldn't she look at him?

"Branwen?"

Or listen to him?

"Branwen!"

She stood and turned towards the door. "If he's okay, I'll get going." Branwen frowned as she turned to leave, suddenly swung back. Another brief touch of a look. Something inside her was screaming. "Do I bully you?"

Caught off guard Cobb wasn't sure what to say. Such questions were a minefield. "No. I mean you can be persistent and repetitive in your requests."

Her jaw slackened, she looked horrified. "Oh God, I'm a nag." She opened the door. "That's even worse. And we're not even a couple!"

"We could be." Cobb doubted she heard him as the door closed behind her. Probably a good thing. He hadn't meant to speak aloud. Hadn't even actively thought it. Turning his head, he looked to the dresser. He knew what was in the drawer. He couldn't let go of-

"She didn't stay long," the boy said.

"No." And he wasn't sure why. She had no reason for coming here. Hadn't said or learnt anything while here. What was with her and Finn? Cobb turned to the boy in the doorway, who was wearing trousers now. An improvement over bruised, skinny legs. "She's a busy woman." She had a business to attend to and to sell. "What's your name, kid?"

Chapter 38
Baron, Pen-Y-Cwm Farm and Guesthouse

Baron watched Shoreham drum his fingers on the arm of the armchair. He understood the frustration, he felt it himself.

"She said she'd put you down?"

A sour look accompanied the nod. "And that we should get out."

"She said that while holding a needle to your neck?"

"No, she said that once she got in the car."

Once she was safe. At least Shoreham had let her go, one less body to deal with. Still, they'd have to find a way to smooth things over. "Did you get to search her car?"

Shoreham nodded.

"Nothing there?"

This time he shook his head. Erudite he wasn't.

"Right, I'm going to search the house." He saw Shoreham eyes light up. "I'll search Branwen's room. You're going out."

"Where to?"

"There's a phone mast up the mountain behind the house."

"Since when?"

"I imagine some time ago, but I only spotted it in the gloom this morning. I want you to go up there, see what you can do to put it out of action."

Agreement reached, they headed upstairs, Shoreham to his room and Baron to Branwen's. Another unlocked door.

Inside Baron looked at the room. The guest bedrooms were country-chic, some edging past shabby-chic, he guessed they needed more time or money to update the remaining rooms. There were cushions and extra blankets to satisfy just about anyone's taste for such nonsense, but still offered plenty of room for the guests' stuff; the wardrobes stood empty, the drawers ready for stocking, the bathrooms clear of clutter.

Branwen's room was different. A lived-in bedroom stuffed full of, well... stuff. Knick-knacks. Didn't look like she threw anything away. He looked at the pile of clothes thrown in the corner. Apparently, she wasn't big on picking up after herself either. Piles of books and papers, magazines – mostly professional – and a fair number of textbooks, crowded the reading chair. It seemed someone in the village kept lizards and Branwen was researching their care.

The top drawer snagged as he opened it, a quick shove in and yank out and it opened, a little too fully, he had to push back for security. The number of frothy, lacy confections of underwear surprised him, they made an odd mix against the solidity of various t-shirt bras and practical everyday wear. He picked up an underwired bra in pink flower lace. The silky fabric moved under his fingers easily. He imagined the pleasure of ripping it off her body of the bounty he'd find below, how she'd react to his force. She'd stood up well enough against Shoreham's nonsense. He slammed the draw closed and looked everywhere else.

There was nothing hidden in here. Nothing anywhere in the house. He considered the possibility that she was telling the truth, that she knew nothing about Whitney or what had happened to him. Baron moved over to the window and looked out. The rough land lay covered in a thick blanket of snow. A few areas where the wind had scoured the snow exposed aggressively hard rock and formed drifts elsewhere. The grey sky glowered at those trying to see, daring sight to distinguish between one tone and the next. Baron squinted, he couldn't see the base of the mast. He hoped Shoreham was doing his job.

***

"Well that wasn't fun." Shoreham grouched as he came into the house an hour later, stamping snow from his boots, shaking the wet off his coat.

Baron, standing in the hallway, kept his eyes on the map on the wall. "Did you disable it?"

"No. Better vandal-proof fencing than normal. I'll need tools to get in."

"Probably something to do with the livestock." Baron muttered.

"What's livestock got to do with tooling up?"

The urge to roll his eyes was only control by the need to concentrate on the map. Shoreham really was hopeless sometimes. "The fence is probably better because it needs to be not just vandal-proof, but livestock-proof too."

A grunt acknowledged the idea as Shoreham, now coatless, came closer. "What are you up to?"

"Studying the map."

"Oh, and here I thought you were waiting for a bus."

Baron turned and gave him the stink eye. He'd killed people for less than that.

"The road at Satan's Turn forks," Baron reminded him. "I was looking for where it goes. It looks like there's a house that way."

"Somewhere the boy could have sheltered."

"Exactly. And somewhere Branwen would know about."

"So, she lied by omission."

"Possibly. You find out if Jones keeps the tools you need to disable that mast and I'll go visit the neighbours."

119

Chapter 39
Jay and Cobb – Peny-Y-Cwm, Cobb's Home

Something was wrong. Jay didn't know what or why, or even how he knew, he just knew Cobb wasn't happy.

"Cuppa?" Cobb moved to the kitchen area, clicked the kettle on.

Slowly Jay grabbed his rucksack and pushed away from the jamb. He moved, by necessity, slowly and steadily, the body needing time to recover. Still, he figured he was doing okay to be this mobile already. He struggled with the clasps. "These are tight."

"It's the newness, it'll wear off," Cobb responded. "Need a hand?"

"Nah, 'salright." Stubborn though they were, the clasps gave way. He looked through the rucksack. "Everything's still here."

"Of course."

Jay looked at Cobb, found the older man watching him. There was something odd about him. Perhaps the standoffishness, but Jay thought there was something more. An air about him, an edge. This wasn't about what had happened earlier. He had seen it before in the cold stare of men pursuing quarry, the remorseless hunt riders, avid for the kill. Worse experience of his life. Until now.

A chill ran through him wondering what kind of trap this was. If this man was another goon after his hide, Cobb would already know what he'd downloaded, and Jay would probably be dead. Unless he had been sent to find out what Jay had done with the information.

As Jay stood again, his head spun, as much from thinking as from his injuries. The cold air chilled his blood. He noticed that the fire had burned low while the fan on his laptop whirled away. He moved over, watching from a distance the CPU usage, as full as possible as the decryption algorithms worked away. Nothing to do but let it run. He looked at Cobb and wondered who the man was.

"Bathroom's that way, if you need to freshen up."

He looked where Cobb pointed. A bathroom break would be good, but was it safe? He'd have to risk it.

"Feeling better?" Cobb asked when he returned to the main room. Cobb was back at the table, in front of the computer.

"More comfortable." Jay sat down again. "Found what you're looking for?"

Cobb shrugged. "What should I be looking for?"

"Didn't your boss tell you?"

Cobb sat back in the chair, regarding Jay steadily. Were he and the raven – what had he called her? Branwen? – were Cobb and Branwen part of Nemesis, the opposition? It suggested he was gathering a certain increased level of paranoia, but considering the circumstances, that might not be entirely uncalled-for.

"Hungry?"

Jay blinked, surprised by the question. "Yes."

Silently, Cobb rose. He grabbed and opened a tin of soup, emptying it into a bowl and setting it in the microwave. While the food warmed, Cobb lounged against the sideboard. The weight of his gaze hung on Jay who wondered what the man was thinking.

A ping announced the soup was ready. Cobb snapped the door open, took up the bowl; Jay saw no sign that he was suffering from the bowl being hot. The big man put the meal in front of him. Quietly Cobb turned again, fetching a thick slice of bread and a spoon. They were put beside the bowl.

"Thank you," Jay said.

Cobb sat again in front of the computer, but this time he simply closed the top. Apparently, the decryption could wait.

"That shut down the program."

"No, it didn't. My coding overrides the operating system to keep the machine running until it's done."

"Neat programming."

Cobb shrugged.

Jay tried not to be affected as he turned to the food and ate. But Cobb watched him, the regard disquieting. If this wasn't an interrogation technique, it ought to be. Jay, already unnerved by his predicament, was rattled more by the steely regard.

"Don't say much, do you?" Jay said eventually, unable to stand the silence a moment longer.

Cobb shrugged.

Again, the silence stretched.

"Good soup." Inane, but it filled the gap.

Silence.

Jay stopped eating and looked at the older man. "Why d'ya bring me here?"

"You were hurt."

Not a flicker of emotion showed. "Why didn't you finish the job?"

"What job?"

"Disposing of me." Jay swallowed.

"Why?" Cobb requested after a few moments.

"Because I'm a threat," Jay announced, sitting up straight.

Cobb cocked an eyebrow. Tipping his head to one side, he slowly appraised the younger man. It creeped Jay out. He was a twig compared to Cobb.

"Not to me, you're not."

"To your organisation."

"What threat do you pose the Mountain Rescue?"

"Mountain Rescue?" Jay asked, bewildered.

"It's the only organisation I belong to." Cobb confirmed.

Open-mouthed, Jay stared at him. "Are you saying that you're nothing to do with those men coming after me?"

"What men?"

"So, you're nothing to do with the music industry?"

Cobb shook his head.

"At all?"

Again, Cobb shook his head. Jay looked around. A radio not in use. No TV. No music player. Way too many books. This was not the home of a music lover.

"Oh."

In silence, they allowed the idea to sink in. Jay struggled with that, mostly because there seemed no other reason for Cobb to keep him there.

"So why are you holding me here?"

Cobb raised an eyebrow at that. "I'm not. You're free to leave any time you want."

"Yeah right, with a blizzard blowing outside."

Cobb glanced out the window. The landscape was white, a few flakes carrying in the wind. "I'll take you into town in the morning then. You can get a taxi from there if you have anywhere to go."

Jay met the steady regard. This man confused him. Jay didn't know if he was friend or foe. "So why are you taking care of me?" he demanded finally.

"Branwen gave me no choice."

"Branwen? The one that was here earlier? The raven?" Jay's voice seemed almost reverent. He didn't like the sound. He cleared his throat under the older man's penetrating gaze and tried again. "The vet?"

Cobb nodded.

"Do the police know I'm here?"

"Don't believe so."

Jay frowned over the curious reply. "Who does?"

"As far as I know, only Branwen and myself. Possibly the village doctor."

That didn't help. He had no idea who the doctor was or what he might do. Doctors had rules, didn't they? Things they had to report?

"So," Cobb said, "since I've been forced into the role of shielding you, would you care to tell me who I'm shielding you from and why?"

Jay looked up at Cobb, considering. The bigger man had a solid strength about him that was more than physical. He was steady in a way no one Jay had ever known was steady. Trusting this man remained questionable, but he was damned sure he would rather have Cobb as a friend than an enemy. The decision easily made, he quickly told Cobb what had happened.

"Thanks for the abridged version," Cobb muttered when Jay fell silent. "Now give me details."

***

Cobb checked the signal and made the call. Branwen answered quickly.

"Where's Hannah?"

"Tunisia."

Cobb frowned. "Fact or sarcasm?"

"Fact." She sounded annoyed and affronted.

"Oh." He thought about it. "Doesn't seem like the kind of place Hannah would want to go."

"It was her boyfriend's idea." The snap came back. "It's not like I bullied her into going."

Again with the bullying thing. "No one's accusing you of being a bully."

She huffed down the line. "Oh, that's right." Sarcasm dripped from her tone. "You think I'm a nag."

"Branwen."

"You said it."

"No, you took it that way. Besides, you don't do either to excess, what's the problem?"

He heard a gasp, a thud.

"I do both? Oh God."

"I didn't say that." This really wasn't a conversation to have over the phone. In his experience when a woman got like this, a hug went a long way. Would Branwen let him hug her?

"You said I don't do either to excess."

That was reasonable, good. "Exactly."

"Which means I do both to some extent."

Cobb closed his eyes and rubbed his head. He had a headache coming on. "Branwen, the only time you've actually bullied me was to get me to help with that lad who'd fallen, then to join the Mountain Rescue. Those are the same two instances that I referred to, exaggerated as persistent repetition. What's the problem?"

"Several people have now referred to me as bullying you."

"So?"

"I don't have any right to bully you. We don't have that kind of relationship."

"I'm not sure there's any kind of relationship that confers the right to bully anyone. And I've given up trying to figure out what

123

kind of relationship we have."

"Oh, that's easy. This is the kind of relationship where you don't give two hoots and I'm leaving town anyway, so it doesn't matter and you'll never have to put up with my bullying you again."

The connection was cut and Cobb stood listening to a silent tone and realising he hadn't had the chance to tell her why he'd called.

***

The wind abated just in time to bring the sound of an engine to Cobb's ear. More people had visited today than in the entire time he'd lived here. Come to think of it, Branwen was the only other human to have stepped foot into the house since he moved in. Jay had already returned to the bed, injuries sapping his ability to stay awake. The boy said he wasn't nauseated, and he was moving easier than when he first got up, so Cobb doubted Jay was concussed, simply in need of recovery time.

Now Cobb headed out the back of the house and grabbed up the wood axe from the log pile. Outside, the world held its breath, no wind, no snow. It wouldn't last, but it meant he heard a car door opening. His long stride carried him quickly around the cottage and he saw the man who had arrived in the Land Rover Discovery – one far too new and clean to be anything other than a hire car. The man was average height, broad, dark haired. Totally out of his element here.

"What do you want?"

The man swung around at Cobb's call. His knees were bent, his fists at the ready, and a mean glint in his eyes. This man was a fighter. Cobb strengthened his grip on the handle of the axe and he rested its shaft on his shoulder, glad to note that the man's eyes noted the implement.

"Hello." The man relaxed and stood straighter, trying to assume an open posture that didn't match his natural inclination.

Cobb held his tongue and waited. The man looked momentarily uncertain.

"I'm vacationing in the area. Having a look around."

That didn't require a response and Cobb didn't give one. He looked the guy up and down. The guy looked back.

"Spectacular landscape."

"Private property."

The way the man's attempt to smile flickered on and off his face told Cobb how hard he was trying. How much he must need whatever he was after. Which had to be Jay and the data he'd stolen. There was no other reason to be here.

"That was quite a crash on the road, Monday, saw the car in the river as I came up."

124

Cobb made a non-committal sound.

"Your car?"

"No."

"Wonder what happened to the driver."

Cobb just looked at the man.

"Did you see him?"

"No."

"Hear anything?"

"No."

The man's look soured as he regarded Cobb. "So much for the Welsh keeping a welcome in the hillside."

"I'm not Welsh. This is not a hillside, it's a mountainside. And you're trespassing." He shifted the axe meaningfully in his hands. "Leave."

Chapter 40
Branwen – Pen-Y-Cwm Village

After a tough day, Branwen wasn't looking forward to the evening ahead. Hopefully that arse Shoreham had left, but she suspected that was too great a hope. She needed to tell Father about McManus and she needed to speak to Emma before that.

"Hi!" Emma called before she walked in. She stopped, looking at Branwen's startled face. "You need to get more sleep!" she told her friend.

Laughing bitterly through her shock, Branwen sat back. "Tell me about it."

"Coming to the Pig?"

Branwen gave her a quizzical look. "Is that legal?"

"Ha ha. Are you coming or what?"

"Twice in one day? Are you turning into an alcoholic?"

"There's something I want to talk to you about," Emma said with a broad smile.

"There's something I need to talk to you about too," said Branwen, standing. The Dutch courage the pub offered was just what she needed. "Let's go."

As they moved down the street, Branwen saw a man disappearing into the pub before them, thankfully Fred, not Ivan. A light shone in the solicitor's office, so they should have a few minutes without interruption or Branwen having to play gooseberry.

Inside the Pig, Branwen was surprised that, for once, the ever-present Dai Jones wasn't actually present. Miracles, it seemed, did happen. Dewi stood behind the bar, leaning back, polishing glasses with a tea towel, while chatting with Fred. Dewi had gone the whole hog this year, no less than three red heart shaped balloons out to mark the day, a desultory display. The last thing Branwen needed. At the bar, the four of them exchanged quick greetings, the two women ordering coffees which Dewi was as happy to serve as any spirit – after all, he made a far better profit margin on the coffee and it pulled in just as much custom.

Turning towards their usual place, Branwen spotted Dai Jones coming out of the gents. Strike one from the list of miracles, she thought, wondering if the old man ever worked. While they'd been waiting, the pub had started to fill.

"How are things with you?" Emma asked as they sat down. "You look exhausted."

"I'm just not sleeping too well is all."

"Trouble at home or work?" Emma's face reflected her very real concern for her friend.

"Neither. Both. You know, just sometimes everything hits at once."

"Yeah." Emma smiled. "What you need is a night out."

"Not tonight. I want to head home to bed. But thanks for the offer."

Emma frowned. "Not with me, you nitwit. With Cobb."

"Oh no!" Branwen groaned. "Not that again."

Emma leaned forward. "Why don't you give it a go? You never know, you and Cobb might be pleasantly surprised."

"More likely," Branwen pointed out, "we'd be unpleasantly un-surprised and wind up hating each other, and I don't want him to hate me."

"Basically, what you're saying is that you're going to miss out on the chance of a lifetime for a lousy, and I might add negligible, downside risk."

"It's not negligible." In her admittedly somewhat limited experience, three quarters, a full six of the eight guys she had ever dated, had been hard pushed to even acknowledge her existence after a couple of dates. She had taken enough insults about her over-independence, how she didn't lavish enough attention on them. Admittedly, Cobb was unlikely to be that way, being independent-minded himself, but Branwen wasn't convinced enough to push her luck. "Besides, he thinks I'm a bully and a nag."

"Bollocks does he."

Branwen stared agog at Emma as she looked up, her greeting echoed by Ivan Evans as he entered the pub. The slender solicitor came straight to their table before the bar. Branwen looked away as the couple met. She hated playing gooseberry to those courting heavy.

"Can I tell her?" Emma implored, looking up adoringly.

"Cariad—"

Branwen cringed at the Welsh term for lover.

"—you can announce it to the whole world."

When Emma turned to Branwen, the vet took one look at the smiling face with the bottom lip caught between pearly white teeth and her sinking stomach told her what was coming next.

"Branny — we're getting married!"

Emma had said it so loud that the whole bar erupted in congratulations, all except one. Fred looked like a dog who'd licked a nettle and stuck out his tongue only to be stung by a wasp. Branwen couldn't mention McManus now; instead she congratulated and hugged Emma then Ivan, wishing them well, and since other well-wishers were pushing in for more congratulations, she suspected only she saw Fred turn sharply and storm to the door.

The reaction worried Branwen. Quickly ordering a bottle of Champagne for the couple and throwing two twenties towards Dewi, she hurried out of the Pig and Whistle after the man she had known since their schooldays.

***

Six o'clock had ticked past when Branwen reached Cobb's. She entered the cottage looking frazzled; locks of her hair had lifted from the once neat braid. Her expression was indecipherable.

"You okay?" he asked.

"Fine." Yet the snapped word, the inability to meet his eye, combined with her virtually ignoring Finn gave the lie to the statement.

She looked at the bedroom door. "How's Jay?"

"Branwe-"

"I came to check on Jay."

The snap was unlike her. She'd changed since they pulled Jay from the car. There had to be more going on than he knew. He moved closer, she moved away.

"You want to keep your distance, so keep it," she growled.

Something cold and hard inside shattered at those words. Keeping clear of her, of any woman, any contact in fact, had been his entire aim in coming here. Branwen had chosen to drag him back into the real world. Now this? Had she really taken the idea of nagging to heart?

"Well, how is he?"

"Ask him. Jay, get out here!" That last was called through and soon Jay appeared in the doorway.

"Hello," he smiled at Branwen.

"Hi, how you doing?"

"Okay." The young man moved across the room to stand in front of her, one hand on the back of a chair to steady himself. "Still not a hundred percent."

"Any dizzy spells?"

He shrugged.

"Come on Jay, I need to know, or we could both be in trouble."

"Why?"

"I'm not a doctor. I'm a vet and a first responder. My treating you is legally and morally questionable, but I'm the best you've got until Doc Pearson gets back on Friday. Now, any dizzy spells?"

Cobb watched. Branwen had no problem talking to Jay, so why did she have a problem talking to him? Because Jay obviously couldn't fight his way out of a wet paper bag right now? Was she scared of him all of a sudden?

128

"Occasionally, usually when standing, sometimes when walking too fast."

"Headaches?"

"Actually no. I mean my face aches, the bumps and that, and I'm tired all the time, but not actual headaches."

Branwen nodded. "Sounds good. Have a seat." She pointed the boy to the one decent chair. "It's likely that you're tired because you need to heal, and because I doubt you've eaten much."

Cobb considered that an affront to this hospitality. "He's had soup, sandwiches and fruit since he woke up. Not to mention half a packet of biscuits. Though I think Finn might have helped with that."

Branwen scowled up at him. "Well Finn should be controlled from that, biscuits aren't good for his digestion." The whine from the dog suggested he understood every word. Branwen turned back to Jay. "You're shivering."

"I'm cold."

Cobb glanced at the roaring fire.

Branwen opened the bag she'd been carrying when she came in. She ferreted around then pulled out a thermometer. "Open wide," she told Jay.

Cobb watched as she placed it under the boy's tongue and told him to hold it. "Any nausea?"

Jay shook his head.

Cobb figured that the instrument had been in the boy's mouth about long enough when he spoke. "Are you sure you've got the right end for that?"

Branwen scowled at him again and Jay's squeal of curiosity turned to a squeak of disgust. Branwen only just caught the thermometer in time.

"Don't listen to him. This is a new, previously unused thermometer." She looked at the result. "All normal." She smiled, wiped the instrument, returned it carefully to the bag. "I'd say you're doing well and in no immediate danger."

Jay looked relieved.

"So, why are people overly interested in finding you?"

"Why'd you two hide me?"

Branwen swallowed. "Getting you to a hospital would have been dangerous in a car and the weather was too bad to call the air ambulance. Besides, once I'd looked you over, I was pretty sure that concussion would be the major problem. But we've kept quiet about you because I'm a vet, not a doctor. Legally and morally it's questionable that I treat you at all, so if something had happened to you, I'd face losing my living and possibly my freedom. Then those two guys turned up the next day-"

"Two guys?" Jay paled. Just as well he was already sitting down.

"What two guys?" Cobb asked, but Branwen ignored him and Jay looked sick.

"A shorter one with dark hair?" Jay's voice quivered as he spoke. "A taller blond one? Both big muscle men?"

Now Branwen paled as she nodded. "Pretty much."

Jay looked away. "Those two beat Frankie up. They turned up at my aunt's place. Oh God, I have to check Sophie's okay." The boy wobbled on his feet, Branwen pushed him back to the chair.

"I'll make a call." Cobb needed to do something. He grabbed his mobile and checked the signal. Another call to Simons. No answer, so he left a voice message.

"They gave me the creeps," Branwen said. "The sort of people that I want to defy just because I can. So, I did. The interest the police-"

"Police!?" Jay shrank back now.

Branwen frowned as she looked at up Cobb, she was as uncertain as he. "They're interested because there is a missing, possibly injured, driver after a road traffic accident. They want to locate you to ensure that you're not out dying on the mountain somewhere."

"Are they likely to come here?"

"They've already been," Cobb advised. "Twice."

"Johnston?"

"First time. Then an Inspector Perkins. He's sharper."

"I should hope so," Branwen said. "There again, it's not difficult to be sharper than Johnston." She looked at Jay, at the worry etched on his battered features. "Okay, you want to tell us what's really going on?"

Jay swallowed, his jaw worked, but no sound came out.

"Clip note version is that Jay here hacked into the files of Nemesis Records and has evidence that Greebo K is a fraud and Alex Berenger actually makes all his music. He also grabbed a load of other encrypted files."

Branwen frowned. "Okay, I've heard of Greebo K, makes awful noisy rap-type music, and so what if it's fake? Most of the music industry is."

Cobb shrugged, it didn't bother him one way or the other. "Alex Berenger is a classical pianist, his persona is the completely clean cut, good guy type. Like Richard Clayderman."

"Who?"

Cobb looked at the two mystified faces before him. "Seriously? I'm only a few years older than the pair of you." Though in that moment he felt ancient. "Alright, think Michael Bublé as a saint.

You've heard of Bublé, right?"

Both nodded.

"I'm still not seeing the problem," Branwen said. "So what if that information comes out? A couple of minor celebrities get damaged reputations. So what? If this Berenger guy is good enough, he'll weather it, if Greebo K is a fraud, he doesn't deserve to. Why send the Goon Brothers after Jay?"

Cobb couldn't help smiling at that. "Goon Brothers?"

She shrugged, a slight blush colouring her cheeks. "It's what they look like. Not the point."

"No," Cobb agreed. "The point is probably the encrypted stuff. That's what we have to find out about."

"How?"

Cobb turned back to the table and the open laptop. He looked at the screen. The Cyrillic fonts had moved to easily readable English. "Seems they're a load of NEF files. Whatever NEF files are."

"Photo files," Branwen said. "They're the raw image file Nikon cameras produce."

Cobb frown at her. "How do you know that?"

She shrugged. "I own a Nikon camera."

"So, all I got was a bunch of photographs?" Jay asked as he and Branwen came to stand beside Cobb. "What's so bad about a bunch of photographs?"

"Let's find out." Cobb double clicked on one and the image filled the screen. "That's what's so bad."

On the screen an attractive young woman was being bent over a chair that looked like some kind of torture device. Her top had been pulled open and down, her breasts exposed, probably bouncing to the way that the fat man behind her was in the act of fucking her. One hand entangled her hair, pulling her head back, the angle he had her at caught light on the tears she was shedding, the way her lips were pulled back in a grimace. This woman was not enjoying the experience.

"Is that Shan Sh'kara?"

The two men looked at Branwen.

"What? I'm not much into music, but I'm friends with Emma, can't miss it all entirely. She," Branwen pointed to the screen, "was on one of those this-country-loves-freaks-without-talent shows last year. Got a fair way through then got outvoted for a crappy novelty cat act. Any idea who the fat bastard is?"

"Don't recognise him, but he's got to be something to do with the record label."

Cobb closed the picture down and sat, searching for Nemesis

Records. It didn't take long. "Richard Granger." He read. "CEO."

"He's a using bastard," Branwen added with venom. "A despicable human being who clearly never heard of the #MeToo movement. No wonder he's sent out the Goon Brothers. The little shit could lose everything if this gets out." She looked at Jay. "And this has to get out."

Jay trembled as he sat down. "But if I release this, they'll kill me. I could use this as a bargaining chip to get them off my back."

"Probably not," Cobb said. "More likely they'd consider you an on-going threat they have to eliminate."

The alarm on Branwen's phone beeped. "Crap," she said looking at the screen.

"Problem?"

"I'm overdue for the milking. The cows will be in pain if I don't sort them out soon." She looked at Cobb. "Get this out. Email the papers or WikiLeaks or something. Don't let that shit of a man get away with it."

Chapter 41
Branwen – Pen-Y-Cwm Farm and Guesthouse

There wasn't enough soap in the world for Branwen to scrub herself clean so she finally stepped from the shower and towelled off.

She'd only seen one picture and her whole being seemed contaminated. That poor girl had to suffer the moment caught in pixels. Branwen couldn't fathom how the girl had got herself into that kind of situation. Could she be that desperate for fifteen minutes of fame? No, surely no one could be that desperate. Struggling to push the image from her head, she stepped from the bathroom to find Baron standing in front of her.

"Hello Branwen."

Surprise stopped her in her tracks. "I thought you'd gone, your car's gone."

"Shoreham had somewhere to go." He moved closer.

She clutched the towel tighter around her. If only they had the money to make a private bathroom. "I expected you both to leave."

"Oh, he'll be back. We're paid up till the end of the week."

"I'll refund you." She tried to step around him, but he side-stepped into her way.

"I don't want a refund."

The memory of what Shoreham had tried to do stopped her in her tracks. She knew Baron was scrutinising her, and much as she wanted to brazen it out, she couldn't find the nerve to face him.

"What I want–"

She thought about what the fat man had wanted. Her face snapped to Baron's. "I don't care what you want."

"Have a care, Miss Jones." He spoke softly, his hand coming up to catch a skein of hair that she hadn't caught up in the towel around her head, winding it through his fingers. "What I want, is for you to tell me where I can find James Whitney."

"What I want is for you to accept that I don't know."

He smiled down at her as he continued to play with her hair. "Oh, I'm absolutely sure that is what you want, but you see, I don't believe you."

"Tough." Cold was creeping into her bones. She wanted to go to her room, finish drying off and get warm.

"I am accustomed to getting what I want."

"Yeah? Well, you're not as scary as your half-wit partn-ah!" she cried out as he tugged her hair and pulled her towards him, leaning in close.

"Oh, my dear Miss Jones, you misunderstand," he whispered into her ear. "Shoreham will stop the second he realises you actually enjoy all this."

"I do not!"

His quiet laugh flowed hot against her skin. "Then why do you have the most charming blush? Why can I see how hard your nipples are even under that towel?"

His hand moved from her hair to her damp shoulder.

"That's because I'm cold." She shoved him aside and stepped past, jolted to a halt as he grabbed hold of the towel at her spine. He moved up close, his lips coming close to her ear. "Shoreham will stop, but I won't let you enjoy it. Remember who's in control here -"

His sentence cut short as she dropped the towel and marched stark naked to her room, carefully closing the door behind her and twisting the key. "I'm in control," she said softly. "I'm in control here, Mr Baron, not you."

Only she wasn't. She was going crazy.

That had to be it. Pacing in her bedroom, trying to pull on a dressing gown that didn't want to slide over damp skin, Branwen saw no better explanation. She was insane. She had to be. What other reason was there for the way her life had turned out? She couldn't blame anyone but herself.

At twenty-nine years old, she had made her choices. She had chosen the veterinary path. She had chosen the actions she had taken concerning McManus. She had chosen to return to Pen-Y-Cwm. She had even chosen not to throw herself at Cobb, which had to be the stupidest damned decision of the lot because he just might have complied, and she got the distinct impression that he would be a fantastic lover.

Groaning at the erotic images flowing all too easily through her mind, she threw herself onto the bed. Burying her face in the pillows, she kicked her feet and screamed her frustration into the muffling down. After a few seconds, she decided to stop being childish and defeatist. Twisting, she lay on the bed and stared at the dark ceiling. *Get a grip!*

She had chosen the veterinary path because she liked animals and her grandmother had said it would save the family money.

She had chosen to take the actions she had concerning McManus, because she hadn't had time to find a better alternative. Fear had controlled her.

She had chosen to come back to Pen-Y-Cwm because the fear had lingered and she'd lost her ability to face the world.

She had even chosen not to throw herself at Cobb, because she feared his control would only shame her more. And it had.

Get a grip!

134

The taking control of her life had already started. She was one step away from selling the business and leaving town. Where she would go remained a question, but as a practice vet she could go anywhere. Forget that. No business hours, no more pampered pets, no more cantankerous cattle. Maybe a zoo somewhere needed a vet. She sighed. That wasn't likely with only domestic animal experience.

The image of Shan Sh'Kara filled her with disgust. The girl probably wasn't even twenty and the man using her had to be twice that or more. The casting couch was one thing, but that? To do something you found so degrading you'd cry through the act? Branwen shivered in revulsion.

And she still needed to tell her father about McManus. Another area of revulsion in her life.

Then there was Baron and Shoreham, how to get rid of them? She couldn't tell her father what they'd done, he'd be furious, and he owned a shotgun.

It was too much to deal with tonight. Huffing out her frustration and depression, she levered herself up. Pulling off her dressing gown, she used its waffled surface to dry herself properly, found a nightgown, threw the wet towel off her head and over the radiator, then thankfully sank back into the bed, allowing much needed sleep to overtake her.

***

Baron heard Shoreham coming a mile off. He moved to the bedroom door and stood at the threshold watching the big man appear at the top of the stairs and come down the corridor. He wasn't as steady as usual.

"Have you been drinking?"

"Had a jar while I ate."

While Baron had been stuck here with home cooked Shepard's Pie, chunky chips and not the best conversation with Iolyn Jones. Branwen had turned up later.

"Get what you needed?"

"Had to go to Aberystwyth, but yeah. Not a town I'll bother with again."

Baron didn't care one way or the other. "Looks like Branwen's found her spine. Why don't you go scare her a bit more?"

Shoreham grinned and turned.

"Door's locked," Baron advised. "You'll have to climb up from outside."

Built of rough stone, the farm house offered plenty of finger and toe holds. Besides, if Shoreham fell and broke his neck, that meant one less loose end for him to tie up.

Chapter 42
Branwen – Pen-Y-Cwm Farm and Guesthouse

The weird dream led Branwen through a distorted version of somewhere both strange and familiar. A big man moved in the distance. She tried to call out to Cobb, but the name wouldn't form.

Cold started at her shoulders and moved down. She felt exposed. The man moved close, fingers gently touched her breast, her nipples peaked and ached. She needed more. Shifting she arched her spine, straining for the touch.

One hand became more possessive, softly kneading her breast and the other hand trailed lower, rubbed over the silk of her nightgown, pressing her pubic hair and questing further.

Eyes fluttering open, she saw the shadow above her, her eyes flew open and a new cold swept through her as she realised this was no fantasy man, but the real nightmare of Shoreham in her room.

"What the hell do you think you're playing at?" she demanded, pushing him away and scrabbling out of the other side of her bed.

"Pleasuring you," he pointed out, staying on the bed.

"It's–" She checked the clock by her bed, wishing she'd gone the other way, closer to her dressing gown. She loved this blue silk negligee, but it wasn't something she wanted Shoreham seeing her in. "–ten twenty."

"Exactly." He smiled, rising. She shrank from his approach. "Too early to be abed." Now he stood over her, staring into her eyes, though in the darken room, with only restricted moonlight for illumination, she could see nothing of his. Just twin pools of black evil promise.

Despite the fear trembling in her gut, she held her ground. "Not when you get up as early as I do."

His fingers ran softly up the smooth flesh of her arms, following the curve of her shoulders, then the line of her collarbone. Revulsion twisted her gut, froze her position, even as his hands rose up the length of her neck. She doubted he'd break a sweat to snap her neck.

"You're very attractive, Miss Jones."

"And you're pushing your luck, Mr Shoreham. Get out." She glared at him.

"My name," he told her softly, "is Gary."

"Bully for you. Now get out, or the only prick we'll share will be the needle I inject you with."

"I fell for that this morning, I won't again."

"I lied this morning, not now." She looked towards the bedside cabinet, where sat a prepared syringe.

He looked too. His features pinched to see the needle, then his lips twitched and he laughed.

"I scream and my father will come running. Twelve bore in hand."

His smile broadened. "As would Baron. How long do you think your father would last, if my friend thought he was attacking me?"

"Is that some sort of threat?"

"No, Miss Jones, of course not. Baron simply doesn't like being disturbed from his sleep. He wakes up grumpy. When he's grumpy, Baron tends to hit first and ask questions later. You wouldn't want your father hurt for the sake of a misunderstanding, would you?"

It didn't matter how much she frowned, if he decided to overpower her, she would be just about as much use as a leaf in a hurricane.

"Get out."

"No."

Mouth pursed, she glared at him. "I am so sick of jerks like you!" She stood to her full height, fists on her hips. "You come up here and think 'Oh yeah, the landlord's daughter, she's fair game.' When are men like you going to realise that we'll welcome you all right – with open arms, not open legs! I'm not some stupid bumpkin who'll just fall for any old line!" Despite her anger she had not raised her voice. His appraising look sickened her, but she wasn't letting this go. Time to really take control.

"On the contrary, Miss Jones," his soft voice whispered down, "I think you're an intelligent woman. I think that's why you're going to do exactly what I ask."

She glared at him. "Or what?"

His grin broadened. "You get hurt."

Her glare was rather weakened by the way she had to swallow. "I am not having sex with you."

"What makes you think I want sex with you?" He moved away, lounged against the footrest of her bed.

"Don't you?"

He looked her over. His appreciation made her skin crawl. "Is that an offer?"

"No!" She noticed where his eyes fell and crossed her arms over her chest. "Okay, you don't want sex –"

"I didn't say that." He smirked.

She went very tight-lipped. "What do you want?"

His head tipped as he considered her. "How about a welcoming smile?"

She looked at him, opened her mouth but no sound came out. Then she clamped her jaw shut, lengthened her spine, glared at him.

"How about you get lost?"

"Oh, come on Angel, you can do better than that."

"Angel?"

"That's what the boy must have thought you were when you helped him from the car. A raven-haired angel."

"I think you'll find angels are generally considered to be blondes."

He shrugged. "Depends on your point of view."

Scowling, she clamped her jaw against her chattering teeth. "Get to the point *Gary*–" she sneered the name "–then get out."

He regarded her. "Tell me about the car crash."

She groaned, throwing up her hands in frustration.

"What?" She glared up at him. "I told you. I found a crashed car, not a driver."

"Really?" His disbelief was palpable. "There are rumours to the contrary."

"Really?" She turned his own reply back on him.

"Tell me what happened."

"I did."

He gave a short, scary laugh. Her pulse raced and she struggled to breathe.

"Got something to hide, Miss Jones?"

Baron said he'd stop if he thought she was enjoying herself. Time to try something different. "Under this negligee?" she asked, clasping her hands behind her back and jutting her chest forward. "What could I possibly hide in here?"

His eyes drifted downward, appreciating the view. God help her, her eyes did likewise; even in this light his erection was obvious.

"Oh, you're good, Miss Jones."

She glanced to the syringe.

He stepped to that side of the bed.

She lunged, her hand almost reaching the sharp. He landed on top of her, pulling her arm away, pinning her down. She wriggled and thrashed beneath him. One arm got pinned beneath her, the other he controlled with his hand around her wrist. With his other hand he grabbed a fist full of her hair and forced her face into the bed linen. She tried to kick and buck, to no effect. He leaned down on her, her noises muffled but sounding of terror. She realised he might suffocate her like this.

He moved to whisper in her ear. "Now you lay still and silent, Miss Jones and I'll let you breathe again. Understand?"

Fear tremored through her body, but she nodded as best she could.

"There's a good girl." He kissed her ear, her attempt to pull away useless. "I'm going to give you room to move in a moment, Miss Jones. When I do, you're going to twist onto your back and lay nicely on the bed like a good little girl. Understand? If you do as you're told I won't hurt you. If you reach for that syringe again, I'm going to hurt you. If you fight me anymore, I'm going to hurt you. Do you understand?"

Though tense, angry, and afraid, she understood. His grip eased, he started to stroke her hair.

"You really do have the most beautiful hair." Soft and silky now it was dry. "Be a good girl, now. Do exactly what I told you."

He eased back and slightly off her. She had to find a way out, a way to out-think him, but for now she had to comply. She turned, twisted until she lay properly on the bed, her head on the pillow. He still had one wrist in his hand, controlling her; he moved it to the other hand, then reached out himself and grabbed the syringe.

Her gasp was involuntary as he brought it towards her. That thing really could kill. Suddenly, he chucked it to the far corner of the room. "We won't be needing that."

He lay on top of her, their faces inches apart, his erection pressed between them. "Very good. You could make a man forget what he wants. Make him forget everything but wanting you."

She swallowed. That was the kind of thing she longed to hear, but not from a man like this. She must hold her resolve. "You disgust me, Mr Shoreham. Men like you should be neutered."

He leaned down, she turned her sneer away from him. He caught her ear lobe between his teeth, suckled, squeezed with his teeth, but didn't bite. She should pull away from him, but she couldn't move. Her breathing hitched. Something deep and lonely inside responded in ways it shouldn't. He sucked harder, her moan a mix of need and surprise. His free hand moved down her body to her hip. Shifting, he reached between them. She tried to move, but there really wasn't anywhere for her to go. His fingers pushed at the silk. The spring of pubic hairs rasped between them.

"Don't you dare."

He grinned down at her as his fingers quested south, pushing the silk between her thighs. Again she tried to twist away, but his strength and weight meant he got exactly what he wanted when his fingers pressed the silk against her vagina and the wet warmth of her arousal sprang up to meet him. He rubbed against her, she swallowed and turned away, her eyes and lips clamping shut as the evidence of her response spread. She shouldn't enjoy this. He moved his hand and pressed the heat of his own erection against her, slowly, carefully. This force shouldn't thrill her, she shouldn't need this kind of attention, but it was the only attention she'd had for far too long.

"Look at me."

She kept her head stubbornly turned away.

"Look at me, or I'll move that silk and fuck you hard."

She opened her eyes, a juddering breath pulling in as she reluctantly turned to face him.

He smiled. "Tell me about the boy."

Whatever she'd expected, that wasn't it. "What?"

"Tell me about the boy from the car."

"I told you, I know nothing about him."

He pressed his groin into her, even as his hand came up to her throat. "Now tell me the truth."

"I have." The hold tightened again. Gasping for air, she looked up at him, her eyes wide and wild. "Please."

"Please?" he asked, not releasing her.

Fear overtook arousal and suddenly she fought him, fighting for breath even as she involuntarily parted her legs and the bastard took advantage to move more intimately against her.

"Please what? Let you go? Let you pull in more breath to lie to me with?"

"Please." She didn't like her small and fearful voice. "I can't tell you what I don't know."

He frowned down at her. "Really?" He released her, slightly.

"I swear. I never saw the driver. I told you before."

"The police say differently."

"Pay the right copper enough money and they'll say anything," she reasoned. "They've got it wrong. I don't know anything about the driver." She swallowed hard, gasping as he rubbed against her again. "I promise." She tried again. "Please, why would I lie to you? I have nothing to gain."

"Why indeed?" He looked her over. The crush at her throat released as he started stroking back the hair above her ear. "Call me Gary."

She blinked. It took her two attempts to force the word out. "Gary."

"Say, 'please'."

Breathing proved difficult. Fear strangled her when he didn't, until he started to sway his hips. Then breathing became difficult for a different reason. She had to force herself not to return the sway.

"Say, 'please'."

"Please."

He left her hair to pull the shoestring strap off her shoulder. "Put them together."

"Please, Gary."

He smiled. "Please Gary, what?" He pulled the other strap off now. Both her hands were free, but they lay useless by her sides.

"Please Gary, believe me. I've not lied to you." Lifting himself up, his knuckles grazed over her hard nipple and her voice gained a squeak. "Please Gary, don't."

His laugh became low and malicious. He squeezed his fingers together, clamping her nipple hard. She gasped at the pain. He looked at the swollen flesh, then smiled down at her. "Beg me."

She whimpered as he continued to compact her flesh. Tears welled in her eyes as she swallowed, whispering. "Please Gary."

He covered her mouth with his. She clenched her teeth, her lips defiantly clamped. Then he started suckling and chewing on her lips. Her hands clawed, straining to push him away. He cupped a hand round her hip, she didn't understand why she let him, but the layer of silk and his trousers might as well not be there. Then she remembered what Baron had said. It was a dangerous game at this point, but it might be the last option left as he pushed against her. She groaned. Relaxing took effort, but her muscles lost tension and she kissed him back, opened beneath him. His tongue invaded her mouth, she tasted some hideous bitter on him, he'd been drinking. She shifted her leg, pushed her hips up to meet his as he broke the kiss to breathe in.

This time she spoke with a deep and wanton tone. "Please Gary. Take me."

He laughed and pushed himself away, walked out, pausing only to unlock the door. Her relief at his departure was only ruined by the groan of utter frustration that echoed in his wake.

Chapter 43
Branwen – Pen-Y-Cwm Farm and Guesthouse

The morning milking got Branwen from her restless bed, gave her something to do besides worry about last night's visitor and stopped her going back to scrub herself beneath the shower – again. The ridiculous thing was she wasn't trying to wash away what Shoreham had done, she was trying to wash away the fact that he had reminded her she was a sensual woman. Emma had a point; she did need a man in her life – just not Shoreham. As she pulled on her Goretex to leave, she spotted the syringe by the door. She picked it up; the needle had survived the throw, and it didn't take a moment to fetch and replace the screw-on cover. If she had to euthanise something, who cared if the needle had been on the floor? She slipped it into the map pocket of her jacket to put back into her kit later.

For now, her mind concentrated on milking. Job done, and leaving the cowshed, she stopped for a second to face the house. She didn't want to go in there, didn't want to risk running into Shoreham. Swallowing her fear and refusing to be driven from her own home, she stiffened her spine and marched into the building. She scrubbed her hands in the kitchen sink, thankful the house was silent. No need to fear running into anyone if they were all sleeping.

Wiping her hands on a towel, she headed out – stopping short to find Shoreham standing in the doorway between the kitchen and the hall that she needed to go down to get out of the house. He didn't move, he didn't speak, he didn't seem to have any expression at all.

Looking at him, she hoped she had achieved a bland expression as she put the towel aside and headed for the hall. At the doorway she halted, stopped by the sheer barrier of him. He literally blocked the way. For a suspended moment, they stood in stillness and silence, watching each other.

Then she decided enough was enough and stepped forward. "Excuse me."

At her request, he turned sideways, just giving her enough room to squeeze past. As she tried to, he caught her arm, pulling her attention back to him.

He leaned down and all those aberrant feelings swamped her again. His breath tickled her ear, his tongue licked her lobe. Heat filled her loins – good God what was wrong with her?

"You belong to me," he whispered.

She shook her arm free. "Did Hell freeze over?" She stormed out.

Chapter 44
Baron – Pen-Y-Cwm Farm and Guesthouse

"Did you fuck her?" Baron asked after Iolyn left them to their breakfast. He'd seen the way Branwen had stormed from the house, slamming the front door and the car door as she got in.

"No."

"Why not?"

"She was too willing."

Baron considered the man he worked with. Shoreham got things done and usually efficiently. But his methods weren't nice and Baron suspected pushing Branwen too far wouldn't get results.

"Did she tell you anything?"

"Not entirely sure she knows anything. Most women would have talked with what I did to her. But she just claimed to know nothing. You know the little cow even had a syringe of something to use against me."

Baron didn't like the way Shoreham grinned.

"Wrestling it off her was fun."

"Did she have nothing to say or were you too busy playing with her to keep asking?"

Shoreham shrugged, a self-satisfied grin on his face.

"That's no use. We need those files."

"We'll head into town. See if there's any gossip there. You get anything from the man in that house?"

"I was lucky not to get a faceful of axe. I tell you, the inbreeding up here must make them all fucking nuts."

Chapter 45
Branwen – Pen-Y-Cwm Village

Branwen sat in her office and shivered. The room was warm enough, but exhaustion chilled her. What little sleep she'd got had been full of contradiction and fear and arousal and she wanted Cobb, but Shoreham's triumphant face kept filling her vision. Thankfully, the phone rang and she snatched it up.

"Jones Vets Surgery."

"Branwen?"

"Pete?" She breathed in relief. "Thank God it's you. Everything okay?"

"Everything's fine."

His voice sounded so relaxed and easy that she closed her eyes and enjoyed the welcome and missed friendship. She'd known Peter Pearson so long, he was her closest male friend.

"Good to know."

"I was just wondering. Have you any plans for tomorrow night?"

Tomorrow night? Thursday night? Doc came back on a Thursday for Friday surgery upstairs and to spend the weekend at home.

"No, no plans. Why?"

"Well," he said. "It's been a pretty full on here, but my last appointment is about four, so I'll get back early with a need to unwind. So, I figured, you know, if you're not busy, we could get a drink when I get back. I'll buy you dinner."

She smiled. "I'd like that, but I'm pretty sure you paid last time we had a meal together, which makes it my turn to pay."

The laugh flowed down the line like honey. "Nothing like a woman willing to pay her own way to emasculate a man. I'm asking you for a date, Branwen Jones, please say yes." She enjoyed his laugh. "Though even I can see how pleading might not be my best option at this point."

"A date?" Branwen swallowed. They had sort of discussed it last week, but now she wasn't sure. Not with knowing that she was leaving. Not after the way Shoreham had left her last night. On the other hand, she needed to talk to Pete; she needed a man; she was so screwed up right now she probably needed her head read.

"Would it be such a bad thing?"

The question brought her back to the issue at hand.

"No," she said. "No, it really wouldn't be. It'd probably be a very nice thing. I'm just not sure that I'm a great prospect for a date right now."

"Branny, you've always been a good prospect as far as I'm

concerned. Other men must be idiots for not seeing what a wonderful person you are, but I'm glad or you'd have been snapped up by now. Besides, it's just one date."

"On Valentine's Day?" She'd nearly forgotten that.

"Okay," Pete signed. "So my timing isn't great, or maybe it is. Does the day matter? I just want to spend some time with you. No strings, no expectations. Think of it as a chance for us to explore if we could work as a couple or not, now we're all grown up. You okay with that?"

She smiled, her innards warm and full of pleasant anticipation. Cobb might not be interested, but Pete was, and that wasn't a bad thing for a night, as long as he didn't freak about her leaving. "I'm very okay with that."

Chapter 46
Cobb – Pen-Y-Cwm, Cobb's Home

Cobb checked his phone: down to one bar. He moved over to the back door where the signal was usually strongest and the second bar wavered in and out. Should be enough. The call rang out, Simons answered quickly.

"Three calls in two days after two years of nothing. What the hell is going on, Cobb?"

"I'm not sure. That's why I need you to check some stuff out. The boy I mentioned before—"

"You mean James Whitney?"

"Prefers Jay, but yeah."

"I looked him up," Simons said. "He's 23 and a doctoral candidate, young man might be more appropriate than boy."

"He looks young to me."

"You look young to me, but if I called you *boy* you'd punch me."

He probably wouldn't, but Cobb took the older man's point. "Okay, but things have moved on this end."

"Where is that end?"

"Wales. I need you to run a check for me on Richard Granger. He's the head of Nemesis Records."

A pause Cobb couldn't account for stretched.

"Anything in particular I should be looking for?" Simons asked.

Unless something had changed dramatically in the last two years, this wasn't like Simons. "Signs of criminal activity. Could be financial, or sexual, possibly violent."

"You're not exactly narrowing it down."

Cobb laughed at himself. "No, sorry."

"What's going on?"

"I was about to ask you that." He trusted Simons completely. He would put his life in the other man's hands if he had to. In fact, he had, many times. And if he had to, he would again. He looked up at the bedroom door. Jay wouldn't hear through that shut wood. "You okay? Judy?"

The sigh was small. "We're fine. Plenty of work on, which would be great if my business partner was around to give me a hand."

A punch in the gut. Or a much-needed kick up the arse. "Yeah." With Branwen leaving the area, he had no reason to stay, and solitude didn't attract him anymore. "Sorry."

"No. I'm the one who should apologise. I swore I wouldn't put pressure on you to come back before you were ready."

Cobb took a deep breath. "Not ready." He let the breath out. "But not as set against it as I used to be either. Look, I've some damning information against Granger. Others think a friend of mine has it. I need to know how far things are likely to go."

Simons noted it. "What's the association between Whitney and Granger?"

"Whitney hacked Nemesis, he stole the information in question. Speak with Frankie Armstrong, he's Jay's neighbour." He reeled out the address Jay had given him.

"Are you going to tell me what this information is?"

"For the time being, it's better that you don't know."

Simons' voice came back in dark tones. "I prefer working with all the facts."

Cobb pushed back his hair. "Yeah, sorry mate, but for now I want this as tight as possible."

"So, Whitney is the friend you mentioned?"

"No." Cobb considered the situation Branwen had described at Pen-Y-Cwm Farm and Guesthouse. There had been no proof it related to Jay, but Cobb wouldn't rule out the possibility. "If you come across the name Baron or Shoreham, follow them up."

Again, that odd pause. Only a heartbeat, someone else might write it off as a pause to write something down, but Cobb knew better. "What's the connection?"

"Not sure that there is one." Silence echoed. Cobb had to say something. "Can you get me the information?"

"Of course." Simons assured him. "Do I take it that the decryption worked?"

"Did you doubt it would?"

"Not much, they're your programs after all, but it's been two years and technology moves quickly."

True, but sometimes not as fast as it should.

"Where are you?" Simons asked.

Cobb started to prevaricate.

"Answer the damn question."

It wasn't like Simons to snap. Something was going on. "Pen-Y-Cwm," he said. "North Wales. Don't bother looking for it on anything more than a local map, it's just too small. Don't be surprised if you can't get hold of me easily. I've no landline and the mobile signal is unreliable."

"My caller ID has you calling from your mobile."

"I am. Signal sometimes works, but it's unreliable."

"Cobb?" Simons stopped him as he made to sign off. "Do you have any weaponry up there?"

The ice outside gathered in Cobb's belly. "Why? Do I need it?"

He heard that swallow again; Simons' discomfort was a worry.

"I know who Baron is, and who he works for. If he finds out you

147

have Whitney, he will come with weapons and no questions. What about your friend? Can he handle himself?"

Cobb considered it. "He is a she. And so far, yes, she has." Had she? The Goon Brothers were here, and Branwen was acting oddly. Had they been putting more pressure on her than he'd realised? The cold in his belly hardened to concrete. Suddenly bile burned inside. "Branwen Jones is not Mary." It wasn't said to reassure Simons. Cobb had to keep reminding himself of the fact. Another worry. In Mary, at least, he could be sure of her abilities, her limits, her training.

"Branwen Jones? Part owner of the Pen-Y-Cwm Guesthouse?"

The frown on Cobb's forehead deepened. "How do you know that?"

"Another time. Are you and her…?"

Simons didn't need to finish the question.

"No." Cobb said. "I made a promise to Mary that I meant. Forever."

"The vow was till death did you part," Simons said. "And I hate to remind you Cobb, but death did you part."

***

Simons' words echoed in Cobb's empty heart. He wanted to be alone. Just him and Finn. No complications, no dependants, no responsibilities. No unnecessary connections. No worries. He'd used all those subtle shifts to make it clear that he didn't want a relationship with any woman. With Branwen in particular. But that didn't make it so. The memory of Mary haunted him, had kept him separate. Was it time to admit, that some part of him had already said goodbye to Mary? When he put his arm around Branwen, it wasn't merely friendship. It was natural and welcome. He had so desperately wanted to kiss her that he'd had to use tourists as an excuse.

Where the whole bullying issue came from he couldn't fathom. Except that sometimes those reactions resulted from being on the receiving end of someone else's bullying. Lately she had been jumpy and snapping, and nervous, and more than ever giving off that don't-come-near-me vibe.

Had he managed to piss her off that much or was he paying for someone else's actions? Clearly the Goon Brothers as she called them were giving her grief or she wouldn't have called them that. How much, and what kind?

He grabbed his phone and dialled the surgery. "Are you okay?" he asked as soon as Branwen answered.

"Fine. What's wrong? Is Finn alright?"

"He's good, I just needed to check on you."

"Well that's…" Apparently, she couldn't find an appropriate adjective. "Sorry, Cobb, Hannah's off and I've got a lizard with Stomatitis. So unless you actually need something, can I go?"

"Sure." The line disconnected before he'd finished the word. This wasn't like Branwen and he didn't like it. Moving on wasn't easy and she was making it that much harder for him. Of course, she had no way of knowing he was ready to move. Perhaps if he told her. What if–

"What if I contact Nemesis?"

Jay's question dragged Cobb from his circular thoughts. The answer didn't need much consideration. "They'll never trust you not to have shared the information and the chances of your getting away unscathed are virtually zero. We went through this last night."

They had, *ad nauseam* in fact, but it didn't change the fact that Jay wouldn't make a decision to send out those images. He should. Branwen was right, exposure was the only way to make Granger pay for what he had done. Cobb worried about what it would do to Shan Sh'kara and the other subjects of even more disturbing photographs in that directory, but the truth had to come out or the abuse would go on.

"Maybe I could use it to blackmail Granger."

"Maybe Granger would sooner send out a hitman."

Jay paled at that idea.

"Or hitmen."

Chapter 47
Simons – Home Counties

Bile rose in Simons' gut.

Coincidences did happen, the laws of large numbers ensured that. But for Cobb to turn up right in the heart of trouble and with names Simons already knew – He didn't believe in fate, but this was too much.

When Cobb had left two years ago, he'd been in a bad way. Simons hadn't wanted him to leave, but he'd respected the man's decision and not stopped him. Now Simons wondered if that had been the right choice. Time to find out about Cobb – was he still the same man?

The Mountain Rescue membership, Simons took as a good sign. It was exactly the sort of thing Simons would have expected of Cobb. He looked through a few articles, only local papers that would never hit national news, and more importantly the photographs. In all of them, though everyone's positions changed, the constant was the woman at Cobb's side. Branwen Jones.

The woman Cobb had mentioned.

A problem? As Cobb had said, Branwen Jones wasn't Mary. Too less alike women it would be difficult to find, but they had attracted the same attachment. An unacknowledged one perhaps, but an attachment nonetheless. Simons switched to looking into Branwen Jones. The guesthouse had once been the family farm and was now a going concern. No gold mine, but it ticked over healthily. Time to look closer.

A vet, studied at Cambridge, but returned to her home town to practice. A practice now up for sale. No good reason to do so came up. Simons wondered why she would cut herself from her main income source. Branwen lived with her divorced father; her mother, an Italian, had returned to Tuscany. Well, that explained the black hair. Not much in the way of a police rec – oh dear.

Did Cobb know that?

***

Research told Simons the Whitney's were an interesting bunch. The parents weren't even heading back to the UK despite their only son being missing. With his contacts, Simons easily got a full report of what had happened, but police records wouldn't tell him everything, he needed to understand the people involved.

He visited Jay's home, spoke to Frankie. The man's eyes remained heavily swollen and bruised, his nose would never be the same again and the cast on his arm would be there for weeks. What Simons had read in the reports left his gut twisted. One of the

150

descriptions Frankie had given for the two men who attacked him was way too similar to another known thug for Simons' comfort. By the time Simons left Frankie, the twists were knots.

Next stop, Sophie Whitney. Approaching the house, he noted the closed curtains downstairs. But not up. He rang the doorbell. As he waited, a young woman stepped from the house next door. He noted that despite the changing bags over her shoulder, no children hung around her ankles.

"Hello," Simons called. "Do you have any idea where I might find Miss Sophie Whitney?" he asked once she'd returned the greeting.

"She should –" The woman indicated the house. Simons watched her confusion increase as she noticed the closed curtains. "She should be home."

Simons started to worry. "When did you last see Miss Whitney?"

The neighbour looked at Simons; he saw the concern build on her face as she thought about it. "I'll go get my spare key." When she reappeared, looking through the key ring she admitted, "Actually you're the second person to come looking for Sophie."

"Who was the other?"

She shrugged. "He went away to look for her at the library."

Simons took the keys from her shaking fingers; the smell assailed them the moment the door opened. "Wait here." He didn't take long to find the body. He walked back to the front door where the neighbour waited.

"She's dead, isn't she?" A very real grief underlined the question. "Yes."

"I'm supposed to be picking my kids up," she said, pacing back and forth on the doorstep, running her hands through her hair. "I need to call my mother, get her to keep them a while." She started towards her own home. "Should I call the police?"

"Yes." Simons saw her shock, but she handled it well and he simply couldn't afford to get involved with more red tape right now. As the woman disappeared into her own home, he walked calmly back to his car and drove away.

Baron shivered in the car. Not wanting to waste the battery, he didn't put the heater on. At least this picking of a shower wasn't falling on him, for all the wind buffeted the car. The rain wasn't doing anything to wash the snow away either. Apparently it was just piled too high and the day stayed too cold.

The ring of the phone he expected to be Shoreham. Granger's snap surprised him.

"Well?"

"Sir–"

"Don't give me flannel man, I want results. Where are those files?"

"We're close." He had to say something.

"Not close enough," Granger complained. "I want a full situation update."

Baron gave him the facts: Shoreham was watching suspect two, he was watching suspect one. Only he wasn't right now, he'd closed his eyes and leant back too.

"Have you searched the man's house?"

"Not yet."

"Why not?"

"He hasn't left it. Besides, Miss Jones seems the more likely candidate."

"You've searched her?"

"Her house and her car. No trace."

"Then search her office."

"And if there's nothing there?"

Granger paused, it was a cold hard nothing. "Then persuade Miss Jones that it is in her interest to tell you where those files are. I want them back."

Baron opened his eyes and cursed the wind. In the darkness of his resting moment, it seemed Branwen had left in her car. He checked his watch. Could be a call out, and she might return, but the certainty was that she'd have to go home at some point. He started the car and put the heater up full whack.

***

"What do you think you're doing?"

An angry confrontation wasn't the way Branwen had expected to be greeted by her father as she stepped into the house. Apparently, she wasn't going to get a choice. Cold fear washed through her, her cheeks burned with a guilt she had no right to. "What do you mean?"

"I had a call this afternoon, some bloke asking about buying the business. I told him it wasn't for sale."

She'd have to make a call and smooth that one over. She sighed. "Shame. Le-"

"You can't sell my business, my home, out from under me. Who do you think you are?"

"I'm not!" The temptation to anger, to argue was almost overwhelming and, her temper already frayed, she had to fight for any control. "Right, let's get this clear. The guesthouse isn't *your* business, it's *our* business. I funded the renovations that got us up to a standard where we could legally rent out rooms. We are equal partners." And if the bank didn't hold a 4% share, they'd never get anything agreed. "If I were to do anything with this business, I would need to notify you first, that's part of the partnership agreement. But this isn't the only business I own. And what I do with the vet's practice is entirely my own decision and I've decided to sell."

His scowl only deepened. "To do what? We're not making enough here for two to live on."

"Could do, if you'd stop clinging to the past and let me develop the business properly. But as it is – no, it won't support the two of us. But one can do it all and survive nicely. And that's what you're going to have to do."

"And what do you think you're going to do?"

She didn't want to answer that question, he wouldn't like her response. "I'm leaving the area."

"To go where?"

"Wherever I want."

"You stupid girl, what do you think is out there? A world that cares?" he sneered. "You're throwing yourself on the scrap heap!"

"Well if I am, that's my choice."

"Have some sense!"

"I've got plenty. And I will not bury myself in the middle of nowhere for no reason. I want to live before I die."

"Oh, I'm not good enough for you, is it? This place isn't good enough, I suppose."

"All I'm saying is, it's not the whole world."

"What part of the world would be?"

"Maybe Italy!" The words left her mouth before she even thought about them. Her father went from blazing anger to cold white hate.

"Don't you dare."

"She's my mother."

"No! This mountain is more your mother than that bitch ever even tried to be!"

"Nan didn't give her a chance and you didn't protect her just like you never protected me!"

The crack as he slapped her face reverberated through her cheek, through the house and split apart some facet of their relationship.

For a moment they looked at one another in shock. Then an unexpected calm flooded Branwen.

"Branny —"

"Don't you ever call me that again." Her voice was flint. "I'm not going to be bullied and controlled by you the way you were by Nan. I want more than I'll ever get here and if you can't support me, at least get out of the way because, if you don't, I will just walk straight over you." Her hands clenched at her sides she turned, stomped straight back out of the house, got in her car and drove away, ignoring her father's apologies and pleas.

***

Baron stood quietly and listened to the Joneses argue. Heard the slap.

He knew that sound. Had heard it between his parents, heard it on several ex-girlfriends. Next came the tears. Only Branwen didn't shed any. Her voice came back hard and strong. Iolyn had just lost everything, and after the car pulled away, the man started to sob.

Baron slipped back into his room, a broad smile full of glee. Women like Branwen weren't easily broken, which made them the most fun to break.

When Shoreham got back from breaking the mast, they'd find out together. For now, he had another job to do.

Chapter 49
Jay – Pen-Y-Cwm, Cobb's Home

Acid burned through Jay's guts. Terror over-rode all other emotions, had been ever since that he'd heard about Frankie's injuries. Cobb didn't understand that. He doubted Cobb had ever been afraid of anything in his entire life. But he made a lot of sense. Some information had to be shared. The public had a right to know. He stood and moved around the room.

If he did this, would he survive?

If he didn't, would he be able to live with himself?

He moved to stand in front of Cobb. "Okay."

The big man looked up from the e-reader in his hand. "Okay?"

Jay swallowed and nodded. "Okay, we'll send that one image to the papers."

***

Cobb stretched and switched on his laptop, making a coffee as it booted up. He'd half expected the news to break last night, but nothing had. He moved with the hot drink to the table, picked up his phone and checked the connection. H+. Not bad for around here. He moved to make it a hot spot, but before he could, both phone and internet connection failed.

Chapter 50
Branwen – Pen-Y-Cwm Village

Pacing her office, Branwen figured she wouldn't be getting any work done tonight. She checked what she had on in the morning to set her alarm clock right. Her cheek still stung from her father's slap. That was the last straw, the decision to leave had clearly been the right one. She couldn't go on like this. But tonight posed a problem. Emma would offer her a place to stay, but would require an explanation and she wasn't ready for that. The pub had rooms, but that would be announcing trouble at home to the whole village. Instead, she made up the bed in her office, straightening to get undressed. Blinding white light spilled into her vision and pain closed in on her. Slumping forward, she fell into blackness.

***

Baron dealt with the unexpected, quickly taking Branwen out of the game. With barely a glance at the unconscious body, he got on with the job at hand – searching the office. The PC was already on. Baron turned to the showing screen: Branwen's appointment book for tomorrow. Using the mouse, he minimised the scheduler and entered the file manager. Searching through the file listing, he hunted for what he needed.

"Branny! It's me, Emma! – I saw your car!"

Baron froze at the call. A quick glance at the front door, then he moved to hide in the rear corridor just as Emma came in. He'd have to deal with her too.

"You're not suppo—" Emma's words froze, and he imagined that she did too, seeing Branwen slumped over the temporary bed. "Branwen!" Fear tainted the tone. "Oh my God!"

Through the tiny crack in the door, Baron watched Emma rush over to check Branwen. When Emma pulled her hand away, he saw red. Blood.

Crap. He hadn't meant to hit Branwen that hard. But Emma was dithering and Branwen was lying unconscious. Time to go.

Chapter 51
Cobb – Pen-Y-Cwm, Cobb's Home

Cobb looked at his phone. A single bar of signal. One that kept wavering in and out. The internet connection stood at G only.

"What's wrong?"

At the question, Cobb looked to Jay sitting with Finn next to the fire.

"The signal's not great." He indicated his phone even as he set it as a Wi-Fi hotspot.

"Not really the time to be uploading a large file."

"The photos really aren't that large, and we're only sending one."

"But it's my safety net."

Cobb didn't need Jay wavering again. "I'm your safety net," Cobb pointed out, but it had been a major discussion point all yesterday evening and long into the night. "But I need to make a phone call. You sort out the email while I do so."

With Jay at the MacBook, Cobb tried Branwen's mobile. No answer. He tried the Guesthouse. Iolyn declared how he neither knew nor cared where the treacherous bitch was. The phone got slammed down even as Cobb realised the slurring was alcohol induced. Whatever had happened, couldn't have been good. He had to find Branwen. He phoned the surgery, straight to answerphone.

"Is there a problem?" Jay asked looking up at him.

"Yeah, I can't get hold of Branwen." Cobb tapped the phone against his lips. Where would she go? Why hadn't she come here? Because he'd kept her at arms-length and she thought he thought she was a nag. He had to find her. "You going to be all right if I leave you alone?"

Fear ramped in the young man's face. "What if someone comes calling?"

"At this time of night? Besides, no one's left to call. The Police have been twice, from the description of what Branwen called the Goon Brothers, one's been here already. Who else is going to come looking for you?"

"One of your friends could come calling."

"Nope," Cobb stated. "No friends to do that. Keep the curtains closed and if anyone knocks, ignore it. With my car gone, it won't take long for someone to figure out that I'm not at home."

"But it's not safe to drive."

Cobb understood the reluctance. "I've got a four by four with snow tires, not a high spec city car. Besides, I'm used to these roads and the lemmings otherwise known as sheep. Who tend not to be wandering in the dark anyway. I'll be fine. I have to find Branwen."

That particular urge was stronger than any he'd felt for a long time.

A noise rumbled in the distance. "What's that?" Panic coloured Jay's voice.

"Thunder," Cobb said. "Don't freak out now. You'll be fine here."

***

Driving into the village without Finn was weird. Blue lights flashed in the dark before he reached the village, pulling his heart into his throat. Stopping by the surgeries, he yanked the handbrake on and stepped out, to find himself face to face with a stunned looking Michael Woolverton.

"What's going on?"

"No idea. Just got back."

The two men rushed across the winter white road, skidding to an awkward halt inside the surgeries' door.

"Too late for the cavalry," Johnston informed him.

Cobb didn't bother with the constable, going straight over to Branwen. She sat in her waiting room, Emma, checking the wound under the pad of cotton wool, sitting beside her. His stomach heaved at sight of the bloodstain on the white pad.

"What happened?" he asked softly, sitting at her side.

"Someone bashed me over the head." Her tone told him what a stupid question it was. She looked up. "Michael! You're back. How's the family?"

His broad grin said a lot. "Mother and baby both doing well."

"Details!"

"7 pound 4 ounce boy, we're calling him Richard, but right now, I'm more worried about you."

"I'm fine."

"Branny!" Emma scolded her.

Branwen turned and glared at Emma, taking the wad from her. "Why don't you go home? I'll see you tomorrow."

"You'll see me tonight," Emma informed her. "I'm not letting you drive home after this. You're staying with me."

"She's right," Cobb put in gently when Branwen opened her mouth to argue. The vet glared at him, but the expression eased quickly under his determined gaze. "You're safest here, stay for tonight at least. And you should get Doc to look at this," Cobb said when he looked at the bump.

"He won't be back till tomorrow evening."

"The roads are open if we go with care," Michael said. "We should get you to a hospital, get that x-rayed."

"No." Her voice held enough determination to stop him. "Sorry Michael. I shouldn't shout at you. But you just got home. So, go home. Be with the family. I'm good."

Michael grunted. "You're playing at being strong. That's what you do. Cobb, take care of her, call me if you need help making her take care of herself."

Cobb nodded and Michael left. He'd noticed something when Branwen looked up and frowned. "What happened to your cheek?"

She hung her head and let her hair cover her face. "Nothing."

An obvious lie.

"Emma." She looked up. More the Branwen he knew and- "Go make up your spare bed. I'll be over when I'm finished here."

Emma's expression grew sceptical.

"I'll make sure she does," Cobb assured the blonde before she would leave.

"Make sure you don't let them bully you," she said, indicating the officers and heading for the door, giving both Cobb and Johnston an unsuccessfully hard glare. "Any of them."

The word 'bully' made Branwen flinch. He put a hand on her shoulder, but she pulled away. Cobb had been watching Branwen, concerned for how unfocused her eyes appeared, the lack of colour in her cheeks.

"Right," Johnston announced, obviously put out by the interruption, "if you are quite finished Mr Cobb, I've got questions for you."

"What?" he demanded, turning back to Johnston.

"Can you give an account of your whereabouts today? Why are you here now at the first sign of trouble?"

Was that jumped up little twat really insinuating he had something to do with this?

"Now just –"

Cobb cut off Branwen's indignant response by placing a restraining hand on hers.

"I've been at home all day. I literally just drove into the village and saw the police cars outside."

As he spoke Inspector Perkins stepped out of Branwen's office.

"Cobb." The shorter man nodded.

"Inspector Perkins."

Neutrality reigned as Perkins turned to Branwen. "How are you doing, Miss Jones?"

"Frayed around the edges, generally intact."

"And you say the first indication you had of a break-in was Miss McGuiness finding you? Where is Miss McGuiness now, by the way?" he asked, without waiting for a reply to the first question.

"She's gone to make up her spare bed for me," Branwen explained. "And yes. There was nothing suspicious before I got hit."

"Why's there a bed made up in there?"

Branwen sighed and slumped. "I was intending to stay the night here. Sometimes I do that if I'm looking after a sick animal."

"There are no animals back there," Perkins pointed out.

"True."

"Did something get released?"

"No. I was avoiding the sick animals at home. Humans," she clarified to his confused frown. "I just needed a night not dealing with humans."

"So, you shouldn't have been here?"

"No."

"No one expected to find you here?"

"No."

"Any idea why someone might want to break in?"

"Not really." Branwen shrugged, leaning forward and feigning interest in her wound to cover her lies. "I've been working on a drug trial and helping the Price-Roberts with what's proving to be quite a successful and lucrative breeding program, but aside from that, the rest's all pretty boring veterinary stuff not likely to be of interest to anyone. Except another vet, possibly, but probably not."

The inspector nodded. He didn't seem overly interested as he looked around the waiting room.

"Anything else you need to tell me?"

Branwen sat straighter. "It might not be the first break in."

That caught Perkins' attention and shrewd eyes pinned on her.

"Wednesday morning, I came in, and got the feeling someone had been in, things weren't quite where I'd left them. Nothing too far off, but everything that little bit out of kilter. Stuff that I usually just put my hands on, not in reach."

"Anything missing?"

She shook her head. "No. I even did a drug stock take, everything's accounted for."

"You're suggesting this was a return visit?"

"I suppose."

Branwen crumpled at the idea, leaning back, her weight falling on Cobb's arm stretched across the back of the bench seat. He should probably move away; instead he curled his hand around her shoulder like he had the right and she leaned in, lay her head on his shoulder.

"What," Johnston demanded in the ensuing silence, "did you see of the crash at Satan's Turn?"

Concentrating on Branwen, Cobb refused to face the constable. "Nothing." Never having liked Johnston, the man's pestering grated on his nerves now.

"What shape was the driver in when you got there?"

That did it. Cobb rarely got angry, but now he channelled all that

160

anger towards Johnston. He shot to his feet. "Look, Constable, someone's committed a crime here and it wasn't me. Why don't you –"

"Cobb." Her hand enfolded his in warmth. He considered how drawn she seemed even as she moved to stand. Instinctively he put his arms around her waist, steadying her as she faltered. Her breathing and rapid pulse were obvious to his touch. She wasn't in much better condition than Jay. She leaned against him.

"If you don't mind, Inspector," Branwen said quietly, "I'm tired and I'd like to go now."

The short man looked over at Cobb's proximity. "What about getting a doctor to check out that head wound?"

She smiled. "It's not as bad as it probably looks," she assured him. "My tiredness has more to do with a general lack of sleep lately than a knock on the skull." For a moment, the inspector watched them keenly. Cobb sensed he saw more clearly than either of them would like. "Can I go?"

Perkins nodded and turned away.

Branwen looked up at Cobb. "Walk me to Em's place?"

"Of course."

Movements slow and careful, he did, less convinced than Branwen that she didn't need a doctor. "Are you really okay?" he whispered as they headed down the road.

"Not really." She leaned against him, like she trusted him to lead her where she needed to go. "I mean, physically I've got a cracking headache, but not a cracked skull. I'm exhausted, but I was exhausted when I woke up this morning."

They had reached the estate agents now, and he turned her to look at him. "Branwen. Why didn't you come to me? I called the farm, your dad seemed in a bit of a state."

"Yeah, we had a row. About me leaving."

The wind blew a hunk of her hair into her face. He pushed it back.

"He doesn't want me to go."

"He's not the only one." Was the need in her eyes, or his imagination? Only one way to find out...

"Oh!" Emma exclaimed as she opened the door to find Branwen on her doorstep and in Cobb's arms. "I didn't mean to interrupt you two."

"You didn't." Cobb quickly released Branwen and moved away from her. "I was just leaving." Looking back at Branwen, he didn't even offer her a smile. "Take care of yourself." He turned smartly on his heel and stalked away.

"I'll have to," Branwen muttered less quietly than she meant. "Clearly you won't."

Chapter 52
Branwen – Pen-Y-Cwm Village

The last thing Branwen needed was the crowd of people who had crammed into the estate agents to nose and grab the gossip. She shouldn't be surprised, in Pen-Y-Cwm this was a major incident. Sat on the sofa Branwen felt claustrophobia crowd her. She needed space, air. The door opened again, bodies moved through the people and she spotted the inspector again. She half-smiled until Johnston appeared a step behind him. Carefully and slowly pushing herself to her feet, she stood to greet the higher ranked officer.

"I need to ask you a few more questions, Miss Jones," he said without preamble.

Branwen nodded. "Come upstairs," she said. "We can talk in peace up there."

Perkins followed her. She hated the way she had to reach for something to steady her, unwilling to risk another fall. Once up the stairs, they found themselves in an over-bright and over-coloured front room that, with its blow-up furniture and lurid lava lamp was a resurrection of the 1960's that got regurgitated every twenty to thirty years. Although not to Branwen's personal taste, it worked for Em. It certainly reflected the bubbly personality of its owner.

"Take a seat. Would you like tea, or coffee?"

"Thank you, neither," Perkins said, carefully lowering himself gingerly into an inflated armchair.

Branwen too sat, and Perkins glanced between her and the still standing Johnston, their animosity obvious.

"Constable," he said, "perhaps you could go downstairs, ask if anyone saw anything, get a head start on the door to door." The resentment was clear in Johnston's voice and expression as he acquiesced and turned. Perkins waited until Johnston left before he turned back to Branwen. "You and Johnston don't get on."

Branwen faced him squarely. "Is that a question or an accusation?"

"Merely an observation."

Branwen picked at the rattan chair she sat in.

"So nothing was taken from the surgery?"

She began to shake her head but thought better of it. "No. At least I don't think so. Nothing obvious, anyway."

"What would an intruder be after?"

This time she shrugged. "No idea. This is a long way to come for a computer swipe and go away empty-handed. There's the drugs we keep, I suppose, but they weren't touched."

"We?" Perkins asked.

"Doc Pearson and I." She pushed her hair back from her face.

"We both have to keep controlled substances on site, so we share a secure room. It's built into my part of the Surgeries. There's only one door and you have to go through my office to get to it."

Perkins nodded. "You always referred to 'them' or 'they' when speaking of your attacker. Why do you think there was more than one?"

Branwen frowned. "Not sure. I wasn't even aware that I was doing that." Except that her most recent attacks had been from Baron and Shoreham and although Shoreham had acted alone she always thought of them as a matched pair. She shrugged again. "Could've been just one, I guess. I can't be sure. Like I said, the first I knew about being attacked was Emma waking me up."

For a few moments Perkins sat still and watched her. Since silence was the weapon so often used against her, she didn't become uncomfortable in the wait. "Do you have any personal enemies, Miss Jones?"

She couldn't help laughing bitterly at that. Perkins obviously took an affront at the reaction. "I'm sorry," she swiftly soothed. "I guess you haven't been in the village long. Yes, I have quite a few personal enemies. Half the village, in fact. Actually," she considered, frowning, "many of them aren't exactly enemies, they're... maybe a bit blinkered about illegitimacy."

"You're illegitimate?"

"No. It's my father as is the bastard, but village memories, and resentments, last a long time."

"Anything more personally directed?"

She considered it for a moment. "Sure, but I've never considered it a problem."

"What about Miss McGuiness?" Perkins asked. "I understand you've been friends for a long time."

"Yes. Since university."

"And the friendship is firm?"

Branwen blinked at him, uncertainty marking her expression. "Yeah. What are you really asking?"

"Might she have attacked you and called the police in a fit of guilt?"

"No! That's stupid." Branwen pulled in a deep breath. "We, that is I —" She tried again. "I have a history. Emma is involved. It has caused some friction in the past, but all long since worked out. Emma has no reason to attack me. The idea is preposterous."

Perkins nodded. "What about Cobb?"

She frowned. "What about him?"

"I understand he doesn't come into town much."

"No, not usually," she confirmed. "He prefers his own company."

"Seemed to prefer your company earlier."

Branwen bit back a sharp retort. "Cobb and I are friends. He has no reason to want to hurt me. And what you saw was just friendly concern. Cobb's a bit of a hermit, but he does care about people. If anyone in the village had been attacked, he would've come running."

"Doubt that," Perkins said. "So, you wouldn't say he has any particular interest in you?"

"It wouldn't matter if he did," she told him, checking Emma wasn't about. "Cobb's the only one who knows, but I'm selling the business and leaving town. Well, sorry that's not entirely true. See, I told my dad earlier. We argued."

"Is that why you decided to sleep in town tonight?"

She nodded. "My life's kind of crap right now, Inspector."

"Any particular reason for that?"

She shrugged. "A series of bad choices culminating in a critical mass probably. Things will get better, they're just rubbish right now. There again, seems the whole world's struggling with worse crap, so I shouldn't complain." She wanted to though. She was stressed, wondering if this indicated the early stages of depression, or if it was just the present circumstances.

"Would Cobb attack you to keep you in town?"

She actually laughed at the idea, but it hurt her head and the mirth quickly died. "No. Besides, why would anyone try and terrify me to keep me here? That's more the work of someone who wants rid surely? Besides, Cobb was only coming into town after you'd arrived. He wasn't in earlier to have been able to attack me."

Again Perkins watched her before speaking, appraised her. "You look tired, Miss Jones, I think you should get some rest. We'll talk again tomorrow."

"I'll look forward to it."

Now Perkins smiled as he stood. "Lying to the police isn't a good idea."

***

"Well would you look at that."

Branwen sat at the breakfast table, her scalp still tender. Brushing her hair had taken too long because she'd had to avoid splitting the skin open. She wouldn't be headbanging for a while, but at least there was no worrying headache or obvious sign of concussion. The typically thick skull had served her well. Now she looked up at Emma coming in with the paper from across the street.

"Look at what?"

Emma placed the paper in front of her. Branwen's world convulsed.

"That's Shan Sh'Kara doing the nasty with some bloke." Emma

164

switched on the kettle. "Can't believe celebrities think it's a good idea to release sex photos. Like it's really going to do their careers any good."

"That's not what this is."

"I bet next thing you know some he-man type will claim he made her cry because he has such a tremendous dick."

Branwen tuned Emma out to read the article. There were less column inches of report than of image. Image received anonymously. Someone accused of abusing the singer, but no evidence other than this, just some speculation. Unfortunately, the speculation seemed to be more slanted towards blaming the singer than whoever used her. And why not show the man? One of them was enjoying the moment and obviously not Shan Sh'kara.

"A woman gets sexually abused, then her character is abused by the papers. No mention of the man doing the abusing. The editor probably couldn't get laid in school. It's sick." Branwen chucked the paper on the table and stood up. "Anyway, I need to get to the surgery, the SOCOs are bound to have left a mess."

"CSIs."

She blinked and looked at Emma. "Sorry?"

"Apparently, we changed a few years ago, and we Brits don't have SOCOs anymore, they're CSIs to harmonise with most other parts of the world."

Branwen grunted, not sure what bloody difference a name made.

"Anyway, you can't work today. You've been attacked, you need to take it easy."

"I will, but I still have to go in to call those with appointments and reschedule because Hannah isn't around to do it for me."

***

Branwen made the call she really didn't want to first. Her father answered on the fourth ring.

"Hi."

His response was a grunt.

"Thought I'd let you know I'm alright."

"Well, you would be," he sneered back. "You always make sure you're alright first."

The dagger he'd set in her heart twisted, the sting in her cheek came back like he'd slapped her again.

"Okay." His disinterest showed, no point going into detail, but there was business to discuss. "Can you go out and check the phone mast? Your mobile number's going straight to answerphone. If we don't report problems, the phone company docks the rent they should pay. If there's a problem, can you tell Cobb, he relies on his mobile." He didn't, but Iolyn didn't know that.

165

Chapter 53
Simons – Home Counties

Simons looked at the front page picture. At least the paper delivery still came early.

Shan Sh'Kara, and not having a great time. Poor girl was only 20 according to the papers, but she looked younger. The man behind her was obscured, though Simons guessed from the pot belly it was Granger. If that came out, it would be extremely damaging. He smiled. Granger would burn for this, but Simons wondered what O'Rourke would do.

He got there, and set up, laser microphone targeted and recording. He watched through binoculars.

"Well?" Demanded O'Rourke when Keel walked into the office. Both looked like they'd had tough nights.

"Don't take it out on me."

O'Rourke closed his eyes and took a deep breath. When he spoke it was more calmly. "Rebecca, you have news for me?"

She inclined her head, an acknowledgement of the efforts he went to, to treat her well. "Indeed sir, it would seem Mr Granger has rushed off up the M40. Your contact said you'd want to know."

"Hmm." O'Rourke considered the news.

So did Simons, was Granger heading to Pen-Y-Cwm?

"Oh, and Mr Salten is here," Keel added.

Simons didn't recognise the name, nor the man who walked in, shook hands with O'Rourke and sat down.

"They can't get to you." The man said without a prompt.

"You're sure?"

"As sure as I can be, sir. You are as aware as I am, that every contact leaves a trace, but we've taken all possible precaution. Cash transactions limit the exposure, but I can't give a cast iron guarantee, only that, to get to any connection to you, there are so many layers of much easier targets that it's unlikely the authorities would keep digging that far."

"How unlikely?"

"More chance of winning the Lotto jackpot three weeks in a row."

Not what Simons wanted to hear.

"Could we cut Nemesis loose?" O'Rourke asked.

"We can cut anyone loose, but it might not be such a great idea with Nemesis. Downloads are taking over, making the laundering more difficult, but they still offer the event revenue stream and that bolsters other lucrative activities. Besides, it's also a good source of young women, and men come to that, who are willing to do anything it takes to get into the entertainment business."

A fact that Granger had apparently found useful and been stupid enough to document.

"It's not the company so much as the man who's the problem, sir," Salten said.

O'Rourke's attention snapped back to the man. "Thank you for your time."

The man inclined his head, stood and left the room.

O'Rourke leaned forward and used the intercom to ask Keel to join him. "I've been thinking," he said softly once she closed the door behind her.

"Yes, sir?"

"We need someone who understands the music business."

Rebecca frowned. "Isn't that why you agreed to bankroll Granger in the first place, sir? Because he knew the business and you wished to diversify?"

"Yes, but that was four years ago, the world has moved on. Granger is yesterday's man. I think we need tomorrow's man today."

Chapter 54
Cobb – Pen-Y-Cwm, Cobb's Home

The morning ground on Cobb, kicking into high gear at the knock on the door. He motioned Jay to hide. He wasn't expecting anyone to come knocking on his door at, he checked his watch, 10:37 a.m. He checked through the window. Iolyn Jones. With Jay out of sight, he opened the door for the older man, a man suited up ready for the Arctic, let alone a snowy mountain.

"Iolyn," he said as he closed the door once the farmer stepped in. "What can I do for you?"

"Just to let you know that the phone mast is down. Looks like some kind of electrical fault, burnt out. Might have been a lightning strike. Though usually with those, there'd be more damage. Phone company says it won't be out to fix the damn thing for several days. You might get a signal from the next over, if you get a favourable wind, but I wouldn't hold your breath for it."

"Cheers."

Iolyn shrugged and headed for the door. "Yeah well, Branwen told me to tell you."

"How's she doing this morning?"

"Same selfish cow as always."

Cobb reared at the unexpected pronouncement. "But after the attack last nig–"

"Attack!" The older man swung on him. "She's saying I attacked her?"

"No..." Cobb had to tread carefully, wondering again at the mark on Branwen's face. "Someone broke into the surgery last night and attacked her. Hit her over the head." Iolyn paled. "She stayed at Emma's last night, probably should have gone to the hospital, but she's stubborn."

"Stubborn. Pigheaded. Stupid." Iolyn grumbled all the way out. None of which told Cobb if Branwen was actually alright or not.

***

Branwen struggled to answer the phone, her fingers so cold the screen didn't register the touch at first. "Hello?"

"Branwen?"

"Yes?" The phone crackled in her ear as she checked the caller ID. "Cobb? That you? I can hardly hear you."

Crackles that might have been a voice came back.

"Sorry. Hold on." She shouted, sounded like she was trying to call across the valley to him without a phone: "Can you hear me better now?"

"Yeah." This time the voice sounded clear and strong. "You

moved?"

"Got in my car. I'm at Cwm Du Farm – lambing issues. Phone mast not down then?"

"Oh, it is, I just drove down the mountain till I picked up a signal. Are you sure you should be working?"

She was pretty sure she shouldn't be, but there wasn't always a choice. "Gotta be, sheep lamb when they lamb." But she needed more than this. "Cobb, tell me everything is okay." She swallowed the pain in her throat.

"What's wrong?"

"I need you to tell me that everything is going to be okay." Branwen didn't like being needy, but right now she was, and she needed to hear it was okay.

"Branwen, everything *is* going to be okay." The certainty in Cobb's voice definitely helped. "Your dad dropped in earlier. You and I, we need to talk. Properly, not on the phone. Promise me you'll drop in on your way home."

Her throat chocked up. She sniffed, but couldn't speak.

"Branwen, promise me."

"Alright," she breathed. "Alright, I will. I'll drop in." No point in pretending she didn't want to. "Have to go home to pick my stuff up. You and Jay okay?"

"We're fine."

"Still, you shouldn't leave him alone, a head wound like that can have unexpected consequences."

"Branwen, this whole thing has unexpected consequences, but even I know potential concussion victims only need twenty-four hours constant observation, not four days."

"Yeah," she sighed. "True. Sorry Cobb, I keep dumping stuff on you. Sorry."

"Wouldn't have it any other way."

The lump in her throat burned. She tried not to sniff, she didn't want him to hear the tears falling.

"Branwen?"

"Still here." She sighed again. "Sorry Cobb, it's just things are getting on top of me a bit at the moment. Sorry, it's…" She didn't know what it was. "It's okay. It's nothing."

She rang off.

Chapter 55
Alex – Belsize Park

Alex looked across the room to where Greebo sat huddled in a ball of misery. His younger half-brother was slumped in a damp mess of tears and snot, a vision of perfect misery. Though dry, Alex suspected his own features reflected the same dark emotion. Hardly surprising, since they had just got back from arranging their mother's funeral.

The phone rang. Habit answered. "Hello?"

"Alex?"

"Yes?"

"It's Levinson," Mark identified himself. "I need to speak to Granger, but he's not taking calls."

Alex didn't much care. "That's not my problem."

"I need a quote about Shan Sh'kara."

Alex sighed. "Fuck sake, Mark."

"Would your fans be happy knowing you swear like that?"

"Would your editor be happy knowing you're harassing a man who just got home after arranging his mother's funeral?"

"Frankly, I doubt the bitch would care as long as she got the story, but I am sorry for your loss. How's Greebo doing?"

It was the first time anyone had asked, but Alex wasn't about to pour out his pain and anguish to a journalist. He was also aware of Levinson's increasingly agitated responses. "What do you want Mark?"

"If I don't get a story, I won't work for the magazine again. Can't you give me something on the Shan Sh'Kara situation?"

Alex sighed. "Okay." Alex paused to consider his words. "That picture is shameful, it is not something I or Nemesis Records would want to be connected with. However, I feel for what Shan must be going through right now, and my thoughts go out to her. At this point I have to ask two question. Firstly, where did the picture come from, and secondly, why have the papers protected the man doing the abusing? No woman deserves that, and no man should be allowed to get away with it." He suspected he sounded a little rehearsed, but he didn't care. "Oh and Mark?"

The voice suggested Levinson had drifted from the conversation. "Yeah?"

"Just remember, you've known the truth and kept it secret too long to take any moral high ground. Don't even think about publishing anything damaging to my reputation. Yours will be so much easier to destroy."

Even knowing that he had the last word, nerves racked Alex. He didn't like the way Levinson had been. He didn't trust the man.

The association with Granger was no longer useful. After the photographs he'd found on the server, he'd lost any respect he'd had for the man. Of course, there was another, much deadlier man Alex knew.

Alone in his room, Alex pulled out the burner phone from its hiding place and made the call. Better to be at the left hand of the Devil than in his path.

Chapter 56
Branwen – Pen-Y-Cwm Village

The last thing Branwen needed on returning to the surgery was a bloody great Mercedes parked in the customer parking area. Doc owned a Volvo, and wasn't due back just yet, she had two appointments this afternoon, and neither of them owned the hunk of expensive metal parked in her spot.

Bloody tourists had a nasty habit of using it as a free carpark, though free didn't last long, because she used a clamping service – Paul was ever enterprising. She also had warning notices posted at driver eye level, and the Merc was sitting right in front of one. The temptation to key the immaculate paint work was near irresistible.

As she stepped out of the Land Rover she dragged her phone from her pocket and photographed the car before sending it to Paul.

"Miss Jones?"

Branwen signed off the call as she turned to the man who had called her. A physically large man, it had been a few years since his waistline had been concave, something the double-breasted suit he wore did nothing to hide. His unsuitable shoes and the camel hair coat might look good in the city – she recognised his accent as London – but here it just looked impractical. Worse yet, she recognised the man. Richard the-using-pervert Granger.

"This your car?"

He glanced at what appeared to be his pride and joy. "It is."

"What animal do you want me to look at?"

That stumped him for a moment. "Oh, it's nothing like that, I merely wanted to speak to you."

"What about?" She saw Perkins getting out of his legally parked car across the street.

"Perhaps we can talk inside?"

"I'm comfortable out here."

He clearly wasn't. "I have some business to discuss."

"Veterinary business?" Perkins was approaching now. At least he wasn't the bulky threatening type.

"Well, no."

"Well this is my business, and these are my business hours, so if you don't have veterinary business, then you have no business with me," Branwen said. "That means you're illegally parked. Move the vehicle or get clamped."

"Miss Jones?" Perkins called her attention.

She'd rather avoid him, but too late for that. "Inspector Perkins. Let's go inside." She reached into the back of the Landy to grab her case; leaving medical supplies around was never a good idea. Then she turned to the fat man again. "Move your car."

"I don't have to."

"Sign says you do." Perkins pointed to the clear parking policy on the wall.

"And if you don't move it now," Branwen said before pointing to Paul approaching, yellow clamp in hand, "he'll ensure you don't move it again without paying a hundred pound fine."

The smile slid from the fat man's face like grease off a hot pan. He reached into his pocket for the keys.

Leading Perkins to the door, Branwen's hands shook so much she took too long to open it. Stepping over the threshold, she flicked on the lights; the dim afternoon meant it would soon be dark. Inside she pulled a width of blue paper from the roll next to the reception desk and spread it on the counter before she placed her bag on the paper.

"What's that for?" Perkins asked as she turned.

She glanced at the bag then back to the man. "Me being overly cautious. I've just come from a lambing, and the bag was on the shed floor, I wiped it off but I don't want to risk transference to any of the patients as they come in. The blue roll is there generally because animals tend to be indiscriminate about where they discharge, particularly when they are frightened, and vets frighten so many of them, so it's always handy." Now she moved over to the disinfectant dispenser, wiped some of the pungent lemon liquid over her hands, wiped those on another wad of blue tissue and then held out her hand to shake the Inspector's hand.

"Sorry, about outside. It annoys me when tourists use my business parking like a free carpark. Still, what can I do for you, Inspector?"

"Follow up from yesterday and I'd like to talk to you about the crash at Satan's Turn on Monday."

She nodded. "Okay. You want a coffee?"

"Dim diolch," he said. "I mean –"

She stopped him with a wave of her hand. "Rwy'n siarad Cymraeg hefyd. Tend to deal mostly in English these days though. Nothing wrong with the Welsh language, mind, but there's a whole lot of modern words, medical ones especially that it just doesn't cover."

"Don't mind waiting if you want to make yourself a drink though."

She shook her head. "So what do you want to know?"

"How are you after yesterday?"

"Sore. Oddly defeated, and rather pissed off. Physically I'm tired but fine."

"Could 'tired' be a problem?"

She nodded. "Be more of problem if I hadn't been shattered for the last couple of weeks. As I mentioned, my life's a bit of a mess right now. Lots of things crowding in and I need a break. Haven't taken any time off since—" She had to stop and think about it. "Wow. Don't think I've had any down time in five months."

"Yeah," he offered a small smile. "That'll leave a body in need of a good rest. You've cleaned up after CSI then."

"As best I could. That fingerprint dust is a bugger to get off."

"True, but we need to take them just in case, as we need yours to eliminate."

"You already have mine."

He nodded. "From the McManus case."

"Yeah, but do me a favour and don't go shouting about that, I haven't even told Dad about it, and small villages can be small minded."

"They can also be surprisingly supportive. Nothing closes ranks as quickly as a small village when one of their own is in trouble."

"Something you encounter often?"

"More's the pity. Did you check if anything is missing?"

"Yes. And no, nothing's gone. As far as I can tell, whoever broke in only searched the computer."

Perkins frowned. "Why do that?"

"Not sure." That was the first real lie and it didn't sit right with her. "That computer is basically veterinary business only. There are breeding plans and health checks on various animals and proud as I am of some of the results being achieved in that area, they are the farmers results more than mine and none of them are so special as to be worth stealing. Other than that, I get some personal emails through, do my business banking from there, but in truth there's not a lot worth finding."

"So, no idea why you'd be targeted?"

Again, she shook her head. Perkins' regard was steady and open. She got the distinct impression that he didn't entirely believe her, but had nothing to go on. There again, that could be her guilt talking.

"Right, Monday, and the crash at Satan's Turn."

"What about it?"

"Well, let's start with what time you got up there."

"Oh." She frowned. "I'm not certain actually, I didn't check my watch. Around quarter past five, maybe. The roads were really slow because of the build-up of snow and more flurries that day. I saw the accident, stopped my car. When I looked at the car in the river, there was no sign of the driver, nor any indication of he or she getting out. Did you at least find out who owns the car?"

He nodded. "A Mrs Margaret Whitney."

Branwen frowned. Did that mean the boy had stolen the car? She hadn't considered that before. "Meaning there's a potentially wounded woman out on the mountain somewhere."

"No, actually. Mrs Whitney is in Malta. We believe her son, James, also known as Jay, has taken the car." Perkins reached inside his jacket and pulled out a photo which he passed across.

Branwen took it and looked. A young, clean shaven blond with intelligence in his eyes. She kept looking, studying the photograph, taking in the fact that he looked surprisingly preppy. "He looks like a kid. How old? Eighteen? Nineteen?"

"Twenty-three."

She found it hard to credit that this was the same young man as was at Cobb's. Though the fact that he clearly had dyed his hair meant her own observation skills were working just fine. "I've seen no young blond men on the mountain."

"We believe he's changed his appearance."

Again, she frowned. "Yeah well, if he didn't, there's a good chance the accident did." She reached out to pass Perkins back the picture.

"What do you mean?"

"Well the windscreen was smashed in, and it's quite usual for faces to hit steering wheels. The kid might well have facial injuries."

"The airbag would have saved him."

"Only from hitting in the initial crash, after that they auto deflate and he could have been hurt in the fall into the river." She shrugged. "But I wasn't there, so that's just conjecture."

"What about Cobb?"

"What about him?"

"Could he have taken the driver in?"

How she managed to maintain eye contact with the inspector she wasn't sure. "If he had, I'd know."

"Because he was still there when you reached the turn?"

"Because I was at his cottage first thing Tuesday morning. To check on Finn."

"I was there yesterday. Who's Finn?"

"The dog. Big wolfhound. I'm fairly sure you would have seen him, he's kind of hard to miss, though it is possible to mistake him for a rug the way he hogs the hearth." She smiled, an expression Perkins mirrored as he nodded. "Finn's not moving much at the moment, still recovering from stepping on that mantrap. Have your lot checked on that yet?"

He nodded. "It was gone by the time we got there."

"Johnston probably warn–" She cut herself off.

"It's not a great idea to cast aspersions on a police officer without evidence."

Branwen shrugged. "Anyway, Finn got hurt and I visited Cobb's to check on him. But if you've been to Cobb's place, you're aware he's alone up there. Just the way he likes it."

"I didn't go into the bedroom or bathroom."

Her smile broadened. "No offence Inspector, but as I think you might suspect, I have much better access to Cobb's bedroom than you do."

"He doesn't like being alone that much, then?"

Branwen's cheeks burned. She could hardly correct the impression that she and Cobb were lovers now *and* keep the secret.

His good-natured smile shone. "Fair enough. Why not call the Mountain Rescue out that night to look for the driver though?"

She sighed. "In all honesty, I'm not really sure. I probably should have. It could be rationalised that I would have been putting more lives in danger looking for someone we hadn't any idea how to find, and we had no clue what direction the driver might have gone off in. But the truth is, I don't know why I didn't call. I did report the accident. I guess I just assumed if the police thought it was important enough, they'd call us out."

"Even with Johnston responding?"

She opened her mouth to answer, couldn't, tried again. "Didn't think of that. But it had been a tough day. I was tired. Guess I just didn't want to take any responsibility for anything." She shrugged, hung her head. "Great, now I've got guilt to add to the rest."

"I didn't come here to make you feel guilty, Miss Jones," Perkins said. "I'm just trying to get to the bottom of what happened to that driver."

She nodded but looked away. "If I could help more, I would."

For a moment in his silence, she hoped he would go away.

"Miss Jones, are you sure you're okay?"

She closed her eyes, tried to find that illusive calm. She thought about the call she'd made to Cobb. He'd sounded so certain when he'd told her everything was going to be okay, she wished she believed it. She huffed the air out of her lungs and looked up at the police officer. "Honestly, no. I'm a long way short of okay. I've already argued with my father, I'm going to have to piss off a good friend, and the buyer who expressed an interest in buying this practice messaged me that he's pulling out of the deal. I've just come from a farm where I had to euthanise a healthy sheep because her lamb was breach, tore her up inside and the farmer can't make enough money from the herd to pay for the animal to be treated and saved. I know it's a business decision and I don't have an issue with that, no matter how the vegetarians and vegans try brow-beating me, but that doesn't mean I enjoy doing it. So, coming down here and finding some rich git parked on my business space, and a policeman asking questions I can't answer, does nothing to make my day better." She took a breath at last. "Sorry, the last thing you need is to be ranted at."

"I've heard worse. Feel free to rant."

"Is that when people usually slip up and reveal the stuff they're trying to hide?"

He raised his brows quickly, with a part smile. "Usually."

"And what did I just tell you that I didn't mean to?"

"That you're more sensitive than you want people to realised and that you're selling the business. Does that mean you'll leave the village too?"

She nodded and slumped back in the chair. "Can I, now it's too late, ask that you keep that to yourself? Only Dad and Cobb know I'm selling."

"It doesn't impinge on my investigations." He shrugged. "No reason I should reveal it."

"Thank you. What's your next step?"

"If you were that driver, what would you do?"

"Well, probably follow the river downstream or the road downhill, but it sounds like the guy might not have been in his right mind. He might have wandered off in any direction."

"You think we might find him dead on the mountain in the spring?"

"I hope not, but it's possible. Injured and disorientated is a good way to get into trouble and die of hyperthermia on any mountain. Especially in the kind of weather we've been having."

She watched Perkins turn to the window and the slowly falling snow.

"And without shelter."

She murmured agreement. "Though there is a tiny chance that he made it to one of the natural caves that would provide shelter."

Now he looked at her closely. "There are caves up there?"

"Depends on your definition of cave I suppose. They aren't deep or obvious, but they do offer some shelter." She refocused on Perkins. "You not local then? You sound local."

"From Dolgellau. But I don't spend a lot of time on the mountains. Unless someone dies up there and luckily we have a pretty good local Mountain Rescue that tends to avoid that."

She inclined her head in thanks for the sideways compliment.

"Could he survive up there?"

She shrugged. "Possibly. Depends if he had any supplies with him, and how badly he was or wasn't injured."

"Do you think he'd still be up there?"

A sigh accompanied the shrug this time. "Again, it's possible, but getting less likely with every passing hour. We've had some bad weather, it wouldn't be a nice place to stay. But again, it all depends on what state he was in after the crash."

"Who else would know about the caves?"

"Anyone in the Mountain Rescue, most locals." She looked him up and down. "Maybe." She dwindled. "Possibly even those two idiots up at the farm."

"What two idiots?"

"Messers Baron and Shoreham. Turned up Tuesday morning. Shoreham's one of those arseholes who comes up here and thinks that just because I'm a country girl I must be stupid and easy."

"Want the local police to come up and warn him off?"

She laughed at that. "That would just aggravate him, make things worse." Mirth vanished. "Actually, there's something I should tell you, before you hear it from elsewhere. Shoreham was... well he was pushing his luck Wednesday morning, so I told him I had a syringe of pentobarbital and since he was the sickest puppy I'd ever met, I could put him down."

"Would that work on a human?"

Branwen nodded. "Of course it would, you only need about 60cc to kill the average human. I need about double that to put down a horse."

"Tell me you didn't have an actual syringe."

She shook her head. "At least not to his neck, I used the point of a pin badge. I do, however, carry sharps as a part of my kit, and I do carry pentobarbital, but it's not in at-the-ready syringes. Wanna look?" Her hand rose and indicated her bag. "Sharps are on the right, drugs on the left, instruments in the middle."

Perkins looked at the bag, but didn't open it up.

Chapter 57
Branwen – Pen-Y-Cwm Village

Branwen was ready to lock up when Granger barged into the surgery.

"The surgery is closed, Mr Granger, come back tomorrow." She tried to usher him out of the front door.

"This won't take long, Miss Jones. Just a minute of your time."

"Okay." Reluctantly she stood back, her arms crossed, offering him a sour get-on-with-it glare.

"Have you seen this?" Granger asked holding a carefully folded paper out to Branwen. She took it, unable to avoid the small article he directed her to.

She saw the name Sophie Whitney and the lady's picture inset against a picture of Jay Whitney who it boldly proclaimed was wanted for his aunt's murder. The kicker was that if he really had killed his aunt, she and Cobb were accessories after the fact.

"You're harbouring a murderer, Miss Jones."

Nothing to do now but brazen it out. "I'm not harbouring anyone, Mr Granger." Not technically a lie. "I'm also a little disheartened to find this inside the paper, but given that there's a photograph of Shan Sh'Kara on the front page to feed the mass appetite for celebrity news and sex over anything that actually matters, not entirely surprised. Now you said you're head of Nemesis Records and I'm pretty sure that Shan Sh'Kara is on your label, so tell me, Mr Granger, why aren't you getting behind your artist?"

The way his lips clamped and his piggy eyes hardened, he was taking that exactly how she meant it.

"Why, instead of dealing with a potentially damaging mess, are you here, in the back of beyond, asking about a man who, as far as I can tell, has no more connection to you than he does to me?"

His patently false laugh sent shivers down her spine. "Oh, nice game play Miss Jones, but really. I know you know where both Whitney and the files I want back are."

She shrugged and tried to act nonchalant. "Really? You live in a fantasy world Mr Granger."

He leaned closer. "I never gave you that name."

Ice washed through her veins as she realised her mistake.

"I never told you who I am or what I do. You have thus proved you know Whitney, and therefore the files."

She swallowed.

"Hey Branny, you there?"

Pete. She wasn't sure if that was good or bad news. Granger

looked to the back where the voice had come from, then hard nasty eyes pinned her again. "This isn't over, *Branny*."

***

"I want that bitch shut up."

Baron watched Granger pace in the tiny space of the gents at the back of the Pig and Whistle. Shan Sh'Kara hadn't yet reacted to the publication of that picture, not even on social media. Which was something of a surprise these days.

"I'll not have her ruin my reputation."

From what Baron had seen of the photograph, the pain the girl had been in suggested that Granger had ruined more than her reputation. Granger's use of a certain struck-off doctor meant Baron already knew what he'd done to the girl. It wasn't nice.

"There's not a lot I can do from here."

"Then don't be here." Granger handed over an address and an envelope full of money. Baron glanced at it.

"Payment up front."

***

Pete walked into the Branwen's surgery as she stood in the middle of the waiting area, staring at the front door as it banged shut. He moved over and flipped the latch to lock the front door, pushed the deadbolts into place. Then turned, saw Branwen's face, the tears running down.

"Oh Branny." He came to her, pulled her into a hug. For a moment she resisted, before leaning into him, her hands resting lightly at his waist. "I heard what happened yesterday. You should be resting, Branny."

"Sorry," she sniffed.

He held her closer. "Don't be. Since Cobb got here I'd begun to despair of you ever noticing me again." He kissed the top of her head and she flinched.

"Branny?"

"Sorry."

"What for?"

How to answer?

"Let's go to mine and you can tell me all about it."

Since 'his' was a bungalow at the back of the plot the surgeries were built on, there wasn't far to go. Now she stood away from him, moving like an automaton to switch off lights, lock everything up, grab her handbag.

At the back door, he locked up and set all the alarms. He put his arm around her and she leaned into him. Even when they had dated during his last year at Cambridge and her first, she hadn't been keen on being held in public, but right now she needed

180

someone. All that had happened had upset her more than she wanted to admit, and her father's slap had been the last straw. She needed someone to take care of her and Pete always had. The world might be ignorant of the facts, but he'd always been here for her.

Thankfully the heating had clicked on, so they stepped into a warm house. The door opened directly into the living space, and Pete steered her towards the sofa then locked the door behind them. The curtains were already closed, he must have closed them when he dropped his bags in earlier. Branwen didn't sit down but stood numbly in the middle of the room. He moved over and picked the bag strap off her shoulder, moving it away from them to a chair.

"Iesu Grist! Branny, what have you done."

She glanced at him. He was staring at her head. Her hand came up and even the light touch hurt. "Bugger, is it bleeding again?"

"Seeping. Sit down."

This time she obeyed, sitting on the edge of the sofa as he rushed to get the first aid kit from the kitchen. He sat beside her and twisted her that he might clean the wound. "What happened?"

"I smacked it up at Cwm Dee, it must have opened up again." She picked up her phone and sent a text, as he did his job.

"I meant, how did you get it in the first place? Who treated you? They should have put stitches in this." She didn't reply. "Branny?"

"You're the first doctor to see it."

"Jesus Branny, you should have gone to the hospital, had it looked at properly. You should have been x-rayed." He stood, but she grabbed his hand before he could go far.

"It's fine, Pete. I've no headache, no concussion, it's just a small split to the skin that's bled bad, as head injuries tend to."

She looked up at him, pleading with her eyes as the words proved elusive. She needed him like she'd never needed him before.

"You need a stitch in that."

She smiled, small, uncertain. "You can do that here can't you?"

"Of course I can." He squeezed her fingers before moving to get his bag. Needles and stitches were beyond the usual first aid kit, but he carried more.

"Barely a flinch," he said as he finished. "You've always been a tough little thing." He cleared his stuff away and sat back beside her. Without a word, she leaned in, her head on his shoulder, her hand on his stomach, his arm snaked around her as she kicked off her trainers and put her feet up on the sofa. She'd missed this closeness to another human. She wanted this with Cobb, but he'd been clear that he had no interest in her.

"You going to tell me what happened?"

"I was in the surgery, pain flashed across the back of my head, next thing I know Emma's there telling me the police are on their way. Nothing stolen. I checked your floor too. Looks like they wanted something from me, but were disturbed before they got anything."

"Do you know what they were after?"

"Yep."

A pause.

"And?"

"I don't have it. Actually, I never had it. I just know about it."

"And what is 'it'?"

"Can't tell you."

"Why not?"

"Someone might come after you."

She didn't want that. She wouldn't put him in the firing line.

"You are staying tonight, aren't you?"

She remembered her promise to Cobb, but after what had happened with Granger, visiting him wasn't a good idea. It would establish the connection, and that was a risk too far.

"I should go home. Smooth things over with Dad."

Pete frowned. "What happened with your dad?"

She told him. She told him why.

"So, you're leaving?" he asked when she fell quiet.

"Yeah."

He squeezed her. "Why did you agree to date me then?"

There was no immediate answer. "Because I've missed this. Because you're the first man to ask for a long time. Because I thought for once, it would be nice if someone saw me as something more than a vet or a target. Why did you ask? We stopped being involved years ago."

"Because I've missed this. You're the only woman I've wanted to ask out in a long time. And I thought it would be nice if you saw me as a friend rather than a professional."

"We've never not been friends."

"I want that to continue. Even if you leave."

"It will." The certainty rang in her voice. "I don't ever want to lose your friendship."

"You won't." He kissed the top of her head again, smelt the disinfectant. "You will stay tonight though, won't you?" They were both aware the bungalow only had one bedroom.

"I don't have any spare clothes with me."

"Stick the ones you're wearing in the washer drier."

Her laugh rumbled through him. "Are you trying to get me to strip for you Doctor Pearson?"

"Well, you've done it before."

A few times and he'd enjoyed every time. As had she.

She turned to him and he took advantage of the new position to press a welcome kiss on her lips. Welcomed and deepened. He pulled her to him, shifting under. He was hard and ready; they were panting as the kiss grew deeper and hungrier. This was some kind of goodbye sex, but she didn't care. Right now, she needed and he wanted. That was enough. His hands moved over her, touching her breasts, cupping and caressing, find her nipple and squeezing gently. She gasped, breaking the kiss and pushing herself up over him.

Her legs shifted until she sat astride him. She felt the heat and length of his erection beneath her. She rocked, and he strained up.

"Is that what you want, Pete?"

"Oh God yes, Branwen," he gasped. Now his hands on her hips pulled her down as he rocked beneath her. "I want you so much!"

She leaned down and kissed him again. Their hands moving, he had to sit up as they started pulling clothes from each other. It took a while to realise that the ringing in her head was actually in her ears. His phone. His mouth was full of hers. His hand caressed her naked back. Only her bra separated their chests. If not for two inconvenient pairs of trousers he'd be rock hard inside her. The ringing changed. His mobile now.

That insistent call was the emergency tone.

She broke the kiss. "You have to answer that." But her lips on his shoulder worked that flesh. They both gasped for air. She didn't want the real-world intruding, but she understood his job. He swung his legs off the sofa, keeping her on his lap. He felt delicious beneath her. He leaned to the side, stretching to reach his phone.

"Christ Branwen, you're gonna make me cum before I'm even inside you at this rate."

She moaned and ground herself harder against him. "I'm close too."

"What?" He snapped into the phone. Concentration on his conversation was impossible over her pulse thumping in her ears. "Can't you call Adams?" Apparently not. "Oh. Shit. Okay." He snapped the phone off and slumped back against the sofa. She didn't want this to end, but it had to. Branwen stilled and looked down at him.

"You've got to go?"

He nodded. She leaned down and pressed a hard, hungry kiss on him, then moved away, bereft in the cold.

Chapter 58
Simons – Home Counties

Simons dialled Cobb from his office phone. A recorded voice informed him that the number was not available and advised him to try again later.

Since Cobb had warned him of this possibility, Simons checked the profile he had on Branwen Jones and dialled her surgery number. The phone rang on and on. Simons checked his watch. At 6:15 he guessed he might have missed surgery hours. Putting the phone down, he turned back to contemplating the case in hand. He needed to identify Baron's partner.

Chapter 59
Branwen – Pen-Y-Cwm Village

Frustrated didn't even begin to cover Branwen's condition. For years she'd been happily celibate, well, happily was stretching it since Cobb had arrived, but she'd done without sex since university. Then Shoreham had come up and got all caveman, something she'd never been that impressed by, and awoken a monster inside her. As for Pete tonight – oh Lord, she suddenly realised Peter Pearson was the last lover she'd had. Pete was clearly as frustrated at their failure to consummate as she. He'd even given her his spare key to use, to be there when he got back. She hadn't said anything because she hadn't known what to say, but even as he'd kissed her goodbye, she'd known she wouldn't stay. Guilt assailed her, she had come so close to using him. Pete deserved better. He probably wouldn't have complained, but he still deserved better.

She should head home, but she wasn't ready to face her father. Or Shoreham. She had a terrible fear that she might well jump the bones of an abusive stranger she felt so needy. She could drop in on Cobb. Only she wouldn't. He was another man she might leap on and with Jay around the option was void anyway.

As fearful as she was of going back into the surgeries on her own, she made herself do it. Inside, behind a firmly locked door, she texted Cobb. Then realised that with the mast down there wasn't much hope he'd actually get the message.

Stupid, stupid, stupid.

***

Cobb looked at his watch again. 18:37. Why hadn't Branwen come? She'd promised him. He checked his phone. Nothing, no signal of any kind. He swore, ran his hand through his hair.

"What's wrong?"

He turned to Jay. "Branwen. She should be here by now. And she sounded in a bad way when we spoke earlier."

"Still no signal?"

Cobb looked again at his phone in vaguest of hope that something had changed. "No."

"You going to go into the village?"

"Sorry, kid. I've got to."

He grabbed up his coat and whistled for Finn. If he went down without the dog again, people would notice. In town he saw Branwen's car in front of the surgeries. He pulled into the car park of the Pig and Whistle. As he pulled the handbrake his mobile beeped to tell him a message has arrived. From Branwen. He opened it.

Granger here. He knows. Can't visit. Can't lead him to you.
That explained it.
He was here now, he might as well check out what was going on.

***

One option left.

The pub.

The temptation to dive into a vat of wine was great. Drinking her problems away, while tempting, wasn't practical though.

Gathering up some of the articles she needed to read, Branwen headed to the Pig and Whistle. Emma greeted her, beckoned her over, but with Ivan at Emma's side, Branwen didn't find it terribly inviting. She smiled and pointed to the reading material. Emma would have to understand.

Pint of cola in hand she picked an empty table and sat down to start reading. Leaning against the bench back, she put her feet up on a stool and forced herself to concentrate on the articles. Anything to take the heat out of her demanding crotch.

Most people preferred to stay home in this weather, leaving the pub quiet, though with the log fire roaring on the far side of the room, Branwen had enough heat for a while. She was comfortable where she was, especially when served the house special burger. The beef in the burger and the bacon topping it were from local farms; she was convinced more organic, less antibiotic breeding and rearing programs paid off in taste.

Lost in the article on the role of badgers in the spread of bovine tuberculosis, she jumped to have a heavy grey head suddenly appear on her thigh. Finn looked up at her, all sad eyed. Glad to be sitting, she looked up at Cobb standing by her feet. Oh God, exactly who she didn't want to see, not with Granger possibly about. Without a word he leaned down and placed a full pint of cola on the table at her elbow. Only now did she see that she'd virtually finished the first. He raised his own glass to her and moved across to sit close to the fire, calling Finn to his feet with a click of his fingers.

He must have got her text. She looked around, recognising every patron. Even the ones who didn't like her or she didn't like. Safe. She was safe here. Mind, she'd thought she was safe in the surgeries and that hadn't turned out great.

Dewi came and cleared away her plate and empty glass; Branwen concentrated again on the magazine. Only she couldn't read it because she was too aware of Cobb being in the room. He shouldn't be here. Heat shouldn't be building inside her just because he was here, not after what she'd nearly done with Pete. He should be in his cottage taking care of Jay. Why wasn't he on the mountain? Why did he have to be here, upsetting her equilibrium?

186

"Hello again."

She looked up to see Granger place his fat arse on a stool at the other side of the table. He put his pint on her magazine. She saw a wet ring soaking in. "Fuck off."

She moved his pint off her magazine, deliberately flicked the liquid he'd spilt over him.

He grabbed her wrist and she saw Cobb tense across the way.

"Let go, or I'll scream," she grated under her breath.

"Give me Jay and the files, or else," he sneered back.

Her lip curled, but she didn't try to pull from his tightening grip. His sweaty palm disgusted her, but he had more reason to worry than she did. "Or else what?"

"Or," he whispered, "I'll tell this entire town all about your dirty little secret."

She didn't dare to look anywhere but straight at those piggy eyes. Whatever he thought he had on her, only one thing scared her. McManus. Emma already knew, and it was past time the rest of them did. Besides, she was selling the business, she was leaving, it would only cost her a few weeks of shame. And she was sick of men thinking they could boss her around.

"Go on then." It was reckless and stupid, and the words were out before she had a chance to rethink it.

Confusion marred his features, weakened his grip; she pulled her arm away.

"Go on," she said. "Tell them." He didn't move.

"Hey Dewi!" she shouted across the bar. "Turn the music off will you!"

Everyone turned to them. Absolutely everyone. Branwen stood up. If she was going to make a production of this, best go all out. "Thank you everyone for stopping and taking note, this man here has an announcement he'd like to make."

They all turned to Granger as he sat with his ramrod-straight back to the room. He looked up at her with hate-filled eyes. "What do you think you're playing at?"

"Oh, no need to whisper there, Mr Granger. Everyone, we're all supposed to be mightily impressed by Mr Granger's credentials as the head of Nemesis Records. Nemesis Records – I'm sure you've heard of them. They're the record label that signed Shan Sh'Kara, she of the photo that covered the front of this morning's papers. I'm sure you all saw that."

A murmur of agreement, and from some, disgust, across the room. She even heard a slap. Apparently someone wasn't in their wife's good books because of that photo. Granger stood up, the stool scraping back behind him. He looked down at her, but she wasn't intimidated. She was already over the edge.

"Well Mr Granger, you have the floor, you have their attention. Time for your big announcement."

Someone laughed. "Hey Jones, you can't have a recording gig – I've heard you sing!"

"True, cats screech more melodically when I castrate them," Branwen laughed along with Ivan. "Come on Mr Granger. What's wrong? Cat got your tongue?"

The pause hung heavily in the air. Now she glared up at the music man. "You come in here, threaten me with an 'or else', you damn well better be ready, Granger, because I'm not that much of a walk over."

When he still didn't speak, someone piped up. "What's he got to say, Branwen?"

Branwen turned to the old man at the bar. "Not actually sure, Dafydd. It was an ultimatum, so either it's the one thing I've never mentioned to anyone here or it's complete bollocks." She turned back to Granger. "Well then, we're all waiting."

Granger went from grinding his teeth to booming out the statement: "Branwen Jones is a murderer."

Three people started laughing. Branwen looked around, not sure how to take that, but she found herself grinning along with them. Neither Emma nor Cobb were laughing.

"She is!" Granger blustered, which only made one person laugh louder. "She killed James McManus."

"No, she didn't." Of all the men she expected to defend her that night, PC Johnston wasn't one. She tried not to notice Inspector Perkins sitting behind him.

"And he preferred to be called Jim not James." She was too shocked by the accuracy of the announcement to pinpoint who said that.

"We know all about that," Dewi said from behind the bar. "She was arrested but the charges were dropped."

"Would have been self-defence at worst, anyway," Irene Calver from the corner shop added.

Branwen looked around the pub. There were mutters and nods of agreement all around. This made no sense. "Wait, are you lot telling me you've known all along?"

"Of course we have, my lovely," Mrs Davis, the primary teacher who had taught Branwen, said.

"Reporters came up here trying to get the scoop on you when it happened," Paul added.

"We sent them packing soon as," Ivan assured her.

"Not having some outsider come here and tell us what to think about one of our own," Dafydd added.

Branwen could only stare at him. It didn't compute. "You and I argue. Pretty constantly. But in all these years you've never thrown that in my face? Why the hell not?"

Dafydd shrugged. "You're my second cousin several times removed. You're family, girl. And you're innocent. Of that, anyway."

Open mouthed she found herself without a thing to say. Her whole world had shifted. "Does Dad know?"

"Of course," Mr Davis at his wife's side stated. "He's the one who asked us all never to mention it to you."

"Wow." Branwen swayed and sat down heavily. "Just... I... Wow." After a moment, she looked up at Granger and all that uncertainty resolved into a cold hard disgust. She stood up again, faced the man. "Well, there you go, Mr Granger. Apparently as long as I keep their pets and livestock healthy, they're not that bothered that I might have caused a man's death. Which I didn't. So, it really wasn't as much of a threat as either of us thought."

"You're not the only one I have dirt on."

A gasp came from behind him. She turned. "Em, if they know about me, they know about you."

"And what about Mr Cobb sitting over there so innocently?"

She looked at Cobb, unable to judge what his lack of reaction denoted. What would he think of her now he knew about McManus, about her part in the man's death? "What about him?" she asked and swung back to Granger. "What makes you think anything you say about Cobb is going to make the slightest difference to the fact that he's a part of this community too?"

Granger faltered.

"Okay!" Branwen turned back to the gathered villagers. "Is there anyone here that hasn't already realised that Cobb's skill set is very military based?" No one disagreed. "Is there anyone here who hasn't figured out that at some point in he probably had some kind of black ops involvement? He's killed men, probably women, possibly children too." He stared at her, wide-eyed. If he'd been a cat the fur along his spine would be sticking up and she'd be afraid of getting her eyes clawed out. "Michael, does that make you think any less of him or his ability to contribute to the Mountain Rescue?"

"Certainly not," Michael assured them both.

"Mrs Davies, does it change your mind about letting him work with the kids at the school?"

"Of course not, I've got all his CRB checks on record." Mrs Davies, still the primary head teacher, stated.

"As have I." Branwen turned to face Granger. "You see, Emma

189

may sell him a house without checking out his past, but I can't employ him without doing those checks, so it's not like he's anything to hide either."

"The locals might agree with you, but what about the customers of your guesthouse?"

Branwen actually laughed. "Are you fucking kidding me? You go tell the world that I've got a real-life Bear Grylls working for me and I'll have occupancy through the roof! It would be the absolute level best unpaid advertising I could possibly get. The kind of clients I get wanting outdoor survival courses would lap that up, they'd be beating a path to my door and I'd be suing you just to keep the story in the papers longer because part of it would be true and any salacious crap you threw in would be enough to get me additional revenue. So please, please go to the papers with that story."

"What about his wife?"

The gasp held the room.

"Don't you dare," Branwen snarled. "Cobb's a widower and if you say one more word about him, or me, or anyone in this village, I will tear down and destroy everything you've built, and I will shame you before the whole damn world. What I'll do to you will make the whole #MeToo movement look like a school yard scrap."

Granger stared at her. Did he sense the soul-deep hatred she had for him, the disgust, the loathing? The swallow said he did. He stepped towards the door, tripped over the stool he'd upended and left in the most undignified manner to peels of laughter.

Branwen eased back her shoulders, took a deep breath, let go of the darkness and came back to herself. "And that ends tonight's entertainment. Dewi, put the music back on."

Shaking, she returned to her seat, to the articles she wouldn't now read. She looked over at Cobb; he looked back. What did it mean? Music played again. The Pretenders. *I'll Stand By You.*

Chapter 60
Branwen and Cobb – Pen-Y-Cwm Village

Cobb left before Chrissie Hynde got to her darkest hour.

He won't stand by me then.

Reading ceased to be an option, she was in revelation overload. Perkins didn't take long to walk over to sit with her.

"Hello."

"Hi." Not riveting conversation, but about all she could manage.

"You okay?"

Was she? She'd been accused of all sorts. She'd been sexually assaulted and said nothing. She'd argued with her father. She'd had to see images that revolted her. She'd been thwarted for sex. She'd faced down an ultimatum. Her best friend, who should really be the one coming over here to support her, hadn't. And the man she most wanted to have sex with had just walked out. She wasn't okay, she was utterly shit.

"I'm fine."

Perkins smiled. "Liar."

She nodded. "Sorry. What else am I supposed to say?"

"Finding out what you believed to be a well-guarded secret is in fact, common knowledge, must be a shock."

She nodded. "You can say that again."

"Want a stiffer drink?"

She really, really did. "Can't, I've still got to drive home. I've been wearing these clothes for two days already."

"What was the original request?"

Numb she frowned at him.

"The alternative to the or-else we all saw. What did Granger want?"

Words proved elusive. Johnston couldn't be trusted, could Perkins?

"Branwen?"

"He wanted what I couldn't give him, because I don't have it. Like you, he wants Jay Whitney and the stolen files."

"If you had met the injured driver after that accident, what would you have done?"

She looked away and shrugged. "Something spur of the moment I suspect."

"Would you have treated his injuries?"

Now she looked at Perkins. Was this a trap? "I'm a vet, not a doctor. I am, however, also a trained first responder. I could give a human first aid and use a defibrillator, but I'm on thin ice for anything much else."

His look was considering. "Want to do something to help a copper?"

Watching his features she tried to figure out his game. "What do you want me to do?"

"Lean forward and make it look like we're conspiring."

Frowning, she leaned forward, whispering, "We are conspiring. Why?"

Perkins too whispered. "Because I want this tete-a-tete to be witnessed."

"Going to tell me why?"

"Not yet. Put you hand in your pocket, pull it out as a fist and put it on the table."

Not at all certain why she was doing this, she followed his instruction. He smiled and placed his hand over hers. She forced herself to stay still for a count of five before she carefully pulled her hand out from under his. He nodded, smiled and stood up, his hand dipping into his pocket as he moved away.

Branwen looked after the inspector, worried about what he was setting up. More worried about the way Johnston frowned.

"Interesting conversation?" she heard Johnston ask as Perkins stopped at the bar with him.

Perkins said something, patted his pocket.

Johnston smiled, but it was more a grimace. "What are you going to do with it?"

What indeed?

"I have to drop into the office, lock it in my drawer for tonight. It's too late to do anything else with it now."

***

"That was, ermm…"

Branwen looked up at Emma. Neither seemed able to keep eye contact. "Better it's in the open."

"Exactly," Ivan said at Emma's side. "No more secrets."

Except Branwen was still keeping so many. "I'm selling the veterinary practice and leaving the area." The words tumbled out in a rush.

"What?" Emma sank to the stool. "You can't. You can't leave. You love this place."

The lump threatened to constrict her throat. "I do love Pen-Y-Cwm." And knowing that tore at her heart. "But I can't stay here. There's too much else I need to do. I want to live some more."

"You can't leave," Emma declared. "You can't do that to me."

Finally, Branwen looked her in the eye. "And you can't keep doing this to me. I've carried the guilt of what happened with McManus more heavily than if I had been convicted. We were best

192

friends right up until that point. Then the guilt settled in. I brought you here so we could hide. I took care of you when you needed me. I gave you everything I could because I love you *and* I felt guilty. I gave you the setup costs for the estate agency when every financial adviser told me it was throwing money down the drain. But you've made it work and I'm so pleased for you that you did. You needed that success, you deserve that success. But every day here that guilt renews because every day here I see you, and I can't get free of it. What I forgot when I came here was that this is the digital age, news travels fast. Turns out everybody knows about what I did and I could have let go of this burden of guilt years ago, but you've never let me. You don't need me Emma, you're a success in your own right, a businesswoman, you're free, there's no need to hide any more. You have Ivan, he'll keep you safe and warm and loved for the rest of your life. Now I have to go find my freedom."

"But what about Cobb?"

Branwen laughed, but even she heard the tears that burned behind her eyes. "He just walked out." She had defended him and he had left. It said everything about their relationship.

"What about Doc, then? Didn't you and he —"

"Emma!" It was the sharpest tone Ivan had ever had to use on his fiancée, and it surprised all of them. "Branwen, you do whatever you have to. You know we'll all be here for you when you're ready to come home."

The dam broke and tears flowed, and all Branwen could do was run.

***

Cobb had never felt more wretched. He'd watched a monster attack a good friend and done nothing. That Branwen had fought for him like a Valkyrie was a source of simultaneous pride and shame. Proud of her actions, ashamed of his inaction. There was nothing he could have done better. She had had to be the one to stand up and risk everything. Apparently, he was the only one in the village who didn't know about McManus. He still didn't know about McManus, only that Branwen may have killed in self-defence. She'd certainly looked like she wanted to kill Granger for a moment there, capable of it too.

He'd also had no idea that she'd run any kind of background check on him. It made sense, but he'd never thought about it, never had any indication that she'd needed to. And she knew he was a widower.

"She knows about Mary."

Finn whined at the name, a heavy head thumped onto Cobb's shoulder.

193

"Is that why she's never let me in?" Cobb asked. "Does she think I'm not ready?"

Did he think he was? Ready or not, there was a job to do. Branwen had battled Granger, but Granger wasn't the only enemy. The Goon Brothers were still around, and he had to make sure Jay stayed safe.

Sighing he reversed the Defender from the space and slowly moved down the side of the pub. He had to break hard not to hit the figure that came rushing out. He looked across the square blue bonnet and saw the startled gaze of Branwen. She was crying.

He leaned across and popped open the passenger door. "Get in!"

She hesitated, before climbing into the car. Finn was closer and she hugged the dog as she shut the door. Without a word, Cobb pulled forward, switching on the wipers once he'd cleared the edge of the building to clear the screen of yet more snow. He'd never known a winter like it.

"Stop the car."

He did, and pushed Finn out of the way so he could see Branwen. The big dog resisted. "Sit down, Finn." The wolfhound had other ideas.

"Finn, sit."

Of course, Finn sat when Branwen told him to.

"Branwen, we need to talk."

"Yes, we do." She wiped her eyes. "And we will. At your place. Tonight. But I'm going to need my car." She popped the door open a crack. "I'll follow you up."

"Bra-"

She cut off his objection with a hard, swift kiss on the lips. "I will follow you up."

The pain where she'd crushed his lips against his teeth only registered after she was gone. A pain worth having.

Chapter 61
Baron – Pen-Y-Cwm Village

The Pig and Whistle was quiet when Baron arrived. Dewi greeted him with surprise.

"Late in the day to be coming to town for a drink."

"You got a room for the night?" It had seemed that Branwen wasn't going to go home for another night, and he'd come into the village to snoop.

"Sure." The barman smiled. "But you've missed the entertainment."

Baron frowned up at Dewi, then glanced at the chalkboard. "Karaoke isn't my thing."

"And changing the board isn't mine. You out for a night on the razz, is it?" he asked as he eased the head off the requested bitter, topped it up and placed it on the bar towel before Baron.

"More a case of leaving the Joneses to battle it out in peace," Baron grumbled as he paid. "He's a curmudgeon of the worst order, then she walks in and they're at it like prize fighters. It's a wonder they get any guests at all if that's the way they always treat each other."

"It's not."

Baron noted the darker tone in the other man's voice. He could easily put the burly barman down, more fat than muscle these days, but what was the point? "Cheers." Taking the change Dewi had left in a puddle of beer, Baron asked for the room number and was passed a key.

"What's happened to your mate?" Dewi asked.

Shoreham was off on the added excursion Granger had given them. "Decided on a late night stroll, for the peace. He'll be along shortly." Baron didn't like the way Dewi watched him. Like the barman didn't believe him. "So, where's room 6?"

***

The little shite stood peeing when Baron went into the gents. He stepped up to the urinal to do what nature intended, standing right next to Johnston. A glance told him what he already suspected, his own was bigger. He saw Johnston looking too. Other men often found his flaccid length and girth intimidating.

"Well?"

Johnston jerked and pissed on his own shoes. Getting a grip of himself and his cock, Johnston shook it off, putting himself away. "That idiot Perkins has a pen drive." He zipped up. "He has the files. I'll get them."

"Where is it?"

"He's taking it to the station. I'm going after him in a minute. I'll get the files, you'll get them tomorrow. You just get me the money you promised."

Baron took a wad of twenties from his pocket, peeled off five, offered them to the officer, but before Johnston could take them, he flicked them into the urinal channel and walked out.

Chapter 62
Branwen and Cobb – Pen-Y-Cwm, Cobb's Home

Branwen parked beside Cobb's Discovery as he called Finn down from the cab. They didn't speak as they headed into the cottage. Unusually Cobb had to use his key to open the door and when he did he pulled up to his full height and stopped. Branwen looked around him to see Jay ready with a frying pan to hit an intruder. "You a fan of *Tangled*?"

Both men looked at her like she'd lost her mind. "Well, I like it." As an embarrassed Jay returned the pan to the kitchen Branwen pulled Finn inside while Cobb secured the door.

"Your ribs playing up?" Branwen asked of Jay, watching him cradle his torso as he moved.

"They're sore yes. Leaves me short of breath."

"Come here and lift your arms up." Branwen was all business now as she removed her jacket and hooked it over the back of the nearest chair. She frowned as she carefully tested the boy's ribs.

The sudden intake of breath told her when she found the wound.

"Right, one to ten, give me a level of pain here."

"Ah! Seven."

"Hmm. Keep your arms up."

"It hurts."

"I'm not surprised." Branwen said pulling his t-shirt and jumper up. "I thought you'd just bruised them." Given the colour, he'd certainly done that. "Now I think one might be broken. You can put your arms down now." She turned to Cobb. "I'm going to have to strap these ribs. Do you have any bandages in the house or do I need to go back out to the car?"

"I got some." He moved to the bathroom.

The urge to rush nagged at Branwen, but she needed to do the job properly. Thankfully Cobb understood and waited patiently until Jay's ribs were strapped and his tops returned.

"Thanks."

"You're welcome. Now go to bed."

"I'm not tired." He sounded like a whiny kid, but at twenty-three he was old enough to face the stark truth.

"I don't care. I need to talk to Cobb and the conversation has nothing to do with you. Make yourself scarce." Only once the bedroom door closed fully did Branwen turn to Cobb.

He stood against the kitchen cabinets, watching her, his expression unreadable.

"You said you wanted to talk. Where do you want to start?"

"Full disclosure."

She nodded. "Fair enough. Right. I had to look into your past before I could offer you a job. I started with an internet search, which wasn't that easy without your first name. I found Captain E Cobb on several honours rolls for military action, but couldn't get much detail, then I saw your name connected to CSC Securities. There's still a tiny photograph of you which pixelated when I tried to enlarge, but I was pretty sure it was you so I phoned them up. I spoke to someone called Simons. Given his tone and manner, I'm assuming he was ex-military too?"

He nodded. "My old CO."

"He told me very little, but enough for me to read what he wasn't saying. He also told me that he was glad to hear you might be getting involved with the world again, but that I should respect your need for solitude and peace, that it would take you a long time to get over the loss of your wife."

Those eyes stayed on her. "So you've known all along that I'm a widower?"

"A month or so after I met you."

"Why didn't you ever say anything?"

That wasn't entirely clear to her, even now. "Not saying stuff seems to be the way I operate. You never said anything either."

"It hurt too much. I didn't want your sympathy."

She huffed at that. "You had it all the same. I just tried not to show it."

"You never told anyone else?"

"No."

"Not even Emma?"

"No."

He frowned at her. "Why not?"

"It's none of her business. I figured if you wanted people to know, you'd tell them. But you didn't, so I couldn't."

His eye contact dropped away. She felt adrift without that anchor.

"I need some answers too," he said.

"Okay."

He turned back to her. "Do you trust me?"

She frowned at the question. "Would I be here if I didn't? Of course I trust you, Cobb. I always have."

"Why?"

She thought about it. "I don't know. I just do. Even before I found out about your past, I just did. Instinct."

"Even though you think I've killed women and children?"

She swallowed, uncomfortable that she had flung the implicit accusations earlier. "Yes."

He huffed a wry laugh. "Why?"

She shook her head. "Because I believe, whatever you did, you did it for the right reasons and I don't expect you took any pleasure in it. I bundle it all up in a box I don't particularly want to take the lid off and call it 'Acts of Duty'. I don't care about the details of what you did before you came to Pen-Y-Cwm. I think that you have this – " She searched for the right words " – air about you. I guessed you had some involvement with law enforcement the first time I saw you. Your past confirmed it. Sometimes I'm just not sure what side of the law I thought you thought you were on."

He fell silent, frowning slightly as he considered her. "Sometimes," he said softly, "I wasn't sure what side I was on. But I did my duty. Except by Mary."

"What happened to her?"

"I'm not ready to talk about it yet."

"So, the full disclosure only works one way?"

"Tell me what everyone else already knows."

She'd known this was coming, but it was difficult nonetheless. How does one say this sort of thing? Quickly. Rip off the plaster, even as the memory choked her. "I killed him."

"That isn't what the village thinks."

Clearly it was too much to hope for that he'd let slide the things she wasn't ready to talk about.

"What's Emma McGuiness's involvement with the matter?"

Branwen closed her eyes. It didn't help. It never helped. McManus was always there. If she wanted Cobb to be honest with her, she had to be honest with him.

"Emma and I shared digs in uni. That's how we met. She was dating Jim McManus. Jim was a passionate man, he cared about everything. You know the type – member of CND, Greenpeace, Amnesty International, the lot. Well, Jim was really into animal rights, an avid anti-vivisectionist. When he found out what course I was on he assumed that I would support him all the way. He didn't like it when I didn't. It's not that I agree with vivisection entirely, because I don't. Some of the things that are done are just plain evil. But I still think it's better to test animals than try un-tested products on humans, though modern tests are starting to override that view somewhat. Anyway, to get off the soapbox and back to the point, at the time, Jim decided I wasn't worth talking to. Which made life kinda difficult since he spent so much time in our house with Emma. In our final year, I worked at one of the nearby bio-labs. The place was attached to the university and some research was done there, but mostly it was just a breeding ground. Mice, rats, frogs. For school dissection classes mostly, but other stuff bred for experiments too. When Jim got wind of where I worked, he went ballistic. Not just with me, but with Emma too. Things at home were awful for ages. Then near the end of spring term in our final year, Jim announced he was off for the evening, so Emma and I decided we'd have a girls' night out to work on our friendship. So, because I was working that night, she came with me. Since that was against company policy, I smuggled her in through a door where I knew the security camera wasn't working. Just before I was due to knock off at nine, a brick came in through the window, quickly followed by three people. They started smashing things up, so Em and I tried to stop them. One grabbed one of the pipes we'd set up for the mice to run around in, and came at me. The first time he swung I didn't duck quick enough and he hit my shoulder, pushing me back across the room. That was when Emma hit him with the microscope across the back of the head. It dazed him for a second, but his mates grabbed her, and he came back at me. This time when he lunged, I ducked at the last second, grabbed his jumper, threw him over my shoulder. The wall that side was all glass window and it didn't break his fall. So, when he went through I nearly plummeted through with him."

"Plummeted?"

"The lab was built on one of the rare hills outside of Cambridge, by an embankment for the motorway. Anyway, ground floor on the outside was second floor on the inside." She took another gulp of air. "I tried to keep hold of him, but I didn't have the strength."

"So the fall killed him."

She made no reply. "By that time the police sirens were approaching. The other two intruders had scarpered, and Emma was standing there, stunned. I only realised who I'd thrown then because he called me by name. I wasn't sure if Em knew, so I told her to get out. I picked up the scope she had used, and told the police I'd been alone. Luckily for me the external cameras gave video evidence of only two departing figures and of me trying to pull McManus back."

"So why did Emma get so worked up?"

"Because the police aren't quite so stupid as we sometimes like to make out." She paused. "They found one of the other intruders, and he told them I wasn't alone that night. Besides, it was hard to keep the description of the attack straight in my head without Emma being in the room. Three against one as fights go, are tricky, and I had to say I was the one who hit Jim. They thought I was lying, then when they dragged Emma in and questioned her, she said that I hit Jim, then she said that she hit Jim, and it all got nasty for a while. But basically, they weren't sure which one of us actually hit Jim. Which was where the problem came from. The fall didn't kill Jim. The crack on his head did. In the end it came down to personalities. They looked at Emma, and then they looked at me and they just figured that I was the one more likely to have hit him that hard. So, I had to cop it."

He frowned. "You had to?"

She shrugged. "Yeah. I'd always maintained my guilt over Emma's. She'd never survive in jail. She barely survived five minutes of police interrogation. Luckily the police and the court viewed it as self-defence and accidental, case dismissed. I literally got away with murder."

"But you didn't kill him," Cobb pointed out. "Emma did."

"But I threw him out the window, so it still feels like I killed him. Besides, Emma's had to live with the loss every day. Don't forget she was in love with the guy. She feels it more keenly than if she'd been charged and found guilty. She can't accept that it was an accident or self-defence. That's why she was terrified of Ivan finding out. She's so convinced of her own guilt, she can't get past it, so she can't conceive of anyone else seeing past it. Though that may have changed tonight."

"You protected her."

She couldn't face him. He must think the worst of her now.

"And you put your own neck on the line to do it. Emma on the other hand set you both up for a fall."

"Maybe, but Ivan has softened that landing somewhat."

"You've spent this week protecting Jay."

She shrugged. "Mostly covering my own back in ca–"

"No, don't do that. Don't try to shrug it off." He moved to stand in front of her. "You went above and beyond for that boy." He pushed his finger up under her chin, forcing her to look at him. "And tonight, you did the same for me." His head bent towards her and she wanted to lean up and kiss him. "Why?"

"Because I could. Because I should. Because I wanted to. Because you're a part of Pen-Y-Cwm too. And no one attacks my family or my home without getting a slap back."

His smile was slow and honeyed. "I'm part of your family?"

It was impossible not to smile back. The fact that he was moving closer just made her smile more. He was going to kiss her, and if he didn't she was going to kiss him. *Just like you kissed Pete?*

She pulled away.

"Branwen?"

Her hands were in her hair, pulling it like punishment. "Oh, I am such a terrible person."

***

Cobb didn't understand what Branwen was talking about, or why she had pulled away. He'd never call Branwen a terrible person. The stress had been building for a while, he'd noticed that a couple of months ago. Putting the vet practice on the market was just the final proof. This last week had put an extra demand on already stretched nerves. The call at lunchtime had been an act of desperation. Was this more of the same?

"Branwen, I meant it when I said everything is going to be okay."

She laughed, bitter and full of self-loathing. "You don't know what I've done."

"Then tell me, it can't be that bad."

Again, with that bitter laugh that held no mirth. "I have been having a crap day."

That was undeniable. He stepped closer and she moved away. An attraction connected them, one growing stronger despite her declaration of imminent exit. Was he kidding himself? Was it growing precisely because she was leaving? The perversity of the human heart knew no bounds.

"And I made a mistake when I told you that I'd come see you." She took a deep breath, her eyes on the floor for all she faced his direction. "I'd already promised someone else that I'd meet them."

"Who?"

"Pete."

"Who?" He remembered. "Doc Pearson?"

She nodded. "We had a date."

A date. She'd never agreed to a date with him – there again he'd never asked. "Why?" The question was gauche, but unstoppable. Judging by her expression as she finally looked up at him, she was also struggling to believe he'd asked it. Her brows drew together.

"Because he asked. Because he's the first man to ask me in seven bloody lonely years!" She shifted and started pacing, keeping the table between them. "It's not *that* unbelievable. Christ, Pete and I've known each other since primary school, have been dating on and off since our early teens. So when he asked, I said yes. He promised no strings, no expectations and I figured it would give me a chance to tell him about selling the business. Then Granger turns up, comes into the practice, says all sorts of things." She stopped and looked at his bedroom door. "Actually, he said some stuff Jay does need to know, but not tonight." The pacing started again.

Tension thrummed from her every movement. She was as tight as a person could get without imploding.

"Then Pete came in. I was shaking, I think I was crying."

Now she stopped, her hand over her mouth, her eyes full of tears again. Stress didn't begin cover this.

"Branny?"

She stared across at him. "I fucked up, Cobb. Completely and utterly."

"What I saw tonight wasn't a fuck up."

She shook her head. "I called Granger *Granger* before he told me his name. I revealed I knew he was part of Nemesis. He never said that. That's how he knows that I'm in contact with Jay. I gave the game away."

It was a rookie mistake, one any training course would talk about. Only she had never been on any such training course, never before having been in the game. It was a fuck up, but he attached no blame to her for it, not considering all she had been going through, all that she put herself through.

"Which is why you didn't come here. You didn't bring him to me. And you weren't followed out of the village. I watched our tail the whole way. Branwen, you really haven't screwed up as much as you seem to think."

Her face was full of pain. Pain, regret and the masochistic determination to say what she believed he wasn't going to like. He'd have to be careful with his reactions to whatever she said. Internally, he braced for impact.

"Oh, I have. Pete and I were going for a drink, a meal. We were going to talk. But I was in such a state, he took me back to his instead."

"His?" Cobb swallowed to control his voice. "The bungalow?"

She nodded. "He cleaned my head up, gave me two stitches. Gave me a talking to about not getting it medically checked out straight away. We talked, I told him I was leaving. We were..." She licked her lips.

His heart shouldn't be hammering, he shouldn't have the overwhelming urge to go find Doc Pearson and rip his throat out.

"Then we were... well, kissing." She couldn't look at him. "And..."

He desperately wanted her to stop, but she needed to get this out and he would cope – apparently, by imagining ways to maim Doc, but he tried not to express that reaction.

"And then we were... doing more than..."

"You slept with him?"

She looked at him. "Could you manage a more judgemental tone?"

He closed his eyes and turned away. He understood that she was struggling, that she needed support and that was often sought in a closeness she wasn't getting from him. He knew that, he understood the need, but he hated the truth that she had turned to another man.

"And no."

Did she say that, or did he imagine it? He turned to face her.

"No, I didn't sleep with Pete, though in all honesty, that's only because the phone rang, and he got called out on an emergency. That's why I was on my own in the pub."

Chapter 63
Johnston – Dolgellau Police Station

Johnston parked as normal at the back of the station. Few attended this station at this time of night; with all the cut backs, it was surprising it remained manned, let alone for 24-7. Of course most nights there was only one man, but one was generally enough. Only one car was sitting in the car park. He didn't recognise the old banger.

He parked and using his Dallas fob to open the door, walked in. The one man would be at the front desk, in case someone called. Moving through the back and getting to Perkins office proved easy. The door had a lock, but the inspector hadn't used it.

Checking the corridor first, Johnston went inside. He flicked on the lamp and tried the drawer. The prick had locked that. Still, it was an old desk, easy to unlock. He pulled his penknife from his pocket, flicked open the blade. Okay, so it wasn't a legal knife, but who checked the local bobby?

Slipping it between desk top and drawer, it was easy to find the locking bolt and push it aside. Grinning, he pulled the drawer open and there amongst the other detritus, lay the pen drive. He picked it up.

Something so small, yet so valuable. And now he had it.

The piss money, though valuable enough to take and rinse, was nothing to what this was worth. It wouldn't get him out of this dump, but it would be a comfortable blanket. Most comfortable he'd had for a while. He slammed the drawer shut, threw the drive into the air and smiled as he caught it. Score one for him.

A couple of steps and he was at the door again.

He yanked it open, strode into the corridor, and stopped dead in front of Inspector Perkins and DCI Griffiths of the Professional Standards Department. Johnston turned; two more police officers were behind him. The bastard had set him up! Good and proper, but he'd not go down easily.

He turned back to Perkins.

Griffiths started to read him his rights.

The inspector stepped forward.

Johnston swung, Perkins ducked, Johnston's own weight carried him forward and his head impacted with the wall. Pain echoed across his brain as he fell to the floor.

Chapter 64
Branwen and Cobb – Pen-Y-Cwm, Cobb's Home

Cobb took the big comfortable chair by the fire, with Finn by his feet. For a moment Branwen saw a Celtic warlord and his faithful hound. Did he sit in judgement of her? Why not? She did. Thoughts of what she'd nearly done with Pete only a few hours ago twisted her gut. Shame warred with guilt. Cobb hadn't said anything since she'd confessed. She didn't know what he was thinking; if there was a way past her betrayal, she couldn't see it.

Her eyes sunk to the floor. She'd totally messed up. Time to go.

"Branwen."

She'd only shifted her weight, hadn't taken a single step. Swallowing the lump and bile in her throat she looked back at him. His hand rose, reached for her. Unsure, she moved over and took the outstretched hand. His palm warm and dry, he pulled her closer, brought her to sit across his lap. Warm and comfortable with him, when he gently eased her head to his shoulder, she complied with relief. Nestled with his arms around her she felt safe for the first time in a long time.

"Do you forgive me?"

His hand moved to her shoulders, his fingers drawing lazy circles. "There's nothing to forgive. Nothing happened."

She shifted away. "What if it had?"

He shrugged. "I've no right to judge."

What did that mean? He pulled her back against him. Relaxing into the invitation, she watched the flames of the fire.

"Why were you crying when you left the pub?"

The words flowed soft and gentle. She'd longed to hear him speak to her that way, to say something that told her she mattered to him. It seemed unlikely now, and with her leaving, it seemed an unfair expectation anyway.

"You left," she said. "You left me."

"It was that song."

"I love that song."

"So do I."

"Then what's the problem?"

He took a while to answer. "It was our song. Mine and Mary's. Played as our wedding dance."

"Oh." What to say? Knowing he'd been married was one thing, hearing about it from him was different. But she apparently harboured masochistic tendencies. "What was she like?"

He didn't respond at first, then he slid his hand under her knees, tensed and shifted from the chair, carefully placed her on the floor beside Finn. "Don't move."

She didn't dare. Cobb moved away. She stared at the orange flickering flames as a drawer opened, a few things were moved aside, then the drawer closed again. Cobb appeared at her side, crouched and lent against the chair. "I fell for Mary the second I laid eyes on her." He held out a photo frame with the picture facing down. "This was our wedding day."

Branwen didn't want to see it, but she had to. She took the frame and turned it over. They'd married in full dress uniform. Branwen didn't recognise which of the services those uniforms represented, but she didn't need to. Cobb sat astride a massive motorbike, his red hair shining in the sun, his hat in Mary's hand as she sat side saddle in front of him. A happier couple she'd rarely seen. Glee shone in both fresh faces and this wasn't so very long ago either. Mary was beautiful, stunning. Branwen could see why Cobb had fallen for her. Now Branwen understood why he wasn't attracted to her. The only thing she and Mary had in common was black hair, but while her own was long, down to her waist. Mary's black hair was shorn to her head, a thin layer of tightly curled afro that revealed large beautiful brown eyes that glittered at the camera over a straight wide nose, full lips and even, white teeth. Her skin was the most attractive chocolate brown Branwen had ever seen. If Mary hadn't been a soldier, she'd have easily been a model. Mr and Mrs E Cobb had clearly been the perfect couple. She didn't know what to say.

"You owned a Harley Davidson."

Cobb chuckled. "Actually, I owned a Kawasaki, the Harley was Mary's."

"Oh. So. Beautiful. Powerful. Loved you to distraction. Owned the perfect bike." She passed the photo back. "I think I hate her."

Cobb chuckled again. "I think the two of you would have been firm friends."

Carefully he placed the picture aside. He leaned forward and put his arms around Branwen, rested his head on her shoulder. "When she was killed, it broke my heart. It broke me. I was in so much pain I didn't want to go on. I bought a cottage in the middle of nowhere, with a dirt track for a road and no phone line, to keep humanity out. I decided to hide away, bury myself. Never wanted to care about anyone or anything ever again. Within a month, I see this figure with hair flying like a raven's wing standing like some mythical siren at the edge of a crag, apparently about to throw herself over and I realised I still had it in me to care. Then you turned around and started brow beating me into helping you."

Bullying again. If she hadn't heard the smile in his voice, she might have got up and moved away.

"And every time you called me, whether the Mountain Rescue or running a course up at the farm, I answered. Not for the person needing rescuing or for the students wanting to learn. I answered for you."

She let that sink in in silence. He did care then. Didn't he? Finally, Branwen asked the question that she had been pondering ever since she found out Cobb had been married. "What was she actually like? Mary? As a person."

Despite two years of vainly trying to forget about her, Cobb found the images came to him all too easily. "She loved life. Loved her job, she was damned good at it too. She was generous, but no pushover. Firm but fair. You and she would have got on well together, for the most part."

She considered that. "Explain, 'for the most part'?"

"I mean–" He shifted so that he could look directly at her. "–for the most part. But I wouldn't have wanted to be around when the pair of you argued. You're both strong, determined, stubborn women. If you'd had a fight, I doubt either of you would easily have backed down to heal the rift." He was smiling now.

"What do you think we would have fought about?" Branwen asked. Besides you, she added silently.

"Religion, for one thing. You're a strong Anglican; she was a complete atheist. She would argue with anyone that there was no God. We often had heated discussions about it."

"You believe in God?"

"Uh-huh," he agreed. "Only not in religion." He considered a moment. "I think that's the biggest difference between the two of you, really. Mary demanded everything be proved to her, occasionally even orders, which was the real reason she agreed to leave the army. But you..." he smiled as she turned to face him "...you'll accept things on faith. For all your cynicism, you're a much more trusting person. I think you understand people better than she did. Mary wouldn't have bothered with me a second time if I'd treated her with the ill manners I greeted you with. She certainly wouldn't have come up here and beaten me over the head with my own stupidity and selfishness till I agreed to join the Mountain Rescue. She wouldn't have tried to draw me back into society the way you have. She'd have labelled me a worthless idiot and left me to rot."

"Then she would have missed out." She wanted to kiss him, but didn't dare, so she leaned her head momentarily against his before leaning back. "Cobb, what's your first name?"

He dropped his eyes for a moment. Then looked back at her.

"I've never liked my name. My family, including my parents, even Mary always called me Cobb. When Mary found out my name, she laughed. Laughed loud and long."

"I'm not Mary."

He brushed her hair back, sending tingles to all the right places. "Erasmus," he said.

For a second Branwen frowned, then smiled. "Beloved."

That stopped Cobb. "What?"

"Erasmus. It's from the Greek for beloved, or desired. I like it."

His look was half frown, half smile, and a fair bit of confusion. "How do you know that?"

"Religious studies in school. There's a Christian martyr called Erasmus. I looked up the meaning. I like to find out what people's names mean – see if they fit."

"Oh." He sat back, a half smile. "I've never had reason to be thankful for my name before." Then frowned as he looked at her. "Does your name match you?"

"Not really," she said. "Wish it did."

"Why? What does Branwen mean?"

"Beautiful Raven," she said.

Cobb smiled again. "Suits you."

Was he leaning in?

"Can I–"

They both turned to see Jay at the bedroom door.

"Sorry, I need the bathroom."

"Go for it." Branwen shifted and stood; Cobb stood too.

"Branwen?"

She turned and looked up at him. "I should go. I…"

"Stay."

She smiled up at him. "I can't. With everything that's going on, I should go home."

A swallow or a gulp? How was she supposed to know the difference? "You're probably right."

She smiled. "Trust me, I am. I've been wearing these clothes for two days now."

He followed when she headed for the door. "Branwen."

She stopped at the call and turned on the threshold. He stood in the doorway, inside the cottage, she outside.

"Everything will be okay."

Chapter 65
Simons – On the Road

Simons cursed the pouring rain that turned to slush and eventually snow as he headed north-west on the M1. Some of the things he had discovered about Granger were unsavoury, not unexpected and not as shocking as some of the low lives he had dealt with. What bothered Simons about Granger was not his actions but his associates, specifically his employees.

Cursing again, Simons told his phone to redial. Again the damn thing told him the number was unobtainable.

Granger was one thing, but the worry now was Cobb himself. Simons' feared how Cobb would react to the news of just who was working for Granger. Simons was struggling to believe it himself. Granger was employing a dead man. A murderous walking corpse.

Gary Shoreham. Real name Graham Denham.

Graham Bloody Denham.

Mary's killer.

Chapter 66
Branwen – Pen-Y-Cwm Farm and Guesthouse

Everything will be okay.

The way Cobb said it made Branwen want to believe.

He stroked her hair again, tingles tickled through her nerves. She was warm and safe, and with him. The heat of his body ran the length of hers, surrounding her. The brush of his breath was on her face. Coming home hadn't been easy, the inability of her father to look at her without a sneer had sent her straight to her bed and a pity party.

In her bed.

Alone.

Her eyes snapped opened.

Shoreham grinned at her.

She tried to jump away, only to find Baron stretched out on her other side. His hand went over her mouth as she tried to scream. On her back now, she found her legs trapped by the duvet. But as Shoreham pulled down the duvet, her left arm came free and she tried jabbing straight up to catch his chin or nose. He caught her hand, forced her arm above her head and pinned it there with his right hand. Then he brought a knife up in front of her face.

Her eyes went wide, staring at the sharp cut-throat razor.

She tried to cry out, but Baron's hand still covered her mouth. Now she tried to drag air in through her nose, but Baron shifted his hand, squeezing her nostrils closed. Fear ratcheted. Her eyes looked between the two men. She didn't know their plan, but it didn't matter: suffocation or throat cutting, she wouldn't survive either. She tried thrashing, but couldn't move. She didn't understand it. She'd locked her door and propped a chair in front of it, so how'd they got in?

"Shhhush now." Shoreham spoke quietly as he brought the knife close. "Promise not to scream and Baron will let you breathe."

She stilled and stared at that increasingly close blade.

"Promise now."

She didn't know how to.

"Blink twice for yes."

She looked at Shoreham. Blinked twice.

Baron's hand moved from her mouth, she dragged in a huge breath, filling and emptying her lungs several times until she steadied her nerves a little. Shoreham's eyes fixed on her chest, there wasn't much she could do about that with one hand held over her head, and the other stuck under the cover. Baron's hand moved away but came back with a pistol – a silenced pistol. He placed it under her chin. Not pushing or controlling but reminding her who had the power.

"If I scream, my father will be in here with a shotgun."

"You won't be alive when he does," Baron said conversationally. "And he'll be dead a moment later."

Shoreham pulled at her top, exposing her left breast, his big hand fondling her flesh. Gritting her teeth, she realised she had to let him do whatever he wanted; objection equated to folly. His interest focused on her breast, she focused on Baron instead.

"What do you want?"

"You know what we want."

As her nipple was clamped again, she tried not to cry out, but shook her head. "Please, no, I don't. Tell me what you want."

Now Shoreham took her nipple into his mouth, sucking hard.

"Urgh." She tried to shift away, but had nowhere to go. "Please stop."

Baron smiled down at her. "Just tell him what he wants to hear."

Shoreham sucked harder, drawing more of her breast into his mouth. It was the least arousing thing she'd ever experienced. As he sucked and squeezed her breast, she clenched her jaw against crying out. When he'd tried this before he'd wanted her to beg him.

"Please, Gary."

The sucking continued, off her nipple now, on the swell of her breast. He bit her.

"Please," she sobbed, the pain screeching through her chest. "Please, Gary. Please stop."

The pressure only got harder, her flesh was going to give way. Tears sprung from her eyes, ran down her face, pooled itchy in her ears. She wanted to scream, but it really would bring her father and however they argued, she wouldn't be the instrument of his death.

"I can't tell you what I don't know."

Her skin broke. She turned her head away, the pain intense, and she started to cry out. A hand clamped over her open mouth. She clamped her teeth on Shoreham's flesh.

"You know exactly what we want," Baron said.

She clamped harder. The metallic taste of blood dripped into her mouth, made her sick. For a moment she looked down and saw the blood, her blood, trickling across her breast. Shoreham was sucking still, biting. She pushed her head back on the pillow. If he didn't stop, he would literally bite her breast off. She stopped biting and twisted her head, he let her go.

"I'll take you to Jay." The pressure instantly eased. Relief and pain washed through her in equal measure. "I'll take you to Jay."

"Good girl." Baron stroked her face with the barrel of the pistol.

"I knew you'd do it."

He got up, but Shoreham loomed over her, his lips blood stained, his grin chilling.

Laughing soft and dark, he sprang to his feet, dragging her up with him.

"Animals mark their mates." He held up his palm and she was horrified to see her teeth marks there, to realise now that the odd taste in her mouth was not fear-rushed adrenaline, but blood too. His blood. "Only death can separate us now."

She stared up at him horrified, forgetting in that moment the pain in her breast.

"We'll finish this later, and I'll hear you scream just as you want me to make you."

She so didn't, but he dragged her towards the door. She pulled back, yanked away.

"Let me dress."

"No."

Shoreham reached for her again, but she dodged him.

"You can't drive to where Jay is. I'll have to lead you there, but I'll freeze before I get there like this, then I'll be dead, and you won't get your prize or your pleasure. Is that what you want?"

Shoreham stood straight and moved close, leaned closer. "Get dressed."

***

Branwen moved around Shoreham, gathered a pair of panties and a bra from her drawers, and in doing so looked down and saw how her breast bled. She turned, reached for her vet's bag. Shoreham grabbed her and pulled her from it, crushed her to him.

"I need a dressing," she said. "Please, I'll do whatever you want, but let me have some measure of comfort given that you've robbed me of any measure of pride."

"I let you anywhere near that, and you'll get another needle or a scalpel."

Baron tutted and moved around them. He snapped open the bag and looked through. All he could find, as Branwen knew, was bandages, it was difficult to get a plaster on a fur covered animal. She tried to wriggle away from Shoreham, and Baron looked up at her. There was a pause while he looked at her, considered her. Then he picked out a bottle of iodine and a wrap of cotton wool.

He passed it over and she used what she could, not rushing, but not stalling. She had to think. She wouldn't take these men to Jay, but she had to make them think she was. Not caring how they watched her, or how Shoreham rubbed his groin, she dressed carefully.

"How did you get in here?" she asked. "I locked the door."
"I climbed."

Shocked, she looked up at Shoreham. That wasn't an easy climb, as she'd discovered as a teenager.

She grabbed a coat, looked to Baron. "I'm ready."

***

The Land Rover was freezing, but under all the nerves Branwen didn't register the temperature. Behind the steering wheel, shrouded in misery and hate, she stared blindly at the silhouette of the dark mountain standing harsh against the glowering sky. She had done her best to patch up Shoreham's bite, but under the thick jumper and fleece the wound pulled with every movement, every breath. She had never before known such cold, hard hate, but now she hated Shoreham. She wanted him dead. She wanted to be the one who killed him. She wished she had the jacket she'd left at Cobb's; she'd never got around to putting that syringe back in her kit.

Branwen parked facing up the mountain towards the bluff. A short way behind her the mountain fell steeply away in rocky outcrops. When she stopped, she put the vehicle in neutral and half applied the handbrake. Her left foot on the brake pedal hidden from Baron's view by the high central console, held them in place.

Throughout the short journey, Baron had sat quietly by her side, but as they had left the farm behind he had shifted slightly, silently laying a gun on his lap.

The only guns Branwen was familiar with were the shotgun she occasionally used for rabbit hunting and the tranquilliser dart gun she had used a couple of times on more dangerous large animals at university. All the same, the dull metal was what she believed to be a semi-automatic pistol, a display of the men's authority.

Authority she wasn't going to put up with much longer. She only had to time it right.

Shoreham stepped from the car, pausing by her window. Slowly he raised his hand, palm out, showing her the blood trail from the wound he would not allow to scab. Smiling through at Branwen's pale face, the tall man's grin was pure malice. Slowly he brought his hand to his face; one wide lap from the heel of his hand to his fingertips wiped the blood off. He left his tongue lolling for a second.

Branwen saw the dark red swathe, swallowed disgust, and turned from him. Even so his laughter echoed, chilling her soul.

In the pre-dawn light, Shoreham moved towards the path. A smattering of flakes fell on the windscreen. That was all she needed – but on second thoughts, perhaps the weather was conspiring with her.

Beside her, Baron sighed and looked out of the side window. Shoreham moved forward, looking for the cave she'd said was there.

The door catch was soft and Branwen hit the ground running, not pausing to look behind her. The crunch told her the car was rolling back.

Legs pumping for all she was worth, Branwen struggled out of her blue padded jacket, revealing the white hooded sweatshirt she had on beneath. Along with white jeans and light tan walking boots, the outfit should help disguise her in the snow-covered landscape. All except her black hair. As she ran she pulled up her hood, covering the betraying raven wing, increasing the camouflage.

She heard Baron jump from the car. Shoreham yelled her name and came thundering towards her.

She skidded around an outcrop, two shots ringing after her. Her only weapon was a superior knowledge of the land, more of a shield really; she pressed on, leading them east while the haven Cobb offered lay to the west.

The wind picked up, the earlier flurries turning into a snowstorm. At what appeared to be a dead end, Branwen pulled up. One look over the edge confirmed she was where she needed to be.

"Jones!"

Branwen swung round at the call, she hadn't expected Baron to be quite so close, nor Shoreham so close behind him. She backed up as both men raised guns. She raised a hand.

"Wait!"

They didn't.

Chapter 67
Baron – Cader Idris

Baron didn't like it. He didn't enjoy killing people, especially if they died before giving him what he wanted. He moved to the edge of the mountain. The body lay on a ledge roughly seven feet below where he and his partner now stood, the wind buffeting round them. The stark blue white of the landscape was marred by two darker shades, one the girl's black mane, the other a rapidly growing patch of blood seeping from her left side.

Standing above her, Shoreham cursed. "Too quick. I wanted to hear her scream. A lot." He raised his gun and aimed at her head.

"No," Baron stopped him. "She's dead already. We have to go back to the farm and take care of things there."

Chapter 68
Cobb – Pen-Y-Cwn, Cobb's Home

Cobb paced. 07:43. The sun was up, and he'd barely slept.

Everything in his gut twisted over and over itself. The way things were with Branwen, he had no idea what to think. He probably had no right to think anything. He'd known she was struggling, that she needed support, but he'd held his support back. He'd known Doc wanted her, yet still he had made no move himself. He hadn't known that Branwen and Doc had that kind of history. If he had, he'd have been more worried.

He could only accept the reality of what had happened. Such acceptance did not come easy. Having so recently decided to rejoin the human race, Cobb was ready for action. He wanted to do something. Anything. He felt stuck, babysitting Whitney while Simons delved into the archives and Branwen faced the enemy front lines. Why hadn't Simons been in touch? For the umpteenth time he checked his phone – still no signal.

He couldn't remember ever being this useless.

Yes, he could. But only once – the night Mary died.

He prayed history wasn't about to repeat itself. He prayed and he paced. By eight, Finn grew tired of watching his master, padded over to his bowl and carried it to the tall man, dumping it at his feet. Feeding the big animal proved little more than a momentary diversion. Cobb took to pacing again.

Not knowing what else to do, Cobb moved to a window and checked through the curtain. No one out there; he hadn't expected there to be.

He heard movement and turned to see Jay coming out of the bedroom. "How're the ribs?"

"Tender, but I'll survive."

He would.

"Are you and Branwen an item now?" Jay asked.

Cobb stopped pacing and glared at the younger man. "No." Unfortunately.

"Why are you so worried about her then?"

"She's a friend and she's in danger." As he spoke, Cobb resumed pacing. "Just because she'd not my girlfriend doesn't mean I don't care." He cared more than he wanted to admit. He had never expected to care for another woman after Mary, so the way Branwen had got under his skin surprised him. She had shown some interest, but nothing had materialised mostly because he'd been pushing her, and everyone else, away.

"Don't you think she can handle the Goon Brothers?"

Cobb didn't even want to contemplate that. "Tell me again about the two men who came after you."

Before Whitney could answer something heavy hit the front door and this time it was not a gust of wind. Both men turned to stare at the wood, at the handle being turned from the outside.

"Bedroom," Cobb hissed and Jay hid, rushing in spite of the pain the movement seemed to cause him.

Finn moved to the door first. One sniff and he started barking, whining and scratching at the door in some canine attempt to open it. As Cobb approached, a slow banging at the door appealed for admission. Something in the slow, weak beat told Cobb that whoever was on the other side didn't pose a danger, yet he refused to be reckless.

He opened the door a crack, seeing with horror the image that greeted him. Finn shouldered the wood aside to get to his friend as Branwen staggered forward, lurching into the house and practically collapsing into Cobb's arms.

Balancing Branwen with one arm, Cobb half-dragged her fully in to the cottage, slamming the door after her.

"Jay, bring a blanket!"

Cobb swept Branwen up, carrying her to the fireside, worried about the amount of blood down her left side, about her white face. Her lips were blue; snowflakes had iced on her eyebrows and lashes, painting her black hair white. She was soaked to the skin.

He snatched the blanket from Jay's outstretched hand and wrapped it around Branwen and her wet clothes.

"Cobb?" Her voice was weak, her eyes glazed.

"I'm here," he assured her. "You're safe." Turning to Jay, he told the younger man where the first aid box was and to be quick.

Gently, Cobb laid Branwen on the floor in front of the fire wrapped in the blanket. Quickly, he removed her boots and started stripping her of the sodden clothing. Jay returned as Cobb struggled to get wet denim and the thermals over broad hips. He placed the box in easy reach. "Anything I can do?"

"Get some dry clothes. From the chest of drawers in the bedroom."

As Jay moved, Cobb opened up the layers covering Branwen's torso. First the zipped-up sweatshirt, then the thin fleece and brushed cotton shirt. Slipping her out of those, he discovered a thermal vest, even that was wet. Whatever she had faced, she had been prepared for it. Luckily so, Cobb thought; without these layers she might have frozen to death out there. He tried not to think of what she had suffered, tried to ignore she was limp and lifeless in his hands as a rag doll. Peeling back the last layer, Cobb noted with relief that the blood was from a wound on her arm and not her chest as he had feared. The simple cotton bra she wore held back a wad of cotton wool and the scent of iodine, blood soaking through from beneath.

Carefully Cobb picked the sodden mass away to reveal what was clearly a bite mark.

"Oh Jesus." He backed away, his hand to his mouth. He'd seen this. Not in real life, but in the investigation of Mary's murderer. In finding out about the man who killed her, he'd found a rap-sheet of escalating violence against women, and a death certificate that he suddenly thought might be a fake.

"Cobb?" Jay stood beside him now as he stared at the wound on Branwen's breast.

Branwen blinked and roused. She looked like death, and when she saw her exposure she pulled the blanket over her, trying to sit up. Jay had to move to help her.

"Cobb?"

She shouldn't be the one worrying about him.

"Cobb what's wrong?"

It couldn't be, it just couldn't be.

"Cobb!" This time Jay shouted.

Cobb scowled at the young man, then focused on the woman he was supporting.

"The men you called the Goon Brothers. What are their names?"

"Does it matte–"

"Yes! It matters," he cut Jay off and looked again at Branwen.

Colour had started to return, but she looked scared, of him. Perhaps she should be. "Jeff Baron and Gary Shoreham."

The names meant nothing to him.

"My phone," she said hoarsely. "In the zip pocket of my sweatshirt. It still there?"

Jay reached out when Cobb hesitated. The now cracked screen lit up when Branwen pressed the button. A few more touches and she showed the screen to Jay. "Meant to ask, were these the guys from London?"

Jay swallowed, nodded.

Branwen turned the phone to Cobb. He looked at the candid shot of the two men by the car in Pen-Y-Cwm yard. It wasn't well composed, but it didn't have to be. One man, Cobb recognised as his visitor. The other he recognised as Graham Denham.

Cobb surged to his feet, kicking the second chair so far from the fire, it skidded and shattered against the wall as he exploded with an unintelligible sound of rage and frustration.

Chapter 69
Baron – Pen-Y-Cwm Farm and Guesthouse

Baron stepped into the cowshed and looked at the taut back of the other man. Shoreham had stewed in silence on the return journey to the farm which was why Baron had allowed him some entertainment for the evening.

Looking around, the shed had become a macabre scene. Without emotion Baron viewed the tableau. Six cows lay eyes agog, throats cut, the straw around them awash with their blood and the excrement of fear.

There was the corpse at Shoreham's feet. Iolyn was already bloating, swelling from multiple lacerations, his bones broken. In his own experience, human bones snapped much the same way as hollow branches. But they sounded better. The added squelch of flesh and blood.

Flesh was an amazing thing. Surprisingly resilient. Amazing that for all the damage Shoreham had done, the body had very little broken skin. The face, of course, was a different matter.

Shoreham crouched briefly to wipe his hands on the straw. Then Baron watched as he rose again, withdrawing a semi-automatic handgun from his jacket. Baron had supplied that gun. The serial number had been shaved off, but then so had just about every serial number for every modern handgun held privately in the UK since 1997. Of course it was an illegal firearm, but not an unusual model. Far more guns lurked on British soil than most Brits would be comfortable knowing about.

Slowly and carefully, Shoreham paced to the cows. In turn he took each head in his hand, turned the lifeless cranium to him. He centred the muzzle roughly an inch away from the still warm flesh and squeezed off a single round into each skull.

He carefully wiped the gun clean of all possible traces of his fingerprints. Holding the iron with a handkerchief, he placed the weapon in Jones's lifeless fingers.

Of course, Baron considered, any forensic investigator would see instantly that the bullets were fired after death because of the way the gore was splattered. But no investigator would ever get to see that much. The best they would have to work with would be charred skeletal remains.

Shoreham struck a match and lighted the hurricane lamp, which he threw into a manger, watching as the dry hay caught.

"You done?" Baron asked.

"Yep." He turned, moving away from the rapidly increasing fire. "You?"

Baron nodded. "Nothing. If she ever had those files, there's no trace now. Come on, we need to get back to the village and complete our alibi."

Chapter 70
Cobb – Pen-Y-Cwm, Cobb's Home

He couldn't look at her. How could Branwen have been harbouring that man?

"Cobb?"

The weakness of her voice scared him, but he had to focus. He had to remember she didn't know who that man was.

"What do you see? Who?"

Bile rose and burned in his gut. "Graham Denham."

"No, their names are Baron and Shoreham."

"The blond is Graham Denham," he snarled, the ferocity of the wild animal only just contained.

Branwen paused before trying again. "Who is he?"

"Mary's murderer."

"Oh, God. Cobb, I –"

"It was a contract hit. We'd just left the army, set up the business. Our second case. Killing Mary was a message. One clean shot through the forehead, from a moving vehicle. Lucky or brilliant, doesn't matter, same effect. And I saw it, just couldn't stop it."

He felt a hand on his shoulder, but pulled away, pacing and pushing his hands through his hair. He'd believed the bastard was dead; letting go of the need for revenge had really only just happened and now it was back, with a vengeance. He marched towards the door.

"Cobb? Where are you going?"

His hand clasped on the doorknob. "To kill Denham."

"Great," Jay's acid sarcasm stopped him. "You couldn't save Mary, and now you're going to abandon Branwen when she needs you? What kind of man are you?"

Cobb swung back ready to punch the stupid boy, but Branwen stepped between them.

"It's okay," she said.

It was anything but okay as Cobb glared at Jay.

"Cobb, if this is what you have to do, then go do it. If avenging Mary is so important to you, go. I understand."

He didn't need her permission, but he welcomed it.

"I left them up on the mountain, but they could be anywhere by now."

Then the sooner he left the better. Turning on his heel, he slammed open the door and slammed it closed behind him.

You're going to abandon Branwen when she needs you?

The accusation cut through him. He wasn't abandoning her, he was stopping Denham. Cobb had to stop that murdering bastard in his tracks.

I understand.

Of course she understood. Branwen always understood, that was who she was.

The kind of person who cried because she thought he'd walked out on her.

He stopped short.

I understand.

What did she understand? What put that dull empty tone in her voice? Didn't she understand she was the most important thing in his life?

He turned back to the cottage, the oddity over the roof catching his eye. The column of black smoke rose high and straight in a surprisingly still morning. Something big was burning. And only one thing sat higher on the mountain than this cottage.

Cobb marched back to the house. Branwen hadn't moved, her head down and Jay protectively at her side. They both looked up, startled, but Cobb ignored Jay walked straight to Branwen.

"Killing Denham is my best way of protecting you, both of you, but that might not be an option anymore. There's smoke rising from the farm."

Her eyes went wide and she tried to head for the door, but he caught her by her upper arms.

"I have to go!" She tried to wriggle out of his tightening grasp.

"You have to stay here."

She scowled up at him. "But Dad –"

He shook her once. "But Denham."

Her face fell in fear. He searched for a more reasonable tone.

"Branwen. You can't go. You're not even dressed right now. I'll go. You stay here, clean up that wound and get some clothes on. I'll go up and see what can be done, you get yourself sorted and I'll be back as soon as I can."

Turning to Jay, Cobb instructed. "Keep her here. Tie her to a chair if you have to." He strode towards the door, pulling on his coat. "Neither one of you leaves until I get back. Understand?"

Jay nodded.

"Branwen?"

Though she didn't meet his eye, she nodded too.

***

Cobb reached the bridge in time to see the local fire brigade cross it, heading towards the farm. He followed quickly. Their presence worried Cobb more. If there had been time for someone to spot the fire, put the call out, and for the brigade to get up here, then the blaze had been going for some time.

When they reached the farmyard, he spotted Doc's Subaru parked safely out of the way and Doc himself making a valiant, if somewhat vain, attempt to hold the fire back with the sluice line used to wash down the yard. Black with ash, Doc looked relieved as he handed responsibility to the professionals.

"I can't find Branwen!" he told Cobb above the sound of the fire and the attempt to stem it.

"What about Iolyn?" the larger man asked.

Doc pointed towards the barn, black and skeletal now. "I could see him, but not get to him. Is Branwen safe?" Doc asked as the two men stood back out of the way of the fire crew.

Cobb said nothing. Branwen trusted Doc, but he stupidly wanted to keep her to himself a while longer.

A few minutes later the blaze became a steaming pile of embers, and soon those too would be gone. A police car arrived, Inspector Perkins. Cobb and Doc Pearson greeted the policeman and were swiftly joined by the Brigade's sub-officer.

"Well?" Perkins demanded.

"The barn and most of the house are gone," the sub needlessly reported the clearly evident. "There are a number of remains in the shed area: six bovine and one human. I believe at this stage that the human is Mr Iolyn Jones, the owner of the farm."

Perkins nodded. "Any other casualties?"

"Not that we've found, but my men are checking the house."

"Anyone missing? Unaccounted for?"

"Branwen Jones," Doc supplied.

Cobb said nothing.

"The vet," the sub added when Perkins didn't say anything, staring intently at the house.

"Yeah." It was almost absent. "Her office was broken into a couple of days ago, this might be related." Perkins looked at Cobb and Doc. "I understand two guests were here this week. Were there any others?"

"Didn't even know there were two," Doc stated.

Cobb shook his head. "Not as far as I'm aware."

Perkins looked at his watch. "I was here an hour and a half ago. Iolyn was alive then and, I believe, alone. He said Branwen had taken two guests onto the mountain."

Perkins looked to Cobb. Cobb had the uneasy sensation of being read like a book.

"Have either of you seen Miss Jones this morning?"

Cobb looked away, hung his head.

"No," Doc said. "I was coming up to see her, to apologise for standing her up last night."

224

Perkins brows rose. "You two had a date?"

Doc nodded. "Then I got a call out and had to leave."

And Cobb suspected the audible regret was linked to what Branwen said they hadn't done.

"So why are you here?" Perkins pressed Cobb.

"Sir!"

The fireman turned to the young officer who had called. "What is it?" the sub demanded.

"I think you'd better come take a look at this, sir."

The man excused himself and headed for the near-burnt-out barn. Cobb frowned after him, wondering what they had found.

Now Perkins called Cobb's attention back to their conversation. "Would you care to explain your presence here, Mr Cobb?"

"I saw the pillar of smoke," the tall man said. "I came to investigate."

"Saw it?"

Cobb nodded. "The column was clearly visible from my cottage. I saw it when I glanced out back."

The sub-officer returned, not a happy man.

Perkins focused on him. "Any ideas on what started the fire?"

"I'll have to wait for the investigators report to be certain."

"So, guess," Perkins snapped. "I want your first impression."

"First impression, an accident. Like the man tripped in the barn with a lighted hurricane lamp, knocked himself out and started the blaze."

"Why would he be using a flamed light?"

The officer shrugged. "No idea."

"A bad habit," Doc offered. "Mains power doesn't reach up this far and although they have a wind turbine and solar panels, the barn isn't connected to the supply. Iolyn and Branwen use paraffin lamps and torches usually."

"That's stupid," the fireman stated.

"It's the way things get done. It's habit."

"So," Perkins summed up, "no definite signs of foul play other than the missing daughter."

"And possibly the guests," Cobb added. If he could put hurdles in front of his enemies, he would.

"Except no one knows who they were."

"Jeff Baron and Gary Shoreham." Cobb tried not to sneer.

"You know them?"

"Not really." Cobb didn't want to discuss it with so many people.

"Erm, actually," the sub-officer put in uncomfortably, "second impressions say this might not be an accident."

The men turned to him, all curiosity.

"There appear to be bullet holes in the skulls of the cows and the remains of a gun by the human corpse."

***

Cobb and Doc looked at each other as the emergency services moved to the barn.

"Is she safe?" Doc whispered.

Cobb looked at the younger man. "Are you in love with her?"

The way Doc hesitated told Cobb everything he needed to so.

"I could be."

Cobb took a deep breath. "That's just familiarity." He watched the others. "It's being lazy. If you love someone you do whatever you have to."

"And what do you have to do?"

He had to keep Branwen safe, whatever it cost. She wanted out of this village and he had to ensure she survived to go.

"If all else fails," Doc said quietly, "go up on The Chair. She's lived here all her life, knows it like the back of her hand. It's one of the things that makes her so useful to the Mountain Rescue."

Cobb nodded and turned back to the man. "Keep your ears open in the village. If Branwen turns up, keep her safe."

"Do you think the police can be trusted?"

Cobb looked at Perkins. He hated the bad rep so many of the police had these days, but men like Johnston made him understand why. Perkins shook the hand of the sub and turned towards them. "That one. Not Johnston."

Perkins was back.

"You don't think Iolyn would have done this do you?" Doc asked.

Perkins shrugged. "He was maudlin enough. But don't worry, I'm not the path of least resistance type, I'll check every possibility. There's nothing more you can do here, you should go."

"*Da iawn*," Doc said heading for his car.

Cobb checked his phone. Still no signal. Perkins did the same.

"Anything?"

Perkins shook his head. "The mast is down. May not get a signal up here for a while."

Cobb swore. "I forgot."

"Problem?"

He looked at the inspector. "I need to make a phone call."

"When you say 'need'…?"

"I mean my business partner."

Perkins brows rose. "You mean CSC Securities that you walked away from two or more years ago?" Perkins paused. "Oh, don't be so surprised, I'm good at my job. I can get Dispatch to put you through."

226

Was that a good idea? Right now, it was the only idea. "I'd appreciate it."

Perkins led him to the police pool car and contacted despatch, giving them the number Cobb gave him.

"CSC Security," came the crisp female greeting. "How can I help?"

Perkins passed the handset to Cobb. "Can I speak to Simons?"

"Well hello, Judy." The voice of the partnership's secretary came mockingly back at him after she had recovered from the shock of hearing his voice again. "It's good to speak to you again after all this time. This is so worth doing backflips for."

Cobb sighed. "Sorry Judy, I don't have time to chat. Where's Simons?"

"Wish I knew," Judy grouched. "There are clients here screaming because he's not working for them. He's left a note that he'll not be around for a while, but it doesn't say where he's gone." She sighed. "He's getting worse for this sort of thing." She stopped for a second. "Since this isn't the first time you've called, you probably know what he's up to better than I do. Not that that would be hard at the moment. Try his mobile, it hasn't changed, but I can't guarantee anything."

"Thanks."

Cursing, he passed the handset back to Perkins.

"Wanna try the mobile?"

"Would you mind?"

Perkins connected to Despatch. It didn't take long to get the message back that the number was unobtainable. Cobb rubbed his face.

"Problem?" Perkins asked.

"Maybe."

"You left after your wife's murder," Perkins said. "The murderer was never caught."

Cobb nodded. "The murderer was Graham Denham. He's one of the guests who was staying up here. Branwen said they were Jeff Baron and Gary Shoreham. I don't know which was which, but the blond bastard killed my wife."

Perkins looked at him. "Can you prove that?"

"You think he'd still be walking around if I could?"

***

Cobb dreaded telling Branwen about her father. He couldn't predict her reaction. Normally he'd expect a calm, deeply hurt response, she wasn't one to rant and wail. But now, after all she'd been through, the physical and emotional abuse, he wasn't sure how she would deal with the death of a loved one, with his suspicions of murder.

The cottage looked unoccupied as he approached. With the low-hanging clouds shedding the first flakes of snow, even the chimney smoke was obscured until he was all but at the door.

Only the sound of his footfalls crunching on the crisp snow broke the silence as he approached the house. The door, when he tried it, was locked. He knocked.

"Answer the door." Branwen's voice was faint and dull, completely lacking inclination. "If it were anyone other than Cobb, Finn would be going nuts by now."

A few moments later, a pale and wan Jay opened the door. Inside, Cobb looked at Branwen while the boy re-locked the door. Her clothes had been dried in his absence, and she was wearing them again, blood stained as they were. She sat calmly by the fire, staring into its bright burning heart, Finn before her, the animal's scruffy head in her lap. One hand moved in an absent stroke over the grey fur. Shrugging out of his thick coat, Cobb asked Jay how she'd been during his absence.

"At first, she paced," he spoke in a whisper. "Then she sat." He glanced at Branwen, then looked back at Cobb. "I think I preferred the pacing."

When Cobb turned, he found Branwen watching him, her expression unreadable.

"My father's dead, isn't he?" she asked tonelessly.

No point lying. "Yes."

No reaction. "Shoreham? The blond one?"

"Probably."

"Can't prove it?"

"Not yet."

She turned to face Finn, ruffling his head one last time, then she moved him and stood. "I'll get you a warm drink, you must be frozen, being out so long." Going to the sink to fill the kettle she absently told Cobb to go sit by the fire.

The two men exchanged a worried look. Jay shrugged, and they parted, Jay to the second seat by the fire, Cobb to join Branwen.

"Are you okay?" he asked softly, stopping close behind her.

She drew in a deep breath, releasing it slowly. "No." She fell silent for a moment, switching on the kettle, then leant back against his chest. He found what he considered too much comfort in the contact. His hands came up to her arms, he wanted more but daren't allow himself that luxury. They just stood there in silence.

"Do you want something to eat?" she asked a moment later. "I noticed a few tins of stew in your cupboard. Would they be okay?"

"Branwen –" Cobb started.

228

"No. Don't." She shrugged off his hands, moved away. "Don't tell me not to worry about such things. If Shoreham killed Dad than he must be getting desperate. It won't take long for something to lead him here, so we're going to have to leave. A good hot meal before we go wouldn't be a bad idea, don't you think?"

Cobb couldn't help but smile ruefully, looking over her head as she kept her back to him. Even in her grief, she still had a clear grasp of the situation and she still displayed good sense in her management of it.

"Besides," she added, "while we eat you can tell me what happened."

Chapter 71
Simons – Pen-Y-Cwm Village

As Simons drew into Pen-Y-Cwm village, the slow pace he had maintained for poor road conditions became a crawl. The road was practically blocked off by cars. Carefully, he parked behind the last of the line.

Stepping out onto the pavement, Simons surveyed the place. The one street was straight, the houses mostly late-nineteenth, early-twentieth century, although the Chapel – Baptist he noted – seemed older. An oddity, a Jackson Pollock among the Turners, was the estate agents. Though tasteful of its type, it stood at odds with the rest of the village.

Only one building stood out as a new construction. That was at the far end of the village. From here he saw the sign on the door. The Surgeries. Someone with a sense of humour had painted a human silhouette on one door and on the other, the outline of a dog and above it a bird. So, the doctor and the vet shared the building.

In a town dominated by the chapel, a close second came the opposite building – the pub. The Pig and Whistle. It seemed the only signs of life were from that building, which seemed weird for midday Saturday. Habitually locking up the Land Cruiser, Simons headed into the watering hole.

The atmosphere hit him the instant he stepped inside. The wall of silence wasn't that brought on by the entrance of an outsider, it was born of fear, anxiety, an atmosphere so thick it could be cut. Whatever was going on, it affected the whole community.

Everyone turned to him. One face jumped out at Simons, not because he had ever met the man, but because it was a face Simons had had burned into his mind two years ago when he had sworn to kill the murderer of one of his best friends. Graham Denham. The shorter, darker man at Denham's side, Simons realised was Baron. Either they hadn't done anything provable, or they were just too ballsy.

Another face moved out of the crowd. Quite an average man, nothing that would be picked out of a line up.

"Can I help you?"

"I'm looking for Branwen Jones."

The statement brought forth any number of unpleasant responses. A blonde, one of only two women in the room, sobbed into the chest of the suited man who comforted her. Judging by the ring on her left hand, Simons assumed the pair were engaged. A number of people shifted uncomfortably, and someone uttered a caustic, "Aren't we all?"

Simons identified the speaker as a tall thin man in his early to mid-thirties. His face, though strained, was attractive and commendably trustworthy.

The man who had originally greeted him glared at the speaker. "Doc." The one-word reprimand had no effect. He watched Simons with hooded, suspicious eyes. The other man turned back to him.

"I'm Inspector Perkins."

Somehow this man being a police officer didn't surprise Simons. Simons was also aware there was a risk either Baron or Denham would know his name, if not his face. He'd have to be careful.

"I have business with Miss Jones."

Perkins eyes narrowed. "Unfortunately, Miss Jones is unavailable."

"Unavailable?"

"Missing."

"Done a bunk, probably," a thoroughly disreputable-looking older man grumbled from his place by the bar.

The inspector's features tightened.

"Don't be ridiculous," the tall man, Doc, stated.

"What's so ridiculous?" the old man demanded. "They –" He threw his hand up wildly indicating Baron and Denham, or Shoreham as he now called himself. "–said she'd had a fight with her father. She's been grumbling about this place for ages. She's probably topped her old man and run off, she set the fire to cover her crime. I always reckoned she was a bad 'un. Capable of killing."

Simons suspected everyone was capable of killing when put in a wrong enough situation.

"Look how she offed Ewan."

"Dai," Doc said coldly, "Ewan was a colt who got hit by a car. She didn't have any choice but to put him down."

"She didn't have to enjoy it so much," the old man grumbled turning back to his pint.

"She didn't enjoy it at all!" Doc snarled.

"She's dead!" the weeping woman wailed out of nowhere.

"Emma!" Doc snapped.

"She's dead!" The blonde stood to face down her opponent. "Burnt with the farm. And no amount of denial's gonna bring her back, Doc!"

"She is not dead!" Doc virtually screamed.

Simons watched everyone shrink back from him, apart from the blonde who was too busy being insensitive. Pushing his hair back, Doc visibly pulled himself together on a carefully inhaled breath.

"The only body found was Iolyn's."

"Then where is she?" Emma pleaded. "Where's Cobb?"

The Doc looked across to the Inspector.

"Cobb went back home. He hasn't seen Branwen either."

"Then where is she?" Emma's voice cracked as tears ran unchecked down her checks. "She's dead. She's –"

Emma appeared to be voicing the opinion of the room, with only Doc seeming to disagree. Perhaps, Simons figured, he was in possession of more reliable information. He would need to separate Doc from the body of the assembly and find out.

"Em, love," her comforting fiancé rose to take her in hand. "This isn't helping. Let's go home."

"I don't want to go home." The petulant statement was accompanied a little-girl pout.

"We are going home," her companion stated and guided her out.

The woman left a wake of silence, a silence split by the ringing of a mobile phone. Several people in the room moved to check. It was the inspector though who answered. He listened, smiled then frowned. Whatever the man had heard it wasn't the good news he had been hoping for.

"Any news?" Doc asked.

The inspector didn't smile this time, but Simons noted his hooded gaze seemed directed towards Baron and Shoreham. Then he looked back at his phone. "Constable Johnston has been arrested."

The shock in the room was quickly followed by visible relief. Simons considered the room, calculated if Baron and Denham/Shoreham had been dealing with that particular officer; if so, they hid their disappointment well.

Suddenly Doc turned to Simons. "Are you the gentleman looking to buy Branwen's business?" he asked. "She left some papers with me for you to look over."

Simons knew that Jones was selling the business, but didn't know what this was about. He had to be careful. "If this isn't a good time–"

Doc moved towards Simons and the door. "No time like the present. Besides, I'm doing no good here."

Chapter 72
Alex – St John's Wood

The only time Alex's heart usually thumped this hard was when he stepped in front of a live audience and had to play and sing alone on stage, sometimes a live audience of thousands. Today he only had to go meet one man. The journey into the offices was easy, but when he got to Granger's office door, a man mountain barred the way.

"I've got an appointment at ten."

The man, 'security', didn't move. "Then you can go in at ten."

Now Alex looked at his watch. One minute to. This was taking punctuality to extremes. Granger had never been that bothered about meeting times before. Not that Granger actually had left the message for him to be here 'at ten precisely.' A woman's clipped tones had ordered that. Unsure what was going on, Alex stepped back and went to the window. He didn't like this. Any of it.

A catch sounded and Alex turned to see the bouncer opening the office door. He went through.

Granger's big chair was turned towards the window. Alex walked up towards the desk, then realised the visitors' chairs were missing. He'd have to stand. Uncertain what to say, he said nothing. Then nothing happened. He waited. Nothing. He tried coughing.

"Yes?"

The blood rushed from Alex's head, he felt faint. This wasn't Granger. That voice belonged to O'Rourke. Why was he here, where was Granger? How much trouble were they in? Alex glanced to the other room. Couldn't be that much trouble, could it?

"I was asked to be here at ten."

Slowly the chair turned. Alex wondered if this was like being on *The Voice*.

For the first time Alex had a chance to see O'Rourke. He looked like a city-type. The suit, the clean-cut hair, the slim worked-out body might be disguising the other man's age. "You were."

"What can I do for you Mr O'Rourke?"

For a moment he quaked in the silence of the older man's regard. "Do you know who I am?"

Clearly he knew the man's name, but that wasn't the question. "The man in charge."

O'Rourke gave a gentle smile. "That's right. I supported this business at start up. I expected a good return. You have had good support over the years, now I want that back."

Alex frowned. "You're the money man. The one who's cash I've been laundering into sales."

A small inclination of his head indicated the man's admission. "I'm surprised Granger had you do it."

"I'm surprised you had Granger do it. Rather than do it yourself."

"The cash transaction and rooting through kids' bank accounts keeps it clean and gets you in the charts."

"Limits your exposure somewhat too."

"Indeed, but my guy can't give cast iron guarantee, only that, to get to any connection to me, there are so many layers of many easier targets that it's unlikely the authorities would keep digging that far."

"How unlikely?"

"More chance of winning the Lotto jackpot three weeks in a row, apparently. I have considered cutting Nemesis Records loose, but I think there are alternatives. It's not the company that's the problem here, so much as Granger."

"He is the boss."

"Was."

Looking O'Rourke in the eye, Alex swallowed. He doubted that this man was ever a fool, about anything. "I see, well, a new conductor can make a difference to the composition. I'm happy to support any change you consider necessary for your business."

"As long as I support yours?" O'Rourke asked.

"I would prefer a mutually beneficial working relationship, sir, but I'm not fool enough to think anything other than that you're the man in charge." At least for now. If he played his hand right, possibly at some future point, he could reverse that position.

"Good," O'Rourke said. "But do remember, Mr Berenger, I like the obedient, not the obsequious."

Alex swallowed. "Yes, sir. Do you know about that?" He pointed to the other door, the one to the chair.

"What do you know about it?"

"That I've never been in there, and that's a good thing."

"Hmm." O'Rourke indicated Alex should precede him. "Go ahead."

Alex didn't really want to. He'd seen the photographs, he didn't want to experience the abomination. But refusing O'Rourke was clearly dangerous too. One night-time visitation was enough. He stopped at the door, hesitated to steady his hand before reaching out. Carefully steadying himself, Alex pushed the door open, but did not enter the room. He felt the older man come to stand at his shoulder.

"Vile," O'Rourke said.

"You can see why the photos will ruin everything."

"I'll send my cleaners in. You want the job?"

Alex turned to face the older man. "Cleaning?"

"Managing Director," O'Rourke said. "You'll need a mentor, of course, and an accountant."

That didn't make sense. "We have an accountant."

"You'll need the one I'll send."

Chapter 73
Simons – Pen-Y-Cwm Village

Simons followed Doc in silence. The village seemed deserted after the crowd in the pub. No one about, the houses dark, dead. At the Surgeries, the doctor opened his own door, allowing the stranger to precede him. As the doc flicked a couple of light switches, Simons noted the lift which seemed odd in a building no taller than the first floor, but he supposed it was for those who had difficulties with stairs. Stairs the Doc pointed him too.

"Peter Pearson," Doc introduced himself, holding out his hand once they were upstairs in the waiting room. "But most everyone calls me Doc."

"Simons," Simons stated, taking the offered hand. Welcoming the good solid shake.

Doc grunted. "So how do you know Shoreham when he obviously doesn't know you?"

"What makes you think I know Shoreham?" Simons showed none of his admiration at the doctor's keen observation skills.

"There was recognition in your eyes when you saw him, yet none in his. And you tried too hard not to react to the mention of Cobb's name."

"You have a keen eye, Doc. Why don't you tell me why I know them?"

Doc smiled, stepping away from Simons and beginning to pace as he considered. "Well, you have to be either a 'good guy' or a 'bad guy'. Personally, I'd rate Cobb one of the good guys. A hard, reserved, kind of good guy, but a good guy nonetheless. Shoreham – well, I wouldn't trust him as far as I could throw him, and I'd genuinely like to throw him, preferably off the Pony Path and into Llyn Cau. There's nothing I can put my finger on, but he bothers me."

Doc turned to face Simons. "Since you aren't now going for my throat, I'd guess you're a friend of Cobb's."

"Does that make me a good guy?" Simons asked, straight-faced.

"A lighter shade of grey, perhaps." Doc sat down in his waiting room, watching while Simons sat opposite him. "What's your side of the story?"

Simons considered. He didn't want to reveal too much but he didn't have time to pussyfoot around. "Cobb and I own a business together. He called me last week, mentioned some problems, things he wanted looking into. Said he was working with Branwen Jones."

Doc nodded. "Things have been a little odd around here this last week."

"Tell me what's happened."

Doc shrugged. "I'm not sure of all the details, but last Monday there was a car crash. The car skidded at Satan's Turn and fell into the stream the bridge goes over. Cobb and Branwen would have been the first to pass the site. They officially say they didn't see any sign of the driver, but there are a lot of people think they might have helped him out of the car, possibly have taken him in."

"Why?" Simons asked.

"Ah well, that's where I run into a bit of a problem. Tuesday morning after the crash, I left town to hold surgery in Llanindra, I only got back yesterday. From what I can make out, the day after the crash Baron and Shoreham arrived at Pen-Y-Cwm Farm Guesthouse, and they look like a brace of pure-bred thugs to me. Yesterday, Baron followed Branwen all day. I have no idea what's happened with Johnston, who's been the local bobby around here for decades. Some guy called Granger turned up, yesterday, I think. Apparently, he delivered some kind of ultimatum, and Branwen shot him down. I'm told she was magnificent in her defence of herself, Emma and Cobb."

"Emma?" Simons asked. "The woman that left?"

Doc nodded.

"That was Emma McGuiness?"

"You know what happened in Cambridge then?"

"I did a background check on Branwen Jones, the name came up."

"Then you know they're both innocent."

Simons didn't quite agree with that interpretation. "Can you explain why people think Branwen Jones is missing?"

Doc swallowed. "This morning I woke up to see a black column of smoke rising up from Pen-Y-Cwm. I called the fire brigade then drove up there. By the time I reached it the place was a burnt husk. A man's body has been found, and that can only be Iolyn, Branwen's father, but no one knows where Branwen is."

Simons frowned. Branwen may not be Mary, but it was beginning to look like she might well have suffered the same fate.

Movement caught his eye.

"That might not be entirely true."

***

As he spoke, Perkins stepped into the surgery waiting area.

Doc shot to his feet. Simons reached to his side, stopping as he recognised the inspector.

"You do realise it's illegal to carry a firearm in this country?" Perkins scowled at Simons.

"You do realise some of us still have the necessary clearance?"

Simons watched the man consider the point. There were enough registered shotguns in the area that one pistol in the hands of a man who knew how to use it was hardly going to make much difference.

"Who are you?"

Simons best defence was silence.

"Do I need to show my warrant card?"

"Simons." Simons said.

"CSC Securities?"

Surprised, Simons confirmed it with a nod.

"Cobb tried to contact you this morning. Couldn't get a line."

Simon reached for his phone.

"Don't bother, once you get into Wales, it becomes patchy," the inspector advised. "So, is Cobb hiding both James Whitney and Branwen Jones?"

Tension yanked Doc's body together. Simons watched the inspector, he was no yokel, but that didn't mean that he could be trusted.

"I was up at Pen-Y-Cwm Farm this morning, got there about half six," Perkins announced. "I spoke to Iolyn. He claimed that Branwen had taken Baron and Shoreham up to the bluff, something they aren't mentioning. I was halfway back to Dolgellau when I got the call about the fire." He concentrated on Doc. "After you left, Cobb needed to make a call, but with the mast down, he couldn't, I let him try the police radio to get Despatch to connect him. He tried to call you." Now he looked to Simons. "Someone called Judy said you were unavailable."

Simons nodded. "She doesn't like not being kept in the loop."

"I know the feeling," Perkins groused. "But I checked out Cobb, and CSC Securities, and you. Be grateful I did, or I'd be taking that gun off you, licence or no." Stalemate, neither man willing to back down, nor fight the point.

"What makes you think Branwen's with Cobb?" Simons asked.

Perkins looked at Doc. "Because the other most likely outcome is that she's dead."

"And because Cobb would be tearing the mountain apart if she wasn't." Doc sank back down to the seats and covered his face with his hands.

It seemed a fairly safe bet that Cobb had a rival for Miss Jones's affections. The hands fell away and Doc faced Perkins.

"Who killed Iolyn?" Doc asked.

Simons sighed. Honesty seemed the best policy. "Graham Denham, probably."

Doc looked confused. "Who?"

"The man claiming to be Gary Shoreham," Perkins advised.

Simons looked at him, shocked the man knew.

"Cobb mentioned the name, so I did some checking, it looks like the same man from the photographs. I've contacted HQ, they're looking into the possible connection and hopefully someone will be up, but the first response I had was that Denham was dead and no one cared."

"Oh, he's very much alive." Though Simons gave no guarantee on how long that would last.

"Those two are saying the Joneses were falling apart."

"Were they?" Simons asked.

Doc shrugged. "Maybe. Their relationship has been strained for years, and I doubt Iolyn would have been happy that Branny was selling the business and planning to leave."

"To go where?" Simons asked.

"Not sure," Doc admitted. "I'm not even sure Branny knows. She just has to get out of here. Part of me is surprised she stayed this long." He looked at the inspector again. "What did Iolyn say?"

"He was drunk. Maudlin." He reached into his back pocket. "He gave me these." He passed two photos to Doc.

"Iolyn and Isabella." Doc looked at the second photo. "Iolyn and his mother." He frowned and looked up at Perkins as he passed the images to Simons. "Why would he give these to you?"

Simons looked at the pictures. The couple looked happy. Isabella was tall and thin, very Italian looking. From what Simons could tell, not having met either woman, the mother and daughter shared hair colour, but everything else about Branwen was very much the Welsh side. He looked at the second picture, and revised his opinion. Branwen looked nothing like her grandmother, so there was more similarity of facial features between Branwen and Isabella than first seen.

"He said they were chains he wanted rid of. I figured I'd take them back when he sobered up."

"Now he never will. Do you think he killed the cattle and set the fire?"

Seemed unlikely to Simons, and Perkins expressed the same thought.

"Denham killed Mary," Simons said.

"Mary?" Doc asked.

"Cobb's wife."

Doc's jaw loosened. "Do I know him at all?"

"Highly unlikely," Simons said. "He's not the most open individual." Simons turned to Perkins, returned the photographs. "So, what have you got in mind?"

"Without a body, I have to assume that Branwen is still alive and we have to do what we can to find her. The farm is covered with the fire investigation, the Mountain Rescue are going to cover the Foxes Path route to Dolgellau and the stream from Satan's Turn. Woolverton is convinced that she wouldn't go over the mountain, and I'm pretty sure she's with Cobb."

"If she is, why won't they just drive off the mountain, through here, they must know that we're all worried?" Doc asked

"They'll also know the risk Denham poses," Simons said. "Cobb may still want revenge, but he wouldn't put anyone else in danger to get it."

Doc and Perkins looked at Simons.

"Branwen or James Whitney?" Perkins asked.

Simons was calm and steady. "Both probably."

"What the hell information does that boy have?"

"The kind that costs lives."

"Reputation destroying photographs?" Perkins asked. He didn't expect Simons to answer so he didn't give much of a space for the man to do so. "Shan Sh'Kara was found dead this morning. It appears to be suicide after the release of the photograph of her. More interestingly, she was signed to Nemesis Records, which was run by Richard Granger."

"Granger?" Doc asked.

"He employs Baron and Shoreham slash Denham."

"He's here," Doc said.

"He's dead." Perkins surprised them both. "I've got uniform protecting his room and CSIs on their way."

"Murdered?"

Perkins shrugged. "I'll wait for the pathologist to tell me that. But no obvious signs."

"That's good."

The other two men turned to Doc.

"Well it is. If Baron and Shoreham worked for Granger and Granger's dead then they won't get paid. They might just bugger off and leave us alone."

"They don't know Granger is dead," Perkins said. "They'd left the pub before I came down from Granger's room."

"Maybe they knew what you'd find and ran."

"This village consists of one road, which I've got patrol cars blocking off. It they've left the village, there's only one possible direction they could have gone – up the mountain."

"Does Shoreham know Cobb's here?" Simons asked.

"Yes."

"Then payment's irrelevant. He had to fake his death to get Cobb off his tail before, he'll not want to do that a second time. He'll hunt Cobb, and if Shoreham believes Cobb cares about Branwen, that would mean torturing Branwen and letting Cobb know about it."

"Then we won't let that happen," Doc said as he stood.

Simons nodded. "We'll get up to Cobb's."

"Why?"

"Cobb's house will be the most defensible position, he'll wait there for reinforcements."

Doc shook his head. "Only if he knew you were coming, but he couldn't get a call through to you. No, they'll go over The Chair."

Simons looked confused. "What chair?"

"The mountain," Perkins explained. "Cader Idris. The Chair of Idris." He turned to Doc. "What makes you so sure?"

"Branwen knows it and when I told Cobb to do it this morning, he didn't raise an objection."

"Could they do it with an injured third?"

"Probably. Branwen can tend a man as well as a dog. She shouldn't, but she could," Doc said. "We've each helped the other out when we've had to."

Perkins nodded. "Then we go after them."

"No."

Simons' objection surprised the others. "*We* go after them." He pointed between himself and Doc. "We need you to coordinate the rest, keep everyone else off the right track and out of harm's way. Out of my way." Because there were things he might have to do that a police officer couldn't be part of.

Chapter 74
Branwen – Pen-Y-Cwm, Cobb's Home

Pain sliced across her breast with every move, but Branwen held the wince inside. That bastard Shoreham had marked her in such a way she was never going to forget him. But that wasn't the only pain in her breast. Her father was dead.

Dead!

The word kept ringing in her head as she finished the dishes. She might not have been as close to the old man as she would have liked, but she still loved him. His loss ripped a new hole in her life that might never heal over. And again, because of that bastard Shoreham.

"What are we going to do?"

She looked up at Jay's question. A bloody good question. What were they going to do?

"We're getting off this mountain," Cobb said. He stood on the far side of the room, pulling things from cupboards, things they'd need to survive overnight on the mountain. It shouldn't take more than 5 hours to walk over the mountain, but with the condition Jay was in, and her not much better, that time would stretch. They'd definitely get to the shelter, but anything further was questionable. Add in the weather conditions and they needed to be prepared.

"What are you doing then? We don't need food to drive away."

"We can't drive. The only road is through the village, and we can't go there."

"Why not?"

Cobb stopped and looked at Jay. "If we do that, it's likely we'll run into Shoreham, and if we don't, there's a good chance that we'll run into the police and that would be even worse."

"Why?" Jay demanded.

"They'll arrest you for hacking," Branwen said. "They'll arrest me for interfering in a police investigation and they'll confiscate your laptop, and if Johnston gets hold of that, chances are that he'll sell it straight to Granger and you'll only have your word against Granger's on the pictures."

"So, we're up shit creek without a paddle."

She shook her head, aware that Cobb was continuing to pack. "If we can't go down we'll have to go up. Get your stuff together."

Chapter 75
Baron – Pen-Y-Cwm, Cobb's Home

"They're gone," Baron stated unnecessarily as he and Shoreham stood in the empty cabin, the wood shards from Shoreham's breaking of the door around them.

With a growl of frustration, Shoreham kicked over the nearest chair, then moved to turn over the heavy oak table.

Baron watched the petty display with no outward sign of his distaste. Baron liked things clean. Neat. A quick easy kill with no trace. He did what he did because he could. Not for the violence or the power of killer over victim, but for the intellectual victory of a winning criminal over the opposing investigating law enforcement agent. Psyche over the physical. Intellectual dominion over sheer domination.

What he saw in Shoreham was a Neanderthal. A beast removed from the general body of the animal kingdom only by its ability to walk upright. A very slim difference.

Shoreham stood with his back to Baron. He rolled his shoulders back and straightened.

Watching him Baron felt his usual indifference coalesce into a distinct dislike. No longer prepared to wait on his rage or his calm, Baron paced back to the door. In the cold of silently falling snow, he checked for clues as to the direction Cobb and Whitney might have taken.

Looking closely, it didn't take him too long to find the tyre tracks. With the snow already filling the indents, he realised it wouldn't have been much longer before this trace too had been obliterated.

Shoreham's footsteps crunching towards him, Baron stood and followed the tracks' trail with his eyes. The taller man stopped at his side.

"We follow them?"

Baron kept his own counsel. They had to go after Cobb and Whitney. If the information Whitney had reached the police, Granger would go down. If Granger went down he would take not only Greebo K and Alex Berenger with him, but Gary Shoreham and Jeff Baron too. This was no longer about what they were being paid to do. This was personal.

And Baron had been playing this game too long now to be taken down by an insignificant pawn like Whitney.

Simons noticed the fresh marks on the road as he and Doc left the Surgeries. After stowing Doc's gear with his own, Simons followed his directions out of the village. The weather had settled into a blanket of snow. The flake curtain obscured the view and slowed driving, but it didn't halt their progress.

"You were convinced all along that Cobb had Miss Jones with him?"

"Hell, yeah. He'd tear this mountain apart to find her otherwise."

That was how he'd been with Mary, why he'd imploded and come here to hide when he'd lost her. "Why didn't you mention that in the pub?"

"The outsiders were there."

Watching the road, Simons considered the doctor's loyalty and the consequences of this potentially deadly game. Simons hoped Doc could be relied on; his conclusions were about all they had to go on at the moment. "Just how close are Cobb and Miss Jones?"

He almost heard the grinding of teeth. "Too close."

"And you and Miss Jones?"

Doc took his time answer. "First kiss at 14 and 17, first time together at 16 and 19. Dated on and off ever since."

"Not that serious then."

"What?!"

Simons shrugged. "That first time is what, fifteen years ago? If that relationship was going to go anywhere, it would have by now. It hasn't, so it won't."

"Depressing thought." Doc slumped in his chair. "You think she and Cobb...?"

There was no way for them to know. But the fact that Cobb hadn't said anything didn't bode well. "Don't know."

"CSC Securities." Doc read the business card on Simons' dashboard. "Cobb, Simons and?"

"Cobb," Simons said solemnly.

Doc thought about that a moment. "Cobb's brother?"

"No." Simons paused, a mark of his sorrow for her loss. "Cobb's wife."

They held a moment of silence. Simons wondered where Doc's thoughts went.

"Branwen's leaving."

Simons doubted Cobb would stay much longer then.

At the bridge, the damage to the wall was obvious, though the barriers had been blown down. "This is where the accident happened?" Simons asked.

"Yep, this is where it all started. Satan's Turn. Take the track there." Doc pointed to the tight turn up to Cobb's property. Simons was unhappily unsurprised when the tyre tracks he had been following all the way turned in that direction too.

The snow fell thicker and faster here. Clumped flakes fell like cotton wall balls on the windscreen, the wipers worked double time to clear the blinding cover but still the cottage remained obscured until they were about twenty metres from it. The dark lump took a while to form a clear image and then all too quickly it became apparent that the door was standing wide open.

First out of the car, Doc ran into the cottage only to stand helpless in the middle of the mess of overturned furniture.

"What a fight," he observed when Simons stopped beside him.

"No," came the certain contradiction. "If Cobb and Denham had clashed here there'd be more blood and at least one body. Hopefully Denham's. No, Denham did this on his own. Rage at finding Cobb gone, probably. Come on," the Englishman spoke as he turned. "We should get after them."

Chapter 77
Branwen and Cobb – Cader Idris

Branwen worried, watching Jay grimace in pain as Cobb bumped the Jeep over the track. Given how bad the crash had been, Jay was less injured than he might be, but he was a long way short of the fitness level needed for the kind of journey they had to undertake. Her own suitability had to be questioned now too. She remained lightheaded from the amount of blood she had lost. The wounds in her arm and breast throbbed like hell and just about every other muscle and bone in her body screeched about the abuse she had given it. But at least she had her fury to keep her going.

Cobb was the only one among them fit for this. Physically at least. Branwen remained concerned about his mental state. Although she understood his reaction to discovering Shoreham's, or Denham's, proximity, she feared what effect that might have on him or his decisions during this flight.

Carefully Cobb drew to a halt, as the terrain became too rugged even for the four-wheel drive. In silence they left the car, Finn grumbling as his front paw touched the cold ground.

"Where now?" Jay asked.

She pointed off to their left. "Over that."

Jay looked up at the blank space of lowered clouds, the outline of the mountaintop just visible before them. Branwen found herself almost glad he had little idea of what they faced. It wasn't easy on a good day. This wasn't a good day. She didn't want to do it. She didn't even want to think about doing it. The prospect was too demoralising.

"Come on." Branwen spoke gently as she moved to take the rucksack Cobb held out to her, the lightest of the three they had with them. Branwen passed it to Jay, helped him ease it over his shoulders. She took and shouldered her own pack as Cobb did likewise.

"Ready?" he asked as she'd settled the load.

She nodded once, bringing up the rear as Cobb led and Jay followed.

***

"Cobb!" Branwen screamed ahead over the sound of the wind on this exposed outcrop. His long legs carried him much faster than she and Jay could manage. Jay leaned more and more heavily on her. She worried that if he leaned too hard on her, the skewed position would twist his ribs out of alignment.

Cobb turned, Branwen saw him say something. Easing Jay to the nearest boulder, she pointed to her ears and shook her head. Finn was already back as Cobb strode towards them.

"What's that?" Jay pointed down the scree slope to the water below. Some days that glacial lake rivalled a sapphire for blue, but today it lay grey and foreboding. Like a howling wolf waiting to devour them, the sound around them it's breath as it stalked its prey. Thank God the snow had stopped.

"That's Llyn Cau," she told him. "That's where I learnt to swim."

Cobb was back now. "We don't have time to keep stopping."

"And carrying on beyond Jay's endurance isn't going to help us either. We need to get to the shelter."

"What shelter?" Cobb frowned at her.

"Penygadair. If we follow Craig Cau around the rim, we'll meet the Pony Path, and from there we can get to the shelter. It's not much, but we should be able to breathe there."

"You're sure there's a shelter?"

She nodded, wondering how he didn't know it, but clearly they hadn't had to rescue anyone from there for a couple of years. "I've known these mountains all my life. Don't forget you're still in my backyard. Trust me."

"Okay."

"If you can help Jay, I'll lead the way." So saying, she took Finn in hand and led, following the curve of the rock. Branwen looked back to ensure that Cobb and Jay were behind her. Jay's arm hung over Cobb's shoulder, the bigger man half-carrying, half-dragging the younger one.

As she looked back, Jay's legs went from under him, the sudden shift of weight nearly taking Cobb down too, his foot slipping on the icy rocks beneath. Jay waved him away and slid to the ground, on his knees, one hand on the ground the other on his ribs. Branwen went back. Kneeling with Jay, she pulled his chin up, forcing him to face her. His eyes were shrouded by exhaustion and clouded by pain. He needed to stop.

"Your ribs?"

He held them as he sat wheezing, desperate for air. His answer was a nod. Loath though she was to do it, Branwen opened up his jacket, pulled off her gloves and examined the bones beneath his sweaters. What she found did not please her. She offered him a weak smile. "You need painkillers."

Jay nodded his thanks before lowering his head again as Branwen took off her pack and started looking through. As she did, she frowned and reached into her map pocket, pulled something out. Cobb asked what it was.

She looked up and slipped the syringe into her outer pocket. "Nothing useful."

247

He didn't seem to believe her as she found the med kit she was looking for. It wasn't a standard med kit, but she'd left it with Cobb deliberately.

"Is there a problem?"

"Potentially, a very big problem," Branwen whispered back. She glanced at Jay before meeting Cobb's direct gaze. "At least one of Jay's ribs is broken."

He frowned. "Not good."

Branwen cursed her own stupidity. "I was wrong. Maybe he cracked it in the accident, and it was okay while he stayed fairly still at the cottage, but today's trek, the way I had to help him, it probably all combined to knock the rib out of alignment. That's why he's having so much difficulty breathing."

"Is there anything we can do?"

"Get him to a hospital quick." Branwen instantly regretted her sarcastic tone. "If he were a dog, I'd suggest it would be more humane to put him down, but since that's called murder when you do it to a human, that's not really an option. I'm sorry Cobb, I'm a vet not a doctor. I can strap his ribs and give him a painkiller. Other than that all I can do is pray that he doesn't puncture a lung or start bleeding internally or some other dread scenario I don't want to even think about."

His eyes said something she wasn't ready to interpret. He reached out to offer her comfort, but she shied away from the contact, her worried gaze lingering on the young man causing a lot of her concern. "Right, I'm only going to give you a half dose," she said taking a small syringe from the bag. "It'll take the edge off without making you useless."

The injection passed easily into his cold skin. She zipped his jacket before putting her gloves on, then stood. She looked at Cobb. "I think your difference in height might be exacerbating the problem. I'll have to help him again."

"You up to that?"

She wanted to lie, but wouldn't. "Possibly not, but it's the best we can do."

She shouldered her pack and helped Jay to his feet. "Lean on me and be careful."

He nodded, leaned in, his head on her shoulder and they started away. "Branwen?" he said after a few steps, and turned his head to put his mouth near her ear.

"Yeah?"

"Why aren't you married?"

Branwen almost choked. The odd question would have made her laugh if its honest answer didn't make her want to cry. One quick

248

glance behind told her Cobb was watching them but wouldn't hear them. "No one ever asked."

"Marry me."

This time she smiled as they walked, denying the overwhelming sadness that washed over her. "Don't be silly."

"No," Jay agreed softly. "We're not likely to get off this mountain alive."

"Don't think like that," Branwen commanded. "Why, even the wind is dying down."

Jay nodded. "I can think of worse ways to go than in the arms of a beautiful woman."

Branwen looked at the tousled top of his head, seeing the washed-out red on blond. He really was an endearing child. "I'm not sure I can find you one of those at short notice."

"Meant you."

"You're delirious," she told him.

"You're still beautiful. I'd die happy in your arms."

Shocked, Branwen paused, uncomfortable more in her emotions than her body. "Well, Jay, I'd really rather you didn't."

"If we get out of here —"

"When we get out of here," Branwen affirmed.

"Will you go out with me?"

She laughed softly. Gently, she smoothed his hair back as a mother might her child's. "No."

Chapter 78
Baron – Cader Idris

Baron had trained as a tracker, but this weather fought them. The snow drifts were blurring the marks of the preceding tires. Eventually, Baron had to admit he couldn't push the Discovery any further. They parked, stepping out into the snow, closeing the last inches of zip and buttoned up windcheater flaps on their jackets. Baron pulled on a thermal hat and turned up his collar. Shoreham retrieved rucksacks from the boot of the car. In silence, Baron shouldered his share of the load, then led the way as they set off after their quarry.

The chill of the day was quickly warded off by the exertion of their pursuit. Of course, he knew the phenomenon would not last long, all too soon nature's cold would be biting through even the multiple layers of their protective clothing.

While the Discovery couldn't be forced further, there was a limit on how far the Jeep would be pushed too. Within minutes they saw the car. Baron also saw the break in the cloud. The low temperature ensured the snow wouldn't melt, but it wouldn't build up more. Baron hoped the biting wind wouldn't sweep the evidence away.

Cold, Baron considered, was not their only enemy. Cobb would have a superior knowledge of this land. That left him not only several steps ahead of the game, but with a clearer image of what the board looked like. With better understanding of the playing field and the rules of engagement, Cobb could play this game out for days. Baron smiled. What Cobb probably didn't know was that Baron and his companion were adept at adaptation to the sport. And of course, he'd be slowed by Jay, who must be injured. That stood in their favour.

Their rucksacks contained all the survival equipment they needed, and more firearms than they were likely to want. Two bullets should do it.

In any other season, Baron knew he could easily survive on the land, but winter lay like a pristine white shroud, the dark crags of the mountain poking through in places like the broken bones of a flesh-stripped corpse. This cold and forbidding place would not help their passage.

Chapter 79
Simons – Cader Idris

"That's Baron's car," Doc announced as they came up behind the vehicle.

"You're sure?" Simons queried.

"No one local can afford a brand new Discovery, and loads of us would like one," Doc pointed out, ignoring the fact that Simons was driving the same model. Now the air had cleared of snow, he saw the other vehicle parked further up the mountain. He pointed. "And that's Cobb's Jeep."

"It is," Simons agreed.

Simons parked. There's wasn't much hope of getting any higher in a car. He and Doc got out, zipped coats, pulled on packs, prepared for the slog ahead. Simons scouted for clues as to where the others might have gone. He found some and followed, Doc close behind, but soon stopped.

"Looks the most likely choice," Simons said pointing east along the trail, where the wind had obscured the footfalls.

"Nope," Doc declared. "That's the Minffordd Path, it curls back down the mountain, and heads towards Minffordd, surprisingly. It's too close to Pen-Y-Cwm. Branwen will head north, probably towards the Foxes Path and Dolgellau or the Pony Path. Probably the Foxes Path."

Simons looked at the east-headed Minffordd Path. That was the way he'd choose, the way he thought Cobb would choose, but he had no idea about Branwen or Whitney. Doc did. He turned west and indicated for Doc to precede him.

Walking side by side they moved up towards the peak of the mountain. For a moment Simons looked around. This part of Snowdonia rose in majesty, though at this time of year, *foreboding* seemed a more suitable description. As they walked, Simons saw signs of recent footsteps. The snow had stopped falling, the wind had weakened but not gone, and the air wasn't clear. Visibility was good enough to keep them clear of mis-step, but not good for seeing far ahead. He could only see two sets of footsteps.

"How tall is Branwen Jones?"

"About five four," Doc said. "Why?"

They were following two men then.

"What's Cobb's current level of capability?"

Doc considered the question. "Cobb's well trained, knows the area pretty well."

"He's been out of action for nigh on two years."

"There are some things you never forget."

"Fitness levels deteriorate." Simons considered; as a doctor, the man would recognise a fit man from an unfit one. "What's Cobb's fitness level like?"

"Good," Doc allowed.

"A match to Baron and Shoreham?" He'd have to change his thinking for ease of communication.

Doc stopped dead and looked at Simons, thinking before he started moving again, before he answered. "Baron and Shoreham struck me as men who spend a lot of time working out. Cobb doesn't. He may be fit and strong, but he is not as honed as they are."

"Cobb is an intelligent, capable man. He should be able to avoid direct hand to hand contact. He will handle the situation." Simons wasn't sure who he was trying to convince.

"Cobb's been hiding out in the back-of-beyond for the last two years. He will not be as sharp, nor possibly as hungry as Baron or Shoreham."

That, Simons considered, was unpleasantly true.

"Branwen's not combat trained. She wouldn't be any sort of a match for either man."

Simons considered the assessment. "But she knows the land?"

"Oh yes. This is her mountain. We're right above Pen-Y-Cwm Farm here." He looked back, the burnt-out husk of the farm clear in his memory if unseen now. "In fact, I think we might even still be on their land, hard to tell at this point. Branwen grew up running over these rocks. She probably knows them better than any other human. That's one of the reasons she's so valuable to the Rescue."

That was the best news Doc had offered thus far.

They carried on, the cold and the wind dragging at them, but neither man was going to let that stop him. A few minutes later, the phone in Simons' pocket started ringing.

"How the hell are you getting a signal up here?" Doc asked as Simons pulled the chunky phone from his pocket.

"Satellite phone." He answered the call. Judy. "When you say *wrecked*?"

Doc obviously heard Simons' question and stiffened at the word.

"Complete," Judy said. "But no human remains. However, they've found what was described as 'a gallon' of blood on a ledge nearby, but again, no body for it to have bled from."

He thanked Judy and signed off.

"Well?" Doc asked desperately.

"Branwen Jones's car has been found, at the bottom of Craig Lwyd, and a small about of blood." Judy had said 'a gallon' of blood, but Simons was well aware that a small amount of blood could look like a lot to someone who didn't understand how it spread.

Doc's hand went to his mouth.

"Branwen Jones, however, has not been found."

Doc nodded. "She has to be alive." He started moving along the path again. "She has to be."

Chapter 80
Branwen and Cobb – Cader Idris

Jay was struggling to walk and breathe. Branwen noted the grey cast to his skin. The shelter stood about 500 meters away, but the way he was leaning on her, it wasn't certain he'd get there. She looked over her shoulder and looked at Cobb, who was looking at his phone. The weak glint of daylight reflecting back on his face didn't illuminate anything happy.

"I gotta rest."

She looked at Jay; he looked terrible. There was nowhere here to sit. "Okay, but you'll have to stay on your feet." He nodded and they stopped. "You be okay on your own?"

He nodded and took his own weight.

She stepped back in the direction they had come, Cobb stepping up to her. "We don't have time to stop."

"He can't go much further."

"We're too exposed up here."

Branwen knew that, but Cobb should understand too. "The other choice is to leave the path, rough shod it over the mountain itself, that's rough and an ankle twister on a good day, but Jay couldn't cope, he needs the trail. Besides, it's the only choice anyone following us has too. What's with the phone?"

"I can't get a line." He seemed distant, raising his voice rather than getting closer to her

"What did you expect up here? Who are you trying to contact?"

He frowned. "Don't you trust me?"

"Do you have something to hide?"

His jaw flexed. "I was trying to get hold of Simons."

"Your partner in CSC?"

He nodded. "It's likely he's on his way here, but I'm not sure. We could do with the back-up. If he is coming, he's no way of knowing which way we're headed."

A true and worrying thought. "Depends, if he's looking for me, he might run into Pete, and Pete would figure this out."

Cobb tutted and looked heavenward.

"What?"

"Well of course, Doc would know." Cobb growled. "What about Jay, he asking you out as well?"

"Actually, yes, but right now you're the one being a dick."

*　*　*

The worst thing about that pronouncement was that she was absolutely right, he was being a dick. He knew it, yet he couldn't help himself. Unable to look at Branwen, Cobb glanced back. A blind man could follow their tracks, and the air was clearing; soon they'd be visible to the short sighted too. They had no leisure to continue the slow pace forced by Jay's injuries. There had to be a way to protect Jay and Branwen without leading Baron and Shoreham straight to them. If these two got to the shelter, maybe he could turn back and draw their pursuers away. Be less of a dick.

He hadn't carried a gun since leaving the army. After all, it was against the law. He'd bet his life neither Baron nor Shoreham cared about that law. Unfortunately, he was betting Jay and Branwen's lives on it too.

He moved up closer to Branwen. Jay was leaning heavily on her, his grey skin sheened with cold sweat. Branwen didn't look much better. Neither was doing well. Maybe they'd have to hole up in shelter and stay there; he could guard it from outside until they were sure the others were out of the picture or a rescue was made.

"How much further?"

"Not far."

"I don't like that we're exposed up here."

"I know but it's still the best way to use the land, and that's all we can do."

Her considered her a moment. "Can you get Jay to the shelter on your own?"

Her head snapped up and she stopped. "Why?"

He nodded. "Our tracks are too visible, I want to go back–"

"But if we're being followed–"

"Then separating may be the best chance you two have."

Branwen didn't look entirely convinced, but she started off down the track and didn't look back. Didn't care enough to look back for him. He sent Finn after Branwen. She took the dog's collar to make sure he stayed with her and didn't try to follow his master. Cobb turned away. He had to stop anyone who might be following.

***

Leaving Cobb felt like a betrayal. Branwen knew he was, strategically, right, but being away from him just felt wrong. She wanted to be with him, but she had to get Jay to some semblance of safety. The boy's breathing rasped through his expression of pain. Branwen had felt his ribs move out of alignment again beneath her hand. She feared for his life and it had nothing to do with Baron and Shoreham.

Two more steps and they reached the stone shelter's door. She didn't need to duck under the lintel of the open door; this was one time to be thankful that Jay's weary head hung lower than hers. The last thing he needed was another cranial blow. Finn rushed inside.

She led Jay into the oblong shelter, taking a moment to be careful of their footing on the uneven floor slabs. Around the edge of the shelter was a ledge, stepping past the driven snow from the open door and avoiding the equally open windows, she found a dry place to set him down. She worried about his clammy skin, wheezing breath and blue-tinged lips.

She took off the light day sack she was carrying and knelt by Jay's side.

"Do you think you can lie down?" she asked, moving to support him.

He shifted uneasily, leaning heavily on her. "I might never get back up, mind."

The flippant remark echoed her own fears. "Don't talk that way."

Easing him back, Branwen carefully unclasped his jacket, then lay it open. Bunching his jumper in her hands, she eased it back. He winced. What she saw worried her. Beneath the white bandages, Jay's stomach was beginning to swell, an angry purple lump. She swore privately. Internal bleeding. And there was nothing she could do about it. Not here.

"Bad, huh?" Jay asked, seeing the deepening frown.

She met his clouded eyes with a steady regard; despite her best efforts, the seriousness of his condition was plainly written on her face. "Not good."

"How bad?"

Branwen didn't want to admit that even to herself. She looked again at the wound, gently laying his clothes back over the bruising.

"I'm not going to make it, am I?" The weak question broke the silence which had fallen like a pall over them.

Finn came to stand by the bed. He whined once and licked Jay's face, his soulful doggy eyes pools of sorrow. Branwen empathised but ordered him out of the way.

Unable to meet Jay's eye, or answer his question, she had to do something, but what could she do? She was a vet. She had sorted out internal bleeding on animals but never a human and this wasn't her surgery. She had no equipment this time and this sure as hell wasn't a sterile environment.

Chapter 81
Cobb – Cader Idris

The mountain top offered no shelter, nowhere for Cobb to hide. But he had to be a line of defence between Branwen and Shoreham. He would not allow that man to rob the world of any more of its light.

Cobb knew his limitations. He couldn't fight two men at one time, not after these past two years. The best hope was to tackle one at a time.

Use the land.

Crouching at the edge of the trail, Cobb couldn't immediately see any way to use it. Baron and Shoreham would be as exposed as he. Two walking men would be more easily seen than one man crouching. Shifting his weight, one foot rolled on stones, and a couple clattered towards the scree. The path wasn't close enough to ensure a fall would take a man over the edge, usually. When someone fell, it was normally because they left the path to look over the lake. There were, however, areas where the path and the edge drew closer.

Staying hunched and low, Cobb moved ten feet forward. Here the path and scree were as close as they got. Made of worn earth and stones, the path was obscured by the snow, in places only the built-up edge marking the way. Shifting some of the larger stones Cobb built a false edge, pushing the path closer to the scree. He looked up to see if anyone was approaching. Though he saw nothing, he had to assume they were there. Running back, he gathered up armfuls of snow; it made an obvious mark, but if they got to this point, that didn't matter. Returning he quickly but carefully covered the edge he'd made. Then he moved back to his previous position.

Cobb hadn't brought weapons with him when he'd left London, never imagining he'd need them again. Now he did, he had nothing. He put his hand to the cold earth, felt the sharp stone beneath. Looking at the trail again he started to smile. He had exactly the same weapon David had used to slay Goliath, only more ammunition.

Quickly fashioning a sling from a strip of bandage from his own light pack, Cobb finally felt prepared.

If he could make one fall, he could stop the other, but people moved away from the perceived source of attack, so he needed to be on the inner lee of the mountain.

He pocketed a handful of stones before moving down the easier slope of the mountain. This offered him a little protection compared to those on the exposed ridge. He settled down to wait, eyes squinting against the falling snow. He hadn't waited long when the figures came into view.

He rolled the stones in his fingers, slipped two into the sling and started to swing it. Only once he was confident of the speed and the mens' location, taking the detour he had contrived, did he loose the stones. The dots disappeared in the air and were lost for eternity before the tall man flinched, stepping to his right and knocking his companion who slipped and disappeared over the edge.

Denham, Shoreham as he now called himself, stepped towards the edge, looking over. Cobb put the biggest of the stones he had in the sling and twirled it, firing off the missile. It landed squarely between Denham's shoulder blades, a foot too low.

Denham turned from where Baron had fallen, and squinted in the direction of the flung stone. Cobb stood. For a moment the two big men each sized the other up. Then with a roar, Denham charged like a deranged rhino.

**

The push from the side toppled Baron; luckily he had an excellent sense of balance. As he fell he twisted and kept a grip on the edge of the path.

Shoreham stood over him, but didn't stoop to help, then disappeared roaring.

With a grunt, and a little difficulty on rocks slippery with ice, Baron pulled himself back up to the path, laying on it a moment to catch his breath and seek some clarity.

Rising to his feet, he saw Shoreham fighting. It took a moment to recognise his opponent, but it had to be Cobb really. Which of them was winning was unclear; they seemed evenly matched. If Cobb was here, Whitney couldn't be far away. Shoreham could deal with the big man, Baron would go for the mark. Whitney and the stolen information were the important things here, not some jumped up grunt.

Easily bypassing the wrestling match, Baron moved forward. The wind picked up again, but held no snow in its claws now. He clearly saw the scraped snow to one side of the path; that bastard Cobb must have done something here, but he didn't know what, and didn't care, as long as he found Whitney.

Marching on, he soon saw the shape of a shelter. The stone construction of the local rock would have completely blended in, but for the white on the ground highlighting that the wind had stripped much of the snow from the walls, marking the outline clearly.

The stone construction gave way to gaps, but no physical doors or windows. Carefully approaching, Baron suspected that the wind would hide what little noise he made. At the edge of the building, the two foot thick walls prevented him seeing inside. From what he knew, Cobb had a dog that rarely left his side, but the animal wasn't with the owner, so there was a good chance it was inside with Whitney. A big dog like that had to be dangerous, have a man's throat out in seconds. He'd have to deal with that first. Baron reached inside his jacket and pulled out a small gun. The Browning was old, but functional, illegal but useful. He had filed off all identifying marks years ago. He checked the magazine then slid a bullet into place. Shrugging off his backpack, Baron turned to the door. At least he had the element of surprise on his side.

Chapter 82
Branwen – Cader Idris

Finn's head rose and his ears pricked up. Though concentrating on the needle of morphine she was injecting into Jay, Branwen still sensed the movement.

"What's wrong, babe?"

Withdrawing the needle, she turned.

Finn stood, barked.

Shadow cloaked the door.

A shot echoed in the cabin. The barking stopped abruptly.

"No!" Screaming, Branwen launched herself at the shadow she now saw as Baron. She dragged her claws down his face.

"You bitch!"

Baron recovered quickly, his balled fist hitting her full force in the gut. Gasping for air, she fell to the floor.

"You should be dead."

He kicked her thigh; pain shot up and down her leg. Baron moved to the cot and grabbed the boy by the jumper. Dazed eyes flickered open, stating clearly that Jay couldn't supply the answers Baron needed, even if he had been inclined to do so. Virtually throwing the limp body back down, Baron turned again to Branwen as she struggled to her knees.

Still struggling to breathe, she held one hand against her stomach. Grabbing her by the hair, Baron forced her head back. Without a full breath, she couldn't scream. With her teeth gritted and lips pulled back, she glared up at him.

"Where's the information?"

"Where's Cobb?" she retorted.

"Dead." He yanked on her hair again. Tears sprang into her eyes. Her free hand came up, covering his, her nails pressing into his flesh. "Where's the information?"

"In a timebomb."

The hand yanked her hair, shook her head, made her teeth clack.

"I managed to get a connection last night, posted it as a time locked page on the surgery website. If I don't get a connection to reset the file at a specific time it'll send all those files to everyone I have ever had an email address for, and the inbox of Reuters and every national newspaper I could find a contact for."

Frowning down at her, Baron didn't know what to believe. Such programs were easily built. He could disarm it – if he could connect and break in. Given time he could defuse that bomb. But time was the thing he couldn't be sure of.

"When?"

She grinned defiantly up at him.

For a moment he glared at her. What was he thinking? He let go of her hair, punching her across the face.

Yelping, she fell sideways. Her stomach ached and her cheek throbbed, her split lip and broken gums bled, but as Baron stood over her, she kicked his ankles from beneath him. He fell heavily to one side.

Despite her own injuries, Branwen knew she had to stop him. She wanted revenge for Finn. For Cobb. For Jay. As Baron fell to the ground, she leapt on him.

In blind rage, she punched again and again. Strong hands grabbed her by the shoulders, forcing her over until she was on her back on the floor, then he knelt astride her. He raised his fist to smash it into her face but she punched him hard in the groin.

His turn to crumple, gasping for breath.

Chapter 83
Cobb – Cader Idris

The match between Cobb and Denham was more even than either man was used to. Tired and breathing hard, they swapped blow for aching blow.

Cobb's fist connected squarely with Denham's jaw. Both staggered, the crushed snow beneath their dance slipping them off balance.

Denham's sudden kick knocked Cobb's legs from under him.

Cobb grabbed the fist flying for his head, twisting it round, forcing Denham to twist with it to avoid a break. Cobb punched him in the kidneys, then another, he readied for the third.

But before he had time to strike again, Denham's other arm crashed on his jaw, catching Cobb off balance and knocking him sprawling to the ground.

Spinning, Denham brought his foot down hard on Cobb's ankle. The tall man cried out. Denham kicked again. His boot connected with Cobb's jaw. The prone man's head was forced back, hit the ground hard.

Blood poured from his nose and mouth, staining the snow. Cobb felt stunned by pain, his brain working through treacle, his senses packed in cotton wool. He had to get back up. Had to stop this man.

Denham stood over him, watching with a grin of triumph as Cobb vainly tried to stand. That hated face twisted into a sneer. "Die slow and painful." This time the heavy booted foot fell powerfully over a twisted knee.

Cobb screamed in agony, his world turning black.

Chapter 84
Simons – Cader Idris

Simons was walking ahead of Doc, seeing the sweep of the land and noting the clearing of the air when he heard the scream.

Both men saw the clear path cut by a handful of people taking the same direction over the snow. The mist-softened sight of two men fighting drifted out of the not so distant.

Simons pulled the satellite phone from his pocket and dialled, passing the phone immediately to Doc. "Tell Murray where we are and to get up here quick."

Chapter 85
Branwen – Cader Idris

The bastard had hold of her, and she couldn't get free. She spotted the dropped gun on the floor, had no way to get to it with Baron holding her down. The memory of her threat to Shoreham came back. As did the memory of what lay in her pocket. All she had to do now, was get to it.

Heart racing, blood pounding in her ears, she pushed at Baron's face as she reached into her pocket.

Please God, let the syringe still be intact.

By some miracle it was. The metallic taste of blood rolled into her mouth past split lips. The syringe between her cold fingers, she fumbled to remove the sharps cover, managed it.

She hated herself for what she was about to do, for taking a life. But he had killed Cobb and Finn. He would doubtless kill her and Jay too. From his absence, she assumed Shoreham was dead. She hoped Cobb had had the pleasure of seeing him go first. Jay was dying and she didn't see a future for her. They had lost, but she would not let Baron win. Only one option was left. Stalemate.

Wriggling, twisting to avoid another punch, she pulled the syringe from her pocket. This time she jabbed a finger into the man's nose, not caring about the goo she encountered as much as forcing his head up and exposing his neck, giving her just enough skin to stick the needle into as she depressed the plunger. His expressed was startled, then glazed, then gone.

His muscles slackened. She rolled aside as the corpse collapsed on her, his grunt nothing more than the expulsion of air from unused lungs.

Silence echoed after the fight.

She heard only her own hard breathing and the condemnation of the ages for murdering a man.

Horrified by her own actions, she stood, stepped towards the door. Baron lay face down and silent – she hadn't put him to sleep, she'd killed him. How was she supposed to live with that? On the other side Finn lay silent, red staining the grey shaggy shoulder. Before her, Jay was deathly pale in a painkiller miasma.

A sob escaped her. They had all lost.

Pain hit her squarely between the shoulder blades. Staggering forward, she turned to see Shoreham's evil grin.

"No," she whispered, shaking her head as he advanced. Tears streamed down her face. How could he still be alive? Was Fate so cruel as to cheat her of any victory?

His face wore the feral mask of bloodlust.

"I'm going to enjoy killing you," he told her in a low growl. "Again." One large hand swiped up, snapping her head to one side. She tried to steady herself, to remain standing, but her foot caught on the uneven slabs and she fell, sprawling next to Baron's corpse. Shoreham moved to stand over her, one leg each side. Unable to move, with nowhere to go Branwen faced her executioner.

"It's gone," she told him. "The information. I posted it on the internet. You'll suffer for this; your employer will go to jail."

He smiled at the pathetic show of defiance.

She leant up, her hands on the floor behind her, her face level with his knee. The solid joint connected with her jaw.

She was going to die.

Branwen realised she was going to die as she slumped over on her side, she wished she had had the sense to do what she'd said. No more fighting back. There was no point. She didn't have the energy and she wouldn't give Shoreham the pleasure.

He knelt over her. Vices grabbed her upper arms, forcing her onto her back. She turned her head, refusing to look at him. Instead she saw Baron's cold dead eyes staring at her. She turned her head the other way. Finn, his eyes closed. She closed her own.

One large hand grabbed her chin, forcing her to face towards him.

"Look at me!"

Closed eyes! Closed! Keeping eyes closed took muscle control. Finn was down but he wasn't out. She had to help him.

"Look at me!"

She opened her eyes, but not because Shoreham had commanded it. Overwhelming hatred assailed her. More hate than she thought possible. She filled her mouth, her split lip and broken gums bleeding into it. She spat the stream of red at Shoreham's face. It hit his right cheek.

They both became very still and quiet, stunned by the action. Slowly Shoreham raised his hand and wiped at the spittle. He brought his hand forward, looked at the bloody mess, turned it to show Branwen, then licked it in one broad swipe from his fingers. She gagged in revulsion.

At the sound, Shoreham scowled, before he slapped her so hard her head snapped to the side, her broken nose moving again.

This time when he turned her back to face him, she struck out at him, but he caught her wrist. Despite the desperate strength behind her struggles, he forced her arms over her head and held them there with one hand. With the other he pulled down the zip of her Gortex despite her attempts to wriggle and buck away from him.

Beneath he opened the no longer white zipped sweatshirt,

ignoring her struggles and venomous curses. He revealed a thermal vest, with the stitching that ran by her collar. Shoreham grabbed it and pulled. Between his strength and her bodyweight, the material parted, exposing her breasts, the left covered in a dressing. He ripped that off, her involuntary cry making him smile.

She was breathing hard, a mixture of exertion, fear and cold. It made her breasts heave as he reached out, one finger tracing the outline of hurt. She flinched from the touch, but had nowhere to go, her back scraping against the frozen flagstones.

Leaning down, he suckled on her. His tongue rasping over the scab, he groaned his appreciation. Surrounded by death, there was no one left to stop him, no one to hear her scream. He had time. She had no fight left and no rescue to come.

He sucked the scab, catching the edges with his teeth, breaking the cover away. Branwen gave a small cry at the pain and he pressed her into the floor with his hips.

A different warmth ran over her breast. Blood. Hers. Laughing, Shoreham rubbed his beard-touched jowls in the flow. When he pushed himself up, he reminded her of a dingo at feed.

"You're going to kill me, so just do it."

He laughed. "Oh I'm going to kill you, alright. Just not quickly."

Chapter 86
Cobb and Simons – Cader Idris

Cobb lay severely injured but alive. Roughly, Simons shook him till the tall man regained consciousness.

Eyes swollen, Cobb had to squint to focus, to recognise his old friend. "Decided to join the party then?"

"Better late than never," Simons joked, as Cobb forced himself to sit up.

"Not too late I hope." Cobb struggled against the pain in his right leg. "Help me up."

It took a while to get him to his feet and once there, he leaned heavily on Simons.

"We have to get to the shelter," Cobb said, although he saw another figure already at the structure. "Doc?"

Simons confirmed it as they moved off. Cobb's fastest pace felt unbearably slow.

Chapter 87
Branwen – Cader Idris

Death.

That was all her future promised. The Grim Reaper had her pinned down. And he was loving every second of it.

His hand raised to hit her again.

There was an explosion of sound. Shoreham jerked, hit the wall, fell towards the floor.

Horrified, Branwen watched him fall on top of her. Her mouth open in a silent scream, she scrambled away from beneath his dead weight, turning to her saviour. "Pete?"

Slowly, Doc lowered the gun. The gun Baron had lost earlier, the one she hadn't been able to reach.

Suddenly she stood clasped to Pete, returning his fierce grip. She was shaking like a leaf. Tears streamed from her tight-closed eyes. Terror and relief warred inside her: glad to be alive; ashamed of having killed; grieving for all she'd lost.

Pete held her tight, trembling himself, burying his head in the mass of hair at her neck. He spoke her name like a mantra, thanking God she was alive.

Chapter 88
Cobb – Cader Idris

He should be grateful for being alive, but when Cobb saw Branwen fly into Doc's arms calling his name, he almost wished himself dead.

Another movement caught his eye. Against the back wall, Denham was mortally wounded, a ragged wound weeping in his shoulder, yet still he clung to life – and he was reaching inside his jacket.

Cobb didn't even think. As Shoreham trained his weapon on Branwen's back, Cobb forgot his pain and stepping forward, swiped the gun from Doc's hand, aimed and fired.

The bullet left a small clean entry wound in the middle of Denham's forehead.

Simons supported Cobb when his anger subsided and the pain returned, led him over to the wall, and helped him sit on the ledge that circled the shelter. Finally, Simons moved to check Jay. For a moment, Cobb looked at the evident shock on Branwen's face. She didn't offer him any encouragement, nor move towards him. Swallowing his hurt, he turned to the prostrate dog.

The second shot had surprised Doc and Branwen and they stood, still together but slightly apart, stunned by this final resolution. Doc saw Simons tending to Jay and pulled himself together, steadying Branwen before he moved away to treat the prone young man.

Branwen looked at Cobb, her face slack and numb after all that had happened. If she had chosen Doc, he had no right to complain. He let his eyes slide back to Finn.

Suddenly Branwen appeared in that picture. Covered with blood and fresh bruising, her clothes half hanging off her, she checked over Finn. Hopeless, of course, after that shot –

"He's still alive," she breathed.

Pain detaching him from reality, Cobb looked on the scene from a million miles away. If he hadn't been sitting down, he suspected he would have fallen. Baron and Denham were dead. Doc knelt by Jay, working to save the man's life, Branwen similarly tended to Finn. Simons had stepped back to let them work and was surveying the scene. It was surreal.

Taking the gun from Cobb's limp hand, Simons turned it over, then turned to Doc. "You used this?"

Both medics looked up at the question.

"Yes," Doc answered.

"I used that." Branwen pointed to the syringe that now lay between two floor slabs. "Pentobarbital. Enough to put Baron down like a dog." She concentrated back on Finn. "It's better than he deserved, isn't it, baby?"

Simons pocketed the gun and moved to the syringe, taking it carefully and ensuring that nothing got left behind. Moving towards the doorway, he sat beside his friend. Dimly, Cobb heard an approaching helicopter.

"You won," Simons said softly.

Cobb glanced to Branwen and Doc. "Did I?"

Chapter 89
Branwen – Glan Clwyd Hospital

Branwen sat in the emergency ward cubicle feeling very cold and alone. And numb. A helicopter had arrived and taken them off the mountain. Jay and Cobb had been taken to separate operating theatres; she had no idea what had happened to Simons or Doc as she was ushered into the emergency room.

The duty doctor patched her up and told her she could go. Her shoulder ached as she pulled on her jacket and she wondered exactly where she should go. She had no money and no transportation. She would have to phone Emma and ask her to come pick her up. A far from welcome prospect. Much as she loved and valued Emma, what she really wanted right now was a dark corner to curl up in and cry. With a sigh, she figured she didn't have much choice and went looking for a phone. Instead of a phone, she found Inspector Perkins by the reception desk.

Perkins spotted her, spoke briefly to the receptionist and moved straight towards Branwen. "Hello, Miss Jones." Taking her arm, he steered her to a sheltered area of the waiting room. "How are you?"

"Alive," she pointed out.

Perkins smiled at the rueful comment. Taking his hand from his pocket, he pulled out the two photographs Iolyn had given him. He held them out to her. "I went to see your father. He passed these to me."

Branwen took the photos, frowned over them. "My parents, Nan," she said softly. She looked back at the inspector. "Why did he give these to you?"

Perkins shrugged. "I'm not sure. He seemed depressed when I spoke to him. Like…" Perkins shrugged. "I'm not sure. Like he was at the end of something."

Branwen nodded. She understood. Family had always been of the utmost importance to her father. Announcing her departure would have hurt and depressed him. She felt sorry for him. None of the women in his life, gran, mother, wife nor daughter, had treated him fairly. She was glad of Perkins' visit, thankful that he had handed the photographs over, unwittingly preserving them. She had family with her now, continuity. Holding the pictures to her, she turned back to the inspector uncaring that tears streamed down her face. "Could you give me a lift back to Pen-Y-Cwm, please?"

Chapter 90
Jay – Glan Clwyd Hospital

Lying in the private room Jay considered himself lucky to be alive. The doctors said he should have been hospitalised hours before he was – but the doctor didn't realise Jay had been injured last Monday. Perhaps some would blame Branwen or Cobb for not taking him straight to a hospital, but Jay knew that if they had, Granger and his hired thugs would have killed him.

Simons arrived, interrupting Jay's contemplations. The older man reassured him that the hacked information was now in the right hands. "How's Branwen?"

"Released yesterday. Went back to Pen-Y-Cwm."

"She's okay then?"

Simons nodded.

"Cobb?"

Simons checked his watch. "In surgery an hour now. Shoreham did a lot of damage to his knee."

Jay nodded and stared at the thin hospital blanket over his legs. "So, no good news?"

Simons shrugged. "Depends what you think of as 'good'. No charges are being brought against you for hacking into Nemesis Records, and Granger is dead."

Jay's head snapped up. "Dead? How?"

"Natural causes," Simons answered. "A massive heart attack. Given the man's obesity and probable stress levels, it's hardly surprising."

Chapter 91
Alex – St John's Wood

Mark Levinson earned two lines of obituary, a car crash, same place as Marc Bolan. Suited Levinson, unable to make a decent name for himself, he made an indecent copy-cat death. Probably suicide, but O'Rourke said he liked things neatly tied up.

Alexander Berenger left the paper on the desk and sat back in the deep leather producer's chair glancing at O'Rourke, his deadly silent partner in the shadows. Granger, Greebo and Levinson had lost, but he had won.

Some minor fines and the odd hushed-up knuckle-rap for his part in the Greebo K set up, but now his own fan base was broader and he was free to release whatever music he wanted and still be assured of good sales. Greebo's lack of talent had again highlighted his abundance of it.

Yes, he smiled as he lorded over his new record studio; he enjoyed owning his own music.

Chapter 92
Branwen – Pen-Y-Cwm

Branwen stood by the rental car outside of Doc's bungalow. Her bag was in the boot. The bag was new. Everything inside was new. The only not new things were two photographs, and even they were in new frames. The other not new thing, of course, was Pete being by her side.

"Are you sure this is what you want to do?"

She smiled up at him, despite the sadness. "Yes. The farm and Dad are gone. The truth about Em and me is out. Nothing left to hide and nowhere to live. At least Mum wants me with her for a while, and I should make some effort to get to know her better. Besides, Thomas has the surgery now. Nothing left in Pen-Y-Cwm for me."

"Me?"

The way Pete smiled and wiggled his eyebrows told her he was joking. They'd said their real goodbye last night. Twice.

"He's alright I suppose. Talbot."

Thomas Talbot, 32, a vet with a very good reputation. "He'll give you a run for your money with the local girls."

"The only girl I want to run for is about to leave."

Indeed she was.

"What do I tell Cobb if he calls?"

She took a breath, swallowed. Cobb. He hadn't called, hadn't come back for her, or at her invitation. She hadn't stopped thinking about him. "It's been over a month, he hasn't called yet, doubt he ever will."

"He needed major surgery on his knee," Pete pointed out. "He's doubtless still in recovery. He'll call when he's better."

"I don't even know what happened to Finn," Branwen lamented.

"They got him to a veterinary hospital in Chester. He's in recovery too. Simons would have said otherwise."

She hung her head. She'd kept her most desperate wishes, most desperate acts from Pete. He had burdens enough at the moment.

"No, really, he would have. I had a long talk with him while we waited at the hospital. He promised that if anything happened to either Finn or Cobb, he'd let me know."

She hung her head. "Sounds like you got it all covered better than I did after what happened."

"Yeah, well." He hung his head and turned away.

"Pete, you did what you had to do." It wasn't the first time she'd had to remind him of that. He was struggling and she felt guilty for leaving him, but if she stayed, she'd be putting the needs of others

274

before her own needs and doing that was what had caused most of the problems in her life. It was time to do what she needed to. "It wasn't something you'd choose to do, and I'm glad of that. You wouldn't be the wonderful man I know you are if shooting someone was easy for you. I'm also glad you did do what needed to be done when you had to. I wouldn't be here now otherwise."

Taking his upper arms she braced herself; she hadn't realised how much of a wrench leaving him was going to be. But it was what he'd asked for: if she was leaving, she was to cut all bonds. Not come back. Not call. Suddenly she wasn't sure she could do it, only she knew she had to – for his sake as well as hers.

"Promise me something," Branwen asked. "Forget me."

His arm moved around her and squeezed her to him. He kissed her hair. "Oh Branwen, I can never do that. You're the only girl I've ever actually loved." He tutted, sighed and pushed her away from him. "But you don't love me, not like I want you to. You never did, and I always knew that. But I will promise you this. I won't die a lonely old man, I'll find someone, but I will never love another half so well as I've loved you, Branwen Jones." The kiss he planted on her lips was tear-flavoured, from both sides. "Now you go find your better life." And he pushed her away towards her future.

Chapter 93
Jay – London

The big car slipped quietly into the traffic, the woman with the lovely legs sitting quietly at his side. Jay had no idea why he'd agreed to get in the car, or why he panicked only once he was inside. An hour from the city they drew up to a large house. A nice place. The car stopped, the chauffeur stepped out, opened the door for the woman, who slid to the side and gracefully got out.

Jay opened his own door and stepped out. The fresh air spoke of recently mown lawn. A very nice place.

"This way, Mr Whitney."

Jay followed the woman to an elegant office where Simons and Cobb waited. Cobb looked different in a suit and tie, scarier. Even leaning on a cane, it was too ready a weapon.

"Thank you, Judy."

Judy inclined her head and left, quietly closing the door.

"NASA isn't going to call." Simons came straight to the point. "I am. I need another hacker."

Jay frowned. "You're a white hat?"

Simons mouth offered a small smile. "Usually."

Chapter 94
Cobb – Home Counties

Cobb stood to the side of Simons' office, Finn by his feet. Despite being equal partners, it seemed better that the offer came from Simons than from him, so he stayed back, watching from behind Jay, where he could keep an eye on the door which opened to the corridor and the office wing of the house. It was odd to be back here, even though he actually owned half the place, well two thirds, in fact. When Mary had died, everything that was hers had come to him, and the three of them were equal in the business.

Being here there were things that reminded him every day of Mary. The way she'd arranged the furniture, the pieces of art and *object d'art* that she'd selected and placed. Her clothes in the wardrobe. None of it was enough to blot out a beautiful raven. Living in the past hadn't done him any good when he'd hidden in Pen-Y-Cwm, it wouldn't do him any good now. Thinking of that place and all that had happened didn't help him much either. So he threw himself into the work, into re-establishing his contacts, his place in the business, his ability to function. Even his physio. Though he listened to the doctors warnings not to overdo anything, he'd made a determined effort to pack up the old to get on with the new. It was the only way to carry on. And even with that he couldn't blot out the thoughts of Branwen Jones – or the memory of her in Doc Pearson's arms.

He swallowed the tide of anguish as he applied himself to the here and now. Be present. Breathe. He had to blot out the pain, even as needles pierced every nerve when he shifted his weight on the new metal knee that had been necessary to replace the shattered old one.

Concentrate, on the here and now. Let the past go.

Out in the hall, he heard Judy moving around even as he listened to the offer Simons was making Jay. They'd spent some time deliberating the details. It was a very good offer; the boy would be a fool not to take it. Luckily, Jay wasn't a fool.

"Do you have any questions?" Simons asked when he was done.

"Yeah," Jay was forthright. "Where's Branwen?"

Simons' eyes shifted over Jay's shoulder and pinned Cobb with a hard look. Jay twisted in his seat and glared at him, drawing all Cobb's focus. Now he had to think about the very thing he shouldn't think about.

"She's in Pen-Y-Cwm." Or so he believed. He dared not check for fear he'd weaken when he shouldn't.

"Jesus, Cobb. Why not just go get her?"

Tightness drew every nerve together. The urge to slap the boy down was as much because he wanted to strike out at himself as Jay.

"When it comes to Branwen," Jay said with a curled lip, "you really are a dick."

The accuracy of the accusation stung. The idea of going to get Branwen was so seductive. He wanted to do it, he really did, but she deserved someone better. Someone who could protect her. "I can't even walk properly at the moment."

"Oh, and that means I'd give up on you, does it?"

Branwen? Finn picked up his head and whined.

"Like I gave up on Finn when his leg got broken?"

Sarcasm and challenge. The tones he'd heard from her the very first time they'd met. Swallowing the lump in his throat, unable to calm the racing of his heart, Cobb carefully shifted, leaning too heavily on the damn cane, to face her.

Branwen.

Here?

Was it possible or was his desperation for her making him hallucinate?

He wanted to run to her, gather her up. Declare his love. Yet he found himself frozen to the spot. He should tell her to go. He could never be good enough for her now. And everyone was watching him, including Judy who had stepped into the doorway when Branwen risked the half step forward.

"Why didn't you call?" she asked.

He'd asked himself the same question. His inability to answer hadn't helped even when the phone had been in his hand. "My leg."

"Has no effect on your ability to make a phone call."

She was right of course, she usually was. "You could have called." God, now he sounded like a dick to his own ears. Little wonder Jay tutted him.

"I did." Her voice was deep and sure. "When you wouldn't answer your phone, I called Simons. Pretty much every day. When I didn't speak to him, I spoke to Judy."

Cobb glanced at the older blond, who nodded. Why hadn't he already known that? Why had he been so afraid to talk to or even about Branwen? Why was he still? Now he met her gaze; she gave no quarter.

"Doc?"

Her lips momentarily compressed. "What about him?"

"You've been living with him."

She sighed and crossed her arms. "My home and everything I owned was burned to the ground. It's all been destroyed. Em's place is a psychedelic nightmare, and I couldn't afford to stay at the

Pig that whole time. But okay, we'll have to deal with the issue of Pete at some point, so let's do it now. I've known Pete my whole life. Pretty much every 'first' I ever experienced was with him. We've been lovers on and off since we were teenagers. I will always love him, just like you'll always love Mary."

"Mary isn't about to turn up and challenge you."

"Pete's not the one I just drove over two hundred miles to be with. Though in fairness when I told him I was leaving the village in February, he tried to persuade me not to, which is more than you did."

Cobb hung his head. He hadn't wanted her to go, to leave him, but he couldn't cage her, that wouldn't have been fair. "That was two months ago."

"Yes, and since then I have seen my life burned to hell. My best friend killed a man to save me and even though he knows he did the right thing he's struggling to come to terms with being a murderer, his word not mine," she added when his shock at the term showed.

"I had to bury what remained of my father, and answer a ton of questions as to why you weren't at the funeral. I met my mother for the first time, which isn't something that should have happened at my dad's funeral. I've sold my business and I have no idea what's going to happen next. I haven't stopped for the loose ends I had to get tied up since you walked away."

Emotion strangled him. All that she'd been through and he hadn't been there for her. She deserved better.

"Oh, Emma wants to know what to do about your cottage. Is it on the market? Are you keeping it? Do you need maintenance done to it?"

"I don't know." He wasn't even sure he cared about the damned property.

"Well I do." Again she showed him the crystal clarity he loved from her. "Someone kicked the door down and the storm blew in. There was water damage. We've boarded it up, but the cottage needs maintenance and if you're not going to live there you should sell it. One less loose end in your life."

Her breathing wasn't right. She was struggling to take a breath. She looked heavenward, licked her lips. When she faced him again uncertainty clouded every feature.

"Loose ends don't help anyone. Is that all I am to you now?"

How could she even think that? She was everything and he wanted her, he just didn't know how to make her stay. How could he even ask when he could never be good enough for her? Finn whined, stood and padded over to her. One thin white hand reached out and fussed the big grey head, tickled the soft ears. Canine love was so simple.

Branwen reached inside her pocket, pulled out a folded, printed sheet. She held it up to show a QR code.

"This is a ticket to Tuscany. Mother wants me to go live with her."

That would be good for her. See a bit of the world, get to know her mother.

Get swept off her feet by some Italian stud. *No.*

"Italy's lovely," Jay suggested.

Cobb had almost forgotten that the boy was in the room. Simons and Judy too. His entire focus was on Branwen; he had never wanted anything in his life more than he wanted her, not even Mary. Something deep inside him screamed that they belonged together, but he had no idea how to vocalise that fact. His stupidity struck him mute. The room was full of expectation, everyone waiting for him to speak. He couldn't. He was making an idiot of himself and they were all witness to it.

Branwen's huffed laugh was rough and bitter as she broke her gaze from his to look at Jay.

"However lovely Italy may be, it's not my home," she said. "Neither is Pen-Y-Cwm. Hasn't been for a while. I only stayed because home felt like being around Cobb." She paused.

They all waited. What the hell was he supposed to say to that?

"Oh, for God's sake Cobb," she pleaded. "Say something."

Say what? What could he say to make her stay with a man so unworthy of her as him?

Her harsh expulsion of air was the sound of a heart breaking. There were tears in her eyes now.

"I'm not good with words," he said.

"The ones I need to hear aren't difficult."

So why couldn't he say them? There she was, the woman he loved, everything he wanted and she was standing right in front of him, pain in her voice, need in her gaze. He wanted to take that pain away, give her what she needed. Dry her tears. He wanted her to stay, to love him, to be here with him however unworthy he was. But she just looked at him with an expression so sad he was immobilised. The only sound was that of his heart thumping to remind him he was an idiot. The silence around him was condemnation. They were waiting for him to act, but he had no idea how.

Branwen blinked and stepped away; Finn moved with her.

"Stay."

They both stopped. She looked down at the dog. Finn looked

between them, owner and friend – which would the animal chose? Finn gave a plaintiff whine.

The sound of air being dragged in straightened her spine as her head half-turned back to him. "You talking to me or Finn?"

"You." Finally the words were there, like a flood gate had opened. "Branwen, if you walk out that door, I'll have lost everything that matters to me."

Twisting slowly, carefully, she faced him, and he hobbled towards her.

"When I first met you, I was lost. I didn't want to live, but you made me. You saved me that day on Cader Idris. But when you needed me, I wasn't there, I couldn't get to you. I wanted to save you, but I failed. Doc had to be the hero that day. I couldn't save you like you saved me. I couldn't be your hero."

Her frown deepened. "I don't need a hero."

"But I do. I need you. You've been my hero for a long time. I can't give you back what you've lost, but if you marry me, I swear I'll build you a throne in my heart and keep you safe there forever."

The frown smoothed; her expression softened. Then she was in his arms, kissing him like her life depended on it. It seemed his did. All the pain disappeared, even the constant ache in his knee. She was here, she was his. He held her tight, but had to break the kiss to breathe. He grinned down at her like the fool he way. His beautiful raven. His.

"You know you just promised to marry me?"

"You know you just promised to make me a throne in your heart?"

"You already sit there." He didn't know precisely when she'd taken that seat, but she had.

Her grin was broad and welcome. "The only chair I'll ever need."

THE END

About the Author
GB Williams

GB Williams has finally left the world of nine to five and offices behind, swapping system design for writing and freelance editing.

She writes crime fiction as GB Williams, and has written novels, shorts and flash fiction.

She has also had some success with steam punk (writing as Abi Barden in the US), paranormal prose, and poetry.

She was born in Kent, grew up in Tonbridge, met and married a Welshman, and now lives in Swansea.

https://gailbwilliams.co.uk/